THE
MIDNIGHT
WORK

THE
MIDNIGHT
WORK

KASSANDRA SIMS

tor romance

A TOM DOHERTY ASSOCIATES BOOK
NEW YORK

To the Turnip, who believed in me even when I didn't.

This is a work of fiction. All the characters and events portrayed in this book are either products of the author's imagination or are used fictitiously.

MIDNIGHT WORK

Copyright © 2005 by Kassandra Sims

All rights reserved, including the right to reproduce this book, or portions thereof, in any form.

A Tor Book
Published by Tom Doherty Associates, LLC
175 Fifth Avenue
New York, NY 10010

www.tor.com

Tor® is a registered trademark of Tom Doherty Associates, LLC.

ISBN 0-765-35394-6
EAN 978-0-765-34394-8

First edition: December 2005

Printed in the United States of America

0 9 8 7 6 5 4 3 2 1

Acknowledgments

IT'S MY FIRST book; we've got a lot to cover.

First off, thanks to my editor, Anna Genoese, who, you know, bought my book! She needs a raise. And to find a genie with limitless wishes.

Thanks to Laura Diehl, Zahra Winston, Carrie Scott, and so many others (who are going to burn my house down for leaving them out), for reading everything I've ever written and making it all better. You were my personal writing clinic for years, and without you I'd be doing something very different with my life. Ok, let's be honest, I'd probably be in prison by now.

Vicky Denniston pops up and saves me from myself on such a constant basis I should pay her to be my personal life coach.

Dee Stiffler not only coined the term hoyay, she also read this book for very integral bits.

Lastly, I want to thank my mom (yeah, had to be done) for never once telling me I should get some realistic dreams.

OCCITANIA

1242

Prologue

THE EARLIEST BUDS of the plane trees burned with the fervor of youth, the luminous green a startling backdrop to the filth and dullness of the camped crusaders. Even if early spring struggled against late winter in the plains, the thin air of the mountains still held the edge of ice and fury in the Pyrenees. The stone of the besieged castle retained the cold, helping the work of winter while defending those behind the walls from those without. Metal crashed against wood and more metal as the knights and soldiers continued with their ceaseless holy crusade. Some in the castle had come to believe the war would truly be ceaseless, that Rome would send Frankish lords after Templars after clerics until every Believer was as cold as a mountain spring.

Two figures stood in the long-armed embrace of late evening, the sun wrapped around them both through the tall windows set at head-height along the stone walls of the room. The woman stood unveiled. Her thick, blond hair shot through with white shone in the sunlight, the white of her gown and bliaut gray in the glare. Her face showed no hint of her decision to surrender and burn rather than continue to wither away and starve. A swift martyr's death instead of a lingering coward's. Her son was not so stoic. Tang from Olivier's salty tears and the ocean coated the back of his throat as he struggled with good-bye.

"Do not mourn for me, my joy," she murmured. The bones in her fingers pushed at the skin with the urgency of famine as she reached up to touch the man's scarred face. "This world is but a prelude to the Truth. I go before you, as so many others have, and you stay behind to find the souls of the lost, to keep the Truth alive."

"Mother, I would go with you to the fires rather than live an eternity knowing you burned." With his voice shaking, he dropped to his knees, his arms coming up to encircle her hips, his face pressed into the rough fabric of her apron.

Her skeletal hand wove through his hair. "You of all, I would save from this world. To release you from this prison of the Evil One, to set your soul free into the world of Spirit and the Good God. My only living child, you are more precious to me than my own soul. But you must choose your path for yourself, and you are needed here. My time has passed, but you were chosen to continue, to endure, to protect the others, to keep those who are born again alive. We have given much, do you think we should fade from the world completely?"

He wept as she spoke, more scared of her death than he ever had been of his own. "I would not give the Evil One dominion over the world. Neither would I see so many die in vain."

"Your piety will see you through this." Her voice

broke as the heavy, oaken door leading to the corridor behind him opened and three others entered. "Take him, but if he wills it to the end, you must allow him to leave this world with us."

Strong arms yanked the dead weight of the man from the floor, away from his mother's frail body. He let them drag him, sagging against his comrades, his cousins, until the line of sight between him and his mother was broken. As the one unbroken piece of him crumbled—the one part of his former self that had held out hope, ridiculous, precious hope, that the siege would end, that the Church would relent, and that they would go free to live as they chose—the man shrugged off his captors to stand by his own volition.

"You will come willingly?" his cousin asked, incredulity pricking out the words like silver gilding.

"I will come because my mother is done with this life, and I am not," he replied. His cousin held firmly on his arm, one step, two steps, and he dropped his hand away. He did not add, again, his distaste for sorcery.

"Don't torment her anymore, Olivier; this is already torturous without you refusing to accept reality." A torch guttered as they passed in the wide, cool, stone corridor leading from the apartments to the warren of passages and caves dug into the solid rock of the mountain. Four sets of feet fell in an uncalibrated rush, leather slapping stone, mail jangling against plate, sighs and gnashed teeth—the constant clangor of their imprisonment atop Montsegur.

"You shouldn't have been chosen, my brother, not with your mother still living and walking tomorrow into the flames," his cousin continued, his hand returning to his arm—this time not in admonition, but in affection.

The shadowy flickering on the wall presented him

the murderous pantomime of all the deaths he had seen. They echoed the deaths yet to come, the deaths of the most devout, the most holy, going willingly into the next world, the world of Spirit. He glanced at his cousin, all black hair and fair skin, calculated and calm, ever the warrior.

"I have never wished for my death more than I have today, cousin," Olivier said. They came to a standstill before a stone door set in a recess in the wall. The escort at their rear stepped around them and tapped a curious pattern of raps against the surface of the door. "But, yet, I am conflicted. Which is worse: to die and be done with the pain and never again know the sweetness of the flesh, or to survive in this corrupt body remembering the sorrow of all my days?" Olivier whispered. Their faith taught that the flesh was a lie, the sensual pleasure a lure set by the Evil One to confound and confuse, that only the soul was pure, that the true world lay beyond this one of the body.

The door rolled open to the side, bit by tiny bit.

"Your heart is that of a poet, and for that I have always pitied you." His cousin again squeezed the man's shoulder in reassurance, even as Olivier considered the exact series of moves that would immobilize the escort as well as his cousin and allow him to escape to the upper-reaches of the fortress. He had no desire for the fate that awaited him. He would rather choose sure, swift death for himself, than what had been chosen for him. He had been chosen for his skill with a bow and a blade, chosen to protect their faith and assure that it would never die completely. With even four of the Faith alive, there was hope to find others.

Before he could make a move, a sweet, textured voice drifted from the darkness behind the opening in the wall.

"Would you flee and let the secrets of our people die in the fires of the priests?"

"Phillipa?" he gasped, joy and horror melding in his stomach. His beloved? How had she been chosen without his knowledge? Anger flashed across his skin, the hum of battle madness that allowed him to kill with an ease that made other men flee before him.

Another voice echoed the bleakest thoughts of his heart: "Would you have them all die in vain when you would live on and keep their memories alive in this world of traps and illusion?"

"Rosamund?" The name rolled off his tongue with a familiarity that did not suit this scene. Those fears, the fear that all of the deaths he had witnessed, and all the ones he had heard of back beyond even the memory of his parents' youths, would have been in vain. Their Truth, their Light, faded from the Earth, stomped out by the lies of the Deceiver and the hands of the Church.

Phillipa spoke again. "Some are chosen to be lights in the darkness, to show the way and lead by doing."

"Like your mother." Rosamund's voice grew harder.

Phillipa's voice spoke of Faith, but his skin remembered her whisper in his ear, her tongue on his skin, and his traitorous body responded to her like it ever did. "Some are chosen to become one with the shadow, to whisper in the night the truths that others cower from."

"Like yourself." Rosamund's anger rustled her words, and Olivier's ardor fled.

The truth of their words, combined with his unrelenting yearning for Phillipa, constricted his thoughts. His will was unified with the women, not for the purity of the faith strictly, but because some part of him was low, was a weak man who could not stand to die knowing Phillipa still lived on.

"I will submit." He thought the words, but the living voice in the darkness was his cousin's.

"You will live on as a testament to those who do not, Lucien." Phillipa's voice propelled them both into the void. One foot in front of another. Drawing breath to say her name—Phillipa—Olivier felt a pain in his back, sharp, cold, that narrowed his sight into a tunnel of nothing.

"We could not kill you." Rosamund's warm lips on his cheek. He tilted to the ground.

"I'm sorry." Lucien—it was fitting that his closest companion and fiercest rival would strike the blow.

"Forgive him." Phillipa was there as well, her breath stirring the hair on his face.

"You are forgiven." Lucien, so near, choking at his words, the thick, wet sound of death. Olivier's fingers scrabbled on the cool, weeping stone of the floor for his cousin. No one explained how the change would come, how he would pass from light to dark, and this was all so sudden, confusing.

A warm wetness flooded down his back, and the tunnel became white dots ringed at the edges in a darkness beyond black, beyond comprehension.

Frantic whispers buffeted his face ". . . dying too quickly . . ."—". . . hurry, hurry, you do it!"—". . . he hasn't . . ."

A new pain kindled what was left of his mind, a horrible, throbbing stab to his neck.

"I forgive . . ." He had no breath to voice the words, but he thought them, felt them in his heart.

CHICAGO

PRESENT DAY

Chapter One

THE FLOORBOARDS IN the ceiling creaked with the rhythmic motions of domestic warfare, which woke Olivier from a peaceful sleep. His dreams of fluttering banners snapping in a late summer breeze, of the taste of honeycomb, the heartbreaking sound of perfect pitch in a well-loved voice broke and crumbled as he opened his eyes. His skin felt tight and dry, his hair brittle when he pulled his fingers through it. Hunger had crept up on him again, while his mind was occupied with his newest canvas and his oldest thoughts.

Climbing out of bed, Olivier decided to put off eating for a while longer. It occurred to him suddenly, like most thoughts of daily life did, that he hadn't checked his favorite blogs and websites for a while. Sometimes the Internet was too much of a burden for him, too much like obligation and work, and he would forget about his email and journals for a time.

The argument upstairs turned to the crashes of weapons of cookery and crockery. Olivier opened his outdated laptop and opened a browser. His unseen companions in the other apartment had moved on to noisy make-up sex by the time he surfed into *Read All Over* for the most recent update on dualist theology and solipsistic musings.

. . . and I stood for about a half hour staring into the window of Marshall Fields wondering how come green and red are the universal Christmas colors. I mean, am I participating in my own culture if I don't recognize the symbolism of the most important holiday of the year? First I thought maybe it was something to do with holly—I mean that's red and green, but then I realized holly was probably associated with Christmas because it *was* red and green, that the color scheme probably predated holly being a whole Christmas thing. Also, how did Santa end up being some sort of oppressor slave-owning figure? Is that related to the Dutch ideas about Sinter Klaus and his slave boy? What the fuck? Do elves get paid?

Olivier laughed while scanning back to see if he'd missed many entries on this blog. He had always had a certain fondness for the pun in name—it mainly being about Dualistic religions, two ideas or things set against each other as opposites, Good and Bad, Black and White, therefore the old joke about newspapers, what's black and white and read all over? He had come to think of the author as someone he knew. He hadn't ever realized before that the girl who wrote it resided in the same city as he did. He, too, had seen the Christmas display in the Marshall Fields window.

He was tired and hungry, and inclined to feel sorrier for himself than usual, with the memory of his recent dreams still fresh and his neighbors screwing loudly above him. Her writing took him out of the world for a time, alleviated the sullen mood he felt building.

He typed out a reply to her:

Who are we but the collected memories of everyone before us, of everything before this time? When the memories fall into the silent void of a future-obsessed world, does that make the dead all the deader? Gone *and* forgotten?

He sent his reply and surfed back through the other entries he'd missed.

December 2nd

Re: the Cathars. Not to flog a dead heretic, but the only other semi-contemporary case of the Church persecuting their own with such venom was with the Templars. Rhetoric aside, we know that the impetus for that persecution was mercenary, so that suggests the Cathar persecution to be as well. Insofar as the Northern nobles and French crown were involved in the Albigensian Crusade, the consolidation of power and rich, fertile lands of the Midi would have been irresistible, but that leaves the Pope and higher church authorities on one side of the equation uncancelled. Were they truly worried for the souls of the heretics, or was there a deeper game involved that history obscures? Conspiracy theories are easy, but it's more difficult to admit that when a millennium passes, the unspoken words of a person's heart are still just as irretrievable as if they died last week. What did the hold-outs trapped on top of their mountain fortress feel when they knew the crusaders were going to win?

November 26th

I think there were two camps in the Cathar ranks, not just the perfecta and credentes (perfected and believers), but also ideological camps of those who wanted to stand and fight to the death, to defiantly spit in the face of the Dark One, and the dissenting rank who wanted to apparently renounce their faith and infiltrate the main body of the Church to further their aims. The first group is represented by the martyrs at Montsegeur, the second by the nobles who joined the Crusading Orders and fled with their enemies to Outermer. (For those who don't speak historian-ese, check the sidebar for links to the glossary. Yeah, I'm boring enough to make a glossary.)

Olivier smiled and mused that the author had gotten one too many comments that she spoke in incomprehensible jargon and had decided a glossary would be easier than answering more. He clicked on the glossary. It was not in alphabetical order, he realized, but, rather, in the flow of her thoughts.

Glossary:

Albigensian: another name for Cathar. The word derives from the town of Albi in France.

Cathar: derogative, never self-applied, term for a member of a sect (called heretical by the Orthodox Catholic Church). This sect maintained a dualist theology—that is a theology believing in two deities, one all good, one all bad. The Good God made the world of spirit, of thought and all things Beyond This World. The Bad God created the earth, people, and all matter.

Credentes: average Cathar. The word means believer. They were a pretty liberated bunch with the women having the same say and rights as the men, all believers having no limitations places on their sexual lives or other physical desires, and a religious license to live it up as much as possible. Since the Evil One created the world and the physical form, the Good God didn't give much of a crap what you did with your corrupt body in this corrupt world. Especially since you could take the consolamentum before death and be forgiven all sins (this is really where the Catholics got pissed). Many credentes were artists, troubadours (medieval rap stars), or even knights.

Perfecta: The fervent believer who gave up all worldly sins (eating meat, having sex, breaking dishes in anger, plotting revenge against your neighbor for stealing your donkey, all the good stuff) and attempted to live a perfect life in order to thwart the plans of the Evil One. Perfecta were we very often noble women, the mothers of knights and higher nobility. (You'd renounce sex, too, if you were sold to your husband as a bargaining chip to consolidate a few more acres of vineyard.) The perfectas were the Cathar clergy, preaching and offering the consolamentum to the dying.

Consolamentum: Cathar last rites. This was the purifying of a soul before death that would ensure the swift return of said soul to heaven. Here we have several "heresies" in one package. First is the denial of the bodily resurrection which was a central concept Orthodox belief, next the renounced heresy of reincarnation (because a purified soul returns to heaven to queue up to get shot back into another, corrupt body), but most importantly the Orthodox authorities were incensed by non-ordained clergy giving a sacrament intended to expiate (forgive) sin. They were out of a job if someone else could absolve you of your transgressions and throw open the gates to eternal salvation. The Church had the single file line into heaven, and they did not appreciate butting.

Outermer: European word for the Holy Lands, but more specifically all of the lands they "conquered" and ruled in far western Asia, from contemporary Turkey to Egypt.

Montsegeur: The castle stronghold where Cathar hold-outs withstood a siege by Crusaders and Inquisitors only to be finally defeated and burned alive. All of them. Rumors persist that anywhere from two to ten Cathars escaped on the eve of destruction, the most common number in folk belief being four, but there has never been anything but anecdotal evidence, sort of like the medieval equivalent of Clem and Buddy in the swamp spying an alien space ship.

Her opinions and conclusions were oddly correct. Though he liked her thought patterns, he generally didn't keep track of modern scholarship on his life history—why bother? Once he'd toyed with sending in a paper to an historical journal detailing his firsthand accounts made safe with the use of third person, clinical and professional. Just to see if he would be denounced for his skewed view of troubadour life, the Crusades, any of it. But when he thought back that far, he couldn't remember enough to satisfy himself, couldn't remember Jerusalem before the massacres, Acre before its fall, Venice when it was still clean and full of salt. Not enough to satisfy, more than enough to haunt.

THE ANGRY VOICES streamed through the night, past where she crouched behind a low wall. She hated the villagers for bringing her to this, for scaring her this way, for representing evil to her in a way far more immediate and dangerous than anything she had seen in a long, long time. Leather-covered and bare feet crumpled what grass and flowers had struggled out of the ground in the drought, crushing them back into the earth from where they sprung. One voice rumbled out of the madness of the crowd.

A male voice, laced with the slithering vowels and twisted consonants of a Piedmont accent raised above the others, "We must burn her to save her immortal soul!"

She fled from her spot against the wall, fled into a field and hoped to find her companions, frightened more of something else than the priest and his rabble. They could only kill her body. She searched the horizon for someone, someone she knew would save her.

Sophie Aubrey woke from her dream with her face pressed into the yellow cotton pillowcase on her own bed. It was just more in a lifetime's worth of similar dreams of being chased by villagers, walking miles and miles and miles with the same companions—one of whom was the Man with the Voice. That was how she thought of him. He spoke in whispers with a half-sung cadence. The radio crackled with static as she turned over. She focused on the babbling from WBEZ, the local NPR station, explaining the difference between Santa's elves and the Sidhe of legend. Before she even opened her eyes, the images from her dream completely faded—gone, but not quite forgotten. Chasing off the last of her sleep, she felt the weight of twenty or so essays, individually stapled, paper-clipped or bound, against her legs. She'd fallen asleep grading again. The exciting life of a teaching assistant! Rolling her head against the headboard of the bed, she wallowed in self-pity; she'd never been a morning person, and waking from a nap of any kind always amplified that morning-anger. Her fingers snatched the nearest paper off the comforter, groping for her glasses in the bed clothes.

The human/elven-interest story on the radio went on to explain how Santa's elves had sought sanctuary with

Santa from a band of evil trolls. Sophie looked at the radio as if the idiot who had written this "humorous" topical report could feel her glare.

Sighing at the fact that her tax money paid for that guy to shop at L. L. Bean, Sophie flipped open the cover of the first essay to scope out the title. "How the Use of Prozac Could Have Prevented Religious Persecution." She blinked twice rapidly, but when she looked back, that really was the title of the paper that counted for a fourth of each of her students' grades. While she turned the page and groped for the purple pen on her bedside table, she knew even if the guy failed, she'd at least have a new story to tell over supper. Religious studies rarely yielded amusing anecdotes that people without at least three years of university education in the field could find even passably funny.

She worked through almost all of the rest of the papers, stupendously boring for the most part, but factually accurate—except for the girl who thought that the modern version of Wicca, all heavy jewelry and Rider-Waite tarot cards, had been the religion of the "witches" burned at the stake in the middle ages—before she fell asleep again.

The holidays wore everyone out, and that was only compounded for teachers of every stripe. For college professors, it meant extended office hours and a steady stream of students with "emergencies," life crises, impending nervous break-downs, and the rare truthful plea for an incomplete for the semester. Sophie, as a Ph.D. candidate, was fielding two classes that semester, both filled with non-majors and freshmen, none of whom appeared to be interested in religious studies in the least.

They all needed to see her during her office hours this

week, however, leaving her very little time to find the "holiday spirit." The cookie bribery was pleasant, at least. One girl went the distance with iced sugar cookie snowmen and homemade brownies—but she was already making an A, so Sophie figured the effort was the result of ingrained ass-kissing.

She got out of bed and headed over to her desk to check her email. Her sister was bound to have answered the blistering email Sophie had sent earlier in the day to refuse the invitation to the family cruise for Christmas. Staring at her computer screen, Sophie hovered the cursor over the button. Sighing, she opened the browser window and strengthened herself to beg off again no matter how much guilt her sister dished out.

In surprise, she stared at her inbox. It was devoid of anything from either of her sisters or her mother. Instead, there were three emails from her frequent IM buddy, Olivier.

> **This might seem abrupt, but I'm planning to meet up with the chat group at the bar tonight. I hope you don't mind and will be there.**

The first mail sent Sophie's heart pumping so strongly she could feel the thrump, thrump, thrump in her neck and wrists.

The second read:

> **Ok, you haven't answered me, so maybe I freaked you out. It was a bad idea. I won't be there.**

Her heart hit the bottom of her feet. Sophie reached for the cocktail that her roommate, Suki, had made her before she'd fallen asleep. It had stood untouched until then, but Sophie swigged the warm drink down in two mouthfuls. Typical Suki: too much lime juice, not enough vodka, with an aftertaste that *might* be gris-gris. It burned in her stomach.

Hesitantly, she clicked on the third mail.

Even if you won't be there, I'm still going to the bar. Maybe you'll show up anyway?

Smiling manically, Sophie clicked on the attachment that Olivier hadn't bothered to mention he'd added to the email. As her word processing program launched, she hoped that it was another of his enigmatic poems that he sporadically sent her. She wasn't disappointed.

This morning I saw a finality in the water spiraling
  down my drain,
Saliva and skin and blood that had once belonged to me
Rushed into the metallic darkness of an unknown world
That is everything we will become and ignore as we
Sip coffee in fake, modern coffee shops while
We avoid making eye-contact with others who are
Consigned to the same fate.

The phone rang, the shrill, false music startling Sophie and making her jump. Gazing around her desk, she couldn't see the portable. The voicemail didn't pick up—it had been on the fritz for weeks since they switched over to digital service. Clicking her computer

off, Sophie sprinted for the kitchen. Making her way
the short distance from her bedroom, through the hall
of the house she shared with her two best friends, Sophie's steps rattled the framed pictures and artwork
scattered haphazardly along the way as she hurried before the phone stopped ringing. She slid on the
linoleum of the kitchen floor on her socks, and almost
took a header into the cabinets, but she got the phone.

"Yeah?" Her breathing was ragged.

"Soph?" The voice on the other end was her roommate, Suki.

"Yeah?" In the background, Sophie could hear the
rattle of cymbals. Suki was at band practice.

"Voicemail still broke? Shit, I was expecting a call
from that shaman guy in Milwaukee." Sophie didn't
comment on Suki's whole magical . . . *thing*. About a
year before, Suki had proclaimed herself to be a witch,
and it'd taken Sophie at least seven months to realize
that Suki did not mean Wicca-practitioner, but actual,
for real, magic-having, warty witch.

Sophie had decided to ignore the whole issue. The
only real change for her had been the addition of Suki's
new cat, Sathan, to the household. Suki called him her
"familiar," but Sophie found he was an ordinary cat who
liked to snuggle, chase bugs, and sit on open books.

"I was asleep," replied Sophie, which was a lot more
polite than "Uh, could you get a grip? But if he calls
while I'm home, I'll take a message."

"Right." Suki knew exactly where Sophie really stood
on the magic issue. "Gonna make my show tonight?"

"Are you kidding? Hell yeah!" Sophie didn't miss
Suki's shows, even the ones played on the street corner
or in some friend's basement. This was a real show,
though, at a real club, only the third ever.

"Got that online 'thing tonight?" Sophie rolled her

eyes. Suki was sort of a matchmaker from hell. She knew all about Sophie's on-line flirtation with Olivier, and being the sort of person who wanted to meddle in other people's love-lives had decided that if Olivier didn't have leprosy or a wife, he was golden. Suki claimed this was the traditional role of witches, and that Sophie shouldn't oppress her.

"Uh huh." She made a non-committal noise, hoping Suki would drop it. She heard one voice tell Suki to say hi to "peanut," a reference to Sophie's less-than-average height. Sophie ground her teeth, and Suki, not much taller that Sophie's 5'2", intelligently didn't pass the message along.

On the other end, people started yelling, and Suki sighed. "Ok, gotta jet. See you tonight, and you better bring Olivier to the show so I can inspect him."

"And by inspect, you mean grope." Sophie said with a laugh.

"*Ew*, boy cooties, I think *not*. Big love." Suki laughed, too. She hung up before Sophie could respond. Sophie put the phone on the cradle, thinking about stereotypes. About how Suki shattered many, by being gay and feminine and punk rock and Asian all at the same time, about how Sophie's expectations of Olivier as beautiful and French and a smoker were all her own stereotypes of a poet. Smoking wasn't cool anyway. Look at Norah, for cripes' sake.

Norah was her other roommate, a television journalist, and so addicted to nicotine she was often found rooting around in ashtrays to find the longest butts left to smoke. Her explanation? "It's too cold to go out for smokes, yo!" Even in the middle of summer.

Sathan jumped down from the counter, where he was *not* supposed to be, and looked up at Sophie. His black fur was shiny enough to gleam even in the craptacular fluorescent light of the kitchen. He blinked once, slowly, and Sophie answered him.

"I'm going out, so I can't watch Food Network with you." She turned, and he meowed at her. "Don't pull that with me, sucker. Who buys you Fancy Feast? I have to go meet the chat people."

Truth be told, but who had to be honest to a cat, they were a whole helluva lot more than just chat people. She didn't just IM with them, but ran joint websites, monitored bulletin boards, organized conferences, the entire gambit of Net life pertaining to pre-high middle ages heresy and philosophy was covered by them. Her group was almost all there for comprehensive references for heresies on the Net in English, not run by the Catholic church, and that particular fact was what made them so tight. Odd obsessions tended to make a tight clique.

HOLDING UP A pink crocheted hat with an orange flower appliqué, Sophie inquired, "Should I wear my lucky hat?"

Sathan paused cleaning his face to look up at her like she was even stupider than usual.

"You know, I could dress you up in costumes and take you with me in a kitty backpack thing. I'm not above it." She waved her hat at him. He chose the better part of valor and went back to the licking.

She discarded the hat and turned back and forth in front of the full-length mirror on her closet door. The long black skirt and black, knee-high boots were fine. She even liked the garnet lambs wool sweater her mother had given her in anticipation of Christmas, but she wasn't loving her haircut. "Do I look fat?"

The cat, being an inscrutable creature, kept his own council.

Sophie wasn't *fat*, but she wasn't skinny either. She'd stopped growing in seventh grade, and five or ten pounds can really settle on a short frame. Really she was happy enough with her figure—her real physical nemesis was her hair. She was on a life-long mission to destroy or conquer it. It was fine but curly in a weird way that seemed different every day and didn't look like much except a bad perm that was growing out, and on top of all that, it was oily.

Sophie ran her fingers through the white and black streaks. It had seemed like the best idea ever the day before: black hair with white tips and streaks, rock-star bangs, and a flippy back. Now she hated it and wanted to yank it all out. Or dye it all pink or something.

She shrugged into her winter coat and tugged on her hat, and glanced back towards her bedroom wondering if she should just stay in and loll around with Sathan; maybe they could watch a few episodes of *Los Vampiros* on DVD and maybe she could finish another bag she was knitting her friends for Christmas.

But no: Sophie was finally going to meet the mysterious Olivier who left such thoughtful comments at her blog and sent her those weird but interesting poems in her email. Someone who used the English language so oddly and beautifully was definitely a guy she wanted to meet. It couldn't be a biological clock thing—at twenty-five she was too young to be thinking about babies and marriage. And Norah would really never let this go if she found out she was meeting up with guys online.

Still . . .

Her stomach fluttered at the thought of meeting Olivier finally. She zipped up her parka and stepped out of the front door, hoping she didn't have to wait long for the El.

Chapter Two

A GROUP OF loud undergrad-looking boys were pounding beers at the bar, sloshing alcohol all over them themselves and each other in good-natured high spirits when Sophie burst through the door of the Nunnery. Their fun was probably football-related, she figured, but she didn't really know. Sports didn't even blip her radar.

At a table near the back of the dimly lit pub, she spotted her crowd. Notebooks, glasses and ashtrays covered the high table where her friends were ensconced. Pulling off her coat and smiling at the boisterous, alcohol-fueled hellos from the table, Sophie searched the crowd for Olivier.

"Want a boost up?" Jordan, fellow Ph.D. candidate at the University of Chicago, winked at her and laughed when she scowled and clambered up on the stool. He was cute in that average but smart way, all shaggy hair, glasses and button-up shirt.

"Ha, fucking ha ha." Sophie waved at Penny as her

friend—and Suki's ex—emerged from the restroom, swinging her curly, red hair back over her shoulder. Her face was a network of freckles working in tandem in an attempt to connect completely one day. Her smile was genuine and lopsided. Sophie sometimes felt guilty for maintaining her friendship with Penny, but they'd known each other almost seven years, and they were friends separate from Suki, from their undergrad days.

"Why do we come here?" Penny laughed and turned her eyes on Sophie. "Right before you got here, I totally got into a bitch-slap fest with Jim Matheson. He was making fun of Ultimate, and then he said something about Chinese people playing cricket." Penny stared at Sophie, her face turning an angry red as she fumed. Hm, Sophie knew never to make fun of Ultimate Frisbee around Penny; that had been the catalyst for her break up with Suki—they both took Ultimate way, way too seriously. But mainly she was having trouble trying to piece together how someone would confuse Indians—who did play cricket—with Chinese people—who, as far as Sophie had ever heard, *didn't*.

"He's an ex-seminarian, what do you expect?" Jordan was himself an ex-seminarian, and his views on people of his own ilk were rather harsh. Sophie could understand that, since she usually reserved her harshest criticisms for people either from Ohio—like herself— or Catholic—also like herself.

The conversation dipped and spun, everyone getting a say even if they had to shout to be heard over the other voices. Sophie enjoyed the hell out of nights like this, but she found herself indulging in a couple too many rum and pineapples to cover the nervousness in her belly that Olivier wouldn't show, that he was sixty and covered in warts, that he was really some Prof she knew, and she hadn't been able to follow the conversation like normal.

Penny leaned over, her head cocked to the side, and whispered, "How come you're dressed up?"

Sophie blushed, a horrible habit she couldn't seem to break.

"I am dressed totally normally," she replied, in what she hoped was a haughty tone.

But Penny bestowed a knowing look on her, making her blush even harder, and just said, "Yeah, whatever."

Thwarted, Sophie sat back in her chair.

As they debated, the companions greeted new members singly or in pairs—two religion students from U Chicago, and one in philosophy; Jordan's roommate and Suki's bandmate, a pretty girl with pale skin and dreadlocks; a Women's Studies student from DePaul who was wearing Birkenstocks despite the snow on the ground and the bone-chilling wind; a few new people who had dropped in on their bulletin boards or chat rooms by accident or recommendation and wanted to see who the faces were behind all the words.

Everyone was turning raucous, defending their intellectual positions with the righteous fervor of alcohol. Sophie decided Olivier wasn't coming—and that was for the best. After all, there was no way any person could live up to Olivier's emails to her, so she never should have gotten her hopes up. It wasn't like she believed in soul mates anyway—she'd been burned far too many times in her early twenties by men who threw around the words "soul mates" when all they really wanted was a sex partner for a few weeks or someone to read over their papers for school.

Not like she'd ever *really* been fooled, but she'd *wanted* to be, and that was somehow worse—like she betrayed herself by letting herself be caught up in words she knew were lies. She knew they were lies because none of the men—boys, really—spoke with the voice of the man in her dreams . . .

Not "dreams," like wishes, but dreams, like Freud or Jung. The ones she'd had all her life, about knights and magic and blood. Like the one she'd had that very afternoon.

Sophie turned and was pulling her scarf out of her sleeve to wind around her neck in preparation for leaving when a voice right next to her said to Penny ". . . but dualism isn't a false, man-made construct—it's in nature. There is male and female, pollen and stamen, fire and water, night and day. Those are all systems of two, opposites, in the world. We see them every day and know they are real and natural without thinking. Sometimes intellectuals out-think themselves by arguing that something that's self evident isn't real. Any thought can be accidentally taken too far."

Her heart rolled in her chest, making her almost motion-sick. She turned, dreading to look. Her mind was probably just playing tricks on her. She'd been thinking about the man in her dreams, thinking about the voice—that didn't mean the man in the bar actually *had* the voice.

Penny had moved over two seats; sitting next to Sophie was an altogether too-attractive man.

His hair tumbled over his shoulders in thick reddish brown waves; his mouth bowed with a full bottom lip; his long eyelashes blinked against the cigarette smoke off his own Camel that was clutched between thick, well-shaped fingers; his wrist was broad and attached to an arm that promised to be muscular and toned.

Penny shouted something at him, and he laughed, his down-turned face lifting up and catching the light well enough for Sophie to see a set of three moles close to his high cheekbone on the right side. The line of his chin was so perfect it looked like the example all other male faces strove to match, square and strong and compelling. His nose balanced the halves of his face, resting between his high cheeks in a way that was exactly right for no reason other than it was. His reddish-brown eyebrows flew in arcs over his large, turquoise eyes. He wore jeans that rumpled perfectly in his lap and a crisp, white button-up shirt that gaped appealingly at his neck to show a patch of white under-shirt. He saw her staring, and Sophie tried to look away, to pretend she was only looking behind him, but he caught her eye too quickly.

The man leaned close to her, and she saw the flash of blue on green in his eyes, tiny starbursts of impossible aqua around his iris. "You're Sophie, right?" His smile became just slightly brighter, enough to make her smile back instinctively. The liquid-smoke whisper of his voice somehow carrying over the cacophony of the bar.

"Olivier?" Loud music and raised voices only barely covered the excited tremor in her voice as it broke around his name.

He nodded in response, smiling, smiling, then laughing. She couldn't think of anything clever to say, couldn't think of anything at all really, except "Thank you, God," as though there really *was* a God who took a special interest in her love life. The God of Beautiful Men? Eros? She would build a shrine, burn a candle, sacrifice a soybean.

Leaning in, so close his lips brushed against her ear, he told her, "Your hair is really cool." Losing his balance slightly, he fumbled almost into her lap, and she caught his shoulder, laughing with him at his clumsiness. If he wasn't a sex-god, she would have thought the accidental fumble was anything but.

An immediate pull told her she wanted to spend time with this man, get to know him in the flesh, not just for his voice, which was almost creepily familiar, but for everything. Before she really knew what she was doing, she opened her mouth and said, "Do you want to come with us to see my friend's band later?" She rested her hand on his elbow, pulling him over so he would hear her over the noise of the table.

"Yeah, I do." He offered her what she saw was an American Spirit cigarette, not a Camel at all, and she took it, cupped her hand around his as he lit it for her with a silver lighter. Their eyes met over the flame and his hand was hot under hers. She tightened her hand slightly, but he pulled away when she exhaled cigarette smoke.

He clicked the lighter shut, but kept his hand under hers. He turned his hand palm up, so that their palms were together, and Sophie would have sworn there was a spark.

But she could also hear that hard voice of rationality in her head, reminding her that she didn't believe in love at first sight anymore, or in soul mates, or in instant connections with almost-strangers, reminding her that a woman like her would do better to look for someone on a tenure-track at a good school, someone with whom she had career ambition and intellectual curiosity in common—and she pulled away, turned back to her drink and the conversation, cursing herself as she did so, but unable to stop.

Olivier just smiled at her like he knew all her secrets, and joined back into Penny's conversation about whether any account of history could be truly objective.

* * *

SUKI'S BAND, JESUS' Pickup, was lame. Extremely lame. The sort of band that only teenagers and people who love the band members gave a damn about. But Suki had the deadly combination of being smart, funny, cute—and in a band. Her shows were always jammed full of screaming people hoping to take her home.

Sophie scanned the crowd and regretted slightly that Norah, her other roommate, hadn't made it. She worked all the time. All the time. She and Norah had suffered through so many crappy performances in church basements that it was a shame she had to miss a real club date. Glancing over at her almost-kinda-maybe date, though, she was halfway glad her friend wasn't there. Olivier wasn't *only* gorgeous—he also bought the drinks.

And he hadn't taken her pulling away earlier as a real rejection, only a pause; he remained by her side, and even held her hand as they walked the block over to the club.

Sophie had felt sixteen again, like she was holding hands with her first boyfriend, her fingers tingling. She pegged him as exotic and European, exciting and used to a sort of casual touch that Americans always sigh at after watching too many Avant Guarde movies from the sixties.

At the coat check, Sophie checked her coat *and* her sweater. She withdrew a handful of safety pins from her pocket and pinned her calf-length skirt up to mid-thigh. The rum and pineapple juice she'd been consuming all night insulated her enough that she didn't care that her tank top was almost completely sheer and her bra was pretty threadbare—lace, but threadbare.

"Rock and roll," she said to Olivier, who had avidly

watched her impromptu punk rock re-clothing. He yanked off his brown leather coat and white oxford to sport a white, holey T-shirt with paint splatters all over it. Most of the women in the coat check eyed him openly as the firm skin of his belly was exposed when he reached over several heads to offer his bundle to the coat check attendant. Sophie felt possessive—and then smug when Olivier's arm slid around her shoulders. That's right, bitches, back off.

"Let's go," he said to her, his lips touching her ear briefly. Maybe it was the rum and pineapple juice again, but she was pretty sure there was definitely a connection.

SUKI EXHORTED THE crowd to cast off the scales from their eyes, and the room erupted in random screeches and hoots, only to be drowned out by the loud thwang of bass, and the rattle, thump of drum-kit, and a long riff of guitar. Sophie was jostled and subsumed into the crowd, screaming with everyone else, and jumping up and down in an effort to see. Before long, her tank top was rucked up, her thigh-highs had rolled down to the tops of her boots, and she kept reaching behind her to make sure her skirt wasn't tucked into her underwear.

On one pass to the rear, her hand brushed the front of someone's jeans. She wrenched her head around to catch Olivier smiling back at her. She had to tilt her head way back to look in him in the eye when they stood—he must have been at least 6 feet. He grabbed at her hand, and she yanked his around onto the bare flesh of her stomach.

They roiled and lunged with the mass, bumping into one another, then rubbing back to front, Sophie's arm over her head in Olivier's long hair, his hand pressing against her thigh, forcing her back against him. The crowd obliged and worked them from the middle of the group, to the edge, until Sophie turned and yanked Olivier by a belt loop into the hallway to the coat check. She had no idea what she was doing—she just wanted to *touch* him, to listen to his voice in her ear. The need for that was urgent, like the hum in your teeth when you haven't had coffee for hours and hours after waking.

All along the corridor leading to coat check, patrons of the club were in various states of debauchery. Sophie was drunk enough to think that if other people were groping in the hall, then it was just fine for her, too. Olivier smelled of cigarettes and linseed oil, ink and glue, and lime from the gin and tonic he'd been drinking. His bottom lip was ridged; when she licked it, she felt the tiny ripples in the flesh. The wall was stucco and hurt her bare shoulders and arms when he lifted and pressed her against it.

He rumbled and groaned, whispering words she couldn't get at, couldn't really listen to as hard as she tried. Her mind clouded some, all her higher thought gone, which was not right, not usual for her even when she was drunk or having sex; her constant background stream-of-consciousness never cut off. But one second she was thinking in full sentences and the next there was nothing in the world but Olivier.

"Sophie," she understood, the syllables compressed and elongated in the French way—*So-PHEE*, like a French sex-pop song. Her name from his lips was the answer to all her life questions.

She nibbled on his lips, felt compelled by his mouth, and his teeth sank into the tender flesh of her own mouth, hard—almost too hard. She tasted the salty metallic flavor of her own blood, and the world tilted,

tilted, sliding like melting paint swirling, colors bleeding together behind her eyes. She felt Olivier meld into her, his breath on her neck, his hands under her ass, holding her, moving her, moving *in* her. She held her breath, scraped her teeth on his neck, felt him shudder underneath her hands. Her legs came up to lock completely against the small of his back, clutching. His hips tilted slightly, and with ever shimmy-slide of his hips, he bumped her inside and out, riding those two points most men didn't even know how to negotiate one at a time.

She came in fast waves, her head falling back and bumping against the stucco, Olivier calling her name, crushing her to him.

Chapter Three

". . . WHATEVER! AND THEN the ferret ran up my leg, and I fell into the camera cords. I broke a fucking nail and my hair was a total disaster . . ." Norah broke off in mid-sentence. "Are you awake?"

Sophie opened her eyes. She stared at the ceiling of her living room. Last year she'd glued a giant map of the Roman Empire to it; the Ikea light fixture stuck perfectly out of Carthage.

She sat up and immediately felt the scratches on her back and both her biceps felt abused. Oddly enough, she was wearing her pajamas, the warm flannel ones with pictures of dancing toast and jam. The fear of dislocation slid over her. How did she get home? How did she get into her pajamas? Sathan shifted where he lay between her splayed knees, yawning dramatically and raking her with his almost-but-not-quite sheathed claws. She winced.

Norah stared at her with a look of exasperated

amusement from her perch in the overstuffed, bald chair Suki had inherited from some obscure relative. She was still dressed for work in a smart, red business suit and very high heels—but her hose were torn from her ankle and seemed to be hanging onto her left leg by two threads. Normally her hair was so impeccable she had been asked on occasion if it was a wig, but the flippy black wings were smashed and knotted. Sophie could tell she was tired, because the cinnamon skin of her face showed darker, chocolate circles under her eyes.

"What happened to the ferret?" Sophie wasn't exactly sure what was going on, but she was very good—from being an undergrad—at picking up random threads of conversation while high, hung-over, or drunk. Black-outs, however, were new for her.

Oh, God, she'd had unprotected sex. In public. Oh fuck. Which was worse, STDs or humiliation?

"It bit me and ran off. I hope it drowned in the toilet or something." Norah looked haughty and rumpled.

The actual facts started drifting into Sophie's brain then. "The trained ferret thing?" It was one of those gigs that Norah had been forced into recently by the newsroom.

Which meant it was daytime? Sophie would readily admit that her grasp on reality was somewhat untraditional, but she'd never lost a whole night before. Sure, her orgasm with Olivier—oh God, had she really had sex in a club? That was going a little too far. She wasn't puritanical or anything, but—but—sex in public was slutty no matter how you cut it. She swallowed hard and tried to focus on Norah. STDs!

"You mean the supposedly trained ferret that was really a blood-thirsty killer beast thing from *hell?* Yeah." Norah kicked off her shoes and lit a cigarette.

"At least you're not the weather ho anymore." Sophie said. She sort of meant it to be nice, but also—well, also *not*.

Norah hrumphed and zinged back with, "So, Soph . . . what happened last night?"

"What do you mean?" said Sophie. Uh-oh. Had the news traveled that fast? Had Suki seen her?

"Well, you *didn't come home,*" said Norah with a grin in her voice "On a school night. For starters." She paused and Sophie didn't respond. "You hook up with that hot bartender?" She took out her earrings and tucked them into her suit jacket's pocket, then began rolling her stockings down her legs. She was the bad influence that made Sophie buy all those thigh-high stockings—somehow on Norah's almost-six-feet model's frame they looked just like they did in lingerie ads. "*So?*" Norah finally said with an edge.

"So what?" replied Sophie hoarsely.

"So you never go home with anyone," said Norah. "Remember? You don't have time for guys, your career comes first, dating is pointless because people don't act like themselves until it's too late anyway. *Remember?*"

"Maybe . . ." Sophie cleared her throat and shifted her feet to dislodge the cat. "Maybe I met someone."

Norah dissolved into laughter and slid off the couch. "The huge, and by huge I mean the size of a *baseball*, hickey on your neck gave that away."

Sophie debated smacking her in the back of the head, or reaching up and rubbing at the offending bruising, but instead settled for, "I think the ferret may have ripped out a chunk of your hair."

Norah's perfectly manicured hand flew to the back of her head, and she began patting her hair. "Really? I'll be right back!"

Payback's a bitch, bitch! thought Sophie, and,

smirking, chalked up a point to herself; Norah's hair-issues were an easy target, though, so maybe she should only take half a point. Plus, apparently she'd have to rummage around in her make-up for some base and concealer. She never wore foundation; it would be too obvious. Turtlenecks it was.

Thirty seconds later, Norah reemerged rolling her eyes. "You're evil," she said.

Sophie stared down at the sofa, picked at a piece of lint on the hideous, hundred-colored afghan her mother had made when she was a teenager. "I guess I didn't realize it was so late when I got home." Which sounded much better than "I don't know how the hell I got home, and do you think I might be deranged or suffering from alcohol-related black-outs?"

"Uh-huh," said Norah with a knowing tone. "Eventually I will expect a full report, young lady!"

"Sure." Norah patted her leg and left the room, and Sophie continued, mumbling, "As soon as I remember."

"You seen Suki?" Norah asked from down the hall.

Oh, hell, Suki would be on the rampage that she missed most of the show.

SOPHIE DRAGGED HERSELF to her weekly Wednesday night class with less enthusiasm than for a sporting round of Ebola. She was confounded by the incident with her Internet date, plus Suki had called her, totally on the warpath—as expected, claiming she'd ditched her concert to go to bed early; where the hell had that come from, bed early? They'd had a massive fight about it—which was mostly Suki being hurt and sarcastic and Sophie being defensive and freaked out—and now she had to go to class and act like everything was normal.

Plus, Suki said she was staying with her bandmate until they "worked things out." Not good. Not good at all. Sophie wondered if Suki had really gotten back together with Penny and didn't want to admit it since Norah and Sophie had been pushing for it since their break-up. She also wondered, kind of meanly, if Suki realized that she still had to pay her share of the rent, even if she wasn't sleeping in the house.

Nothing was normal. Sophie was not the kind of girl who kissed on the first date, much less had sex! In public! Against a wall! She planned to visit the school clinic the next day. She was on the pill, an old habit she'd never given up, which was good because Olivier was way too hot for them to not have sex, like, *constantly*. Still, she was a complete moron not to be more careful with him. She wasn't fifteen. She had no excuse. If he'd given her an STD, Norah and Suki would have ammunition for the rest of her life.

Despite being appalled with herself, she couldn't help the rush of heat to her face thinking about him. Her tongue came out of her mouth slightly and pushed at the crack in her lower lip, where Olivier had bitten her. It hurt, a little, pulled her back into reality. But only a little. She'd been doing it all day, would come back from daydreaming into the pain of her mouth, realize what she was doing, and try to busy herself with something else, a distraction, anything. She would see the flash of his strong, blunt fingers, huge around her wrist or against her belly, and felt a blush start high on her cheeks and spread to her ears and neck.

As she slunk into the classroom, she was pleased to note that the chalkboard announced the cancellation of class. The flu was her friend!

She was less thrilled to catch sight of a familiar male form leaning against the wall of the building when she exited. Sophie's heart thud-thud-thudded, and her mouth went dry as Olivier slipped away from the wall and walked towards her. Ice clung to his hair, shining blue under the street lights.

"That's not a happy look." He wore a heavy pea coat, but no hat or gloves, and just looking at him froze her. Except looking at him also warmed her up, made her stomach clench with anticipation.

"I . . ." And suddenly she was embarrassed. Her mind went to disease again, and TV shows about charming serial killers, and the warmth in her stomach turned to ice.

"I thought you might want to have a drink sometime. I have an entire library of books you might like . . ." Sophie shuffled a few steps back, and he broke off. She'd always been sort of wary of strange men—all small women, Sophie reasoned, have to be aware of their precarious situations in cities. She had no weapons, and there was hardly anyone around that part of campus at this hour.

If he had just *called,* or sent her an email, that would have been kind of romantic and alleviated the tension. But to show up at her school, outside her class, as though he'd been *stalking* her . . .

"What are you doing here?" She didn't really know how to be anything but blunt, especially when she was nervous. He pinned her with an unreadable expression.

"I wanted to see you again." That much she could have figured out. And as much as she wanted to tell him off about how inappropriate his behavior was, the streetlight behind her head lit his face when he shifted slightly, and he was as beautiful as a painting by an Italian master—perfect lines and thick hair framing his face like he'd been composed just so.

"How did I get home last night?" She wouldn't let

him put her off by prettying at her. She was better than that, her mind and her cynicism gifts she'd use against whatever pull he exerted on her baser self.

"I walked you, don't you remember?" His voice was meant for bedroom moans and dirty whispers, whiskey-burned and cigarette-scarred. And she did remember that, his arm around her waist, laughing with his head thrown back and his white teeth catching the streetlights. But she knew that was wrong, she could remember not remembering.

Her confusion must have registered, because Olivier tilted his chin up slightly while turning his face to the side. "You don't have to be scared of me."

That was exactly the wrong thing for him to say. Sophie tripped over herself and slid on the ice as she spun around to run away. She lurched off the curb and didn't even get one hand out to break her fall as the frozen concrete came up to meet her face.

Chapter Four

COLD AND PAIN wrapped around and around, dragging at her breath and skin. Her hair broke as it froze. Her skin purpled and blued and cracked off. Then fire broke through the cold, searing away what was left, lapping up her bones and teeth, crumbling her soul from the inside.

MEMORY FOUND HER dreams.

The scent of wet earth and grain trampled under foot. Rye and millet ground together with leather-clad feet passing back and forth, back and forth, walking and running in panic.

Fear colored every breath, every thought fully formed, or waiting to be born, or fading into the still-birth of forgetfulness. Fear like a shadow of the un-seen. She felt all the lives in the village, all the chaotic madness of terror focusing. Focusing on the words of the priest. Focusing on her.

Her own fear gave their shadow fear true life, spinning it into the night like a living being, frightening them all the more. She tasted the blood of the priest on the back of her throat, felt the slippery clots caught in her back teeth, but knew the life lost that night would not be his—but hers. She heard the fairy's taunting voice in the back of her mind cursing her forever for trying to escape him. She felt the geas laying on her like a yoke.

HER SLACK FINGERS gripped at thick, strong ones clutching her hand. Sophie woke with a moan in her throat, her waking body continuing the rhythm her sleeping hips had found. She lifted one leg to angle her partner better, twisting slightly to find the exact right spot. Lips worked below her ear where skull and neck met, pulling her thoughts, her will, her ability to speak out through her skin.

Perfect, perfection, but she had no words, no real thoughts, just this second followed by that second, the body around her, inside her, part of her obliterating the universe, God, death, infinity.

"*Sophie . . .*"

That name was wrong, not hers—

His wet lips locked on hers, the ridges rubbing her smooth mouth. The tang and salt and metallic taste was just that *thing*, that exact thing, and she tore her mouth from his, bit down on his neck as eternity spilled down her throat. Wrenching her teeth from his flesh her spine locked and she screamed his name.

Olivier.

SOPHIE WOKE THE second time face down in the sheets, her right leg cocked to the side. She felt fantastic. She wasn't sore or bruised, and her mouth didn't taste like a boiled shoe. She rolled over and felt a sharp pain in her scalp. Trying to sit up, she discovered she was sitting on her hair. Her hair that should have been shoulder-length was now down to her butt, at least—and what looked to be ten different shades of red and blond. A golden reddish blonde was her natural color—exciting when she was eleven and voraciously reading about Nancy Drew, titan-haired girl detective—so that wasn't *too* strange, except for that it *was*, because she'd started the night with black and white striped hair that she had paid eighty dollars to attain.

That puzzle was soon forgotten when she looked down at her breasts. Like most women, her breasts fluctuated in size—in her case from a B to a C depending on her weight—and were decorated with stretch-marks. That had been the case when she dressed for class the night before. Overnight her breasts had plumped, firmed, and become as smooth as the skin on her . . .

As she tore the sheet away, she realized her whole body was smooth and toned, not lumpy or scarred in any way.

"It happens to everyone." Olivier sat naked in an armchair near the bed. Her first opportunity to see him out of his clothes, and she suddenly regretted the club sex for a totally different reason—his body was the fulfillment of every adolescent day-dream she'd ever had. His pronounced collarbone swooped into broad, heavy shoulders. The muscles in his arms and legs stood strong and defined under his golden skin, even in repose. His chest was smooth and hard, standing out above the ripples in his stomach. Sophie immediately raised her hands to her face to cover her blush as she let her eyes follow the pronounced V of his pelvic flexor leading to his—his—

She felt even stupider for blushing when Olivier smiled at her. His interest in her interest was obvious, and she felt about fifteen.

"Am I psychotic? Is this, like, some psycho-drug in-duced reality?" She used her hair to cover herself, like a mermaid in a painting.

"Do you feel crazy?" He looked at her quizzically.

"All the time." Which was the absolute truth. She'd had a hard time distinguishing reality from fantasy all her life—starting from when she was a little girl who talked to people who weren't there. Of course, she'd thought they *were* there, but that didn't make that okay. Usually her oddities suited her—not too many people could say that they'd picked their course of study be-cause people who weren't there had told them to, be-cause someone in a dream said they were supposed to—but sitting in her new lover's bed with a new body she was distrustful of herself and her thoughts. "What the fuck happened?"

Olivier made a displeased face. "You fell in your haste to get away from me and broke your stupid neck." His face softened, and he leaned forward with his forearms on his knees.

His explanation left quite a bit lacking, and Sophie went from feeling dislocated and confused to scared. "What? How?" She reached up and rubbed the back of her neck.

"The flesh is treacherous and corrupt." He ran a hand through his hair, pushing it away from his face then shrugged. "The Dark One pushed you, maybe you're just clumsy, maybe there was a patch of ice or a pebble under your foot."

The Dark One? The flesh is treacherous? Was he playing a joke on her? That sounded like rhetoric from the heretical sect she wrote her Master's thesis on—the Cathars. They were a medieval French group, almost a cult, who rejected the Christian God, claiming he was really the Evil One, the Devil, and that the real, Good God lived beyond the Earth in a world of pure spirit. They had been persecuted into oblivion by the Catholic church. Or so Sophie thought.

Olivier paused and tilted his head up slightly to look Sophie better in the face, watching her closely. "Do you treat everyone you make love with similarly?" He didn't look angry so much as annoyed, but Sophie was acutely aware of how much bigger than her he was, how he seemed extremely unbalanced, and she felt an odd impulsive desire to please him which was unlike herself.

"Only the scary stalkers!" She tried to put heat into her voice, but she sounded petulant and childish. "My neck feels fine." She glared at him in what she hoped would look like defiance but felt more like terror.

Olivier's expression closed off completely, and he sat up straight. "And I don't have a wound in my back down to my spine."

This guy just kept getting creepier. "Could I get some info here? Did you drug me or something? I feel screwed up and I think I'm hallucinating. Who the hell is the Dark One? Where are we?"

"Ah, okay, there's your personality. I was wondering where it went." He smiled, and as hard as Sophie was trying to hate him and remember that he was a potential serial killer, he was just too beautiful to not want to just give up or let him kill her. "You fell. How, who knows. I hadn't gotten an opportunity to discuss certain matters with you. It was a waste—your youth, your mind gone, and me frustrated for eternity over what you might have had to say or might have thought. I don't have much patience with unsatisfied desires. I never have." He grinned again.

Eternity? "Yeah, fine, whatever. I wanted a real answer, because you seemed really cool . . ." And by cool she meant romantic and *hot*. Sophie flung the sheet away from her body and wiggled out of the bed. ". . . and I—I don't know, but this is so fucked up." She spotted her jeans and shoes on the other side of the studio apartment and just grabbed one of his shirts along the way to them from the piles of laundry strewn all over the floor. She was really uneasy about how he alluded to the Cathar heresy of the Middle Ages as though he were personally acquainted with it, and then ducked her questioning him about that. She had sort of known he was interested in the topic in general, or else he wouldn't have been on their chat threads at all, but his odd way of phrasing set off alarms in her head.

"You should really wait to leave." He was there, right there, so fast, and Sophie didn't see him move at all. He held her bicep loosely—not enough to hurt, but tight enough she had to rip her arm out of his grasp. "Just wait a couple hours. There are things you need to know about the way this works—"

"Please fuck the hell off." Sophie stepped into her shoes without worrying about the cold and not wearing socks. She stole his coat off the floor because she didn't see hers, and stomped to the door. She looked down at her feet as she realized her center of gravity was the same. All the other physical changes, and she was still the same height. Even her hallucinations were rational. She was so boring.

"I didn't do you any favors by keeping you in this evil world, but I thought you were smart enough to ask the right questions." His voice was soft, the vowels not always quite right. He spoke to her back as she undid the locks on the front door. "You're a vampire."

As he said it, she knew, intrinsically, instinctually, like breathing and sweating and bleeding, that it was true. Which had to be magic, or something that ignorant people like her would call "magic." Some pull tugged at her belly, a need for something that the word "blood," the first word she associated with "vampire," glimmering in her mind, seemed to fulfill. Maybe she wasn't hallucinating after all. Which was really sort of worse.

She paused, took a deep breath, and stormed out of his apartment knowing that she should get some answers, interrogate him some more about that Cathar thing, about *why!* The corridor from his door to the elevator was only about six steps, even for her short legs, and she made them in a haze of terror and anger. She jabbed at the elevator button over and over in her agitation. Was she insane? Through the wall next to her she could hear the soft sounds of two people engaged in early evening activities, supper, laundry. Their conversation floated to her, sesame green beans versus asparagus. The elevator pinged and opened just as the beans won out.

So, yeah, that was weird. But it could all be in her head. She fretted during the short ride from Olivier's floor to the lobby, but as the doors rolled open and the bustle of the lobby overwhelmed her, anxiety bled back into fear. A hundred heartbeats buffeted her incessantly thrumming at a hundred different cadences and speeds. A man turned to walk into the elevator as she stepped out, his friendly smile immediately eclipsed as she rushed by him to avoid the shush of his heart murmur. A girl by the large Christmas tree had a racing pulse. A middle-aged woman brushing passed

Sophie out of the street possessed a laboring heart forced to squeeze too hard to move blood through clogged arteries. Sophie hit the sidewalk at a run, her feet barely touching the icy pavement and salted slush as she raced through the darkness of the night, looking for the El. She got half a block down and realized she had no idea where she was. Slowing down she tried to get her bearings. At the next corner she realized she was in Wicker Park on Milwaukee and luckily headed in the right direction to hit Western and hail a cab. The street formed a sort of wind tunnel and gusts hit her hard enough to make her walk harrowing enough to distract her.

On Western she stepped instead to the curb to hail a taxi. Luckily, she barely had to wait before a yellow cab pulled to the curb. The wind was whipping her hair around her face hard enough to sting. Climbing in the backseat she told the driver, "6642 North Glenwood."

"No problem!" The guy was way too chipper for her mood. He headed down Western towards Devon.

The cabbie was a young man with a huge grin and thick, black hair. He chatted amiably to himself after Sophie croaked out her address, pulling jerkily into the flow of traffic with his horn blaring and fist raised to the sky. In the strobing light of the streetlights they passed, Sophie could see the thick vein in the side of his golden skin throbbing. Music blared out of the stereo, rich with vibrato and the exotic, Arabic musical scale. A woman warbled and wailed, the only word that Sophie knew in Arabic, *habibi*, sweetheart, repeated over and over in a lament that was unintelligible, but universal.

"Pull over here." As they passed Clark Street the words skidded out of her mouth before she could stop them.

The driver looked in his rearview with a smile.

"I take you to your door, no problem!" Turning onto Greenview, he continued the sentiment, but Sophie was passed hearing anything but the song of his blood, sweet, rich, necessary like salt and sugar.

"*Stop here!*" She lunged into the back of the driver's seat, gripping him by the shoulder, and he obeyed with a screeching of the tires. He didn't even manage to get the car into park before her teeth were in his neck, the chunk of flesh between her upper and lower teeth bitten off in her rush, the meat flowing down her throat with his life. His spicy, complex life full of love and anger and Allah calling him, medical school and his baby brothers and his love of birds and parasites and the ocean, exploding into her like true love after an orphaned existence.

She opened her eyes to find his body slumped against the steering wheel. Panic waited on the edge of her mind, but before she would let it in, she leaned over the seat and flipped the glove box open. Rummaging around, she found a pocket knife, a good sized one, and she sighed with relief.

She yanked the man's head back by the hair, exposing his gaping throat, and sliced. Her strength was far more than she'd anticipated, and she hit bone all the way across. Where her teeth had torn, she cut in a circle to excise the actual teeth marks. Wiping the knife on the front of his shirt, she pocketed it. Lastly, she knocked him on his side and pilfered for his wallet. She took the whole thing.

Climbing out of the car, she wiped her face on the inside of her shirt. She stared at the car for a moment—why wasn't she more upset about killing a poor stranger? She flipped open his wallet. Mohammed Hinar, twenty-four years old. She pushed deep into her own brain, trying to feel guilt, or sadness, but all she found was fullness, satiety. And curiosity. She instinctively knew how to obscure the—the kill. How did that work? She puzzled at that. Had she always been a murderous lunatic waiting for an excuse? She'd always had a temper, a bad temper, but the worst she'd ever done before was break some dishes.

She needed to talk to Norah or Suki about this, about why and . . . terror stumbled into her mind. She did not want to do this whole vampire thing alone, especially if it meant attacking taxi drivers in the street. Especially if she was really a deluded, murdering nutso.

Sophie looked up from Mohammed's wallet, looked around. No one was paying attention to her. She felt her mouth—bloody. She licked the blood off her finger, and turned toward her house. Reaching into the pocket of Olivier's coat, she felt a jagged piece of paper. She pulled it out. It was the back page of a book, ripped out and torn again in half. In a scrawling, heavy hand was written:

> *Sleep broken like a branch underfoot*
> *by your piercing voice*
> *by your very existence.*
> *You think I see through you*
> *but instead my thoughts are reflected*
> *from the incandescent surface*
> *of everything you are,*
> *you represent.*
> *Your future is my past,*
> *and like the snapped twig,*
> *once undone I can not be mended.*

The blocks to her apartment on Glenwood were filled with the caress of the fresh snow falling from the night sky while she wondered if the poem was about her. Did he have scores of minions floating around the city, an army of girls he met on the Net and converted into creatures of the night? She ignored the rushing of her blood demanding she return to Olivier—had he put some kind of bizarre vampire homing device into her?—and she formed a new plan for how to make this experience bearable.

SOPHIE SLAMMED THE door behind her as she entered the three-flat. Her body felt light, tense, like she was waiting to be attacked at any second as she climbed the stairs to the second floor. She always had bric-a-brac in her pockets, so she'd been able to braid her new, long hair and get it off her neck, but it was still heavy and annoying—plus now it had blood in it, because she hadn't licked it all off.

That was why she'd started cutting her hair short in the first place—not the blood. Long hair looked pretty, but it was hell on the muscles in the neck and shoulders. She was framing a plan to hack it off with sewing shears when she heard the television in the basement.

She was pleased to share her real-life, honest to Satan (apparently her deity of choice now) existentialist crisis with Norah. Because she knew it *was* Norah in the living room. Sophie didn't stop to consider how—just a feeling in the back of her throat, the way certain scents could be tasted just by smelling them, like licorice or cinnamon.

Norah was ensconced on the battered blue plaid couch, eating a container of yogurt and commenting to herself and Sathan about the repeat of her favorite show, *The Up-State*, she was watching. Sophie was confounded by the normalcy of the scene. How could her home be exactly as she left it, with everyone acting just like themselves, when she had stepped into a bad, low-budget sci-fi movie?

"If your man did you like that, would you just be all 'Oh, he must have had a bad day?' Hell no! She is so stupid." Norah looked up and chewed thoughtfully. Sathan meowed meaningfully. "Did you go to the spa without me?"

Sophie was sort of surprised that this was the only response to her radical alteration. "I had a strange day," she stammered.

"You mean night, since we lost you yesterday. *Again.*" Norah glared, as if by going missing Sophie had put a kink in her plans not to care about anyone. Sophie knew Norah was more disconnected from reality than she herself was, that Norah had less patience with people, less sympathy for the human condition— but sometimes Sophie found herself wondering if Norah maybe really *didn't* care about anyone at all. She pushed that thought out of her mind, though; Norah had never been anything but one of her best friends. "So, you went to the spa, or what?"

"Um, in all the time you've known me, have I ever just up and gone to the spa by myself?" Sophie flipped Norah her middle finger. Ah, ok, that felt natural still.

"Uh, no. I'm just sayin,' what the hell?" The commercial ended, and Norah's interest in Sophie did as well. She turned back to the screen, lifting and dropping her spoon into the blueberry Yoplait with no comprehension that *everything* was just *wrong*.

"I'm a freaking vampire." Sophie sighed and collapsed onto the couch when Norah didn't bother to look away from the screen. Or comment on her blood-splattered hair, clothes and skin. Olivier's shirt smelled uncomfortably like him, like paint and linseed oil. She plucked at it restlessly. That must be why she wanted to run back to Olivier, crawl inside his skin, cover her lips with his blood—or it could be the poem.

She shuddered at her own thoughts. They were kind of gross. The part of her brain that she guessed used to be human thought it was icky. The part of her brain that knew how to disguise a kill thought it was hot. She pressed her thighs together, hard.

"What? A what? You been watchin' too many episodes of *Los Vampiros* and lost your mind?" Norah laughed in real amusement. Sathan lifted himself out of Norah's lap and stalked over to Sophie. He extended his pink tongue and began licking the bloody patches on her hand. She just let him. Why not?

"No, I was made into a vampire by an Internet stalker who turns out to be a nutcase or something! I could not make this up if I tried!" How stupid did she sound? Sophie wanted to cry. How could she make this believable?

"I think you *could* make it up, but why?" Norah laughed. "I laugh. See? You make me laugh." She sort of looked over out of the corner of her eye, laughing, true, but more interested in the television. "Now really, is that a water bra, 'cause I need to hook that up."

"Look, bitch, I'm a *real* vampire, and I'm about to open a can of neck-sucking on you!" Sophie kicked her heel against the couch in frustration. She didn't want to hurt her friend to prove her point, but what else could she feasibly do? This situation was not doable alone. Sophie *needed* Suki and Norah to make it through this.

Sathan purred loudly, having hit upon the cache of blood in her hair. He began to knead his paws in her boob as he licked. Sophie tried to rearrange him.

"You're so cute when you throw tantrums." Norah

chuckled again. She patted Sophie's knee, an absently affectionate gesture she always made when Sophie was "cute," and that was enough to turn her sorrow and anxiety over into the soft buzz of anger.

Sophie felt her teeth shifting, the canines elongating and the lateral incisors sharpening. The rest of her teeth realigned to allow the movement of the front ones—even her jaw moved a little. The mechanics were really kind of neat. Eventually she would have to stop and think about it all. Sathan jumped clear of her.

She bared her teeth and breathed in. The complex scent of Norah filled her beyond capacity: menthol cigarettes, beer, coconut pomade, yogurt, cold creamsweatcopperpollutionbloodsaltmetalblood—

"Fuck," Norah breathed. She looked scared. Sophie had never seen Norah scared before.

Sophie tried to run from this strange feeling, one step, two steps launched her out, and her toes brushed the carpet on the stairs and the floor of the landing. The front door flung wide, and she was in the night. In the frozen night full of terror and the terrified, the lovers and laughter and colors she'd ignored until then or never had a name for. She ran down the sidewalk, not thinking, just hungry, starving, dying, pain in every nerve ending and there, so many noises, breathing and thumpthumpthumppety.

Sophie opened her mouth to scream, to bite, tear, claw, and . . . *Olivier*!

"Come here," he said, and he was holding her tightly, her arms clamped to her sides, his arms suspending her slightly from the ground exactly where he'd stopped her from flying over a parked SUV and feeding from the plump middle-aged stock-broker lugging his briefcase out of the backseat. "I think you might be hard for me to figure out." There was surprise

in Olivier's voice, amusement, and something dissonant. Sophie hated him with the fire of ten thousand
burning suns.

"I'm starving!" She heard more thumpthumpthumps
close by, so many, and he held her as she struggled
against him. He sank down to the ground, hiding between cars, and he pressed her face into his neck. She
tore and bit and made him hurt.

Killhimkillhimhatehatehatedie, she thought.

When she came to herself, Sophie was kneeling
over Olivier, who was coughing up blood clots. His
beautiful face was splattered with gore and his own
blood. Sophie's body was on fire with the urge to have
sex with him—everything tingled, even her eyeballs,
even her hair. Then Olivier gave a rattling cough, and
Sophie started to cry.

"Why did you let me do this?" She had wanted to
kill him, to burn him alive, to rip out his throat. But
she'd done one of those, and she felt like throwing herself in front of a truck.

"I . . ." Rattle cough. "Deserved it." He reached his
paint-stained fingers to his throat, but Sophie beat him
to it, pressing her hair into the wound. She felt the tis-
sue move beneath her fingers, felt the veins mending,
the skin healing.

He deserved it? Even if he did, who said things like
that?

She pulled her hair away from his wound and stood.
Her pant-legs were frozen to the ground with blood,
and she had to tug them up to get upright. Sophie left
him on the ground, still bleeding, but healing rapidly.
She walked slowly back to the apartment, scowling at
the people who stared at her.

Norah was on the phone when Sophie got back. She
hung up when Sophie walked into the living room, not

even saying good-bye to whoever it was on the other end of the line.

The scared look was gone from Norah's face, replaced with a horrified fascination, kind of like what Sophie herself was feeling.

"Do you want to be a vampire or not? I think this shit might suck by myself." Sophie was so lonely. Who was she going to tell the details of her insane story to with no one to believe her? And if she didn't turn Norah into a vampire, would she eventually just kill and eat her?

Sophie definitely thought she could live without that sort of guilt.

"If you really are a vampire and not just on a mad killing spree, then hook me up." Norah looked anticipatory, but a little reserved—probably, thought Sophie acidly, she was worried that Sophie would just kill her, instead of making her an evil child of the night with a bunch of superhuman powers and the ability to, like, do cool shit and take over the world.

"Okay," said Sophie, approaching her. "Keep in mind I've only seen this done in movies."

"Oh shit," said Norah, and then Sophie's teeth were in her neck, ripping the smooth brown skin, tasting the blood. Norah tasted like home, like best friends, like confidences over soda pop and crying over ice cream, the best of everything, complete acceptance.

Chapter Five

IT TURNED OUT to be pretty instinctual. Which made sense. Sex was instinctual, so why wouldn't other, more arcane forms of procreation be?

Which came first, the sex or the vampirism? Sophie snickered at her thoughts as she watched Norah change.

Norah's coma-like sleep seemed unnatural—but what wasn't natural about this? Suki always argued that if things existed and were possible, they were therefore natural. Sophie was slightly disbelieving of that argument, but she had to admit that it was either believe this was natural or believe that she was an evil hell demon.

She didn't feel like a hell demon. Even if, maybe, she acted like one with that cabbie.

Norah's hair lengthened and thickened. Her figure, kept painstakingly thin for television, filled out proportionally, and her skin took on the tawny glow usually only achieved in facial-cleanser ads. After a while, Sophie got bored watching Norah's fingernails and eyelashes grow, and went to take a shower.

She examined her body more closely as she did. It was similar to her regular body, but off. Her skin was soft, almost hairless, and she was impossibly toned. She had muscles in places she hadn't previously. After she wrapped a towel around her hair, she wiped the condensation off the mirror to get a look at herself. Her mouth was fuller, cheekbones higher and sharper, eyes slightly larger. Her nose was the same. She opened her mouth to see that her teeth were perfect, white, and human looking. She was vaguely like herself. Enough. But not enough that Norah shouldn't have wondered when she'd had massive cosmetic surgery. Was this some side-effect of the turning? Did she have some sort of magic that covered up her alteration to people who had known her before? She figured it must be something like that. It made a twisted sort of sense. If every vampire had an extreme make over, surely that would tip off their friends and families and cause the stakes to come out.

Evolutionary adaptation by magic. Why not?

Norah was awake when she came back. Disoriented, but awake, and staring at the ceiling. Sophie crouched next to her.

"I want a steak. Tartar. Or maybe a kidney?" Her eyes were a startling hazel with bright green around the irises, and her mouth was pomegranate red. The way her eyes stood out now made Sophie want to go back to the mirror to see what color her own eyes were.

Wait, how come she had a reflection?

She filed that away in the *Don't forget to ask Olivier some time, if you ever see him again after you ripped his throat out* part of her brain.

"Uh, yeah, no," she replied to Norah. "You want to feast on living flesh or some Vincent Price crap."

Norah narrowed her eyes at Sophie. "Damn, am I gonna lose my job over this? I can't go out in the day-time to do remotes if I'm gonna crumble into a pile of dust!"

"Look, we gotta get you something to eat before you freak out, but I think we should find a criminal or something. I know we joke about eating babies all the time, but I think the literal application might be slightly more emotionally damaging." Sophie stood and held out her hand to Norah, who took it, and struggled to her feet.

"Yeah, what you just said. No babies. They might be juicy sweet, though." Norah looked a little too inter-ested in baby eating for Sophie's comfort.

"They will not be juicy sweet," said Sophie firmly. "We can find ourselves a rapist or something."

Norah sighed, but agreed, and after Norah scrubbed her own blood off her skin, they ventured into the night.

THE BEAUTY OF the winter was crystalline blue, stand-ing opposed to the molten gold of summer. The air smelled of angles, the unknown geometry of what re-mained unseen. As they passed over their threshold into the harsh December night, the winter pressed in on them with potential. What was unseen was theirs.

They had both, without speaking of it, opted for soft-soled sneakers and dark coats. Stocking hats hid their hair, long scarves their faces—all survival mech-anisms that could have been innate, or could have been from watching too much *CSI* and *Law & Order*.

Sophie watched people rush down the sidewalks, hunched over against the wind and stinging sleet. A group of twenty-something men passed close to them, their ambition and desperation clogging the back of her throat, causing Norah to cough.

Norah began to lunge at everyone who came within scenting distance, but they were too exposed. Sophie tugged her across the street and toward a park known as a haunt for drug dealers and prostitutes.

Norah gave her a look, her eyes startling in the sodium streetlights, dangerous and frightening. Sophie couldn't imagine herself looking even vaguely similar. She really did want to find a criminal, someone they didn't have to regret killing too much. Maybe they should move closer to Cook County Jail? Pulling Norah down to crouch behind a stand of winter-hardy bushes, Sophie prepared to wait until she smelled or "sensed" crime.

The sleet turned to freezing rain, making all movements hazardous, and painting the world into a postmodernist dream landscape of elongated tendrils trailing from tree limbs and the leaves of bushes and crackling around garbage cans. Norah made a whine that was close enough to a growl for Sophie. She let go, and watched as her friend ran—sailed—at a guy in a really big SUV with a "Jesus Saves" sticker on the back. Sophie told herself that he must cheat on his wife with prostitutes. She stood as a belated look-out, but there wasn't really anyone around, the weather having trapped them indoors. Even most of the hookers had left.

"Maybe," Sophie said as Norah wiped blood off her face onto the man's sleeve, "we should knock over a blood bank and lay up some supplies?"

OLIVIER DIDN'T MAKE another appearance that night, although Sophie *felt* him. She kept turning around to make sure he wasn't following them. Maybe he could turn invisible?

"What I need," she announced to Norah when they got back to the house, "is a manual for this. Like with Frequently Asked Questions and a help file and everything. To learn about turning invisible, flip to page thirteen. For the history of vampires, including where they really come from, see pages seventeen through forty-six. To find out if Anne Rice is really a vampire, see paragraph three on page eighteen."

Norah snickered. "You know what I need? A drink." She pulled a bottle of gin from the cabinet, and two tall glasses.

"Ice, ice, ice," said Sophie. Norah rolled her eyes, but Sophie remained firm. They might be Children of the Night, Creatures of the Damned, or whatever, but they could still be civilized.

"Anyway, I'm serious." Sophie leaned against the counter and bit at one of her nails. There was a bit of SUV-guy blood stuck under there. "What if there are rules that we don't know about? What if God wrote a vampire bible?"

"What if God wrote the real bible?" said Norah. She handed Sophie a gin and tonic. "Either way we're probably going to hell."

Sophie frowned into her glass. "That doesn't sound like fun."

Norah shrugged, took a long sip of her drink, then said, "Hey, all the fun people will be there with us, right?"

Sophie sighed, closed her eyes, drank. There was about a half-ounce of tonic water in her glass, two ice cubes, and enough gin to pickle a liver or something. She drank the whole thing in three swallows, and didn't even feel buzzed.

"Can I ask you something?" That was very weird. Norah rarely asked permission for anything, from the last shrimp to the remote control.

"No, never ask me another question as long as you live under pain of death." Sophie made a fake-serious face.

"Too late. Might as well ask." Her smile was all sunshine and daffodils, real in a way few people besides Sophie ever saw from her. "How did you get all vamperized?"

"You remember that guy from the Internet?" Norah nodded, smiling. "He says I fell and broke my neck. That I was going to die anyway, and he saved me."

Norah squinted her eyes. "See, did I tell you dating people you meet online was dumb?" She paused, seeing the serious expression on Sophie's face. "You don't believe him? You think he lied about what happened?"

"I definitely fell. I know that part's true. He was all super-stalker when I went to class, and I got scared, slipped." She pushed a piece of hair out of her face.

"For good reason." Norah shook glass, knocking the sole ice cube against the glass. "But it's better than getting wrinkles, right?"

Leave it to Norah to think murder was better than lines on her face.

"Do you think being vampires means we can drink more without being sloppy drunk?"

"I never get sloppy drunk," said Norah, which Sophie knew was a lie. She stared at the bottle of gin on the counter, raised a perfectly-arched eyebrow at Sophie. "We could always experiment."

Sophie nodded. Norah swiped the gin off the counter and followed Sophie into the living room. Sophie felt kind of euphoric, filled with power, but also sad. Too bad for that man's wife that her husband really *was* a cheating jerk who had to get himself killed by nasty vampires.

"Let's watch *From Dusk Till Dawn*," suggested Norah with a wicked grin, and Sophie laughed, pushed her moral concerns about vampirism out of her mind.

"Can't go wrong with George Clooney," she agreed.

"Plus we are way hotter than those nasty-ass vampires," said Norah. She took a swig right out of the gin bottle, then passed it to Sophie. So much for civilization.

NORAH AND SOPHIE had actually managed to get incredibly tipsy—although not quite *drunk*. Vampire metabolism *rocked*—they'd gone through two bottles of gin and one of tequila. They'd also moved on from *From Dusk Till Dawn* to *Interview With The Vampire*, deciding that hot Brad Pitt vampire action beat hot George Clooney vampire killers hands down.

They heard the phone ringing, but didn't bother to stop their discussion about who would taste better—people who ate fast food or vegetarians.

"Vegetarians are healthy; that must be better." Sophie let out a large belch.

"But all that fat in the blood, Soph, just like bar-b-que," Norah replied. Sophie stopped to consider that point. "Do you think that was Suki calling us?" It had taken a while, but the whole phone ringing thing had finally gotten through.

"It better have been, ho! She can't just run off and not come home for days at a time because she totally misunderstood what happened when I had sex at the club and then had a black out. I mean, that's totally not my fault." Sophie broke off when she noticed

Norah standing—weaving—over her with the phone in her hand.

"The hell? Sex, what? You can't just *say* things like that!" She punched in the code for their voicemail. "Was it with George Clooney, because if so and you kept it a secret, I will suck you dry!" She hit the code to get the messages.

"Olivier's hotter than George, dude, and he's like our sire, or something from *Los Vampiros*." She wondered if that meant they had to obey him, which lead to some pretty drunken ruminations on not being responsible for her own actions because of someone else technically being "in charge."

"Shit, there's like a hundred messages. Screw this!" Norah punched the phone off. "Is it almost dawn or something? Ima pass out." Norah stumbled towards her room, and Sophie fell catatonic on the sofa.

Chapter Six

A BELL TOLLED somewhere in the distance, she thought in the lower town. Her companion stood facing an alchemist, even from behind she knew her friend was threatening the sorcerer into helping her. The man's terror filled the room, choked her. The shutters of the window to her right stood open letting in the scents of garbage and human waste.

"You shouldn't, not even you, this is an abomination," the alchemist stuttered out. She knew he was right, but also that it didn't matter. "You'll regret this!"

SOPHIE WOKE AND answered the phone on the third ring. "Hello?"

"Soph?" It was Suki. Sophie sat up on the couch and wrestled with her hair that had somehow managed to get tangled almost all around her body. "Are you okay?"

"Wanna be a vampire?" Sophie thought there was probably a slick way of dealing with all of this, but she couldn't think of one to save whatever was left of her life.

"No, I don't fucking want to be a vampire!" Suki was angry. Really angry, and the shock of it made Sophie's brain frizzle slightly. What did she have to be mad about? She was the one who ran away from home and didn't call and hadn't been around when she was really, really needed. "Didn't you get any of my messages? Why are you so stupid!"

That last part wasn't a question. Sophie was starting to get mad. "You always wanted to be a vampire, ever since we were thirteen. What is the problem here?" Sophie had enough to think about without Suki being a bitch about this. Suki was the only reason she and Norah had started watching *Los Vampiros* anyway—well, Suki and because the lead vampire guy was totally hot. Guys like that didn't really exist.

Except for Olivier.

"In *theory!* It's cool to talk about what I would do, killing people and wreaking evil across the land, but it's different when I have to eat people to survive. Humans are not vegan!" Suki was ranting, which wasn't really like her. Sophie tried to hold back her anger, which she began to recognize was actually blood-lust, to find out what was going on.

"Why aren't you surprised I offered to make you a vampire?" That was definitely the most pressing question Sophie could think up.

"If you had *ever* checked your messages, you would know. I knew this was going to happen! Oh shit, this is bad. Have you already made Norah one, too? Please say no, please." Her tone changed so suddenly from anger to anxiety that Sophie was scared, too.

"How could you *know* this . . ." Sophie started.

"*Fuck*! Listen to me. You've got to meet me. As soon

as you can. It's already dark, okay? Come as fast as you can to the Orchid Lounge. You know where that is?" Suki talked with the forced calm one used with children and large snakes.

"Sure, it's where you meet your Wicca buddies." Sophie—even though she was now a vampire—was still bad at repressing her instinct to mock Suki's witch thing.

Suki didn't bother to sigh or get upset. "Yeah. Bring Norah. Don't do *anything* else first. Promise me."

Sophie sighed for them both. "I promise." But she was totally lying. First they would eat. Then they would shower. Then they would meet Suki.

"I should have warned you about the—well, about this. About this before, when you told me about your dreams. I'm sorry, Soph." The tone of her voice held regret, and something inexplicable, beyond sorrow. Sophie's stomach clinched.

"I think I might like being a vampire, really," said Sophie, "and you knowing all this is freaking me out."

"Trust me, you couldn't be more freaked out than me. And you enjoying it is pretty much what I'm freaked out about. I told you not to meet mysterious strangers, didn't I?"

Sophie tried to frame a response, but couldn't think of one. Before she could say *anything*, the line went dead. She stared at the phone for a few seconds. Maybe Suki was madder than Sophie had thought. She *69ed the call, but it was blocked. Huh.

She headed upstairs to see if Norah was up yet.

NORAH WAS SITTING at the kitchen table flipping through the paper and sipping coffee.

"Talked to Suki." Sophie shuffled over to the counter and poured herself a cup of coffee.

"Good. Is she half-dead or sommat?" Norah asked, indifferent.

"Half nuts. She doesn't want to be a vampire." Sophie said it like she meant it—wondering how anyone could pass up such a plum deal.

"Well she's got that whole witch thing going on." Norah scoffed, and even though Sophie felt kind of the same way about Suki's witch thing, she got indignant on Suki's behalf.

"She brought up a pretty good point, though. Humans aren't vegan." Sophie sipped her coffee, waiting for Norah's response.

Norah flipped her off and lit a cigarette. "You're kidding, right? Look, you're not an omnivore who *chooses* to live off of animal products even though you *can* eat only vegetable matter. You're a *humanivore* and have no choice."

"Louis in the *Vampire Chronicles* ate rats." Sophie responded harkening back to the previous night's movie-viewing, not that she thought any tack would work on Norah. Mainly, she was just yanking her chain, since Norah thought any diet that wasn't the all-alcohol-all-the-time-diet was ridiculous.

"That's still not vegan, idiot." Point. Definite point there.

"Yeah, she also seems to be generally distressed about our new lifestyle change. She wants us to meet her at the Orchid pronto."

"I don't really do pronto." Norah smiled, almost her regular smile, all curved mouth and a touch of teeth—but now with added teeth.

"Yeah, I'm aware." Sophie knew it was pointless to express her creepy feeling of "wrong" to Norah. She always thought intuition was more like indigestion and that Sophie and Suki got stressed out over nothing too easily.

"I was thinking we need some new things." Norah's tone was so even and reasonable, Sophie knew there was mayhem under it. "Maybe a snack with a side-order of robbery." Her smile picked up the true humor.

Even Sophie had to admit stealing seemed to be within the moral limits of a child of the night. "Sure, why the hell not? But first we have to meet Suki." Sophie felt a knot in her chest loosen.

If her two best friends were with her, nothing could be totally unbearable. That was the point, right? If she had Norah and Suki, eventually the little piece inside her that was drawing her toward Olivier would go away.

Not like she didn't want to be with Olivier. But he was a creepy blood-sucking fiend from beyond the grave. So was she, but he was creepier. And she was mad at him.

"Norah," she said. Her friend looked up. "Listen, I think we should cut down on the killing frenzy. Just until we understand what's happening better. Maybe knock the victims out and rob them, but leave them alive."

The burst of laughter was unexpected. So was the choking fit that followed it. Sophie just stared until Norah calmed down. "You're serious? Oh lord, girl, you're insane. This is like that saving spiders thing, innit?"

"Hey, spiders are alive, ok. It's not my fault the world has a jihad against them."

"Oh, this is going to be fun. Vegan, bleeding-heart philosopher as bloody-thirsty murderess. I love it." She paused and stubbed out her smoke. "Ok, bring the first aid kit, we ain't killin' a soul."

* * *

IT TOOK LONGER than Sophie anticipated to get ready to go out.

"I always figured that vampirism and lycanthropy were blood-borne illnesses. If real. I'm still not sure this isn't all a drug-induced hallucination." Norah kicked a pile of clothes out of her way and held up one of Sophie's long velvet skirts. It would come down to about below her knees—it hit Sophie's ankles.

"Lycanthropy? You're joking, right?" Sophie snorted at the mere idea of werewolves. Sophie wiggled into a pair of jeans and sighed at their uncomfortable fit. "I need new clothes."

"Yeah, werewolves must be real, too. We have sworn mortal enemies now. I mean, I guess they're our immortal enemies. Whatever, I always thought it would be cool to have a mortal enemy," said Norah blithely. Sophie stared at her. "What? I think that ferret the other day was a wereferret. It obviously knew I was about to be vamped."

"You're such a freak." Sophie wrapped a bunch of old clothes in a cotton blanket and hefted it up. "I'm gonna give this to charity before we start our bloody rampage. Why don't we have a slave or something if we're all evil?"

"We have to capture him. What, did you think vamping came with a free slave? How about you super-size that by making it a sex slave?" Norah tied her hair at the base of her neck with a silk ribbon.

"What other kind is there?" Sophie said, and they both laughed.

"I WOULD HAVE sworn there were, like, ten charity bins between here and house." Sophie lugged her ungainly burden and grouched. "Did you remember the first aid kit?"

Norah patted herself down and came up with her cigarettes and lighter. "I didn't bring the stupid first aid kit. That was a joke."

Sophie didn't laugh. "How will you keep your victim from bleeding to death then? Snow on the wound?"

Norah looked over at her with raised eyebrows. "There must be some sort of instinct that'll tell us if the person's dying or something."

"Now who's relying on the *Vampire Chronicles*?" Sophie asked, feeling triumphant. Norah hissed at her a little—the same angry hiss she did when she was alive, but with her vampy teeth out. Sophie sighed. "Whatever. It would have been helpful if I'd gotten a manual or something." Sophie dropped the clothes onto the sidewalk. The effects of the gin and tequila were fading, and Sophie was ready for more alcohol. "I want a drink. Do you want a drink? Let's just go meet Suki."

"As if you had to ask." Norah replied. She scanned the block. "Leave that shit and let's go to the Orchid." Norah kicked Sophie hard in the shin when she tried to pick the blanket bundle again. "Fuck off with that, come on."

Another block down on the opposite site of the street, wedged between a condemned bodega and a liquor store, was the Orchid. The neon sign above the door now read, however, The Alchemist's Orchid.

"When did they change the name?" Sophie asked.

"No idea, who cares?" Norah tossed the butt of her cigarette onto the sidewalk as several Latino teens emerged from the liquor store.

"Whooo, mami, whatchu` doin'?" One made a lewd gesture and grabbed his crotch.

"Uh, what?" Sophie flipped him off and the kid made to approach them.

"He doesn't have anything to steal," Norah grabbed her arm.

Sophie felt ready to cause some mayhem, but fate intervened in the shape of a bluish gray doorman with a club, wearing a pelt.

"Don't be drawin' attention over here." The tiny man menaced the women with his club. A couple of nails glinted dully at the tip. The troll stepped back beneath the lintel of the Orchid's entrance. He huffed and stomped in place, glowering angrily at the duo.

The Latino youths drifted away down the opposite side of the street, hooting and yelling at each other, all awareness of the vampires and a troll-type guy having apparently evaporated into the December air for them.

Norah stared open-mouthed at the troll.

"Didn't there used to be a human door guy here?" she asked in a voice that indicated she very much thought so.

"Uh-uh, always just me. I'm a crossing troll." He hopped up on a high backed stool and perched on three threadbare velveteen cushions.

"What the hell about Ray Ray, big black dude?" Norah pointed at the doorway.

"I'm Ray Ray." As much as possible, Ray Ray looked self-satisfied.

Norah turned her head to glance at her friend. "That's weird right?"

"About as weird as him being a fucking troll with a naily stick thing, yeah." Sophie replied.

"Succubi or vampires?" Ray Ray whipped out a PDA from under a cushion. He looked down at Sophie and batted his ridiculously long eyelashes.

"Vampires. How did you know we were one or the

other?" Sophie bumped towards the door as Norah got impatient and started shoving her.

"The way you lot look, you have to be vampires or succubi, unholy good looks." Ray Ray sniffed. "Go on in."

Norah propelled Sophie through the front door of the Orchid.

Sophie felt like she was on an invisible fair ride. First she tilted all the way over 90 degrees, then back again 180 degrees before falling back on her feet, lights streaming in front of her eyes and her stomach dropping out.

The troll issue was forgotten, at least by Sophie, as she took in the interior of the bar. Under their feet, moss and lichen grew on ancient flagstones so copiously the slate was almost completely obscured. As the floor ended, a small stream began, bubbling and trickling away from one side of the establishment to the other. On the other side of the brook, tables were set on a sturdy wooden floor strewn with empty bottles, cigarette butts, and detritus better left unexplored.

"Why does weird shit still surprise me at all?" Norah ran a hand over her hair to smooth it, then marched away towards the bar that could be dimly glimpsed sitting along the back wall beyond the tables.

A giant oak tree grew beside the stream, cutting the room essentially in half, its roots splayed out all along the bank, dipping into the water and rising in rippling bumps through out the bar.

Norah tripped on a root as she marched toward her aqua vita and pitched right into a table full of pale people bedecked in capes and low-cut gowns, knee-boots and breeches. Jewels glittered on their fingers, throats and ears.

Sophie watched as one of the figures leaned forward and offered Norah a hand. "What clan are you from, sister?" Black hair cut in severe bangs, long, pointed nails, a too red smile. Sophie knew a lot of kids like that—they all hung out at the mall and listened to bad guitar rock and thought they were Goth. Whatever. Sophie ditched her intrigued friend and headed for the bar looking for Suki.

She parked herself on a stool that appeared to be sprouting directly out of the long bar, and waved at the normal-looking bartender. He was middle-aged, balding, rotund and red-faced.

"What can I get you?" he asked. He smiled warmly, wiping his palms on the front of his shirt, leaving a streak of something yellow next to lots of other, variously colored smears.

"I'm looking for Suki Tsai. She's about my height and age, with black hair and—"

The barkeep cut her off. "Little wee witch. I know her. She was here earlier."

"I was supposed to meet her. Are you sure she left?" That wasn't Suki at all, to leave when she demanded you do something for her. She was reliable, especially when she was angry. What was going on?

"She isn't here now. I know that for a fact." He wiped the bar in front of her. "So, what'll you have?"

"Uh . . ." Sophie really didn't want to ask, but she figured this was the place if she did. "You got anything with blood in it?"

The bartender blinked at her. "Anything you want can have a shot of blood added for ten bucks."

"Fine, make it a bloody Bloody Mary with extra Tabasco." She sighed and rested her chin on her hand, pointedly not looking behind herself when there was a sudden bang. Why would Suki act like that on the phone and then be gone? It had taken them a while to get to the bar, but she'd lived with both Sophie and No-rah long enough to know that would be the case. How could she have known about the vampire thing? Why was she so mad about it?

As she gazed at the pocked and marred bar top, a napkin slid into view. There were words scrawled across the surface in a messy and ornate hand.

Your right sock lies in mute accusation under my bed.
The hand-knitted wool reminds me of hands I've never
seen lovingly knotting and pulling, constructing love
with each click click of the needles. It reminds me of
other hands you'll never know stitching thread into the
long forgotten cloth of a life I remember when I think
of you.

Looking up, Sophie saw that Olivier had slid silently into the seat next to hers. She wanted to tell him that his almost poetry was truly horrible. She loved it, but it was horrible. In the dim light of the bar, she watched him not look at her, his fingers tapping on the bar with no actual rhythm. His hair was pulled back in a ponytail—not the usual sort that men with long hair wore at the nape of their necks, but high on the back of his head like a girl might, like she usually did. It looked strange on a man, but he managed to make it sexy. A smudge of dark paint streaked the side of his neck. He sported a black leather European-style motorcycle jacket, the plain sort that was all clean lines and a simple zipper up the front with a piece at the neck that snapped on the side—she'd taken his jacket, she suddenly realized. She was wearing it; it was hanging on the back of her bar stool.

She couldn't bring herself to criticize his seemingly

heartfelt prose-poetry when not so long ago she'd ripped out his throat. Even though that was totally his own fault.

She touched her hair. "Why do I look like this?"

He tilted his chin up as he turned to look at her. The bartender set her drink down and scuttled off. His feet made clacking noises—Sophie leaned over the bar to see what kind of shoes he was wearing and leaned back just as quickly. He wasn't wearing shoes; he didn't even have feet. He had eight legs that were black and hairy. Her stomach turned over a little. Crossing trolls instead of bouncers she could deal with. Spider bartenders? Not so easy.

Sophie picked up her drink and sipped through the two straws as Olivier rubbed the tip of a finger along the outline of his bottom lip.

"I've thought about that a lot." Swiveling his seat around, he hooked a foot into the rung on Sophie's stool and rested it there. "I think it's to make it easier to cull victims. In a modern way, one could describe it as an evolutionary adaptation."

"The prettier you are, the more disarmed people will be, the easier it is to kill them. Makes sense." The drink was fantastic. Salty and spicy, although she didn't want to analyze the underlying flavor too much.

"If you care, I liked you before. The way you looked. Authentic." He tapped the bar with two knuckles, and almost immediately a large glass of red wine was set before him.

He smiled at her charmingly as he took a mouthful of wine.

"You don't have to say shit like that now. You liked me chubby and covered in stretch-marks? First, you already fucked me, so cut the shit. Second, I guess it wouldn't matter even if you hadn't fucked me." She tried to cut a dark look at him, but Olivier just laughed.

"Your face wasn't meant for angry looks. You're just cute."

The table where Norah had paused to chat with the coven erupted in hysterics, and the couple turned to look.

"You were faster at that than I had anticipated. I thought I could at least talk to you first." He polished off his drink in a couple of long pulls. She figured he meant turning Norah. Sophie finished her drink as well and noticed for the first time that both of his ears were pierced.

"I didn't want to be alone." The truth was so obvious Sophie felt no need to conceal it.

They watched as one of the other vampires offered Norah her wrist while two more restrained her by the shoulders so she wouldn't get out of order.

"You never *were* alone, but your point isn't lost. I remember the feeling of absolute emptiness when I was first . . . turned."

"Do you have a cigarette?" Sophie patted her pockets out of habit.

Olivier looked up at her. "You quit." He smiled. "Or so you say, but you were smoking the other night as well."

Sophie froze, then lit on fire with immediate fear. His tone was low and strange, plus the fact that she was weirded out that he would know that at all.

"You're very dramatic." He smiled again, and the odd atmosphere dissipated. "You talk about it on your journal."

Yeah, of course she did. How could she have forgotten how they'd met? This situation had chased all the normal thoughts from her head leaving only the unsettling newness of a remade world.

"Did you always look like you do now?" She didn't really know what to say to him, so she thought she'd keep the conversation in safe territory.

Pulling a pack of American Spirit cigarettes out of the inside pocket of his jacket, Olivier shook his head. He tapped two smokes part of the way out of the paper packet and offered them to her. Sophie took one, put it in her mouth and futilely patted her pockets for a lighter.

Olivier produced a Zippo and lit her cigarette. She cupped her hand around his, a reflex reaction to steady the flame and bring it to her cigarette. When her fingers touched his skin, which was rough and rather cold, she shivered, let her eyes close. She breathed in the acrid smoke of her cigarette, taking comfort in the old ritual, and let her hand rest on his for a moment too long.

But when she opened her eyes, his face was kind, not judging her, not showing that he thought something was amiss. She let go of his hand and he lit his own cigarette, then snapped the lighter closed, dropped it on the bar, and shrugged out of his coat. He let the cigarette dangle from the corner of his mouth as he flung it over the back of his seat. He extended his arm towards her and traced a line up the flawless inside of his forearm.

"I had a scar there, an ugly, deep scar. I had them all over my hands and arm, one splitting my top lip at the indentation, one on my cheek, and many, many more." He paused to draw on his cigarette, dropping his hand into his lap.

"Were you in a car wreck?" Sophie didn't always say the right thing. Olivier laughed, shaking his head side to side; a few stray hairs came loose from his ponytail.

"Hardly." He paused as another glass of wine appeared in front of him. "I looked similar to how I do now, in the same way that you look similar to how you used to, but this is sort of a Platonic Ideal of who I was, the most perfect me that could have ever been."

She hadn't taken much time to examine her face in a mirror—except for her eyes—because the alterations to her body were so great Sophie was scared to look for her face in a glass and see someone else look back at her. Being confused and disoriented with reality wasn't such a huge leap for her—although it hadn't been this bad since she was a child believing her dreams would come true, or had come true some time in the past to other people—and she figured she'd adjust to this new self, but she'd do it in her own way. Mainly by ignoring all that for as long as possible.

"Do you kill lots of people?" She was tired and worried about the whole Suki thing, and so words just seemed to pop out of her mouth.

"No more now than I did before I was this." And that wasn't any sort of actual answer she wanted.

Norah bopped up being trailed close behind by a girl with bright red hair sporting a Morticia Addams get-up of a formal gown bedecked in silver spider webs.

"Who's this?" Norah's mouth was smeared with blood, and she lit a cigarette off the butt of another.

Olivier answered. "I'm the one who set this all in motion." He extended his hand, and Norah reached to shake it, but Olivier pulled her forward and licked the traces of blood from around her mouth. Sophie gaped, but the Goth vamp chick rolled her eyes in boredom.

"You should get home before you collapse." He turned to the bored girl. "Even for us there are habits best left alone." He tossed his burnt-out cigarette on the floor and hopped up to step on it. "I'll go with you, in case you collapse."

"What the hell are you talking about?" Norah's tone was incendiary, but one of her knees buckled, and Sophie had to dart out an arm to keep her from falling.

Olivier turned to glare at the interloper, and she slunk off in a slithering of her skirts against the wood of the floor. "Opium." He yanked his jacket on and grabbed at Norah's elbow.

"I feel strange, like I'm about to be grounded." Norah let him steer her towards the door as Sophie stood and put her waist.

Sophie felt it, too. Not the opium, but the feeling like she was in trouble with her—very sexy—babysitter. She frowned and fought the feeling. Just what she needed—some sort of warped Elektra complex.

Norah passed out before they got out of the bar, necessitating a taxi, which made Sophie remember her last taxi ride, and shivered.

Chapter Seven

"ONCE FEAR SETTLES in, truly comes to live inside you, it's the same as bone and gristle and sinew—not just *part* of you, but an integrated facet of the whole of you." She's trying to make the other woman understand, to truly understand, but she won't. She's stubborn and *believes*. She believes so fully, she has no room for the fear or for a comprehension of someone else living with it inside them. She won't listen!

"You can't escape fate. How do you not see that yet? You can't do this. Leave well enough alone. Calling on forces you can't control is madness." In the utter darkness of the room, she can feel the people moving above, the magician and his servants, she can hear stray thoughts of supper and drink. But mainly she feels what's inside her, fear bending to terror.

"Rosamund—"

Voices and music woke her with the name still spilling off her lips. Sophie sat up and rubbed her groggy eyes. Flipping out of bed, she saw she wore

Olivier's old, ratty shirt still, but also a pair of cut-off shorts with no underwear. Episodes of lost time were becoming requisite, and she didn't even really wonder about it.

She schlepped downstairs and into the kitchen to find Norah and Olivier eating eggs and sausage while Olivier held forth on the finer points of robbing people.

"You can't let them see you. Sneaky might be hard in five inch heels, so I suggest athletic shoes." He smiled and took a bite of scrambled eggs.

Norah laughed. The Pretenders' "2,000 Miles" blared out of the radio when a commercial for carpeting ended.

"We eat?" Sophie made a production of jabbing the eggs in the skillet with a spatula and sniffing the sausage.

"The no eating thing is a myth," Olivier replied behind her.

"We're totally alive. No escaping the toilet and showering and everything else," Norah chimed in.

Sophie turned around to watch them eat. "You couldn't have made something I'd like?"

"I thought you'd be happier to not be undead," said Norah around a mouthful of sausage.

Sophie could tell Norah was put out by her lack of enthusiasm, but it wasn't like being a vampire had too many benefits so far. Sure, it seemed cool, sort of, but it came with too many strings: she still had to use the toilet, still had to eat, still had to pay rent, and she definitely still had to deal with Olivier. Plus having to drink blood and kill people and everything—Sophie figured that after five or six centuries of that, it would get a little annoying.

She sighed, and faked it. "I totally am, but why didn't you make me something to eat, too?" Sophie was absolutely starving.

"There's toast and oatmeal in the microwave." Olivier answered. And when she checked, lo, there was.

"So, we're not like mythological vampires? Then how come so many of the stories agree on those vampiric facts? That doesn't make sense."

Olivier eyed her over her coffee cup. "What we are, perhaps, can be called vampire, but only because we have died in a way and live on blood. There are others who are what you think of from folk tales and Dracula stories."

Norah sat her cup down, hard. "Wait, we aren't even proper vampires? This sucks."

"Life is what it is—myriad and confusing. There are several variations on vampirism that I know of, ones that live off of other bodily fluids, not blood . . ." He gave Norah a meaningful look and Sophie was totally grossed out by that concept. "Others who fall to dust over time no matter how much they consume. Those whom Western humans normally think of as vampires exist. There are many here in Chicago, they breed like rats. You met some last night." Sophie noted that his normal unending tolerance didn't seem to extend to regular vampires—he was a vampire snob. Weird.

"Where's Suki?" she asked, but Olivier was back to explaining how to climb walls or something, and no one answered her. So she ate her toast and oatmeal, and waited for a lull in the conversation.

"Back on that whole robbing people thing, huh?"

"Now that we know we don't have to eat people all the time, we're just going to rob them and knock them out or something." Norah sipped her coffee.

"What do you mean about eating people all the time?"

"We only have to feed on *blood* once in a while. When we feel like gnawing someone's face off, that's the signal." Norah's voice was exactly the same,

Southern Ohio laid-over with received California-television pronunciation. Her face, though, was mesmerizing. As Sophie's brain registered the caffeine, and her eyes focused all the way, she became entranced by her friend's soft, smooth complexion, rounded cheeks and dimpled smile. Her hair fell around her face in shiny curls, perfectly framing her features.

"Do I have egg on my face?" Norah rubbed her chin with the back of her hand. The action drew Sophie's eyes to the clock on the wall behind her head.

"It's four o'clock?" She spit toast all over the floor and nearly choked on what was left in her mouth. Her heart sped up, and academic panic fluttered in her stomach. "I had First Century Texts at two! Oh God."

Sophie had planned to lead a discussion group. She knew the material backwards and forwards, so she didn't even bother to make notes for her fellow students in case she had to call in sick—she was just going to do it from memory. Crap. Professor McMillan was probably totally pissed off at her for not calling in to let him know she wouldn't be there.

"I'm so screwed. McMillan didn't call?" Sophie looked from one face to the next.

"Someone called from a blocked number." Norah shoved the portable phone across the table. "Why do you care? Hello, *vampire*! What're your going to do with your Ph.D. anyway? Bore all the other creatures of the night?"

"What am I going to do if I *don't* get my Ph.D.? Steal and wreak mischief like you? One major life adjustment is enough for one week. What, I'm going to be a vampire *and* have no career?" snapped Sophie.

Olivier lounged in his chair and smiled at Sophie from under all his hair. Her mouth watered, but she also wanted to rip out his throat again. "You can convince your professor you were in class with a simple coercion. I tend to side with your friend on this issue, though. You're making a lot of work for yourself that will most likely end in frustration anyway, when you have to give up your career and tenure or risk discovery."

"He's in charge, right?" Norah sounded sure, even if her statement was phrased as a question. "I'm calling in and quitting work." She picked up the phone.

"Are you insane? After how hard you worked to get promoted off the weather desk? What happened to your dream of being a major market anchor? What the hell? Not to mention all the 'dates' you had to go on." Sophie couldn't believe this. She and Suki were the ones who had to listen to Norah complain about all the nights she spent listening to self-involved producers and station executives talk about their lives while they tried to grope her.

"What? I just wanted a career that could make a lot of money and make me famous. I don't have to *make* the money now, and fame is no bonus here. Think of mobs with torches and pitchforks." Norah banged her coffee cup onto the table, and moved her finger to turn the phone on, but before she could press the button, it rang. She looked at the display. "Blocked." She tossed it to Sophie.

"This better be good," Sophie snapped. Strange pops sounded down the line followed by an eerie, dislocated sound that Sophie couldn't quite place. Her stomach turned over. "Hello?"

"Sophie? Are you there?" The voice sounded like it came from down a well, down a deep, creepy, Japanese horror movie-type-well.

"Hello?" Every hair on Sophie's body stood up.

"Sophie, Sophie, don't accept any invitations, Sophie, don't trust anyone new."

The words were elongated and clipped in the wrong places, crackling and hollow. Sophie pinched the phone between her index finger and thumb, afraid of holding it too tightly.

"Suki?"

"Yes, it's me, Sophie. Horrible things will happen now—" Suki's voice cut out and the line kicked over into reverb loud enough to make Sophie drop the phone, which bounced on the linoleum with a thud. The line remained connected, squealing out a terror-inducing dissonant loop.

Olivier picked the phone up and clicked it off. "That was your friend, no?" The first thing that registered with Sophie was the strange word-order Olivier had chosen. An non-English phraseology that gave away his origins. That grounded her, was semi-normal.

"Did you just get a call from beyond the grave?" Norah was obviously going for flip, but was just as apparently covering fear.

"Don't say that! It was Suki—she can't be dead!" Sophie rolled through fear, panic, curiosity, and settled on determined. "We have to find her."

"Yes, we do. What do you suggest?" Norah looked at her with her "on-air" face, calm and trust-worthy and vapid.

"I'll go talk to her band. See if anyone's talked to her." Sophie knew Norah couldn't come along, since she'd threatened at least two of them in the past with physical violence. Ah, Norah and bar fights—so fun. Sophie debated passing on all of Suki's nonsensical message, but decided against it. Suki was probably just doing some witchy thing. "Olivier can teach you more about the art of robbing. Or something."

She looked over at him. No matter how intimate their connection was, she still didn't really know him.

She couldn't tell the inscrutable face he wore from the other inscrutable face he donned the night before, nor the one that pointed out her breakfast to her earlier.

Then he smiled, an expression that brought dimples onto both his cheeks.

"Since I failed to convince you previously to let me help you learn about this life, I will take this as a do-over." He nodded.

"A do-over. You play golf?" Norah looked at him with a perplexed face.

"I didn't know that term was sports-related." His smile dimmed slightly.

"Ok, you're a freak." Norah looked at Sophie. "Is he at least as good as he looks like he would be in bed?" She didn't even wait for Sophie to blush before she started laughing.

Sophie steadfastly didn't look over at Olivier, but buried her nose in her coffee cup. When she glanced at him out of the corner of her eye, he was staring at her and still smiling, just a little, just enough to make her stomach flip-flop.

Chapter Eight

STREAMS OF HOLIDAY shoppers bobbed and shifted down the sidewalks of Michigan Avenue. Dirty snow, piled knee-high, impeded access to the street, disallowing jay-walking and crushing the crowd in on itself. A woman with two small children dressed in identical red ski jackets stumbled, her gaudily wrapped packages faltering. Olivier watched the activity in the reflection of the window of Bulgari, and before the stumbling woman's purchases could hit the pavement, he swung around and caught the packages in one hand, and steadied her with the other.

Laughing nervously, she straightened, taking her shopping back with her eyes cast down towards her knees where her children clutched at her. The woman pushed her straw-colored hair back under her hat and smiled up at Olivier. The second her eyes met his, she was his. Some special, unnamable something that was *her*, hovered outside of her skin for an instant, ready to flee back to the collective pool of perfection and happiness beyond this life, but Olivier broke the connection, his smile brightening as he turned back to the window.

Inside the blue and chrome interior of the jeweler's, one of his two most recent accidents tugged at him through steel and concrete and all the intervening human fluttering. He didn't object to Norah's fun, especially because she hadn't needed much of a lesson to learn how to get what she wanted without bloodshed. Much bloodshed, anyway. Women seemed instinctually more adapted to comprehending and using coercion instead of fangs—a lingering remembrance of who they were before, of ways of getting through a human life full of obstacles and hindrances that men constructed the world to make for them.

That didn't keep her from decimating a tiny *chi-chi* boutique on Oak Avenue, however. Norah had ripped out the eyes of the shop clerk before Olivier even saw the signals of her hunger, and when the scent of blood hit the air, she had killed the other two employees before he bothered to suggest its necessity. She was too stuffed and sated by the end of the minor massacre to listen to him explain why carrying a gun or a knife is helpful in situations like that. He cleaned up after her, and he didn't hold a grudge about that. He was the elder, that was his duty to the young.

If she, and the absent Sophie, would stop and listen to him for more than ten seconds at a time, he could explain the world to them. Since they were not prepared to listen to him yet, he could only follow them around to clean up after them, and hope they didn't get into too much trouble before they learned.

Olivier was the same way when he first became a vampire, full of anger at the world, pain at all his loss. No one was able to talk to him or tell him anything.

He'd nearly destroyed himself and the others before he was sensate enough to realize that his life would be different.

Eventually they would understand that when they were humans, the worst they thought could happen to them was death. Now . . .

Olivier's thoughts were interrupted by Norah's emergence from the store. As she turned towards him, she lifted her left hand to push her hair back, and a ring of three huge blue diamonds set in platinum winked in the streetlights. Her smile eclipsed the jewelry, and her laugh, as it tumbled out of her mouth one shocking, radiating note at a time, startling genuine, human shoppers into stillness as they passed. Olivier saw a man in his early thirties pause, arrested in his bustling, pass a shaking hand over his face, then move on—his automatic fight or flight response engaged without awareness of why.

She extended her hand to him, a small silver box rested on her palm. "I brought you a present." When he didn't reach for it immediately, she continued, "It's the twelve days of Christmas, after all." Norah looked up at him with a closed expression of patience, the sort of patience Olivier had for them, the sort of patience one has for a particularly slow child.

The thought made Olivier smile. This one was all control and strength. He could see fate plucking at him in her. She might have not been his intention, but he knew this was where she was heading from her birth into life as Norah Kuti. He was long used to feeling some greater hand directing his assumedly self-impelled actions—and at some times that hand was stronger than at others.

Olivier opened the box withdrawing a sapphire blue velvet jewelry box and pocketed the silver, cardboard one. Nestled inside were a pair of platinum hoop earrings. Norah plucked the box from his hand. He tilted his head back and allowed her to thread them through his ears.

"I thought bling might be a little much." Her fingers were warm where they touched his skin. "I got Sophie pink diamond earrings."

"She'll love them." Olivier fell into step with her. They walked down the sidewalk, death weaving amongst the vulnerable—and, if he let these difficult women, Norah and her maker, they could make him feel comfortable with that.

THEY STOPPED TO eat in a bistro with burnt sugar walls and weathered oak furniture. Olivier approved of the aesthetics. He slid into his seat and the waitress appeared at his elbow, all solicitations and flirtatious smiles. His eyes flicked over his companion, who was busy intimidating the coat check boy, and considered calling her his wife to give himself at least a small amount of room to enjoy his meal.

Offering the wine list, the waitress made sure to bend over as far as possible so that her blouse could gape open. He was sure that when she passed the table again, there would be two fewer buttons fastened.

"A bottle of Chateau Patreuse. Two glasses." His cold tone did nothing to dim the interest of the server.

"Yes, sir." She flounced away as his companion sat.

"You have an admirer." Norah laughed. "But does she steal you presents?"

Olivier returned the smile. "I'm sure I could convince her to."

"Where's the rest of your harem?" She leaned well back in her seat, the emeralds in her ears catching stray bits of light that her ring didn't bounce around the room.

"I lost them to Barbary pirates and the women's lib movement." A couple from another table bumped into their waitress. Norah watched the actions of the customers and the employee with singular focus, her pupils dilated and her nose held slightly high.

"I want to find a new place to live," Norah announced.

As their glasses were set on the table and the wine was uncorked, Olivier rapidly considered the situation. She would procure a new home whether he agreed or not, such was always the case.

"Unless you have far more patience than I suspect and plan to accrue the wealth necessary to buy a new home, you realize you'll have to kill, enthrall, or maim?"

What one becomes as a vampire is determined by who one was as a human being. Olivier was always a killer, and his cosmology did not perceive death to be a finality nor necessarily negative. He believed her capable of ruthlessness. She had advanced to a high, sought-after, difficult to attain position as a human woman, as a vampire she could be a scourge.

"I know." Norah sipped her wine and didn't avert her eyes when he returned her gaze. Power games, she wasn't timid or afraid of him. Respect was something modern people didn't seem to really understand. She respected no one, only suffered the people she chose to. Sophie had Norah's loyalty, but he was nothing to this woman.

"You think you do," said Olivier. He knew he sounded moody, but he didn't care.

The first man Olivier had killed was a Frankish scout he and his brother found in the pear orchard while they practiced archery. His brother had signaled, and through the low-hanging branches Olivier could see the glint of steel and the darkness of a black head.

He had taken aim, meaning to shoot the spy in the shoulder, and put his arrow straight through the man's eye. He was eleven. He got better with his bow.

"Even if you have some romantic idea that murder is your true nature now and that you will bring death easily and without regret, the believing doesn't always make the reality," he finally said. Norah's eyes were hard when he looked into them. If he were younger, he might have quailed. As it was, he was almost amused. All the women he'd ever been fond of were difficult.

"I don't have to kill anyone, I can just make someone into my thrall-whatsit and make him do what I want, like live in a closet while we take over his house and car and bank accounts." Norah sipped her wine and raised an eyebrow. Olivier assumed "we" was she and Sophie. He wondered how *she* would feel about this plan. He wasn't sure of her yet, either. Rarely had he seen someone so close to the change become obsessed with something like a missing friend.

That could either be very positive or point to some serious instability.

Norah gazed at him in a calm, steady manner that spoke of façade and indicated to Olivier that this was a pre-existing fantasy from far before he had met Sophie. A revenge plot. Unsurprising; every turning contained some form of a revenge plot. Some were nurtured over many years and subtle. Most were murderous impulses given a real outlet and opportunity. His own had revolved around avenging his mother's death. He spent night after night picking off Frankish knights and peasant soldiers, slaughtering them in more and more creative ways. His nightly adventures always included at least one clergy member, always, until too much Church attention was diverted to finding the "demon" ravaging the countryside. If he had been alone, a solitary, new creature, he'd have perished rapidly in the sortie sent against him.

"Who is this person?" He knew the standard list: boss, ex-lover, parent, annoying neighbor.

"Paul Winters—the asshole who slept his way into my job." The waitress arrived right then smiling.

"I thought I knew you!" She burbled with excitement. "You're on WGN news. I loved that story you did about the dog dyeing parlor. Who would have known it was just food coloring that turns poodles pink?"

Norah narrowed her eyes slightly. But Olivier cut in before anyone could be hurt. "She'll have the carpaccio. I'll have the baked brie with apple compote." He rested a resisting hand on Norah's elbow. "And another bottle."

The restaurant had started to fill up as they sat there, and people bustled around them, shaking snow out of their hair and hollering amongst themselves about the existence or not of a coat check.

"It says a lot about feminism that men are using their bodies to get jobs, does it not?" Olivier was baiting Norah, and he didn't try to hide it, let a grin accompany his words.

"Being a bump on the road of progress wasn't really my career goal. I didn't spend years fending off the grubby mitts of every male in the newsroom to have Adonis in Calvin Klein drop his pants at the first opportunity and rob me of real chance." Gesturing with her wineglass, Norah drew some attention from other patrons. She ignored their open stares and surreptitious glances to gaze imploringly at Olivier.

Women were his weakness, they had always been

his weakness—women and desire—and this one un-
doubtedly had an instinct for that. "I'll listen to your
brilliant plan while we eat." He knew he had been too
sarcastic as soon as the words left his mouth, before
Norah even tightened her lips and frowned.

"Wait, why do you get to tell us what to do, anyway? If we disobey you, can you make our eyeballs
explode?" She leaned forward, eyebrows raised expec-
tantly.

It wasn't just his tone, though; Olivier had been expecting that question for some time. In fact, Norah had
listened to him far more than he'd been expecting her
to. Those who were like Norah in life, and then turned,
were never inclined toward obedience.

"I have no say whatsoever on anything you do, aside
from having survived . . ."

He didn't bother to finish since the woman was almost to the door anyway. He was sure she could hear
him, but he would leave her be for now. There was too
much trouble that she could get into for him to really
truly worry about it now. As soon as she ran into the
fairies, she would be back asking for his advice.

His mind turned to the unfinished canvas in his loft.

The waitress appeared with their food. She juggled
the two plates in her arms looking at the empty seat
across from him. "Uh . . ."

Olivier stood, withdrew a money clip from his back
pocket, and counted out more than enough cash to
cover the meal and a fifty percent tip. "Why don't you
and your co-workers enjoy the food we won't eat and
share the wine we won't drink." He let his vowels drift
a little, pouring France back onto his tongue with a lingering smile.

"If you're lonely, you should come back by and ask
for Morgan. I won't run out on you like that." She bal-

anced the plates against her chest, and he winked at her as he grabbed his jacket and left, his mind fully occupied with his art.

SOPHIE DIDN'T BOTHER to call around to look for Suki's bandmates. She knew all of the band members intimately, although second-hand, from listening to Suki talk about them. She knew on the weeknights that they didn't practice, Alma, the drummer, would be at home with her son doing her homework. She was in her final year of nursing school, and the band was her only real leisure activity.

She took the El to Old Town, fighting her hunger, the thread of which wound up from the soles of her feet, up her legs, into her belly. She knew when it crept up further, she'd be in real trouble. She hoped she could make it to Alma's and away before she lost it.

Alma lived in a condo building that her parents had helped her afford after the baby. Sophie hit the buzzer labeled "Alma Garcia, YO!" and waited a couple ticks for the "Yes?"

"Alma, it's Sophie Aubrey, Suki's roommate."

"I know who you are!" The door rang the signal it was unlocked, and Sophie scuttled to get through before she missed her chance. Her record was four times that she'd had to get someone to hit the unlock button before she finally made it on the other side of the security door. But she'd had a couple drinks that night, and it had been another, way older, building.

She climbed the stairs, the musty smell of snow melting into carpet over-laid with industrial cleaners and cooking smells rushing her like a rip tide. Sophie could see the benefits of the frigid air of winter—it dampened the billions of smells ambient in the city.

On the second landing, Alma was standing at the second door down with her head stuck out the door, smiling. Her honey skin shone, clean of make-up, and her face was simple and young with her hair pulled back to show it off. She wore a navy blue track suit and thick socks.

"Come on!" She waved at Sophie. "It's freezing out here!"

Sophie hurried up. Alma held the door open for her and stepped back. Her apartment was a riot of scents—apples, onions, garlic, meat, burnt metal from the radiator, shampoo, the distinctive scent of blood. Sophie took a steadying breath as Alma locked the door.

"Where's Benny?" Sophie knew he wasn't in the apartment; his heartbeat was absent.

Alma hustled around her, down the short hallway into the living room, Sophie followed. "With his dad. Don't get me started."

Even if Sophie hadn't been on a mission, she wouldn't have asked someone she only sort of knew for personal information like that. People tended to over-share with her, and she tried not to encourage it if she could.

"Uh, ok—" Sophie started. Alma pointed to the couch, nestled between the television and her drum kit, and Sophie shook her head. "Look, this is sort of weird, but have you seen Suki tonight?"

Alma flopped onto the bold, primary colored, floral couch. "I knew something fucked up was going on."

Sophie didn't like the sound of that at all. "What do you mean?"

"You know all that stupid gris-gris and amulet stuff Suki is into?" Alma asked.

Sophie nodded. "I hadn't realized *everyone* knew about it," she said.

"Oh, it's cool. My mama, she's into Santeria. Suki hit me up about it when she first got into that lifestyle. I hooked her up where I could, but I don't believe in any of that. Whatever, but the past week, she was sketchier than usual. She was wearing a charm and everything."

The hunger thread began slinking up from her belly, and she knew she had to cut this off. "What kind of charm? Why?"

Alma looked at her hard. "You cut your hair? Something's different from the last time I saw you."

Sophie almost, almost laughed at that. Cut her hair? She figured this, combined with Norah's initial reaction to her altered form, that humans couldn't really see the fundamental difference between the human form and the vampire form. She would worry about that later. "I've lost some weight. What kind of a charm?"

"You look good." Alma smiled, trying to be friendly—but Sophie was hovering right on the edge, Alma's heartbeat began to thrum louder and louder. "Against fey creatures, something like that. Fey? Whatever. Do you want—"

"Thanks, but I gotta go," said Sophie abruptly, and the rest of Alma's polite invitation to *something* was lost on her as she flew out of the apartment, not noticing the stairs or the foyer or even the person she fed from until after. She ran and ran, not noticing how far she fled.

Sweet, green like grass, sadness, hopelessness, fear, futility and painpainpain that made Sophie want to laugh, exult, spin out into the night in cartwheels. The overwhelming, personality-*subsuming* need faded, still there, but in the soles of her feet again, like being asked if she was hungry, and her response was "I could eat" rather than being famished.

Sophie wiped the warm, sticky blood off of her face with the back of her hand and stared down at her meal—at her *victim*. The face was dirty and bruised, surrounded by bleached hair. The skin of the upper chest was grayish in the faint light of the alley. Blink: tight dress and heels and skimpy coat. Blink: face young, too young. Sophie ran out of the alley the opposite way from where she entered. Glancing up at the street sign she saw she was on North Avenue.

She needed to find Stacy, the guitar player from Jesus' Pick-up.

Every time she blinked, she got a freeze-frame of the under-aged prostitute. Not good. Was Sophie's ending of her life worse than her continuing to live it? She stumbled along the sidewalk oblivious to the cold of the wet snow that had begun to fall, to the people glaring at her, trying to bank down the euphoria she felt from the blood in her belly spreading through her system like opium. Shoppers yapped to each other, full of cheer and the fake brightness of the Christmas season, as she passed. No one said anything to her, the Midwestern friendliness oddly absent.

"Here, let me get that." Sophie's head snapped up to see Norah holding a hand full of clean snow. She smeared it across the bottom of Sophie's face. "You know the city's gone to hell in a handbasket when a girl can run up and down the street with blood all over her face and nobody says anything. Or did you kill whoever did?"

Sophie reached up and rubbed the numb skin where the snow had melted, taking the blood away with it. She looked up at Norah's smiling face. "How did you find me?"

"Is that a joke?" When Sophie didn't answer, Norah laughed, turning towards the restaurant where Stacy worked and pointed. "Ok, so that place over there? You were going to show up at it eventually. So, being a stealthy night-stalker, I came here and waited."

Norah's presence made Sophie feel almost normal. "Ah, this was a complex plan," she said, and swiped at her forehead where she could feel blood tightening her skin as it dried.

"Multi-layered. Took me weeks." She tugged Sophie off the sidewalk and into the street, dodging cars to cross to the restaurant. "You find out anything yet?"

"Maybe." She wiped the last of the moisture from the melted snow off of her face with her coat sleeve in the warm glow of the amber lights on the outside of the Lux, an up-scale "fusion" joint. "Suki was freaking out about something. She was afraid of 'fey' creatures."

"Gay guys?" Norah looked down at her with a lifted brow, threading her arm into the crook of Sophie's, and pulled her in the front door. "Like they're gonna steal her Prada shoes or something?"

"Like Suki wore Prada?" Sophie rolled her eyes, and Norah giggled. "I would guess maybe more like trolls like Ray Ray? I killed a hooker just now." The second part just fell out of her mouth without her consent.

Norah's face was utterly blank at the hostess approached. "You a pimp, girl." She winked. Sophie was sure she shouldn't have laughed at that, but, honestly, she couldn't help it.

"A table for two?" The woman was all blond hair and cleavage and costume jewelry. "The wait's about forty five minutes to an hour. You can wait in the bar."

Sophie started to explain, that no, they were here to talk to something.

"Sure." Norah said.

"Name?" The hostess smiled her bland, haughty smile.

"Jones." Without waiting for a reply, Norah tugged Sophie towards the bar. They weaved through the other patrons waiting to be seated, all the way to the very end of the room where a closed door led into the kitchen. Shoving the door open, Norah pulled Sophie into the forbidden zone. She let Sophie's arm drop. "You just gotta act like you belong."

Sometimes Sophie forgot that Norah's job helped her develop a whole hidden skill-set. Like brazen trespassing. "Sure. We belong. Let's find Stacy."

"Then we go thrall Paul," Norah said. She sounded insistent; Sophie would have to deal with that later. Thralling did not sound like the sort of thing baby vampires were supposed to do.

Sophie followed Norah as she forged a path through the kitchen staff, weaving and slithering as needed. No one tried to stop or question them. Sophie was kind of shocked that apparently Norah was right about just acting like you belonged.

Stacy found them. She sat at a small table set against a wall with a white board adorning it above Stacy's head. The menu for the night was scrawled in black and blue ink. "Sophie, Norah!" Stacy called, a smile on her face.

Norah made a beeline, the kitchen staff seeming to fall away from her as she progressed.

"I would ask you what the hell you're doing here, but I know it's Suki." Her brown ringlets were pinned back and hidden by a white kerchief. Sophie knew she was high up in hierarchy of the kitchen structure, but she didn't know much about restaurants besides what she'd learned from the Food Network.

"When was the last time you saw her?" Norah got down to business.

"Last night. She was going to meet some of her

coven members. They had some major casting going down." Stacy offered up the plate she'd been eating from. Sophie automatically declined, used to never eating anything without knowing exactly what sort of meat or dairy product could be present.

"What kind of casting?" Norah ignored the plate and chugged on with the interrogation.

"Protection, I think. I'm not really sure. She came by, but I was swamped. We had two people call in sick and another that's still in training." Her pleasant, round face pulled into as close to a hard as expression as it could manage. "I know something's very wrong. I just don't know what. She wouldn't tell me, really. She said the more I knew, the worse it would be. That sounds bad."

"Yeah, that sounds bad." Sophie couldn't agree more.

"Do you think it was something illegal?" Stacy wiped her sweating forehead with a napkin. "It seemed like it could be something illegal."

Sophie wondered if Stacy was trying to convince them or herself. She was Suki's closest friend in the band, very close, and Sophie had always figured that the whole "magic" thing was a shared occupation. Stacy's comments made her think that she was trying to mislead them, or that Sophie had been completely wrong about her and Suki's shared hobby.

Norah looked over at Sophie with a questioning head tilt.

"Yeah, it's probably illegal, but that doesn't have all that much meaning to us now." Sophie sighed.

"Oh, ok. So, that was true, then." Stacy stood and put her chair as well as the table between the vampires and herself. "The liquid diet thing. I thought it was just another rant Suki was on, about fairies and prophecies and vampires and inverted spells."

"Uh?" Norah eloquently asked.

"Please leave," Stacy said firmly. Her pulse had hitched up, but from the outside she betrayed nothing. Sophie applauded her courage, and was glad she'd so recently fed, because otherwise the scent of Stacy's fear would be sweeter than chocolate. Combined with Sophie's anger at being discriminated against, she wasn't sure she could control herself.

"Fine, I have better crap to do anyway." Norah turned without further comment, tugging on Sophie's sleeve.

Sophie paused for a moment to glare at Stacy, who didn't budge. "You could be more helpful, you know," said Sophie. "Who knows what's happened to Suki?"

"Whatever happened to her she brought upon herself," said Stacy, and then made some kind of movement with her fingers. "You are uninvited here, vampire."

Sophie made a noise of disgust, and let Norah tug her out of the kitchen. Stupid witch.

"Stupid witch," she muttered under her breath.

"Just because somebody got different eating habits don't mean they're evil," said Norah over her shoulder.

"Yeah, you're totally not evil," said Sophie.

"Don't be sarcastic with me," replied Norah, shouting a little to be heard over the crowd from the bar. "You're the one who got us both into this mess!"

Sophie absolutely refused to respond to that.

Their return trip through the restaurant was just as uneventful as their first. The night broke around them like glass as the exited the screaming hum of life in the cloistered building. The over-stimulation only asserted itself in its absence, and Sophie pulled in a lungful of sharp, cold air to savor it.

Norah turned to her, hands on hips. "Whatever," she

said to Sophie. "That was weird. She was weird. Suki's obviously more insane than I had thought." People jostled them as they walked, and Norah glared appropriately.

"No more insane than us being the stuff of nightmares." Stacy had been maybe right to be scared, to want to banish them as soon as possible.

"We didn't even threaten her." Norah sounded annoyed. "Not like I will Paul, when I thrall his ass."

Pulling up, Sophie tugged on Norah's arm so she had to turn and face her. "I think we need to talk about that."

"I'm going to get my revenge on Paul by turning him into my slave." She was pleased, really pleased, with this disclosure.

Sophie tried to count to ten, but only got to four. "Oh god." In the interest of full disclosure, Sophie decided to inform Norah about her reservations about her "thralling" plan. "Have you thought out the logistics of having a slave boy?" They talked about having a house boy all the time, but Sophie was not exactly in top form after the Stacy thing, the prostitute thing, and Suki going on some magical bender—plus, a house boy to do their laundry in a thong was totally different from thralling a complete asshole.

"You didn't just say that." Norah laughed and almost tipped off the curb where she was trying to hail a cab. A guy with about a hundred shopping bags sprinted up to and managed to open the door of the first cab that stopped. He slithered inside.

"*Hey!*" Sophie and Norah both screamed as the taxi took off.

"What the hell?" Norah looked about ready to gnaw out a couple of throats. They started back down the sidewalk.

Sophie wasn't finished trying to make her point.

"Look, I'm talking about the real-life scenario of having to take care of someone, to have them lingering around all the time, of having to remember to feed them, make them bathe themselves, dress themselves, all the boring deals of life." Norah huffed and Sophie smacked her on the arm and tried to appeal to Norah on her own level. "Hello, totally tedious."

A taxi coasted up to the curb directly next to them, and as she opened the door, Norah looked over her shoulder. "Look, who said he should be happy and comfortable? We're talking about making him suffer."

"No, really? I thought you were going to buy him a pony." Sophie hopped into the car, wiggling over as Norah bounced further in. She said to the cab driver, "Sheffield and Irving Park," and then turned back to Norah.

"Just make your point," said Norah. She smoothed her hair with her gloved hands.

"Why don't you just kill him and cut out the agonizingly boring part of exacting a protracted revenge? You aren't Lex Luthor, even though you pretend you are in your head." Sophie thought if she made it sound really bad, like *murder* bad, maybe Norah would see the folly of her reasoning.

Killing for food was totally different than killing for fun.

The driver looked at them in the rearview but said nothing. Sophie glared at him, and he looked away.

"Lex Luthor? Ok, let me bust some Lex Luthor on you. If we just kill him, then someone else inherits his stuff. Probably the probate court, 'cause no way Paul has ever thought enough about dying to make a will. So, then we're kicked out of our new place by court officials. If we hex him, then we just take his things and no one says jack shit."

The c.b. in the console of the cab warbled and cackled, and both occupants of the backseat frowned in annoyance.

So this was about stealing his stuff as well as enslaving him. Sophie could see the click and whirl of Norah's brain on that one. Paul's place in Lakeview was great, fabulous, and he had tons of cash, inherited money. His being independently wealthy was one of the reasons Norah hated him so much for being a back-stabbing job thief—he didn't even need the promotions.

Finally Sophie admitted defeat, not because it was right, but because she figured she'd get another opportunity to intercede for Paul. "Yeah, ok, you've thought about this too much, but I get it."

"Thank you," said Norah sarcastically. Sophie reached over and pinched her on the thigh, hard.

"Shut up," said Sophie. "Don't you think we're kind of stupid about this shit?"

"What shit? Being vampires?" She bared her teeth at Sophie and hissed, and Sophie laughed. "Whatever," said Norah. "We're doing all right, I think."

The cab driver made a small noise, and Sophie looked at his scared eyes in the rearview mirror.

"Don't worry," Sophie said to him. "We won't kill you."

"Like hell," said Norah and jerked toward the front seat. The cabbie stopped short, and both women were thrown against the seats, first forward, then back.

Sophie sighed in annoyance. "Norah, can you control your homicidal impulses for one second so we can just get home? Please?"

"Out!" said the cabbie. "Out of my cab!"

Sophie and Norah exchanged glances, and Sophie realized that Norah really did want to kill the cabbie. That was totally disturbing. She slid across the seat, reached over Norah, and opened the door. Then she pushed Norah out of the cab, threw ten bucks at the cabbie, got out and slammed the door.

"You are totally going to get us caught by the vampire-killing brigade," said Sophie, looking down at Norah in the street.

"Bitch, I cannot believe you did that." Norah scowled at her.

"Come on," said Sophie. "Let's walk home. Maybe we'll eat a frat boy on the way."

That perked Norah right up, and she forgot about her wet ass as they made their way home through the darkness.

Chapter Nine

WHILE SOPHIE HAD dreamt her first post-human dreams in his bed, Olivier had snapped a series of photos with his ancient Nikon. The inner curve of an elbow. Three stray curls tumbling across the vacated pillow still baring the indentation from his head. A crooked knee.

As he developed the photos, he played with the negatives. The silhouette of her face he superimposed on the etching of the shield of a long-dead knight, her profile becoming his standard. Another, taken after she'd rolled onto her back, he double-exposed with a nest of garner snakes wrapped around her throat. The second one he planned to use in a collage he had started a few years before that used a snake motif to play off the Christian idea of Original Sin. With her own fascination with religion, she would probably be interested to see herself as a metaphor.

The false intimacy of the internet had made him feel like he'd known her for years and years, and her own reactions to him—her negation of his own take on the world, had pulled him up and made him rethink not only his own thoughts but her thoughts as well. Who did she think he was? What did she think their relationship had been? Did she even think of him at all aside from when they interacted directly? He had no way of knowing, or ever knowing, who they would have or could have been together without the bond of what they were as blood-tied. He remembered being in love, the fear of it mainly.

More than that, he remember the obsession after Phillipa died. The feeling of wanting something he could never have had been unusual for him, and he had not coped well.

He knew that many of his kind used the excuse of modernity, of social progress, to explain their distance from the newly made and from humans. Olivier had always felt disconnected from others as well as connected to every other person in a vital and immediate way, that was the paradox of his life. Even as he could feel the membrane of self-awareness separating him from someone else, he could feel the chime of similarity, of shared consciousness.

He imagined that was the case before his death, but he couldn't remember that time.

Sophie was all post-modern and new, a product of her time, of a time when a woman such as herself could live her life freed from the constraints of family and class and the need to work from sunrise to sundown at all the menial and necessary tasks of the household.

Olivier loved modern women. He loved their freedom and absolute belief in themselves and their identities. His way had never been to manipulate love or allegiance; he didn't like the ashen taste of respect from honor and duty. His love had always been freely given and he wanted nothing but the same in return.

When he'd met her, he saw in Sophie everything her generation promised—and something more that he couldn't name or place, but that screamed in his mind unceasingly.

As he stared at his work and thought about Sophie, he felt an urge for hot chocolate and decided to slip on his shoes and head down to the café nestled into the first floor of the building housing his apartment. The ghost of the taste of chocolate tugged him out of the door with his left shoe not even firmly on his foot.

Olivier wasn't trying to excuse himself, or explain away poor impulse control, when he said he had never been one to deny himself his desires. He had fathered two children by his sixteenth year—one by a married lady in his mother's retinue, the other by an Andalusian singer. Sometimes he'd wonder, when he saw a stray person on the street, if they were his descendants.

His mother had had a few words for him after the she discovered the details of the first child. She found him in the sunshine, Olivier could remember that, the sun on his face and reflecting off the gold in her hair and at her neck.

"This world is full of peril, of traps and shining gems of great worth. But all is for naught, all that twinkles or draws the eye was constructed by the Evil One to make us forget the life of the soul, to pull us down into mindless satisfaction of our bodies." Sometimes in the memory, she spoke like that, in rhetoric.

Other times, she told him: "Love is the most beautiful trick of this life. We forget our souls happily and run smiling into oblivion. Congress with another is the physical, lower aspect of that flight to lose one's cares of the world, pain and hardship. It is only in your nature to be desirous of loving comfort, but always remember the hand of Him is on you."

Olivier suspected both speeches were his own construct, since they were filled with ideas he'd played over for many years. His memories were like that, untrustworthy and compounded amongst themselves. He doubted all of his memories of his true life, of his life in the light, in battle and in the Faith. He could remember remembering, but that was all.

The lobby of his building sparkled in surreal red light cast by the huge Christmas tree bedecked with the names of needy children. Two of his neighbors from down the hall, one an intern at some large corporation, and the other a piano teacher he often heard practicing, tumbled in from the street laden with packages, their faces made lurid in the strange light, their smiles disconcerting.

Olivier waved at them, but didn't stop. His mind threw out a flash of the photos he'd taken of them for their Christmas cards—S&M sex-kitten elves torturing a blow-up doll Santa—and he told himself to remember to stop by their Christmas party with a bottle of something strong.

He used the hallway from the lobby that fed straight into the café; that amenity, matched with the corridor to the drug store and bodega, was one of the main factors in his decision to live in this building. Being trapped inside during the day was a serious pain.

Of course, he was old enough that he could go out in the sunlight if he covered up really well, wore a lot of sunblock, and fed until he was overfull, but that was so bothersome. Easier to live at night.

Sliding into his usual chair at the counter of the coffee shop, Olivier waved to Greg, the barista.

"Espresso?" Greg yelled over the sound of the milk-steamer.

"Hot chocolate!" Olivier yelled back. As he settled

onto his seat, as a weird sensation crept up the back of his neck.

"It's always chocolate with you." A familiar voice slithered over Olivier's skin, into his ear and his brain.

Olivier closed his eyes and rubbed his eyelids with the side of a finger.

Automatically, he switched to his native tongue.

"Is this a coincidence?" Olivier opened his eyes as Greg set his drink in front of him. His oldest companion, his cousin—a word that had little meaning after so much time—stood smiling his own, private smile. Olivier knew this signaled something bad, Luc always brought chaos and insanity wherever he went, but he was glad for the company.

"That answers a question I had. Who is she?" Luc picked up Olivier's cup and sipped from it.

He didn't bother to deny that it was a girl, or to remark on how Luc knew it was. Olivier knew his own story and was aware of his own habits. He didn't bother to explain to Luc that this time it was different—Luc wouldn't believe him. His eyes were drawn to the only face more familiar than his own.

Olivier sighed. Luc nodded to fashion with his ragged but affected hair cut, the liquid obsidian locks falling loose around the pale, pale skin. He was the same, always the same, as Lucien the knight, Luc the sorcerer.

"A religious studies student." Olivier plucked his cup back from Luc.

"Sounds promising. I suppose she's really a Zoroastrian or Mithras aficionado." Luc rapped the counter with one knuckle. "A Turkish coffee," he said to Greg in English.

"No, her real interest is in heresies, I think. You can ask her yourself if you want to quiz her. She's already one of us."

Luc laughed, his persimmon lips falling open in invitation to the world, white cheek firing with stolen blood, head thrown back in the abandon he owned. Most of the heads in the café turned to look at him—half in silent terror, half in inexplicable lust. "You never did have any patience. So, you brought her in, and she confessed that she believed the Holy Grail was a person?"

Olivier looked over at Luc then with a half smile. "You're still angry about that? Why do you care what people think? Sometimes I think you took a knock to the head that's stayed with you." The myth that the Holy Grail was a person was one of Luc's enduring obsessions—enduring since the Crusades. How Luc had managed to take his duties as a crusader so seriously had always escaped Olivier. Luc took all oaths seriously, even ones given for a reason, to achieve some greater end. At one time to get to the Levant as a European meant taking up the cross as a crusader, and Luc did so with a fervor Olivier recalled edged in dust and blood and wine.

"While I may never have been as devout as some . . ." Olivier snorted and Luc made a rude gesture. Piety had never suited Luc. "I still find some beliefs more anathema than others. Modern people are well educated but gullible." Luc rubbed his face, seething. Olivier was always amazed at Luc's ability to become heated over ideas and ephemera. He was at heart a zealot—rather, a believer with no belief left to him.

"They have lost all sense of the mysterious with their science," Olivier said, trying to soothe Luc, "and they seek to make mystery in the wrong way. They crave what they cannot understand. It has always been so." He and Luc both had seen myths form and dissipate, secret societies appear and fall to legend. Man needed to believe in something, not unlike Luc. Wasn't they why they were what they were, his friend and he? Wasn't that why they had lived this borrowed existence until this very day so they could debate meaning or lack or meaning in a pointless circle of familiar words? For Luc the object of belief was less important than the righteous pull of the belief itself. Olivier had always been glad Luc was his compatriot and not his foe.

"Why don't you see that turning an unspeakable mystery into the bastard-born offspring of a prophet is debasing on a level that even these heathens today should be ashamed of?" Luc was beginning to get heated, one of his favorite reasons to hate the infidel set up for him to rail against. It had been more than thirty years since the last time he and Olivier had sat side by side, drinking coffee and arguing about life and religion—and yet they now picked up their conversation almost exactly where they had left off.

"Why do you even bother caring when you know both the myth and greater myth it rests on is false? You lost your faith long ago, why . . ." He was going to say "Why don't you move on?" but he arrested his argument. There was no reason to have this whole fight again. Although he was beginning to think that all he had ever done was relive echoes of a set of ten experiences, the same conversations repeated, the same activities duplicated . . .

"You never change, staring off into space. Are you thinking about sex?" Luc made a face as he drank his coffee, ready to let the fight blow away like the steam on his drink. Luc knew Olivier was jousting with ghosts in his mind, not occupied by sex, but he was graceful enough to let the conversation go. Luc read people well, that was part of his charisma, a talent he was born with.

"I was thinking exactly what you said, that nothing changes." All of life was confusion and incomprehension, striving for some unnamable something that didn't exist to begin with.

"Except that everything does. Heraclites and the stream of change, my brother." Luc sighed. Olivier remembered then that they were more alike than different—way down deep, in who they really were beneath the false trappings of living and the meaningless differentiation of appearance and habit. Their souls were similar. Luc loved ideas and art and all things of the mind. They shared that, even if Luc was more cunning than Olivier under his flip façade, reason and calculation to Olivier's heedless action. Luc was the obvious target for criminals and creatures looking for an easy mark, with his bluster and flash, but underneath he had fifteen escape routes from any room, could memorize the lay-out of a town on one walk-through, gave up chess before Martin Luther was born because there was no challenge.

"So, is your new girl a Believer?" Luc was excited despite his easy cynicism. His faith might have been gone, but the chance that one of their long, long lost people might be among them was something to celebrate. It had been only too rare an occasion.

They had spent their first several centuries determinedly searching for the reborn souls of their coreligionists. Decade after slow decade of weaving among villagers, of listening for stories of strangely wise children, of changelings, of witches, of odd birth marks, of any sign they could invent or imagine to give a sign of their loved ones returning to them. Like they had been taught, instructed, admonished to do. Their only reason for existing was to find the reborn souls they almost never did. Luc channeled his passion into that for long centuries, because that was the task they were appointed to, had survived for.

"I don't know yet. The situation is more complex than I had realized." Complex was a simple word used to describe that which was messy.

"She ran off and turned her friends." Luc finished off his coffee and laughed merrily, an evil gleam in his eye. "Definitely one of us, then."

"And here I was looking to you for sympathy." Olivier had been far worse, however, when the same thing had happened to Luc; so he supposed that when nothing ever changed, when you made the joke the first time, it was inevitable you would be the brunt of the joke the next. But he wasn't sure yet if Sophie was one of them or not—if he just *wanted* her to be one of them. "What're you doing here if you didn't already know about her?"

Luc looked at him slant-ways. "And how would I have known about your little . . . accident?"

Sometimes, Olivier almost gave into Luc's continued power-plays, his need to feel like he was besting Olivier after all these years. His first impulse was to argue, to let the see-sawing of masculine one-upmanship rage on. But that was only Luc getting to him, because that was never who Olivier was.

"Because you have a magic ball or mirror?" He smiled, and Luc returned the gesture.

"Ah, my friend, how ignorant you still are." He sipped his coffee. "I have an imaginary friend who tells me these things. He's a wombat. Do you know what a wombat is, my old, ignorant friend?"

Olivier didn't look at him. He also didn't believe Luc was serious about the wombat, not after that sorcerer they knew in Vienna with the marsupial familiar who poured boiling oil on himself.

Chapter Ten

CONVINCING NORAH TO wait over the day to attack Paul Winters hadn't been simple, but they'd been close friends since middle school, had made the decision to attend college in Chicago in tandem at seventeen, and had functioned almost as a diode ever since. Sophie professed utter weariness and pulled a "cute" face. Norah was pissed, but Sophie wheedled with how she hadn't gotten to go on the "shopping" spree. She hit the goldmine on that one, Norah getting caught up in giving Sophie her earrings.

There was a day-long reprieve for sleeping and plotting, and Sophie took the opportunity to finish grading papers. She debated delivering the papers to the department at U Chicago herself, but ultimately opted printing out a FedEx label and sending them overnight. She drank a little from the FedEx guy who showed up to pick up the package, but didn't kill him—her students deserved to know their grades, and besides, he tasted bad, like hopelessness, lost dreams, clinical depression, Prozac or Wellbutrin, a longing to fall in love. She decided that antidepressants were bad for vampires and concluded she'd have to figure out a way to avoid eating people who took them. At some juncture.

The overwhelming longing the FedEx guy felt for love made Sophie think of Olivier, of all the things she could be throwing away if she didn't give him a chance. A chance at what? A chance to give her some mind-blowing sex again? A chance to show her what it could be like to live forever with someone who wrote poetry about her smelly socks?

Instead of doing anything productive after the FedEx guy left, Sophie sat at the kitchen counter with her laptop, sipping coffee with a lot of sugar to mask the blood left on her tongue, and skimming through emails to avoid thinking about Olivier. Sathan hopped up on the table and sat in the middle of her keyboard, refusing to budge and then biting her and rabbit-footing her with his rear legs when she attempted to dislodge him. Eventually they came to a stalemate with Sathan ensconced on her unplugged computer, any typing postponed until a cat-free zone could be achieved.

"Where do you think Suki is?" Sophie asked her companion. He licked his paw and rubbed his face in response.

"Yeah, I think it's probably best to stay chill about it, too. Calm, cool. No need to flip out or file a police report, right?" She scratched him on his chest and he promptly rolled on his back stretching his legs over his head.

Rubbing his belly she continued their discussion. "I mean, if I called her parents and she's just pulling a prank, she'll be pretty pissed off, don't you think?"

Sathan grabbed her hand with his front legs like he'd bite her, but instead he licked her palm.

When Norah finally woke up, she was just as determined to go through with the entire Paul Winters debacle. Sophie knew Norah's intentions by her even more silent than usual morning—evening—routine. She drank her coffee, flipping through the *Tribune* with a smirk. When Sophie got a look at those antics, she changed into black, to hide the blood, and pulled her hair back as tight as she could, pinned it all up on her head.

She had enough intelligence to realize her entire wardrobe might be pretty goth in the not-too-distant future. Shower, change, snack on crackers, wait for Norah to motion her towards the front door.

The smile on Norah's face as she shrugged into her Burberry coat—new thanks to the recent rampage—was the one normally associated with shoe sales and investigative reports. Sathan meowed appallingly at the door as she slammed it. Sophie knew she was sunk, even as she followed onto the sidewalk, looking for a cab.

"YOU REALLY JUST want to walk in there and, what, look him in the eye and be all 'I thrall you, sucker!'?" Sophie gazed at Norah in annoyance.

"Pretty much, but more menacing than how you did it." Norah brushed by her and started up the steps to Paul Winters' home. The red brick three story home hulked on the sidewalk declaring to anyone who passed by that the owner was ludicrously wealthy and had a great realtor. Paul Winters—rich as sin, beautiful to the point of ridiculousness, aware of both of the above to the point of insufferableness.

The neighbors two doors down were obviously having a Christmas party; people spilled in and out of the front door in a constant stream, shouting to each other. One young man took a slide off the steps and thumped—boom boom boom—on his rump.

Sophie shivered in the wind, then followed Norah up the steps of the brownstone. She had to admit she hated the guy herself. She examined her feelings, and realized that her issue wasn't with thralling him and humiliating him and taking all his stuff. No, her issue was mainly the *logistics* of having a human pet, not the morality of doing so.

An entire three story condo in Wrigleyville did have its appeal, though. There was even a cemetery nearby—who knew when that would come in handy for a vampire? The neighborhood wasn't what Sophie would have picked—full of the sorority girl types who always looked down at her and made snide remarks about her mismatched outfits in whispers intended for her to hear, but she was sure picking off a few of them wouldn't be so horrible.

"Of course he'd live here," Sophie groused as she climbed the stairs of the stoop as the front door was opened by a grouchy-faced Paul dressed in a suit and tie.

"What the *hell* do you want?" Paul was such a stereotype of middle-American perfection that even his conversation sounded programmed. His shiny black hair curled perfectly around his face in a way that wasn't artificial but true, genetic superiority. The pale skin of his face held a ruddy flush that spoke of a high temper. Sophie once imagined that it also spoke of pure sex, a kind of enhanced passion, but after his gross manipulation to get the job Norah'd worked years for, she'd revised that opinion. No one who would do such a thing could possibly be interested enough in another person to be good in bed. Even if he had a mouth that looked like something from an Italian painting.

He held the door open with one large hand braced against it above his head, his other hand pointed at Norah's face. "I'm going to get a restraining order against you."

Norah stepped closer to him. Sophie couldn't see her face, but she did see Paul's hazel eyes lock and his expression of haughty anger turn to interest. His pale cheeks flushed with the cold, turning a boyish, mottled pink.

Sophie wondered why Paul didn't just charm his way through life with that face, and his trust fund, and his requisite six feet-four inches that made him into the poster boy for strapping, good old-fashioned America. He even grew up on a farm—granted it was a horse farm that was more of a lark for his parents than anything that produced food or livestock.

"Sure, yeah. You're right, I need to change." Paul shuffled back from the door pulling it all the way open for them as he did.

"That was fast." Sophie stepped into the foyer behind her friend. They both looked around at the faux Arts And Crafts furniture and beige-toned paint.

"I think he must moonlight as an ad for Crate and Barrel." Norah flung her coat onto an ox-blood leather armchair sitting next to a coat rack.

"Well, we can get some hot contractors in here and rip out this ugly marble floor and maybe put in slate, and paint the walls red . . ." said Sophie. The room totally had potential. She glanced at Norah for her opinion— Norah was the better of them at color schemes. But Norah stared back at her dumbly. "What? You're going to do this no matter what I say, so I might as well enjoy it."

Which is how she felt about most of what her best friend got up to anyway.

"Excellent strategy." Norah smiled. "Except I hate slate, how about—"

There was a thump from the top of the stairs, soon followed by Paul running down to stare at them in shocked anger.

"What the *hell* are you doing here?" he yelled.

Sophie laughed at how limited his phrase book appeared to be.

"Hey, shut up!" Norah shot at her. Sophie tried to pull a sober, serious face, but Paul had no shirt on. To Paul, Norah said, "I told you to go change into jeans and a sweater and go to Janine's party down the block! Get out of our way!" She stepped directly into his line of sight, and his anger visibly bled out of him and was replaced with a pleased and eager puppy-like expression.

It seemed like it would be kind of helpful to be able to affect people like that, but it also seemed like a lot of work. Norah was practically working up a sweat with her stare.

"Oh, right. I forgot. Do you want me to get you anything first? A drink or anything?" Paul threaded a hand through his hair, the red stone in his class ring bright against his dark hair.

"No, you moron, just go change, and hurry up!" Norah sighed, and Paul hustled up the stairs.

"Shit, this plan already sucks." Norah looked murderous as she proclaimed the obvious. Sophie bit her tongue to keep from saying, "I told you so!" Norah continued: "Now I have to watch him all the time? This was *not* the idea."

"We could kill him," Sophie jokingly suggested.

Norah shrugged. "Yeah, but we'd have to hide his

body and figure out a whole will thing . . ." She started up the stairs, and before she disappeared on the second floor landing, she turned back and looked at Sophie. "What's the plan?"

"What makes you think I have a plan?"

"You always have a plan."

Sophie laughed. She did usually have a plan—or three. Swiftly she ran through the options. What was completely plain was that Norah would not give up on the Paul revenge thing, so Sophie saw the endgame there as Paul being enthralled or dead. There were no other logical conclusions. She didn't like the guy, but killing him because he was annoying and made Norah bitch and complain didn't really sit well. Which made her wonder where her vampiric bloodlust had gotten to. Maybe she didn't have any bloodlust at all? Didn't she hate anyone enough to want to slaughter them and their entire kith and kin? She pondered as Norah ran through a stream of anti-Paul invective under her breath, tapping her foot against the marble floor with impatience. When Sophie scrolled back in her mind to high school and still had no one, she gave up on trying to formulate her own revenge massacre.

When she refocused on the matter at hand Sophie realized the only option they had was to ask Olivier for advice because he was the only authority they had. That wasn't the best case scenario, Sophie knew, but that was the best that it got for now.

"YOU WILL WEAR THE BATMAN SHIRT AND HURRY UP BEFORE I BEAT YOUR SAD ASS!" Norah screamed from upstairs. And then: "BECAUSE I'M YOUR MASTER AND I SAY SO!"

Sophie giggled to herself even as she felt a creeping unease about Paul. It was wrong to impose their will on his. But those thoughts were followed closely by awareness that killing—even to survive—wasn't acceptable at all. Especially considering that she didn't even used to eat gelatin or honey because those products came from animals.

The din from upstairs abated, and she looked up to see Norah standing on the landing looking down at her.

"What's the plan?" Her hair was askew.

"Olivier." Sophie buttoned her coat, frowning.

"Good start. He should at least know someone who knows someone." Pleased with herself, Norah sounded almost giddy. Sophie waved at her and stepped out onto the stoop.

To FORTIFY HERSELF, Sophie stared at the Angel Tree in the lobby of Olivier's building for a while. She didn't really have the time to dawdle, but she figured that if Norah was going to end up killing Paul, she'd kill him whether or not Sophie waited a few minutes before going up to Olivier's apartment. She wanted to disappear from here, find a better plan to cope with Norah's insanity. There was at least a fifty percent chance that she'd end up in bed with Olivier within fifteen minutes of entering his apartment. She couldn't look at the guy without wanting to jump on him.

And that was totally not like her. Usually she was crushing on the unattainable and falling in love with people who didn't even know her last name. Sure, she'd let herself be convinced that relationships were more than they were, forever and soul mates, but that was more of a problem of falling in love without a net than any confusion of good sex with love. It was emotional. Or so she told herself when the sex was unsatisfying and kind of annoying. This thing with Olivier . . . there was no way they were soul mates, not really. No way that all the stuff that had been floating around in her mind was true. Maybe he did have the same voice as the guy in her dreams—so what? That could be her mind playing tricks, fusing a memory with a dream. Happened enough with other things.

Sophie's brain was insistent that it didn't mean anything, that their chemistry was just that: chemistry. Pheromones or something, stuff on their skin reacting when they touched. That didn't explain, though, why her heart raced at just the idea of seeing him, why her palms were sweaty and her body tingled, why she wanted to touch him and be near him.

It was kind of annoying, actually, because Sophie absolutely did not believe relationships could be built on one-night stands.

What did they have, really? At odd moments she thought of the light in the club turning his hair from brown to red to gold, the curve of his jaw, the crease by his earlobe, the lines on his bottom lip. She didn't just want to have sex with him all the time—she wanted to get to know him better, to listen to him talk, to read his horrible poetry. That wasn't just lust. He said interesting things, and . . .

Sophie wished Suki was there, instead of wherever she was. Probably in trouble. Maybe she screwed around with someone's girlfriend, some mob guy or something. That was no more outlandish than being turned into a vampire, right? Suki always gave the best advice on Sophie's love life. Sophie tried to think of what she'd say—probably, "So have a lot of sex, get a lot of orgasms, and get out. What else are men good for anyway?" But Suki didn't even believe that men were good for orgasms, so probably not.

The Christmas tree seemed sort of sad without lights. No sparkle and glamour, just squares of blue paper with the names, ages, and Christmas lists of needy children in the area who anyone who took a card could help in the season of giving. Sophie sighed as she read the names on the Angel Tree—Jimmy Welch, Britney Powers, Veronica Jackson—and wondered if they had had Christmases with no gifts, if getting onto the Angel Tree was their only chance of one day of pleasure in sad lives of desperate poverty and abusive parents. Two years ago the whole U Chicago Divinity School had adopted Angel Tree children, each department picking one. Sophie's department, the Religion Committee on Historical Human Sciences, picked a three-year-old boy with a nineteen-year-old mom who was laid off in November from her minimum wage job. The department kitted them out with presents and groceries, even a tree. The look on the mom's face had been Sophie's Christmas gift to herself that year.

She plucked five of the cards off the tree and stuffed them into the pocket of her coat. Just because she was an evil baby-eating blood-sucking fiend didn't mean she couldn't give back to her community. Or Olivier's community. Whatever, kids in Wicker Park probably needed nice Christmases just as bad as kids everywhere else.

The elevator pinged and opened immediately when she pushed the button, and Sophie stepped into the carriage thinking about all the gifts that Paul's money could buy. Maybe they could even arrange some sort of system for a certain amount of groceries every month for the families . . .

Enslaving Paul was wrong, but Paul wasted what he had, wasted all the luck he'd fallen into with his birth. Really, Sophie and Norah were just—well, they were just sort of like the karmic avengers.

Olivier opened his door as the elevator doors closed

behind her, like he knew that she would be there or something. The passageway between his apartment and the elevator was miniscule, this portion of the building being composed of lofts, each taking up half the floor. His front door faced another, identical door, with the elevator set at ninety degrees to them.

He pushed the door completely open and rested his hand on the knob, beckoning to Sophie with the other. She fingered the Angel Tree cards in her pocket and shuffled across the small space and into the apartment, noticing for the first time how the outside of the door was covered in fingerprints in a wide pattern around the doorknob in a hundred different colors of paint.

Olivier noticed her gaze as he slammed the door shut. "I forget to wipe my hands off before I run out for coffee sometimes."

"Naturally," she replied, wondering where the paintings were.

Windows dominated the two exterior walls of the space. Floor to ceiling, lines of glass broken only by the wooden panes that held the glass in place. The kitchen jutted out near the far wall with the bathroom beyond that, and another, smaller room constructed in what appeared to be a homemade manner from plywood and cardboard. She hadn't noticed any of this the first time she'd been in his apartment, but she figured that was okay. After all, the first time she'd been in his apartment, she'd been . . . distracted. And dead.

A thought struck her. "Why don't you have shades for the windows?" Streetlights gleamed across the street to the north, and through the eastern windows she could see all the closed blinds and drapes of apartments in the next building. "Wouldn't you burn up or something?"

Olivier moved behind her; she could hear him

breathing and his bare feet moving on the wooden floor.

"Magic," he said, and she turned to see him smiling.

He made Sophie's stomach hurt. She didn't really know him at all, and she found it difficult to judge what could be a joke. And that . . . that made her kind of annoyed, kind of upset. She didn't *want* to know him better; she wanted to know everything about him. She didn't want to want to know him better; she couldn't stand not knowing him. Not touching him. Her fingers itched to brush across the dent in his lip again.

"Are you for real or making fun of me somehow?"

His smile collapsed, and he tilted his chin up slightly. "I'm for real. I wouldn't mock you for not knowing something—because that's my fault."

Sophie sighed. She hadn't meant to make him go all serious and dour. "Look, chill out. You don't have to apologize or anything. I hate people who apologize all the time. And it's not your fault. I haven't exactly been listening to you." Pulling off her gloves and tucking them into her pocket, she turned away from him and looked around.

Against one window was a pile of photography equipment, a jumble of lights and cameras and cases for lenses. She shrugged her pink wool coat off, and before she could turn, Olivier was pulling it all of the way off and carrying it over to a series of hooks set into one of the interior walls.

"I had the windows charmed by an alchemist," he said over his shoulder. Sophie watched his back shift under his thin, faded blue T-shirt.

"Is *all* magic real?" She wandered towards the kitchen area, noticing the dishes piled on the counter, the pot left on an unlit gas burner. The refrigerator was covered in magnets and little bits of paper, black and

white photos in various sizes, the subject matter sometimes obscured enough that she couldn't discern what
it was.

On the other side of the kitchen, she found the actual art area. The floor was covered in flecks of paint,
and several, huge canvasses were set against the lean-
to room and windows.

"I don't know what you mean by *all* magic." Olivier
followed her at a bit of a distance.

In the bright light of a double row of halogen track
lights, Sophie examined the unfinished multimedia
work nearest to her. Various shades of blue and metallic paint had been built up to form a texture similar to
tiny waves moving in the same direction in a looping
pattern from one side of the rectangular surface to the
other. Text had been inked to parts of the work, she
leaned closer to read it, and found it was written in
some sort of archaic French . . .

Getting closer, she realized it was something close
to Provençal. She'd studied many languages over the
course of her academic career, and she'd spent a couple of years on the various dialects of southern and
coastal France. She'd started trying to teach herself
Latin from the Encyclopedia Britannica in elementary
school, moved to French and Spanish in high school,
then on to Greek, Latin, and various Romance languages in college to augment her religious studies.
Languages had always fascinated her.

Obviously her entire life had been lived so that she
would recognize a centuries-dead language used in a
collage by her crazy vampire lover.

Sophie was about to comment on both the lover and
the Provençal when she got a good look at the figure in
the picture pasted to the painting. A prone woman,
asleep or dead, had been cut out and affixed to a raft-

like contrivance, reminiscent of the famous painting of "The Lady of Shallot," but the photo placed in the painted river was disconcerting, almost frightening.

Sophie flicked her eyes at Olivier who was staring back at her unblinkingly. "That picture is strange. I mean, this is really amazing, but freaky . . ."

Olivier blinked once, then ran a hand through his hair, smiling. "You don't recognize the person?"

She frowned and turned back to the black and white figure. She started to shake her head when Olivier spoke. "That's you."

Sophie felt frozen fingers run up her spine and clutch the base of her skull. She recognized her altered face, her long hair that trailed into the painted waves, the hair that even now had managed to tug itself free from the pins she'd restrained it with.

She straightened up without looking back at Olivier. She rapidly flipped through reactions: freaked out, scared, curious. The wheel stopped on accepting this strangeness as what had to be traditionally obsessive vampire-type behavior. Didn't vampires stalk and obsess in books, like, constantly? Glancing back at Olivier, who had crossed his arms over his chest and lifted his chin, she decided to not address this art/obsesso situation presently, but instead filed it away for something to be ruminated over at a later date.

"So, magic is real." She rounded Olivier and walked briskly back to linger near the front door. He followed at a slower pace.

"Yes. It's real. I'm not anything approaching an expert, though." He sighed slightly behind her. "You don't have to be scared of me."

Laughter escaped her before she could help it, the sort of nervous laughter she got at funerals and when she was being reprimanded, and she turned to look at him. "Yeah, I sort of do have to be. You freak me out. Listen, I'm totally conflicted here, so could you be a little sympathetic?"

His face was hard for her to read, but she thought maybe he was trying to make himself impossible to gauge. He didn't have to try. Would she be like that eventually, closed off and opaque to everyone and anyone? "Fine. Much magic is 'real'—as real as anything."

"Don't get existential on me, Olivier," she ordered. "I'm not in the mood for one of your I'm-a-broody-poetic-unsouled-being answers."

He glared at her. "You need some kind of magic to force someone to be a permanent thrall," he said. He uncrossed his arms and started picking through a pile of laundry, finally extracting a pair of mismatched socks.

Sophie froze. Could he read minds? Did he know how much she wanted to act out every sordid sex fantasy she'd ever had with him? "Thrall?" Her fear made it hard to elucidate her thoughts. "What're you doing?"

Olivier pulled on his socks and shoes, and grabbed a coat off the hooks on the wall, snatching hers as well and tossing it to her. "Taking you to someone who can tell you all about thralling spells."

He stomped to the door, opened it, and extended his hand into the doorway with a sarcastic flourish. She marched to the elevator and pressed the button, refusing to look over at him.

"How do you know what I want?"

"Norah told me." His words were bitten off, clipped, his teeth clenched hard enough to make the tendon in his jaw stand out. "Besides, new ones always want to thrall someone. Revenge schemes are universal."

"You don't know how to do it yourself?"

"No, that's not the way I do things, but, and here we

have a situation I would happily remedy if you would so graciously allow it by not running off somewhere when I try to talk to you, you don't know me very well." The sarcasm wasn't lost on Sophie, and she wished she'd been nicer about the art for a second before being annoyed that *he* was angry at *her*. Who was the weird stalker-lunatic-vampire here?

The elevator pinged and Olivier stepped in. His expression had softened, and he looked depressed. Sophie had never been able to stand hurting people's feelings, going so far as to write long, effusive notes on the papers she gave low marks to in the classes she TAed.

As the elevator closed behind her, she tugged at her coat, watching Olivier. He looked back at her with a wry smile. His eyes were four colors at once—aqua and gold and green and bright blue. So beautiful, it was very obvious he couldn't possibly be anything like human.

"Look," she said, "I loved your painting . . . it's just, I'm having a bad week—understatement of the year—and I didn't know what to say, because, well, that was strange, were you taking pictures of me when I was asleep?"

Olivier blinked a couple of times, then smiled broadly, exposing his front teeth. Sophie's heart skipped a beat. Was there a name for falling in love with your murderer, like there was for falling in love with your kidnapper? Her life had been kidnapped, and she was getting sweaty-palmed for the guy because he wrote bad poetry and was sensitive about his art.

The elevator opened, and he grabbed her elbow, steering her towards the front doors of the building. "You didn't hurt my feelings by not commenting on the art, but thanks for worrying about it," he said, his voice raspy, his mouth pressed to the side of her head near her ear.

She suppressed a shiver but couldn't control the rest of her physical reaction to having him pressed so close to her, her body remembering his touch and the sound of his whispered endearments. She swallowed hard.

"I'm just pissed about having to introduce you to Luc so soon." He pulled back as they stepped into the street, but she caught his arm and linked hers through it. She smiled at him as he grinned slightly, tucking her hand into the crook of his elbow.

Sophie wasn't so sure that he wasn't lying about her non-appreciation of his art. Half her life had been spent around one sort of artist or another, and she knew they could be strange and prickly about the work they produced. She hoped some show of kindness might placate him where her words couldn't. Plus, she had a hard time keeping her hands completely off of him.

"Who's Luc?" she asked, and his arm tensed under her grip.

"This idiot I know," Olivier answered.

OLIVIER KEPT HIS silence as he led her from his apartment to the Damen El stop. Their train hit the station almost exactly as they did, and Sophie glanced harder at Olivier wondering if he had more arcane abilities that she didn't.

"Just lucky," he said as he tugged her into the compartment.

They stood with people shoving in behind them, grappling amongst themselves for the seats, juggling packages and leftovers from restaurants and parties.

Normally, a Wednesday after midnight would find

this portion of the El, servicing to many bars and
clubs, filled with concert goers or loaded nine-to-fivers
on their way home after a few, but so close to Christmas every stripe of citizen shared the spirit of the egal-
itarian, drunken season. Sophie swayed against Olivier,
his thick fingers braced against her lower back and
knee pressed into the back of her thigh to steadier her,
and she skipped her eyes from face to face in front of
her. She paused on a teenaged girl with an expensive
dye-job—purple under-layer and white over-layer—
with the requisite facial piercings and patched coat.
Concentrating, Sophie picked up her conversation:

". . . and I was all *as if* you were there, because we
were there all night, and we never saw you, why do you
have to lie all the time?"

The girl paused and looked up. Her expression became stunned and vacant and then, as she searched the
crowd, not finding what she expected or needed to see,
panicked. Sophie could feel her fear, could feel some
great pressure in her fingertips, in her toes, in the skin
of her face tingling . . .

Olivier knocked her forward with his knee, bouncing her into his chest. The motion looked natural, like
a loss of balance from the train hitting a rut in the rails.
She struggled to stand on her own, anger pushing out
the strange stinging in her body.

"A little hungry?" His hand on her back restrained
her effectively, and her own hand resting on his hip
made their stance appear amorous. Up that close, she
could smell linseed oil, cigarettes, coffee, and cloves on
his clothes and skin.

Before he mentioned it, she couldn't have said what
the slight anxiety sliding her into her consciousness,
the sharp sliver slipping just under her skin, was. She
had been under a little stress in the last couple of

days—being turned into one of the undead would do that, plus that whole maybe-falling-in-love thing, which she was trying not to think about, not to mention her best friend missing and calling her with strange messages—and feeling unease had become pretty normal for her.

But when Olivier named it, Sophie realized *this* unease was hunger.

"Are we almost there?" With awareness came an exponential increase in the need. Tendrils of electrical shock flashed out from her belly to the ends of her fingers and toes, to the top of her head, searing along the path.

"Next stop." Olivier snaked his arm up the back of her coat until it rested between her shoulder blades, forcing her to press completely into him, her panting face wedging into the space between his neck and collarbone. "Have you ever thought about the texture of cheese?"

The thrum-thrum of the life around her faded slightly as her laboring brain processed what Olivier had just said. He continued in the same vein, "The texture of cheese is essentially what makes it cheese and not yogurt . . ."

Sophie tried to concentrate on his babbling, but the scent of his skin yanked at her, the artery in his neck standing in relief in his gold skin. Her lips parted, and her tongue flicked out to bump along in a swift rhythm along the artery. Olivier drew a stuttering breath, his hand on her back tugging hard enough to rip her shirt slightly and the collar gave, his fingers pressing into her skin.

The train halted, and passengers shoved into and around them. One guy, who looked like a scary biker, shoved at Sophie so hard she stumbled away from

Olivier and almost all the way onto the platform. She spun on the man, her right hand extending to catch his coat. The look of stricken terror on his face made her smile, forced several notes of laughter out of her constricted throat. Olivier stepped into her line of sight, though, and the man was free to menace other, less dangerous, Chicagoans.

Sophie concentrated on her own feet as they traversed the platform, descended the stairs, flew along the pavement of the sidewalk. The trip seemed infinite and rapid at the same time. She stared blindly at Olivier as he tugged her through a doorway, and she was plucked from her feet, jiggled around a bit, then set back right side up in a room lit with candles and oddly glowing orbs.

"No Ray Ray?" Sophie didn't wait for an answer, though. She made a beeline for the bar, rapping the surface with her knuckles until the affable barkeep strolled over on his eight clacking legs, already uncorking a bottle to pour up a large glass of a dark, viscous substance.

"Side entrance." Olivier slid into the seat to her right as Sophie gulped down the blood. As the first mouthful slipped down her throat, the world came into sharp focus—as if she'd been living underwater for years completely unaware of it. She drank more, and her body felt splendid, her skin elastic and moisture-rich, her soul resting in it with a perfect fit.

Sighing elaborately, Sophie offered the glass towards Olivier. He shook his head. "I take mine the old-fashioned way." He lifted an eyebrow.

The world was remade, all luster and shine. Sophie polished off the rest of her drink. "Wow."

The bartender smiled. "Only the finest virgin's vintage here, my lady. Packs a punch."

Sophie smiled, licking the remnants from her top lip. "*Blud*!" she said in a ridiculous Transylvanian accent.

Olivier laughed. Sophie watched him, the curl of his eyelashes, the sheen of his hair. With her index finger, she reached into the mostly empty glass and collected a swipe of blood on the tip of her finger. She leaned forward and wiped it along Olivier's mouth. He didn't withdraw, allowing her to play, only catching her wrist when she started to lean back. His tongue darted out to clean his lips, his hand drawing her closer to him. They stopped a breath apart; she stared at his mouth, watched him stare at hers.

They were interrupted by a voice with a thick French accent from behind Sophie. "Ah, the happy couple." She flung her head around to see who was speaking, and would have sworn she heard a low growl from Olivier's direction. Could she growl as well? She was about to be lost down that thought track when the rude guy leaned closer to her. He was braced on his elbows with his back against the bar, his ankles crossed in front of him. His rockstar haircut, too long in the face and cut raggedly about chin level, obscured one eye, and his full, red mouth was turned up at one corner in Gallic mockery.

He sort of rolled on his side against the bar, getting his feet under him, and reached out his left hand to push her hair back from her face. She caught his wrist just as he made contact, shoving him back. His smirk bloomed into a full smile, chased with a laugh.

"You are as expected." His glance flicked over her shoulder to Olivier. "Not that I'm complaining."

His self-assured smarminess made her want to punch the smile off his face. She jumped off her seat to get her feet under her, and spun around with her hands held loosely at her side. She hadn't been in a fight for several years—not since her junior year of undergrad in that bar brawl Norah started—but she figured her new body could probably deliver on any promises her mouth made now.

"I don't remember asking you to get in my personal space." Her normally low voice took on gravel, and several patrons near them at the bar picked up their drinks and slithered off.

Olivier flicked his eyes towards her but kept his neutral expression. Luc just laughed again.

"A woman like you doesn't have to ask me," he sleazed at her. She remembered Suki's spooky voice down the magical phone line: "Don't trust anyone new." Even without that warning she would have hated this guy for being the sort of man who used sex as a weapon, who knew exactly what women would do to be with him, who never passed up a double entendre or sexual joke.

"How about if I ask you to fuck off?" Her voice picked up a snarl, and she seemed to see the minute movements Luc made in slow motion. She watched him open his position, and knew exactly how she could dig her teeth into his throat and yank just. . . .

"If she attacks you, I'm not helping you." Olivier's rasp broke through the mayhem in Sophie's mind.

"Not even if I ask nicely?" The laughter was still in Luc's voice, but the edge of Sophie's inexplicable anger was blunting.

She watched him. If possible, he was even better looking than Olivier with a pouting bottom lip and ridiculously sharp cheekbones. He was dark to Olivier's gold: black hair and amber brown eyes. The mocking expression seemed to fit on his face in a mold so ancient that sincerity might make his skin crack.

"You must be the idiot." Idiot wasn't the word that

Sophie would have used to describe Luc. Dangerous probably would have been. Swiftly followed by self-obsessed and sexy.

Olivier smiled, his dimples denting his face in real amusement. Luc looked at him, his own grin only brighter still.

"You talk about me this way? I'll never recover from your betrayal, brother. *Idiot?*" The insulting name was compressed, a French word, not English. He ran a hand over the crown of Olivier's head. They made eye contact and Sophie felt dislocated, not just that she was missing something vital, but that she knew nothing, absolutely nothing, and that all her belief in her own world, her own reality, had been like a child playing dress up. These two had answers, had seen history, that she didn't even know the questions to ask about.

"Sophie wanted to ask you a favor." Olivier pulled his cigarettes out of the pocket of his jacket glancing over at her.

She was so out of her league here that she just figured she might as well not care. "I need a thralling spell." She felt so stupid saying that. Especially to Mr. Sex-and-Violence. But if she didn't come up with a way for Norah to keep Paul under control, something bad would probably happen that would end in someone's True Death. Eternal Sleep. Whatever vampires called it.

"*This* is not what I expected." He looked her up and down and flicked a glance at Olivier, who just shrugged. "A life-bond?"

That sounded horrible and fucked up, but oddly like what Norah would want. "If you say so."

"Who is this person? What did they do to you?" Luc looked bored, like he was trying to look bored on purpose, like he'd spent centuries cultivating the perfect look of boredom and disdain, and Sophie was annoyed by him again.

"Look, I don't have to explain myself to you. Do you know where I can get this life-bond thing or not? I'm a little pressed for time." She shook her head for emphasis, her hair fluttering out and whipping around in what she imagined was a great effect.

"*C'est vengeance?*" Luc lifted an eyebrow. Okay, she really hated this guy.

"*Je parle français,*" She shot at him. "And even if I didn't, I would probably know you asked if this was revenge. Not all Americans are uneducated churls."

Olivier laughed, and Luc switched to another language that he spoke too quickly with too much compression of the vowels for her to parse.

"Yeah, she is," Olivier replied in English. He turned to Sophie. "He'll do the spell."

Flipping some bills onto the bar, Luc pulled himself fully upright with a sigh. "I can do this spell for you, *mon ange*, no trouble, but could you ever find it in your heart to like me one little part?"

"Whatever." Sophie spun out of his reach as he went to touch her hair.

"She hates you." Olivier's words rode soft laughter. Luc replied in his secret language, probably the same one from Olivier's painting, in what sounded like mock pain.

NORAH HAD GIVEN up on trying to manage Paul about fifteen minutes after Sophie left for reinforcements. She had tied him up with bed sheets, gagged him with his own underwear, and stuck him in his walk-in closet. If she had felt any pity for him, that was quenched when she saw that all of his shoes were in individual Tupperware containers with Polaroid pictures of the contents taped to the outside of the boxes. After depositing him on the floor, she had adjourned to the kitchen to polish off his cache of excellent champagne.

"Why does he have Dom?" Norah held the bottle out, talking to herself. She had tugged an armchair in from the living room and tossed the ugly breakfast nook table and chairs out into the backyard. She sat in comfort, the built-in sound system pulsing out jazzy Christmas remixes, observing the miraculously clean kitchen. The chrome appliances shone, the marble countertop gleamed. *Him* having this sort of life really wasn't fair.

Not that she believed in fair, but until Paul happened to her, she'd believed in karma evening out all of the peaks and valleys in life. She'd worked so hard, twice as hard as anyone else she knew, to get where she was. There wasn't just the fact that she was female, and even if the general population was unaware of it, journalism was still a man's game. All the Paula Zahns and Jane Paulys only proved that beauty queens could have careers as talking heads after they stripped off the bathing suits and stopped taping their breasts together.

On top of that, she was a woman of color, which gave every colleague she'd ever had the excuse to dismiss her as "affirmative action." She'd been turned down for internship after internship and job after job with a "we already have a minority—an Indian" or a "we have a black female already," as though her only qualification was to make the station look good.

Norah hadn't been born embittered and vengeful. She and Sophie grew up in a model Cincinnati neighborhood—Hyde Park—full of professionals with families, successful arty types, and old families who never took buy-outs for their trendy property. Her parents were professionals—her father a lawyer and her mother owned her own publicity agency—and she'd been raised to believe that hard work paid off no matter what your skin color. Her parents forgot to tell her that her gender would be the bigger obstacle. Their expectations were what drove her, what made her refuse to move into print journalism or back to school for some other form of media studies. She refused to fail and disappoint them.

Norah had met Paul Winters when she was at Northwestern's Medill School of Journalism, before Sophie even transferred to the University of Chicago. He'd been in almost every one of her core courses and part of the same extracurricular organizations that were essential to getting anywhere in journalism. Eventually, because who would resist, she started dating him— which really meant more like sleeping with him and catching meals together every once in a while.

Which she thought would make the fact that they both were hired on after their internships at WGN easier. She knew the guy, or thought she did. They had been broken up for years—since before they even graduated—but when he told her boss that they'd hooked up, that Norah had told him that being with him would consolidate her position, that even if he did better than her, they would be married one day anyway, her boss believed him. Just believed him.

She'd been on human interest and the weather ever since.

With her familiar, angry memories somewhat comforting to her, she dozed off, all the energy expended from wrestling Paul taking its toll—along with the champagne.

Norah felt cold crabs scuttling up the back of her

neck and knew that Sophie was back. That knowledge was borne out as Sophie's red and blond hair popped around the corner of the kitchen, her step jaunty, her arms swinging. Norah returned the smile on Sophie's face, and was about to open her mouth to once again mock the nubby pink coat Sophie wore when two more figures followed her friend into the kitchen.

The first was Olivier, whom she didn't really hold any sort of grudge against, since without him where would she be but striving at a job with a glass ceiling and window shopping at Neiman's? The second was a beautiful man in extremely expensive wool pants, cashmere sweater, and wool overcoat—black on black on black—sporting artfully disheveled hair and forceful black stubble on his cheeks. Quality man, and quality clothes. Norah had trained herself to recognize both. Plus this guy had charm oozing out of his perfect pores.

The pretty man inclined his head towards Norah, then said something in French. "You never asked," Olivier replied to him.

"My name is Luc. I've come in answer to a plea made by your friend." He winked at Sophie, who glared at him. "You have a troublesome person you cannot kill?"

On cue, there was a loud thumping from upstairs. Norah sighed. "Something like that."

Luc smiled, turned on his heel, and started towards the stairs. Norah exchanged a look with Sophie, silently asking, "Who is this fool and what the fuck are you doing?" Sophie's glance back told Norah everything: This fool must be friends with Olivier or something.

Norah turned and followed behind him, wondering what exactly this was going to entail. As they climbed the stairs, she heard everyone else close behind. She didn't see any chickens, black candles, or goats, so that was a start.

On the second floor landing, Luc unerringly headed towards the master bedroom and the closet within. He looked over his shoulder and flung open the closet door, meeting her eyes with a smirk that was supposed to mean something. What that something was, Norah didn't know, and didn't give a rat's ass to know. He dropped his gaze down to the squirming figure of a stark naked Paul. The bruise on his forehead where Norah'd hit him with a lamp to subdue him stood out on his skin an uneven conglomeration of purple and black.

Luc pulled up the legs of his pants and squatted over Paul. Pulling off his gloves, he asked "Rapist?"

"No, why?" Norah frowned. That was a disturbing yet intriguing probe. Insightful for a man.

"Happens enough. Complex revenge is usually for a good reason. Rape is a good reason." Luc touched the lump on Paul's head, and Paul promptly passed out.

Norah wished he'd stayed conscious to get the full experience of being hexed.

"It's work related." Norah suddenly felt that her anger had an inadequate source, or that Luc might think so, and she didn't want to justify herself to him.

"Ah, yes, women's ambition can definitely kill." He looked back at her with the same smirk as before, and she pressed her face into a scowl. His accent turned his barb into a come on, and the effect was so cartoonishly sleazy she wanted to laugh.

Sophie and Olivier appeared in the doorway. Olivier frowned and Sophie looked anxious. "Before we continue any further, I have to warn against this course."

Norah hadn't figured Olivier for a bore or overly moral.

"Ah, I have to agree with my friend." Luc smiled ruefully. "Revenge, for our kind, often goes wrong in ways we cannot foresee." The voice of reason rarely looked like the denizen of a Paris bordello.

She clicked over his words for a second. "So, you're warning me not to do this—not because it's wrong, but because something bad could happen? Bad how?"

Sophie pushed around Olivier and came into the bedroom. She looked curious.

"Death, mayhem, chaos, war. There are many options." Luc licked his bottom lip.

"Whose death?" Sophie asked with a tremor in her voice.

Olivier turned to her, his face obscured to Norah. "Often the bystanders." He paused, Luc staring at the side of his face. "I've seen it rebound on the revenge-seeker. Magic isn't controllable. It's alive in a way we don't understand; one action can ripple through a life and exert a force we don't see. Like modern films about time travel disrupting what happened before the traveler disturbed the order of events." Time travel? This guy was a freak.

Sophie looked around him to meet Norah's eyes. Sophie thought this was a bad idea, it was written all over her face. So why did Sophie trust these guys? Who knew what their agenda was? How did she know anything they said was true?

There was no way Norah was wasting the chance, now that she was free from the constraints of a normal life, to get the sort of control over her life and other people she'd never had. People were their food source, that annulled any other objections to using people otherwise.

"If Norah wants this, then we do it." Sophie was still staring into her eyes. They understood each other. Sophie knew what Paul had done to her, seen his aftermath. Their was a loyalty between them that went deeper than reason or good sense.

"Norah?" Luc smiled at her, the twist of his mouth every promise of murder she'd ever thought.

"Yes. Do it." Her voice didn't shake at all.

Norah wasn't sure what she was expecting. She knew that real life isn't like a movie, that there wouldn't be a swell of music or a sharp camera angle to zoom in on the life-changing moment, no makeup girl to dart in during a commercial break and powder the sweat off Norah's forehead.

Action just led to action in a line until the final second.

"We need a third," said Luc. He didn't look up from Paul's body.

"I'll do it." Sophie plopped down on her knees next to Norah. There were, Norah knew, different sorts of friends—ones who hold your hand when you're in the hospital, ones who buy you chocolate when you have PMS. And the rare friends who never had to be asked to help, because they just *knew.*

Sophie was every one of those, whatever Norah needed, and she hoped she was the same sort of friend back. They balanced each other—Sophie's shaking hand holding onto Norah's steady one proved that. Norah would kill, protect, rampage through the world having fun, while Sophie sat home and drank rat blood and worried that Norah was killing someone's child.

But that, Norah figured, was what friends did—balanced each other. Like Olivier and Luc, one kind of a loser weirdo artist, and the other an urbane man of the world.

Once Sophie was kneeling and holding Norah's

hand, Luc yanked Paul into a sitting position, and deftly wrapped the bedsheets around his torso to leave his arms and neck free.

He flipped a metal disk out of a pocket at Norah. She caught it in midair, turning it over to examine it briefly. Scribble scrabble, the requisite pentagram, letters. Was she supposed to know what the hell the thing was? "Seal of Solomon. On reverse, the canta of binding," Luc explained.

"Whatever that means," said Norah. It was pretty, whatever it was, in a Sophie kind of way, like a necklace she'd wear or something. Sophie squeezed her hand tighter.

"We must all three touch the seal." He guided it to Paul's chest with a finger. Sophie scooted close, and without saying anything at all, pressed a finger to the metal. She looked almost excited. Norah watched as Olivier slid up to stand directly behind Sophie, his eyes intently focused on her.

Norah met Luc's stare.

"You're sure?" he asked her gravely. "His life will be yours, and his death will come only at your hand." He didn't blink, and even as she wavered slightly in her certainty of this revenge, she imagined she could see a spark of challenge in Luc's up-turned mouth.

"Do it." She wouldn't be challenged by a man, let alone one so aware of his own power.

Luc's right hand grabbed her wrist. The disk was flattened between her palm and the skin over Paul's heart. Sophie's finger was there, too, cold against the warmth of the metal and Paul and Luc. Norah drew in a breath, and Luc leaned close to her. Flash—he bit his own wrist—whoosh—he pressed it to her mouth and she instinctively bit down, his blood flooding in with a taste of age and incense. Sophie offered her own wrist without having to be prompted. Norah watched as Luc bit her almost softly; she didn't cry out or flinch.

Luc held them all out over the metal disk, dripped their blood onto it, said something in a language Norah didn't know—not French. Maybe something older. She felt the weight of it in the back of her skull, dragging at her eyes and mouth, pulling the blood through her veins and out of her skin. The scent of honey and oranges and something unnamable, something burning overwhelmed her, pulled her out of the room and into a void where her body felt far away.

"Now bite him." Luc's voice sounded in the fragile shell of her ear, in the dark stillness of her mind, perfect and unique, everything she had ever longed for that had no name. She could feel him near her body, feel his breath in her ear, but her body was not her, was only part of her. Something hung in the void with her, some important knowledge chimed like the memory of a bell. She strained to hear, words in languages she had never known and always known straining to her in the nothingness. Skin pressed against her lips, her distant mouth, and her teeth sank into Paul's throat knowing absolutely that the mixture of his power with her anger would be twisted by the magical disk into a curse. She knew so much, the sound of Spanish sparrows in flight, the glimmer of candlelight on the Seine, the scent of saffron crocuses, the taste of ashes on her tongue, the blistering of a leather whip to her skin.

Pain brought her back to herself. The pain of her flesh and sinew knitting itself back together in her wrist. Blinking rapidly, Norah felt the *something* receding, withdrawing, and she knew it was for the best, that with the connection came a loss of self, but she still regretted it slightly. She was scared of what she'd touched, scared to explore why she now knew instinctively that Luc would hunt now, kill men who beat women, who killed the defenseless. She decided to ignore those displaced and inexplicable thoughts.

Luc's laughter bounced off the plastic boxes full of shoes and garment bags of clothes. "Let's drink the rest of that champagne I saw earlier."

He slid to his feet and yanked Norah to hers, twining his soft fingers with hers. "Beautiful, do you have any more enemies?"

He looked her up and down like the villain in a bad action movie, and she liked it, liked him. Knew he meant her no harm, not the sort of harm she's regret. She laughed, the taste of Paul's blood still thick on her tongue. As they left the room, she twisted her head back to see Olivier help Sophie up, her face radiant and joyous, his pulled into extreme displeasure.

Chapter Eleven

THE CHAMPAGNE WAS bright, light, and cold. Sophie wanted it to wash away the last few days, but it just made her drunk. Drunk was fine just then. Drunk meant she could ignore Luc flirting with her friend, ignore her flirting back, ignore the violence that seemed to tingle under her skin with every breath.

Luc charmed the windows of the condo while bickering with Norah about the music—was he the alchemist who charmed the windows in Olivier's loft? He didn't look like an alchemist—then again, did Sophie look like a vampire?

His voice matched the way he looked in a way that seemed intrinsic. He was an archetype, and Sophie listened to the conversation flow from room to room wondering if Luc had been the template the archetype formed from.

"Christmas music makes me sick," Luc huffed, flicking the tips of his fingers against his thumb, like someone ridding their hands of excess water after washing them. The glass of the kitchen windows turned blue, then slid into an oil-slick of iridescent reflection. After a couple seconds, he tapped the surface with a knuckle, and it returned to normal glass.

"It's traditional," Norah claimed. Sophie hoped Luc won the argument about the damned Christmas music; Bing Crosby made her ill. Mostly because he made her think of her father, who had the most pure, beautiful tenor in the world. He always talked to himself and often his mumbling ruminations would segue into humming to singing, no matter where he was—the grocery, the car, his office at the University of Cincinnati.

Sophie wondered a little about Olivier's father. About his life in general. How long had he been alive—well, around? Did he remember his parents? She doubted her father and his could have anything in common—hers being an English professor—and Olivier obviously being old enough to perhaps predate universities.

The arguing pair moved into the front room so Luc could attend to the windows there.

"Anything that's bad or boring, tradition is always the defense. Just admit you like that idiotic songs of your baby god." Luc's voice drifted back into the kitchen. Well, Luc was definitely not a Christian. She glanced over at Olivier and wondered if that was the case for him as well. Luc could just be jaded—being a vampire probably did that to a person—but Sophie wondered about their backgrounds. If they spoke Provençal or Occitan, they could be from Languedoc. They could be one of several non-Christian sects that flourished in the Middle Ages. But that would also make them a thousand years old. She looked harder at Olivier.

How could he possibly be a thousand years old?

He didn't look a thousand years old. He didn't *act* a thousand years old. In *Los Vampiros*, the oldest vampire was eight hundred years old, and over the course of the series he drifted away into nothingness, disinterested in modern life, getting sick from the chemicals in everyone's blood.

But, Sophie reasoned with herself, maybe the people who made *Los Vampiros* had never actually met an eight-hundred-year old vampire. How would they? So maybe old vampires actually did act like Olivier and Luc, simultaneously amused and bored by humans.

Olivier sat in the burgundy leather armchair next to her own, matching, seat. He had kicked off his shoes and pulled out a pad of paper and a pen from the pocket of his coat and was busily scribbling in a language that she hoped wasn't English since she was completely unable to read it.

"What do you think of the Paul thing?" Sophie's voice scraped out of her throat.

"Revenge is often an impulse with those new to this life." Olivier replied. She wondered what it would be like to live for three hundred years, for five hundred, for more. The idea of it even slipped from her, sliding away like complex math and reading music.

"How well does this zombie thralling thing work?" She leaned her head back and imagined she could feel the dawn sprawling across the continent on fingers like knives.

"About as well as any magic. At the worst possible moment, something will go wrong." His pen scratched on the paper in a rhythm just beyond Sophie's perception. That sounded right. Norah always talked about the worst possible scenario, and Norah was well-versed in that sort of thinking.

"Hm. Is Luc evil?"

The pen paused. "When you say evil, do you mean in the vernacular sense of something bad or intolerable . . ." He took a breath, his voice falling quieter still than his normal, almost whisper "Or do you mean some primal force beyond human comprehension?"

"I mean, will he hurt my friends? Besides, all the world is the second kind of evil, just a film, like a cataract on the eye, obscuring the reality of the soul." Sophie took a sharp breath, unsure of why she spoke those words. They came right out of one of her dreams.

She opened her eyes to see him standing over her, his notebook crumpling in a clenched fist.

"Do you believe that?" His tone was strained and his expression pained.

"*You* do." Her eyes were too heavy to care about him or his feelings. He couldn't tell when she was baiting him; he was innocent, trusting in a way that was strange for someone so ancient. She drifted away, a dead woman on a rickety raft on a river of exhaustion and champagne, the nag of hunger and sleep tugging on the edges of her consciousness.

SHE DREAMS OF an alchemist's laboratory. Whizzing contraptions sit on broken tables next to scrolls and amphorae and glass vials. The room smells of burning metal and dust. A woman's voice rises in anger behind her, but she doesn't turn. Her right hand clutches a scrap of parchment; Hebrew words march up and down in columns on the paper.

"What you have, we do not want." The woman is angry, very angry, and Sophie can feel a matching flare in her chest.

"Ah, you do not know what it is I offer, to want it or not." The second voice is wind through tall grass, a carillon chiming, glass breaking.

Looking at her feet, she sees the body of a man, his robes hiked up over his naked hips, his face obscured by his skewed cap. The figure sprawls within a five pointed star, painted on the floor with blood, each point adorned with a bright bauble of jewelry or glittering glass curiosity.

"Rosamund." Her mouth forms the name, alerting the woman behind her that the alchemist is dying, closing in on his last shallow breath.

"You offer us death, as you give it to this servant who called you forth. You are an abomination." A snarl frays the edges of the woman's voice.

"As death is my province, so you are my creature, you and all your kind."

Voice like blood drying on cool skin, screams of children, the crackle of fire. The figure looks around Rosamund, looks right in her eyes, his a whirl of madness, a promise of torment beyond comprehension, the dark desire that no one speaks aloud.

"Phillipa," says the fairy. "I see you. I see your soul." He laughs, full of hopelessness. "You will be mine. You will serve me. My geas was laid on you before your conception, before this life was promised to you, because my world is infinite and terrible. I have only been waiting to be invited in."

A satin-covered duvet cradled her as sleep faded and her dreams chased themselves back to where they lived during the waking hours. Sophie scrunched down into the soft folds of the comforter, her hair wrapped around her neck and shoulders, offering to strangle her with little or no effort, and moaned. She had never been a morning person, and in her short life as a vampire, she didn't see that improving any, even though her morning was now night. A man's voice, raised in song, plucked her from the bed and compelled her to swing her bare feet over the side of the bed and investigate.

She was only wearing her tank top and panties from the night before, so she stopped to dig around in the oak chest of drawers in the room, tugging out several different sorts of women's clothing: several bras, all different sizes and colors; two pairs of size 2 corduroy pants, one yellow, the other white; socks with ruffles, pompoms, and snowflakes. Sophie wondered if Paul kept some sort of trophy collection of the discarded clothing of the women he slept with. The closet was more helpful. It was packed with designer clothes, all of the pants too long for Sophie's short legs, but she withdrew a black velour skirt that fell to her ankles. On the next hanger was the matching hooded sweatshirt. Slipping them on, she could hardly miss the Baby Phat labels inside. She doubted she'd remember to ask Paul about this wardrobe, but for the present moment, she was curious.

Jogging down the stairs, she assessed her need for caffeine and hunger for other substances. Caffeine: definitely. Food: not so much. Blood: hell yes.

The voice grew louder, and Sophie recognized the tune and words to "Angels We Have Heard On High" sung in a voice that could only be Olivier's. She found him in what was once the formal sitting room area to the right of the staircase, now strewn with anything conceivably able to be converted into art supplies.

Olivier broke off singing as she walked into the room, looking up at her from a nest of wire, twine, wire cutters, beads, feathers, and many objects Sophie couldn't identify.

"What're you doing?"

"Making Christmas tree ornaments for my neighbors." He twisted a loop of wire back on itself, and Sophie recognized a half-formed star.

"Okay, I'm not awake enough for that conversation. Let's try: where is everyone?" She yawned.

"Paul is off having his half-lived golem life. The others didn't sleep here." He looked up at her through his reddish gold eyelashes, tilted his head to the side in a way she figured meant "what did you expect from them." She snapped her teeth together hard enough to make an audible click. He offered her no comfort that Norah would be alright. Her caffeine-free thoughts slid around her head, rolling around until she wondered if Luc was more of a threat to Norah or the other way around. She gave up.

Sophie turned around and headed into the kitchen, Olivier's seriousness too much for her so early.

She slammed open and closed cabinet doors until she found the coffee and coffee grinder, but it took her ten minutes to negotiate the complicated coffee pot. Why didn't Paul have a French press or something that Sophie could work half-asleep?

Finally, after what seemed like an epoch of Man, she had her coffee. After she'd polished off one cup, she felt ready to cope with Olivier over the second. He was already standing in the doorway silently when she turned to find him. He was barefoot, as usual, and shirtless, his jeans riding low enough on his hips to display a few curls of reddish pubic hair. She had three options: she could keep her comments to herself, she could say words about how sexy he was, or she could push him up against a wall and have her way with him.

Sophie could *taste* his skin on the back of her tongue, taste his blood gushing over her face, taste his kisses pressed to her face and mouth and neck, the salt of his sweat, the tang of the wire residue on his fingers; she could feel his skin, elastic under her fingertips, his body rocking against hers.

She took a deep breath, her knees weak, and went with the first option: to say nothing.

"Did you have any plans for today?" He came all the way into the kitchen and leaned against the center island.

"Let's see. Work on my thesis? No, I guess not. Call my mom? Nope not ready for that. Hide in a closet and hope that Norah can't find me when it's time to bury the bodies?" She sipped her coffee and made a face at the oily surface left from not grinding the beans well enough.

Olivier watched her for a few seconds, and Sophie began to feel uncomfortable. Finally he said, "Do you want me to leave you alone?"

She considered that. Here was the embodiment of the new chaos in her life offering freely to get the hell out of the picture for a time, maybe forever. However, with her friends gone, that would leave her completely alone, and she'd never done alone well. Plus her knees were still weak from that waking fantasy. She definitely wanted him to leave. But he took care of her, and every time he looked at her, it was like a caress of fire. So maybe he could just stick around while she sorted out her feelings.

Sitting her coffee cup on the counter, she shook her head. "No, I guess I don't really. No, what I really need to do is look for Suki. I should hunt down her coven members. I wanted to take Norah along with me so she could intimidate them. Too bad I got ditched for some underwear model vampire guy."

"I could go with you." Olivier smiled and Sophie's chest constricted at the sight.

Sophie took another long sip of coffee. She had been wrong: Olivier was definitely a post-two-cups kind of guy.

"Fine, let me take a shower, find something real to wear, and I'll take you up on your offer.

Brushing passed him, she left the kitchen and headed for the stairs.

IN THE END, Sophie was forced to wear the stupid Baby Phat ensemble because there were no other clothes in the house short enough for her. When she came downstairs from her shower, it was with her hair tied up in two braids and then looped together over the crown of her head and pinned into place with almost the entire pack of bobby pins from her purse. She'd spent more time on her hair than she had in the shower.

Olivier was sitting at the kitchen counter reading. He'd obviously raided Paul's clothes, since he sported a grey pair of wool-flannel blend slacks and a white and grey button up shirt with no tie. It suited him almost too well.

She felt a hollow feeling in her stomach and examined it: was that *love?*

No, it was hunger, real hunger, for toast or something. He held a plate out to her that was stacked with multigrain wheat toast. Olivier, Mind-Reader Extraordinaire!

She took a piece. "I'm surprised Paul has carbs in the house." Inhaling the toast in no time flat, she grabbed another piece and ate that, too, while crossing to the refrigerator to drink some juice straight from the carton.

"Modern people live in the promised land of milk and honey. They don't appreciate what they have, understand what hunger is." Olivier didn't sound angry, more confused. Drinking the last of the juice, she watched him watch her.

"How old are you?"

He licked his lips. "How old do you think?"

"Were you a Templar?" That was one of her theories, one of the several, and as she'd showered the image of Olivier in the white smock with the red cross had leapt into her mind fully born, with contusions on his face and blood leaking from his mouth.

"I've been many things, and that was one, yes." He stood and headed for the door. "Luckily for us, witches should be easy to find on the Solstice."

Sophie knew avoidance when she saw it. Oh yeah, she surely did. The Templars were decimated, burned at the stake en masse and excommunicated for being heretics, for blaspheming against Christ and worshiping false idols. Most scholars thought that was libel by the king of France and the Pope to get their grubby mitts on the Templars' hordes of cash.

Sophie wondered if Luc had been a Templar, too. Probably—Olivier and Luc seemed to communicate silently, with an ease that spoke of a lifetime—*lifetimes*—spent together.

SOPHIE TURNED UP the collar on her pink wool coat and followed Olivier out to into the cold to do creature of the night business.

The itchy fingers began to tug at her skin as they drifted through Lakeview. She watched Olivier's back and took in the mixed scents in the frigid air—car exhaust, pine, sugar, so many people smashed into a confusing leviathan of Human. Her eyes fell off Olivier and slid of towards a group of tweens jibbering animatedly on the corner in front of them. One turned towards them and her smile fled into a grimace, her wispy blond hair fluttering around her face in a stray breeze from a grate in the sidewalk.

Olivier stepped slightly to the side, breaking the eye contact between predator and meal.

He burst into what sounded close to hysterical laughter, startling everyone within a half block radius and nearly causing Sophie to pee on herself.

"What?" Twisting her head from side to side, she searched the street scene before them and behind them for something funny.

"That." Olivier sort of jabbed his head at the gang of tweens.

"What? Their half-Japanese patois?" Sophie tended to wonder at all of that anime culture teens partook of and how she could absolutely not comprehend it, and worried that she was getting old.

Her thoughts ran into a tertiary rut regarding youth culture always wanting to be incomprehensible to any outside perception. She'd been that way once, ten years ago, wanting to be mysterious and have a lot of secrets, be alluring to everyone. Now she was, with her vampire powers, and it wasn't as much fun as she'd thought.

She opened her mouth to ask about the Secret Vampire Guide to Ruling the World and Using Your Crazy New Powers—if there was one, how could she get a copy, and would it teach her to use the power she could feel thrumming under her skin but couldn't quite seem to access. But Olivier spoke, interrupting her almost-questions:

"You're full of surprises. Who would have thought your natural prey would be children?" Olivier chuckled again.

"*What*?" Arrested in her thoughts and walking, Sophie grabbed his arm and yanked. "My what?"

"You're naturally inclined to want to feed on girls of a certain age." Sophie couldn't reconcile the jaunty, amused tone he took with his words. "Everyone has their natural prey."

"I have to eat pre-adolescent girls to survive? Oh god." She stopped in the middle of the sidewalk, causing passersby to curse her, and looked at him hard. "Is this a joke? I mean, is this hazing of some kind?"

Olivier laughed again. "Um . . ." he began.

"Okay, no, that was stupid, you're not the practical joking type."

"There you're wrong, so very wrong, but this isn't that. I'm trying to be a good teacher; unfortunately my personality gets in the way."

They started walking again. Well, Olivier did, overflowing with good cheer, smiling at other pedestrians, an almost-giggle leaking out periodically.

She caught up with him and demanded, "Why do you think this is so funny?" Sophie was pretty peeved at his behavior, finding her personal tragedy far more serious than all that. Tweens? Little girls? Didn't they have enough to deal with without her out to rip and tear and feed on them?

"It's just absurd. Like all of the world." They stopped at a don't-walk sign. "Luc? His natural prey is violent criminals." Olivier smiled at her and lifted an eyebrow with glee.

"So? Wait, you mean everyone has a different thing?" That seemed fairly reasonable, not that she was ready to be in any way reasonable yet. What was this b.s.? Why couldn't *she* get the criminal element?

"Anger won't get you anything except bitterness. But if you're set on that, I invite you take your rage out on Luc personally." They rounded a corner, and as Olivier spun gun-shot quick and snatched her to his chest, Sophie caught a glimpse of a large church hunched across the street from them. "Just because you *want* to eat a certain kind of something, doesn't mean you *have* to." He wrapped an arm around her waist and tucked her hair under her hat with the other hand.

What was going on here pretty much completely escaped her. Her breath caught on the back of her tongue. "Like being on a diet?"

His face hovered so close to her own she couldn't focus on the features properly. Heat from his exhaled breaths melted the ice on her eyelashes. "Exactly like being on a diet."

Olivier danced them around in a tight circle, smiling and running his thumb under her jaw line.

"Um, what're you . . ." His bottom lip touched her top, the skin freezing together slightly, making the parting sticky and slow.

"Watching someone who was on the other side of the street." His fingers slid to the back of her head, and his tongue skittered across her mouth lightly before he retreated entirely and laid a finger to his mouth whispering "Shhh."

He left her standing on the corner staring at his jaunty figure in bewilderment as he jaywalked over to a house set to the side of St. Mary of the Lake church. Something turned over in her stomach.

To occupy herself, Sophie thought about the differentiated inclination to kill a certain kind of person. It made a warped sort of evolutionary sense. Nature wouldn't want a predator to hunt one sort of human into extinction, like all the women for example. Or maybe it wasn't natural at all; it could be a magical codicil to the spell or whatever that made vampires in the dawn of ages, the sorcerer—the god? The evil god? The devil? The Sumerian shaman? Egyptian aliens?—trying to spread the death around a little more evenly.

Her thoughts broke off as she caught sight of Olivier in the street lights talking to the figure. The second man wore skirts, his ample belly jutting out from his body, and his bald head covered by a small scull-cap. Sophie didn't wait for them to cross the street. She ran full tilt, dodging around the traffic over to where they stood next to a denuded, naked winter tree set in the sidewalk.

As she approached, the priest turned to her, his eyes glassy, his hand pressed to the inner elbow of the opposite arm.

"What the . . ."

"Drop your hand," Olivier's voice whispered, with its natural note of command—not natural, thought Sophie dizzily; *compulsion*—and the man obeyed, dropping his hand from his arm exposing a slashed sleeve that gaped open to display a deep wound that trickled blood sluggishly.

Sophie almost collapsed on the spot from need. Every muscle in her body clenched, her own blood zoomed in her veins with a maddening song, her teeth shifted and rearranged in her mouth. Instinct obliterated reason. Blood flooded her mouth without her feeling her body move. She drank and the forgotten colors of a secondary spectrum paraded before her closed eyes. She smelled wine and incense, heard children's laughter and bells tolling. The very name of God seemed on the tip of her tongue. And she saw all the faces, young, young faces twisted into grief and pain, tasted tears and shame and their horror. Their terror tasted sweet.

Finally sated, she pushed the useless body away from her with a forceful shove. Pathetic vessels of utter frailty. She laughed at the banal placidity that caused them to be perfect victims, always one breath away from their meaningless deaths.

"Maybe that was a little too much." The voice splintered her thoughts, and Sophie inclined her head to look up at Olivier.

"You bit him. Is that wise?" He was trying to control her, and something inside her howled to prove to him he was not her master. With his age he should know, that even that stupid, creeping, crying creatures that they were, teeth marks and no blood did tend to point in one direction.

"With these—" He kicked the sprawled body of the priest. "—it doesn't matter. They take care of it amongst themselves. He was moved from parish to parish. They covered his vile, corrupting actions on children, turned a blind eye to his addiction to innocence, to his desire to bleed everything good there is out of children with his warped sexuality."

She watched him watching her. " 'Revenge is often an impulse with those new to this life.' And sometimes the impulse never fades?"

He backed away from the body, walking backwards down the block with a smile. "Someone will notice this scene soon. The glamour barely survives the victim."

Victim? Clearly Olivier was conflicted, for all his bravado and ancient retribution schemes. She caught up with him, reaching high to grab the back of his hair, just enough to get his attention without really hurting him. "What will you do when the Church collapses and there are no more priests to kill?"

He grabbed her wrist and yanked her into a shadowed doorway. "You definitely had too much to drink." His voice wasn't angry, just spiced with some unreadable intonation. Hunching down, he pressed a knee between her legs and lifted her slightly. "Want to share?" His teeth sunk into her neck before she could frame a response, and the world spun away. The universe was the body pressed to her, the tick-tick-tick of something gathering in her belly, pulling tighter, the tingling in her fingers and toes. Fingers shoved passed the waist of her skirt and into her underwear, thick, cold fingers that she pushed up into, shimmied her hips hard to wedge those fingers into the right place. The loop between the teeth and the fingers closed completely within seconds, sending her body into a rictus of orgasm.

As her mind settled back into a more Sophie-like order, her heartbeat slowing, she thought: *Olivier really has a thing for public sex.*

He buttoned the lower buttons of her coat. They didn't make eye contact, but that was her doing, not his. She opened her mouth to say something to him, and before she could his hand was on the back of her neck, spinning her around to face him. His eyes held hers, the yellow street lights bleeding the color away into grey on grey, and she felt like she'd been in this position before, many times before, marching back in a line as long as her life.

"What's going on here?" A bright light blinded her.

"My wife had something in her eye, and I was getting it out for her." Olivier was back to his amused with the world tone.

"Uh-huh. Well, move it along." The cop dropped his flashlight.

They moved it along.

Chapter Twelve

CITY LIFE WAS such that strange strangers and odd behavior tends to be below noticing or simply gaped at and forgotten again instantaneously. Sophie knew that, and yet was still surprised at how totally oblivious people could be. Take, for example, a beautiful man standing on a street corner turning in a Widdershins circle reciting Shakespeare in pig-latin while his female companion wipes blood from her neck with handy wipes at exactly midnight. Perhaps remarkable while being witnessed, but not nearly the weirdest occurrence in the day of a city-dweller. Not when, upon second glance, they were gone anyway.

Sophie wasn't sure how she'd react herself to witnessing such a thing; last week maybe she'd have been a little freaked out for a minute, and then walked on. Now she was the female companion, actually *doing* the weird things.

"Who would have known you were fluent in pig-latin?" Sophie looked around what appeared to be an art gallery connected through vaulted arches into other galleries on either end.

"It took me forever to memorize that password. I think I got an extra hard one since I pissed the guardian off once." He ran a hand through his hair and approached one of the doorways, touching a mark etched in the wood.

"Why are we here, anyway?" Sophie hung back. "I want to look for Suki—we have to find her coven—"

"We're here to look for Suki. Her coven is unimportant." Olivier looked at her over his shoulder. "Come on."

"I do not think Suki is here," grumbled Sophie under her breath, but she followed him around the room. She gazed at the nearest painting hanging on the beige wall directly in her line of site—a village at night, thatched houses set close together with candles burning in each window, when she squinted she could make out three figures hanging in the grey sky, astride brooms—when the painting faded and recongealed into a macabre scene of a woman in habit with her neck set at a strange angle, blood pooling between her legs. The picture next to it was a child's scrawl of a Dracula character, complete with blood dripping from its fangs onto the ground.

"What is this place?" She turned to Olivier who was already watching her ogle the artwork. The art here was almost as scary as Norah hungry. Next to the kid's sketch was a parade of men and women, most with one or both of their eyes gouged out, hobbled at hand and foot being led by men on horseback dressed in knightly regalia, Templar crosses emblazoned on pennants and surplices.

"All of the art in the world." His face gave away nothing. "We're somewhere I haven't been before."

His voice sounded off slightly, the pitch wrong, neither his crushed velvet whisper nor his sexy-stranger timbre.

Sophie considered that for a second. Why not? Who knew what the guy thought, really? "How does that work? Seems like a lot of art has been made in all of time." The answer was, naturally, magic, but she was curious how he would explain it.

"Some things are so beyond comprehension pondering them leaves you with more questions than you began with." Waving his hand for her to follow, he exited the gallery and strode through the next. Sophie spotted a child's drawing of what appeared to be a pear tree with an ax embedded in the trunk, a half-recognized tableau of fruit, pomegranates and apples, in a bowl with a hovering fruit fly, and a brace of dead rabbits next to a couple of leeks before they emerged into a completely different sort of gallery.

Fire blazed from the confines of every frame in the room. One depicted a ship alight in the midst of a night battle. Various public buildings and palaces burned in every state of immolation from recently alight to near collapse. Directly to her right was a twenty-foot tall tableau of a witch burning, the victim's mouth open and swallowing flame. Sophie watched Olivier purposefully stand with his back to that work. In the center of the room a real fire burned low in an open ring of stones containing several bricks of coal.

Olivier approached the stones and coals and fire. Sophie followed him and watched as he dropped a wondrously detailed sketch of someone's ear into the coals. She blinked rapidly as a tiny figure coalesced amid the shifting flame. Its torso burned a white so bright she had to avert her eyes to its extremities where the flickering limbs waved first blue then yellowish orange at the tips. The creature leapt from a coal directly onto the paper Olivier had dropped with what seemed to be considerable glee. In a flash the drawing was nothing but ash as the tiny, flaming feet rushing over it, stomping out a fiery jig.

"You bring me the best gifts." A voice like snapping wood rustled out of the creature. He turned a mainly indistinct face to Sophie. "Oh, *her!* Let me burn her again!" He stamped around his coal floor in a circle waving his arms above his head.

Olivier's expression turned blank, hard, unreadable. "Your jokes don't amuse me. Words like those will cause me to leave you without my gifts forever."

"Poor blood-drinker, lost them all to the flames." The coal the imp stood upon glowed orange where his feet made continuous contact. Sophie couldn't tell if he was mocking or commiserating with Olivier. "I will always have you here with me."

There was so much going on Sophie didn't understand here. Her mind tripped over her thoughts trying to order the questions she had. Burning her again? *Again?* Olivier lost everyone to fire? Who was everyone?

In the painting on her left, a picture of a dancing bear kicking a gypsy into a bonfire melted into a portrait of a very angry-looking Luc done in superb Italianate style. She focused, came up with a coherent question—Olivier could paint like that?—then decided she was better off not thinking about any of this.

"*Those* you can't consume with your vicious dancing." Olivier's voice was colored by a mocking thread, a tone she had never heard him use. This was not the same man who was patient and curious, but always kind. Except for that whole turning her into a vampire and stalking her part. Which could be his version of patience.

Tiring of crouching over, Sophie dropped to her knees next to Olivier.

"True, true. Did you come to tell me a story?" Hopping from coal to coal, the imp stoked up the fire enough to make Sophie uncomfortable. "Give me more to consume, more, more, and I will answer a question!"

Olivier grinned and pulled out two more drawings. These were far more detailed and perfectly rendered than the ear. The one in his left hand was of Sophie sleeping in a chair, her head back exposing her neck, her hands oddly clasped together politely. The one in his right hand was of Norah laughing uproariously at something, Luc's hand on Norah's shoulder, her posture bent in mirth.

The imp jumped in place. "Yes, *yessssss*. Those. Give them to me!"

"One question for each picture. One for me, one for her." He waved the papers in the air.

"Yes, two questions! I agree." Almost the entirety of his miniscule body glowed white and blue at the prospect of the sketches.

Olivier dropped them both in at the same time, and the imp whipped around in circles, cackling, his feet beating out a rhythm only he comprehended.

"He enjoys destroying beautiful things." Olivier's murmur zinged her straight in the belly. Sophie watched the paper curling into ash from the center out, each little footprint smoking as the fiery creature raced along.

"Not destroying—consuming." She could see that, he fed on the sketches like they fed on blood. Needfully, heedlessly. "Why is he here with all the art in the world? That seems pretty stupid." She turned her eyes back to the painting of Luc dressed in a black velvet smock shot through with silver thread and beaded around the neck in pearls. His anger flared in oil and egg tempura, in perfect shading and light on dark contrast. He was a masterpiece.

"This is his jail. He's serving a sentence for one of the great medieval fires. I don't know which." Olivier drew a breath, and the imp shrieked.

"ROME ROME ROME!" The crackling voice remonstrated. Sophie tore her eyes away from the fearsome Luc, the after image of the imp's figure still flashing in front of her retinas, and gazed on the figure sort of sideways.

"I give her my question. She has them both." Olivier whispered in a low, gravelly tone.

"YES!" The imp hopped up and down.

"Ask him a question." Olivier nudged Sophie..

"Like what?" What did one ask a fiery critter that appeared to have limitless knowledge?

"Anything you want."

"Have I lived another life? Is this the first time I was born?" The dreams, she'd always had the dreams, since she could first remember she'd wondered if they were more than that.

Olivier looked extremely peeved.

"*Auto-de-fe!*" The imp did a somersault over that thrill. "You have lived before, blood-sucker, as have all of your kind. Over and over and over!"

"Ask him something else," Olivier grated out. The anger throbbed off him, she could taste it bitter like lemon peel.

"Is my friend okay?"

The flames stilled somewhat, the flickering slower. He leapt in place instead of running in circles. "Ask something more specific."

And that wasn't reassuring. More specific how? Was it the word "okay"?

"Is she in danger?" She couldn't bring herself to ask if she was alive.

The feet began to move again, round and round, the flames that simulated hair flickering orange. "Danger!! No one you know is not in danger! He will come! Oh, yes, he will come! She can't save you. NO!"

Sophie's skin turned to gooseflesh even as she sat inches away from glowing coals a living fire. He? Everyone was in danger?

Olivier stood, pulling Sophie up with him. His fingers bit into her arm and she jerked away slight, but he only pulled harder.

"Bring me oil on wood!" The imp called after them as they exited the fiery gallery into another hall where portraits flickered in gilt frames.

Sophie gazed behind her and saw the flames recede back to the low bank they rested at when they had first entered the room. "How does the offering thing work? How does it know those things?"

Olivier's jaw clenched, the tendon at the joint bulging. "Fire shares a collective consciousness— what one spark sees, they all see. That's what I know, the mechanics of it elude me." He paused, teeth grinding. "Why did you ask him that?"

"How could you have lived for centuries and have no furniture?" Sophie shot back.

He stopped abruptly, swinging around to look her in the face. "What?" His face showed true perplexity.

"You've been painting for hundreds of years but only have ten canvasses in your apartment. You don't even own a chair, just a bed. I can't imagine someone as poetic as you are not growing attached to *things*. You don't throw anything away." Over Olivier's shoulder, a painting bled from a dour-faced woman in Regency gear to a skipping child followed by a puppy.

Olivier stared at her for another couple of seconds, then smiled slightly. "That isn't my permanent home. I move around a lot and keep all of my accumulated material at one location."

"Which is in France?" She figured if he'd given up that much, she might as well go for everything.

He tilted his chin up slightly. "No." There was a finality in that syllable, enough of it to tell her that she had found an issue.

"But Luc sounds like he probably lives there." Which was both an understatement and a probe.

"Luc and I rarely agree on anything. He lives in Paris." The pronunciation of Paris was given as the French way, with elision of the 's'. "Why did you ask about your prior lives?"

If he thought she was going to give up that easily, he was very stupid. But for now, she let it drop, because the painting of the child and dog had morphed into a glaring clown leering out of the frame with extreme menace, and she wanted to move along before it came to life.

She ambled along, passing into a gallery of surrealism—like the rest of the paintings weren't surreal?—Olivier close behind, his hand still attached to her arm, but no longer biting into the flesh. "I have dreams."

"What sort of dreams?" Olivier pressed.

"Vivid dreams where I . . . live in another time, where I do strange things. Sometimes I'm running away from villagers who want to . . . to kill me. Other times, and this is weirder, I'm on some kind of quest, a quest to find dead people. It's not anything I can explain, or that you could understand." She recognized a Dali hanging next to a crayon scrawl.

"If I did understand, would you believe me?" He

sounded so serious that Sophie laughed. She turned, but he wasn't smiling.

"Um, no way." The dreams were a central aspect of who she was, something she'd lived with her entire life, like the "imaginary" friends she had as a child that she had always known were real. These were the things she only ever told Norah, and only because she felt like she had to find one person to understand her, who knew all her secrets, even if no one else would ever really get it.

Olivier looked at her steadily, as though he did believe her, did understand. She stood wondering if she had found some important truth, something that people had died and lived and worked to discover, or if Olivier was using something sacred to her to manipulate her somehow.

"Tell me something. You need to be absolutely honest about this." He braced his feet shoulder-width apart and clasped his hands in front of his torso. Sophie could imagine his palms cupping the pommel of a sword and realized that might exactly be the pose he now held. She was suddenly very scared of him. Of what he could do to her, of what he had already done to her, of what she really wanted from him—which was the answer to a longing, the last bar in a song she'd been singing all her life without knowing the entire tune, all the answers to questions she couldn't even frame.

"Do you believe in God?" He stared into her eyes, and she couldn't look away. How many ways could he kill her? He was worse than a ninja who could kill with his pinkie, that was for sure. Maybe he would be willing to kill her with orgasms.

"Sometimes."

"What do you believe is the nature of God?" He didn't blink and neither did she.

She hesitated. Their prior conversation, her admission, didn't really meld with this. Unless all of her other suspicions about his origins—Languedoc, this comments about evil, his apparent belief in reincarnation—led her to one heresy: the Cathars.

Her life obsession.

Drawing a deep breath, she told him the truth. "If God exists, he must either be removed from this world, beyond comprehension regarding the pain and suffering of humans—and apparently vampires and fire-creatures—or he must be evil and revel in the torment that people under-go, hoping to draw everyone into unending misery. Or both."

She'd had years and years to think about this. She just couldn't believe in a universally good God who would allow the suffering that existed in the world. She couldn't accept that the all-good, nurturing God of Christianity would allow someone like her father to be killed by a fifteen-year-old heroin addict who'd been abused all his life by his parents. She could not accept that a God who would sacrifice his only son would allow her father to bleed to death on the sidewalk not two blocks from a hospital. Her father who had worked at soup kitchens and been in the Peace Corps and had seven dogs because he couldn't stand the idea of the pound where they would be euthanized. For years, she'd toyed with Cathar belief, their veganism, equality of the sexes, and righteousness appealing as much as their belief that this life was really hell.

That seemed reasonable to her.

"Do you truly believe that a God who could make this world as it is couldn't be the source of love and all that is beyond comprehension?" asked Olivier, but he sounded like he already knew her answer.

"Love, maybe, but love isn't all good. Love causes suffering, death, betrayal. I don't believe a good God would kill children or allow wars to be fought in his name, if he, or *she,* were aware of this world enough to know it."

Olivier smiled broadly, his cheeks dimpling. "Then we have far more to talk about." He relaxed his stance and reached out to brush his finger against her heart. "I haven't found one of our kind for many, many years."

"You really are a Cathar," she said dazedly. Her life kept bringing the bizarre. He couldn't be a thousand years old, could he? She looked at him hard, his smile, the sheen of his hair, the vibrancy of his stillness. This wasn't a creature that had survived for close to a millennium, surely.

Olivier seemed to fold in on himself after his admission and questioning of Sophie. He turned from her, ignoring her statement, and ambled away, through gallery after gallery, with her trailing behind in befuddlement. She was trying desperately to reassess her situation and her view of this really unfathomable person. He stopped in front of a painting of a pack of hunting dogs in repose. Their tongues dangled out of their mouths, heads resting on paws, the background full of men in red hunting gear sitting astride horses. Olivier spoke several lines in pig-latin and stepped into the picture frame offering a hand back to her. She avoided his touch and raised her foot, then the other, to step into the frame behind him. Her feet slogged through what felt like liquid lead, so heavy that once she planted her leg, she couldn't withdraw again as hard as she tried. She looked down at a swirling mess of black and rainbow paint, and when she looked up to ask what was happening, Olivier's head was backlit by a streetlight.

"It's disorienting." He turned his head toward a lurching, drunken pair of young men.

Sophie had really had enough for about six life-times. "I am sick of this weird shit," she declared. "I need to go back to my apartment and pack up the crap I want to bring back to Paul's. And then I need some hot chocolate or something."

Olivier flicked his eyes from the drunks to the tips of his shoes. "You want to go alone?"

No, absolutely not. She wanted him to accompany her, throw her down onto her own bed, and finish what he'd started with his fingers earlier.

"Uh, yeah," she said.

Contrary to what she wanted, but probably safer for her mental health. *And your heart,* a voice nagged at her, but she ignored it.

Something else nagged at her, too; he'd said one of *us* . . .

Had she known him before?

As she turned to leave him on the sidewalk, she figured he'd just trail her at an appropriate, vampy distance, but a girl did need her useful fictions. Like independence.

WHEN SHE GOT home, she found an empty walk-up with the neighbors' 24/7 Indian ragas blaring out of their stereo.

Sathan blinked at her from the doorway of the kitchen, stood and stretched, then walked in circles around Sophie until she bent and picked him up. "You love me, right?" She pressed her cheek to his whiskers and got an answering lick. Since she was feeling self-destructive and freaked-out, she went whole hog: she checked the voicemail.

One of her colleagues from school:

This might come as a shock to you, but it really is the night for your group work presentation. Don't worry, I got your back with a story involving you, the mob, and a truckload of contraband bananas, but I'm not sure how well received it was. You can pay me later. I don't accept bananas as currency.

Her mother:

Babe, mom's just wonderin' how come I haven't heard from you in a while. I guess you're busy with school and holiday stuff.

Sophie could hear her mother's dog, the only one of her father's she kept after he died, barking energetically in the background.

Tippy says hey. Now, if you change your mind about the cruise, we can still get you a ticket. Your stepdad is on this Internet thing where people sell their tickets last minute, and all you gotta do is say it, and you got it! Anyway, so your sister called me during The Valley *last week, during the commercial, did you know that one boy and that other girl are a real couple? Damn, someone's at the door, love ya, babe!*

Some underpaid guy:

This is Blockbuster Video, you have two movies that were due back on the twelfth of December, Meet Joe Black *and* Gia. *Please return them at your earliest convenience.*

Norah's mom:

*Norah, I saw your latest piece on the news, and
I thought I'd tell you that even if it wasn't what
you were going for, you comic timing is brilliant.
Maybe you should give up on news and just go
into acting. People have done it. You're so beautiful and talented. I know if you set your mind to
anything you'll accomplish it. That ferret was
possessed. Give me a call so we can discuss your
brother's presents and what time you want to do
Christmas supper.*

Her own mother, again:

*This is mom again, hello, Norah and Suki, did
you get the socks I knitted you? Sophie, you need
to call me so I can give you all the contact information for while we're away. I couldn't stand to
think that you couldn't get a hold of me if something were to happen. I figure we can do presents
after we get back, that's what your sister said she
wanted to do anyway, to come out while the rates
are cheaper, but rates are always cheap from At-
lanta. Oh, and I got a email from that yarn shop in
your neighborhood that they have alpaca on sale
this month. Go get me a bunch and I'll pay you
back! Mom loves you.*

Stacy:

*Suki! Don't make me call your mom and tell
her no one's seen you for days. I know this is obviously some drug-binge, but other people might
be concerned.*

Suki's mom:

Do you see any surprise here that you don't bother to call? Not even this year with a Christmas list. Maybe I should focus on the offspring I have who deign to speak to me. I love you despite your copious faults.

Suki:

Sophie? Norah? I know you did it. I don't know when it is there now. Don't trust him! He's trying to get free. Only you can free him!

When Suki's voice rang out from the receiver, Sophie dropped Sathan, who didn't even meow in protest. Suki's voice was as tinny and wrong as before, and Sophie replayed the message over and over, and as she did, the words would change slightly, Suki would breathe in different places, the blips and wha-wha-whooshes between the words would change place.

Rationality had fled, especially since the fire creature had told her she was in danger, and she dropped the phone on the floor and tore ass towards her bedroom, ran flat out and leaped on her bed, throwing the covers over her head. She made sure every last strand of her hair was covered, and not even an edge of her clothes was exposed. Sathan found her under the fortress anyway. He snuggled up in the hollow created by her knees being bent up to her face. His loud purring definitely wouldn't distract any creeping things that might jump off the ceiling at her. "Shhhh," she told him. He answered by purring louder.

She tried to calm herself thinking about Norah's mom, about how they had to move on, deal with their pasts or let them go. Maybe Norah was going to ignore her family, let her picture be put on milk cartons or in the post office or something. Except she was slightly too visible for that. There was probably already a missing person's report out for her. She should have listened to all the messages to see if the cops had called, if they were looking for her, too. Sophie would eventually call her mother—after Christmas, after the memories of her father had faded a bit, after she'd gotten a little more used to the whole vampire thing.

She wondered if Norah would bother to carry her cell anymore—she used it only for work, and never talked on it otherwise. Sophie hadn't ever bothered to get a cell phone. She had a hard enough time remembering to answer emails.

Depression crept into her consciousness on fingers shaped like her mother's voice. Where was Suki? What was out to get them? Was it all pointless? Had she been turned into a vampire just to get killed another way? Had she been killed in another life and was just repeating that somehow? Why couldn't that have all happened before her dad died so she didn't have to live through his funeral?

The comforter made her feel safe, and she started to think about the packing. What should she take? Everything, she supposed, and sort out the crap from the non-crap later. What about boxes? She had to wrap up the clothes for charity in a sheet, surely they didn't have any empty boxes folded up in some closet . . . suddenly the concept of procuring packing materials was just too much.

She was acquainted with the ways of death, the formality of buying new, somber clothes, of occupying one's mind with flower arrangements and casket options and obituaries for the paper. When her father died, she'd walked through that like everyone did, in a locked-knee daze of denial and shock. Only later did she have time to realize deaths of her mother and stepdad were always looming somewhere in the distant future. But right then she looked in the abyss and it blinked back. She would *really* outlive and bury them. Her sister, her brother-in-law, her niece and nephew, all of her friends besides the obvious one, Suki if she was still alive, and babies born that very instant. Eternity in a changing world full of people who were of a different time, a different concept of time, from her.

The weight of gravity pressed her back, back, back into the bed, feeling like the weight of every death she would pass by. Would they die and be recycled, the same souls looking back out at her through unrecognizable eyes? Would she remember enough to sense the similarity, a small tell like a fondness for banana margaritas or hatred of saxophone music? Were those the aspects that even made them who they were at all?

She remembered her father's funeral, the scents of chrysanthemums and old-lady perfume, the looks of shock and studied blankness on the faces of her family and her father's friends. How many times would she have to endure that?

"Why did you check the messages?" Norah slid a hand under her head and helped her sit up.

"I thought if we were moving . . ." The tears flowed, but she already felt better with someone to look after her. She'd never done well alone, have never been a loner or lived alone or even wanted very much to be alone for longer than an hour at a time.

"You'd come here by your idiot self and work yourself up into a big depression over how nothing's ever going to be the same and everyone's going to die." Norah hugged her, then sat back. Sophie took in her designer jeans, the coolest ox-blood leather coat on the

planet, and a sweater two shades off from the coat. Sophie checked herself at Norah's exact description of
her behavior—they had always thought almost exactly
the same, but with Sophie tending toward emotional
over-analyzing and Norah to ruthless and rational
over-analyzing.

"Where have you *been*? What are you doing here?
Why aren't you out wreaking havoc and causing some
arcane, vampire-hunting club to set Chicago as the
newest hotspot?"

Norah combed Sophie's hair back up into a neat
braid. "Packing, same as you. Why are you still surprised when we show up at the same places without
making plans or buy the same shoes without mentioning liking them?"

That was, indeed, a good question, because she *was*
endlessly shocked by that. "Because I have a tiny rat
brain?"

Norah hugged Sophie to her tightly for a moment.

Luc's head popped around the door, a smile on his
lips. "Are we ready?"

Sophie tried to frown at Luc, she just really had a serious, unexplainable antipathy towards the guy. But he
was obviously important to Olivier, and so hating him,
really hating him, was pointless. People came with their
friends, that was how it just was. But were they really
just friends? They didn't look alike, but could they be
cousins or half-brothers . . . or maybe lovers? Sophie
almost giggled when she tripped over the last thought.

"Send in the clowns!" Norah made a flourish with
her hand, and Luc smiled brighter while fading back
from the doorway. Soon, Sophie heard noise enough
from the front of the apartment to drown out the thrum
of sitar from the first floor neighbor's.

"Where did you get movers at two in the morning?"

Sophie wasn't suspicious; she *knew* something messed up was afoot.

"We made them. That's where I've been all night. With Luc—he's been teaching me." Norah was smug. Not a good thing.

"Made them how?" Sophie looked her dead in the eye.

"Check it out for yourself." Norah looked way, way too pleased. Oh lord.

Sophie closed her eyes, took a deep breath and marched out of the bedroom and down the hall towards the kitchen. As she was about to walk through the doorway, a figure lurched out, arms laden with a So-phie's brilliant, retro, bright yellow coffee pot her sis-ter had bought her in Italy—even remembering to get the converter bit for the plug—head lolling in an un-natural manner from shoulder to shoulder before jerk-ing up-right again. It shambled with a stiff gait down the hall and towards the open front door. Soon it was followed by a similar figure carrying a box that rang with a metallic rattle, probably full of cutlery and those silver, Russian cup-holders they kept breaking the glasses to.

Blinking rapidly, Sophie turned back around to find her friend standing in the hall behind her. "Zombies?" She lifted an eyebrow.

"Did you kill all these people to make them zom-bies?" And it really said a lot about her peer group that that was the most likely scenario she could conjure.

"Do you know how long that would take? Puh-leez." Norah scoffed. "Grave-robbery, an untapped market for labor. We got them fresh—or not-so-fresh—from Rosehill Cemetery."

Another zombie appeared from Norah's room and bumped the two women into the wall as it ambled by clutching several boxes. Luc followed the zombie, his ever-amused expression annoying Sophie.

"Necromancy? Is there anything you *can't* do?" Sophie pointed at yet another zombie who carried up the television from the living room.

Luc flicked the tip of his tongue over his bottom lip and laughed. "Do you really want to ask me that before you get to know me better?"

She supposed there were many ways to take that, but she decided to take the worst way and be repulsed. "Don't make me projectile vomit."

Luc and Norah broke out in hysterics. Sophie would even swear a couple of the living dead were chuckling.

"You are uptight. That is unfortunate, but sometimes it can be fun to mend." Luc kept on smarming at her, and Sophie felt her teeth begin to edge around slightly. His expression altered, the humor becoming curiosity. "Ah, you have a temper. Olivier is predictable like that."

Luc brushed passed her and started barking at the zombies in French. Sathan stalked out of the kitchen and up to Luc, rubbing his slutty cat self all over Luc's shin. Luc stooped down and picked him up and continued on his way to oversee the zombies.

"So, Sophie hates Luc, check," Norah said to her back as Sophie watched Luc hurry the undead along.

"I just don't like men who hit on me all the time." Even as she said it, Sophie knew that it was pointless to defend herself.

"I know, oh, don't I know," said Norah, and rolled her eyes. Sophie scowled at her.

"He's pretty cool, actually," continued Norah. "He made a tree do a dance for me." Norah sounded as near besotted as was possible with her general hatred for the entire world.

"So, what, you spent the whole day with him, and then—"

Norah cut Sophie off with a laugh. "Girl, do not even go there. I don't sleep with vampires on the first date."

"You sleep with everyone else," grumbled Sophie, and wished for Sathan to bury her fingers in.

"What's up with you?" Norah stopped in her tracks, grabbed Sophie's arm. She peered at Sophie closely. "You wanna tell me why you're acting like being vampires ain't the best thing since *Los Vampiros* came out on DVD?"

"I just . . ." Sophie could feel the tears welling up behind her eyes. She swallowed hard and pushed them back. "I want chocolate and to watch videos. Why don't we just head back to Paul's? Can the zombies be left alone?" Sophie'd had enough of this stripe of insanity for the evening. Norah nodded at her. "I haven't even told you about the fire-sprite who lives in a huge art gallery yet. Or how Suki left a message on the answering machine from . . . wherever she is."

"At least she ain't *dead*," said Norah.

Luc's head jerked around the doorframe. "He took you there?" Sophie squinted at him; he appeared to be forcing the insouciant façade now. "What were the paintings in the first gallery you entered?"

It was an odd question in the middle of a strange week, and even though she knew the answer was somehow going to be important in an insane way, she just didn't feel like prolonging this conversation. "A horror show."

Luc's composure cracked a tad bit more, the smile completely sliding off his face. "What kind of horror?" He didn't pronounce the 'h' in horror at all.

"Torture, rape, Knights Templar, people burned

alive," Sophie answered. She didn't wait for him to ask more, just grabbed her coat from the hook by the door and hoped Norah would follow close behind, because she didn't feel like being alone with the mover zombies.

She did follow quite close behind bundled against a cold that didn't really affect them.

"What? Knights Templar are evil? Who knew?" Norah asked as she flipped the collar of her coat up.

"They killed lot of people for stupid reasons," Sophie answered. She felt a lecture on Cathars rise to her throat, but choked it back. Norah definitely wouldn't want to hear it, and she was pretty sure Luc and Olivier had lived through it—not that either of those jerks was around. Where had they gone?

A car pulled up to the curb and Norah opened the back door.

"Zombie driver?" Sophie asked. She wasn't sure that sounded exactly safe.

"Just Paul." Norah replied.

"So, that's a yes." Sophie smirked. A thought hit her. "Why don't the zombies smell like putrefied flesh?"

They slid into the backseat jostling each other, then lounging back against the supple leather of the seat. Very nice, Sophie thought.

"Some spell or something," Norah was always dismissive of the mechanics of anything she could get someone else to do for her.

"There's a 'canceling icky odors' spell? Why don't wizards go into marketing? Also, I suppose that makes sense because you don't want to get busted by the townsfolk due to the smell of the nasty toe of a dead criminal you've had on the table for six years." Sophie occupied herself thinking up other useful spells: a stain-out elixir that really, really worked; a love potion that was good for a week, until the person was on your nerves or eating all your food out of the fridge; an ever-full gas tank; a way to project an image of yourself to family holidays so you could stay home and eat fudge and watch television.

". . . and he says we can be apprentice witches if we want." Norah finished. Sophie had cut back in on the conversation at the exact wrong part.

"Huh?" she asked. Norah gave her the blank expression of 'you're-an-idiot.'

"Okay, to recap: Luc knows everyone; he wants to introduce us around; there's some kind of crazy guidebook we're supposed to have that Olivier never gave us; we can learn magic; he has some sort of secret identity." Norah patted her perfect hair.

"Yeah, he was in a cult when he was alive, and I think he's on an epic quest to keep the cult alive." Sophie was good at explaining things without any real facts or big words. Generally her friends didn't want all the boring details anyway, just the violent or beautiful highlights. "And I *knew* I was missing a guidebook! Damn it."

"What?" Norah said before bursting out laughing.

Sighing, Sophie regretted even mentioning this at all. Somehow she felt like she should have discussed it with Olivier before feeding any pertinent observations to her friend, then felt extremely disloyal for thinking that. "Oh, it's all so boring and long. It's about one of those groups I tell you about all the time."

"The Templars?" Norah interjected. Sophie allowed that she had, perhaps, gone on about Templars a little too much a year ago or so when she was studying the validity of the heresy charges against them.

"The Fire-worshippers?" Norah tried again.

"How many times do I have to tell you they're called Zoroastrians?" Sophie glared and saw that Norah was just getting a rise out of her. "No . . ."

"Cathars!" Norah laughed and snapped her fingers. Okay, Sophie could admit that had verged on obsession there for a while. Well, for a long, long time. It wasn't always fair that they had been friends since middle school.

"Uh huh." Might as well fess up when busted, an explanation of why she thought Luc and Olivier were, indeed, Cathars, when Norah clucked her tongue.

"That's so boring! Why couldn't they have been pirates?" Norah sighed dramatically. "Yup, pirates are way better than religious nuts." Norah nodded vigorously with her comic face. Sophie sighed. Maybe she *had* talked about Cathars a little too much.

Luc FINISHED UP with the golems—he'd never taken to that ridiculous word zombie, and refused to use it even if it did have a certain currency today. Luc didn't respect all traditions, but he had the few he cherished for no real reason. Mainly because he was stubborn. He left the golem movers in the basement of the unfortunate Paul Winters' condo, all the boxes deposited and unpacked. He made sure the cat was sent over to the new house in a padded box with a hole in the top, just in case.

Olivier was as easy to find as ever, lingering at a 24-hour diner near Paul's house. Was there coffee? Was there pie? Was it near his newest baby vampire? Olivier would be there.

Luc sauntered through the doorway, knowledge all over his face that Olivier had first followed Sophie to her old apartment, seen Luc there, and decided he trusted him with her safety. Trust between them might not be universal, but it was automatic and sacred in certain areas—like protecting their own. It was quite apparent that Olivier thought the girl, Sophie, belonged to them, was perhaps one of them reborn, and until he knew otherwise, Luc would respect that.

But not solemnly.

Sliding into the cracked vinyl booth across from Olivier, Luc rubbed his hands together and blew on his fingertips while grinning. "You took Sophie to the Great Gallery?" There was a tremor of glee in his tone. He never hid his feelings from Olivier; the attempt was pointless and exhausting. He valued having one person in his life whom he could consistently disappoint and still always count on.

A couple heads turned when he spoke. One was a Latin-looking man who was obviously trying to puzzle out what language was being spoken.

Olivier looked Luc directly in the eye, the habit that had made him disconcerting and powerful even when they were very young. "You obviously know I did." He leaned back and placed his arm on the back of the booth, tilting his chin up and brushing his hair back with his free hand. Luc laughed. He'd once seen a documentary on body language on Italian television, and he scoffed at "experts" who touted that baring your chest made a person open and vulnerable. A smart man knew that to look vulnerable was to truly have the power.

Luc watched him for a long moment, waiting to see if Olivier would have one of his odd bursts of spontaneous sharing. Looking for portents or auguries had never been Olivier's way—in life he had said sorcery was a tool of the Dark One to trick people into loving the world better; as a vampire he had found magic mainly pointless and often dangerous. That had been before Phillipa's death.

After that he'd hated magic for centuries, hated all magical creatures—even became a known scourge to them after he killed an entire band of fairies who were bleeding the Bavarian countryside under the cover of the Reformation.

Eventually, Luc's impatience took over and he had to ask. "What paintings hung in the gallery that you entered into?" Lore and wisdom stated that the paintings a person was graced with on his first trip to the Gallery held the story of that specific life and all the others that had come before. Rosamund was known to take great interest in that fact, for centuries lugging humans through the portals just to discover if someone she felt a connection to was a lost loved one from the Time Before. She had found a few, even turned them.

They'd all died quickly, unable to survive as vampires.

Luc had never much believed in the fable of the Gallery's telling, but Olivier had.

Olivier wore the blank face that he thought gave away nothing. Luc read there anxiety. "There were many."

Luc gave up on any attempt at subtly. "Who do you think she is? Your mother?" The delivery was as deadpan as he could force, but a grin tipped his mouth.

"*Lucien.*" Olivier shifted in annoyance, and Luc laughed that he had been able to slip one in even after all this time.

The waitress hovered near the table and Luc dismissed her with a wag of his head, settling back in the booth with his legs splayed. "I never thought you were that depraved." He smiled, but the truth of the situation folded it into a frown. There could only be one person

Olivier would seek so hard. "Do you even remember Phillipa enough to know if it could be her?"

"Do you remember the sound of the screams of the burning?" In a rush, Olivier leaned forward so that their faces were inches apart. "If you couldn't, would you ever admit it?"

This ground was truly treacherous. The memories of the best loved were more than cherished—all they had of who they were was the memories, and yet that did not preserve them over the centuries. Some nights Luc dreamt of the rattle of armor, of the song of mail against sword, of the righteousness of Truth. He woke from those dreams wondering if they emerged from long dormant memories or from snatches of television recreations about his forgotten life. He loved to watch historical recreation on television, computer generated models of places where he walked and sang and drank. Every so often the surreal images the computers kicked out were even more right than wrong.

He sighed. "Were there paintings of burnings?" Phillipa burned on wet pear boughs, the smoke killing her before the fire could do its work. Olivier's mother walked into the flames with her arms outstretched, ready to meet the world of Spirit. Luc had always marveled at the righteousness of women, of the continual sacrifices they made through time, through successive lives. Phillipa sacrificed herself to save them, Olivier's mother's sacrifice had been made in the mistaken belief she was saving her doomed religion.

Olivier blinked twice and polished off his coffee. Luc knew there had been a painting of a bonfire.

Ah, Phillipa, Olivier's true love. Luc felt the burn of bitterness in the back of his throat that Phillipa reborn had found Olivier, but Rosamund . . .

Now a young fledgling with no knowledge of centuries past, but while she walked the earth a vampire, she hated him for centuries, avoiding him, never losing her fury and single-minded pursuit of their reborn kin. She never gave up, never faltered, never questioned. No route was too questionable, too difficult, too expensive for her to ruthlessly follow it to the bitter end, in order to resurrect something lost a thousand years before.

Once he had shared her purpose, her loyalty to the Truth, that which made them what they were. If not for the Perfects, the elders, trusting them to carry on and keep the faith alive he would have never smoked a cigarette, tasted refined sugar, seen Moliere.

He stared at the pattern of the Formica tabletop, unable to remember why he and Rosamund had parted ways, following the twists and turns of memories back to the haze of youth, the screaming of the righteous as they were burned to death for heresies both real and imagined, the soft flesh of Rosamund's body moving underneath his own. Through one heresy to the next they had threaded hoping to find sparks of the Truth, time and again finding nothing.

Olivier coughed softly; Luc looked up and their eyes met. Luc nodded sharply. Olivier knew what he was thinking, just as he knew what Olivier was thinking—if Sophie could survive being a fledgling, she might actually make it, might be able to stay with Olivier this time.

"So," said Luc, pulling himself together before his outward appearance began to match his inner thoughts—he always did try to leave the maudlin brooding to Olivier. "You didn't give them the handbook?"

Olivier laughed, banged his empty coffee cup on the table. "You're still insisting there's a guidebook? What happens when someone wants to *read it*?"

Luc lifted one shoulder and let it drop. He decided now was as good a time as any to discuss what had to be. "I've heard troubling rumors."

Olivier's eyes dropped to his lips. One of his many ways of trying to give away nothing.

"Rosamund." He flicked his eyes out of the window of the coffee shop watching heavy snow backlit by dirty city street lights.

"No one's heard anything?"

Luc snapped his eyes back to Olivier's face. "If you haven't, then no, no one's heard anything." Which lead to two obvious conclusions: she was dead—or, worse, she had stirred up some madness with the fairies again.

PATIENCE HAD NEVER suited Luc. Even when he had eternity to wait, to think and ponder and strategize, he had never found a way to bide his time. Olivier refused to act until he was at sword point or his dick ached, and Luc found that to be his worst personality trait in a personality full of flaws. Olivier's actions were always dictated by physical need or odd caprice; he wasn't a planner.

His artwork changed, if the personality didn't. Collages of snakes and photos and bits of hair; Luc squatted to get a better look at one. Fetishistic in a way Olivier used to hide, so sentimental. How could he be otherwise and be who and what he was? Luc never understood how Olivier could adapt with rapidity on the outside—to speech patterns and technology and social norms—but never on the inside, to realize a thousand-year-old cause was pointless, worse than pointless, a tragedy.

They had tried and tried and tried to save their religion, to make converts to thwart Catholic clergy, but that had come to nothing. To less than nothing in a time when people who even professed faith rarely had any. The worse tragedy was being alone in the world, of rarely finding the souls of their lost comrades, of their families and lovers. Luc's family was just a memory of a memory. Names that hadn't even ever been recorded on the lists of the martyrs.

As he looked at the photo of Sophie, Luc wondered. "Are you just another in the ever-futile quest to find them?" He brushed the tips of his fingers against her paper cheek.

"You've lost all heart?" Luc had been waiting for Olivier to speak, waiting for him to signal that they would have a conversation, acknowledge the ceaseless struggle between them. He stood and turned.

"I never believed like you, brother, not enough to keep trying after failing and failing and *failing*!" His words crescendoed into eye-popping anger. "Even if they are among us, how could we ever find the right ones? How?"

How do you find a thousand souls amongst three billion? Why should he even believe they *were* among them still? How much more futile was Olivier's real quest to find just one soul? Phillipa's.

"Veronique . . ." Olivier began.

"Veronique! Yes, the *one* in how many years, how many years that march on and on and on? Will we go another thousand years and find one more? I'm done with this." He said so, but he always said so when he was confronted with Olivier and his unyielding sincerity of belief. Veronique had been three hundred years ago. At least. The one soul they had managed to find— who chose to stay with Rosamund anyway. Lost again to them.

"The Evil One tests us, but . . ." The Evil One? Luc

couldn't believe that Olivier believed that nonsense, that smoke and confusion, still.

"Don't speak to me of that!" Flying across the room, Luc snatched the back of Olivier's head and brought them brow to brow. "Do you really still believe in that?" Their feet slid into a locked pattern of alternating toes, Olivier rested his hand gently on Luc's elbow. "Do you really believe she's Phillipa?" Luc twisted the only knife he had, twisted but felt the knife in his own belly. Hurting Olivier brought him nothing but more sorrow.

"I have to believe, brother," said Olivier, "for if I do not, I am less than nothing, I'm a joke of fate." His tone didn't sound resigned but truly hopeful.

Hope was something Luc had lost before they even became vampires.

Hope was something Luc had lost when Toulouse burned.

Luc watched hope roast with the women and children, watched and could do nothing after the fact, so many and more dead. His mother and sisters and him a day's ride away, harried by Franks who believed in nothing but gold and gems and comfort. Then he more than believed, he *knew*, that their enemies were sent against them by the Evil One, that this world was nothing more than hell, the hell they had to live to go to heaven at the end. His fervor had been complete, ecstatic. And then he watched his city burn from a day's ride away. Knew without pause that every woman he loved had been raped, tortured, and burned alive.

Luc's faith didn't die as much as transmute into the sort of rage that even a thousand years, when the source of it had crumbled to oblivion, was still a glass shard under his skin ready to cut and break out.

Oliver was staring at Luc. Luc stared back. Finally Olivier said, "Why did you come here?"

Luc had waited for that question, knew that Olivier didn't want to ask it. He always wanted everything freely given, hated to take, to ask, to force. Twisting his fingers into Olivier's hair he let his scent wrap around him, rolling his forehead against his cousin's. Olivier made no move to break or push away. He just waited.

"Years ago, several now, decades, I felt . . . something. Like a memory of a place that had changed, a field that is now a building, and I felt like I was falling. I wanted to come then, but . . ." He caught his breath remembering the fire and blood and screams of magic so dark that even more than twenty years gone it was a weight on his skin. "I was detained. Then I said every year or so, 'I will go to him.' "

"And then one day you did." Olivier brushed his hair back from Luc's face.

"And then the pull became too much and I did." He didn't add that the need had been so great that he couldn't feed or sleep or fuck without the constant thread of wrong ruining his pleasure.

Luc released Olivier's hair, and let his forehead fall to his shoulder. "I know it's her, brother. But it might not matter if she hates me anyway." Olivier was afraid.

Luc lived every second with his own lack of faith, lack of reason to go on, but in the face of Olivier's cracking resolve, he couldn't cope. They had roles, and this did not suit them.

"I will stay until this is played out, brother." Luc imagined he could smell burning flesh under the agony cascading off of his cousin. Women were the source of all that was right and new in the world, but they were also the source of all the grief of the ages.

Chapter Thirteen

WHEN IT CAME down to picking through it, Sophie was a little depressed by the collected oddments of her former life. A box full of cards from her mother and grandparents—birthdays, holidays, random—a march of cartoon animals and almost-clever jokes and puns from her first year until the current one, her grandparent's handwriting getting shakier and shakier to mark the progression of her adulthood and the ending of theirs, her mother's scribbling never altering, but never legible either. Yearbooks and school photos from her youth came wedged in the back of an old Adidas shoebox along with a napkin from an old boyfriend's bar mitzvah, the crushed and battered corsage from her junior prom, and a bunch of notes passed between her and Norah in long-forgotten classes. The memory card from her father's funeral in an envelope with the news articles about his stabbing, and his obituary. The envelope was tucked into the page of her father's favorite part in *The Wasteland*.

There was more, but the walls were starting to press in on her, and she needed distraction. Other than Sathan stalking through the remnants of her life trying to find the best place for a nap. Zombies tended to provide that in aces, she'd recently learned. Before she wandered out of her new room to see what the latest high jinks the zombies had perpetrated, Sophie stripped her new room of the vacuous, cookie-cutter art—seascapes— that Paul had decorated the egg-shell walls with.

First order of business—some serious zombie re-decoration! Off-white really wasn't a fantastic color-scheme for a vampire.

She found Norah in the kitchen explaining in small words the finer points of decoupage to a middle-aged woman in an ill-fitting churchy dress of navy blue wool. A demolished hat perched precariously on her rat's nest of hair. Her mottled skin gave no indication of what her race had been when living.

"Arg! How can you get so close to them?" Sophie wrinkled her nose, as Norah turned to wink at her. How could this be her life?

"What? We put the non-purification whatsit on them." Norah sniffed loudly. "You can't smell them!" The last was emphatic, as if she had just won some sort of argument Sophie wasn't aware of.

"I mean how they look, you idiot." She glanced from the corner of her eye at the purpling all over the dead woman's face and screwed up her own. "Ickarama." She wondered if she was supposed to think this was normal now that she wasn't human.

"You're the idiot," Norah shot back.

"You are!" Sophie said and started to giggle. Okay, this was normal.

"I *keeeel* you!" Norah screamed and launched her-self at Sophie in mock attack.

"Would this be a bad time to interrupt?"

Sophie let out a shocked screech at the unfamiliar voice as Norah swiveled her head around so fast it should have popped right off her neck.

It was just Paul. Who . . .

"Aren't you under a compulsion to go to work and do normal stuff?" Sophie definitely appreciated that he was garbed for work—black dress pants, shiny black shoes and matching belt, and crisp white oxford.

"Normally I'm not at work at three A.M." He said it with a slight twist to his lips. Was that a personality peeking out? What?

"What do you want?" Norah glared at him.

"I have to pass along a message." He slid a hand into his pocket and cocked his hip out. That was definitely a smile.

"What sort of message—from Luc?" Sophie felt a niggle in her throat and at the base of her spine. Something was wrong.

"Close, from Suki." He smiled, really smiled, all blinding white teeth and dimples and fluttering eyelashes. Norah coughed slightly. Sophie went cold all over and then flushed, her fears confirmed. She circled around him, circled so that she could try to get a grip on what was happening. How did this pertain to Suki's messages? Paul wasn't new; she hadn't just met him. She'd known him as long as Norah had.

"I'm here to invite you to join her, to cross over to where Suki is."

"Do you want our souls; will you enslave us, steal our free will, transport us to another dimension, harm us physically, emotionally, mentally, or in any other way that I can not name because I am unaware of it at present?" Norah tilted her head and waited for him to answer her questions. Sophie was nervous enough to laugh, a sharp giggle that she tried to stifle. The fact that Norah was raised by a lawyer asserted itself at the oddest of times.

Paul's grin didn't dim, and that was really frightening. "I have no desire to bind you in servitude, nor harm you in any way." He paused. "My life is your life. I am only the messenger."

Sophie turned to Norah. "Do you think he's aware of what's happening to him? I don't just mean being some sort of magical conduit, if that's even true—but that he's bound?"

Norah shrugged. "Who cares. You get what you dish out. Tough titties for him."

"Okay, so—do you think Suki's really sending us a message?"

"How else would he know anything about her being missing?" That was a good question, the issue that she'd already stumbled over.

"How do we get there? How do we get to Suki?" Norah looked unimpressed and suspicious no matter what she said about believing him.

"You simply decide you want to be there, and then you will be there." His smile faded, and the normal, thralled expression returned to Paul's face.

"Okay, that was weird." Stepping forward a couple steps, Norah waved her hand at Paul. "Were you just possessed or something?"

Paul blinked. "Yes."

"By what?" Sophie demanded.

"Something . . . I don't have any way to explain." He stuttered to a stop.

"Well, that sounds—" Norah turned to Sophie. "What the fuck are you doing?"

Sophie looked down at herself and realized that she was fading out, her body becoming translucent. "Decide to come with me!" Sophie screamed as Paul's kitchen faded out completely.

The fade-out didn't feel incremental. One second she was standing in the middle of her appropriated kitchen, the next she was gazing not at ridiculously expensive Italian appliances but at a vast lawn of silvered turquoise grass blowing in a soft wind.

To her left, in the far distance, evening had begun to drag itself across the sky with red and purple fingers. To her right, in the near distance, a grove of trees reached up to brush its foliage into the swirling dusk. A wide path formed a break in the trees through which Sophie could see glass twinkling in the sunlight where it was set in stonework. Definitely a building, but she couldn't make out what kind. Wind blew fabric around her legs, soft, sheer fabric, that when she looked down turned out to be burnt orange and gold.

Norah popped into view similarly dressed—in a modified sari cum toga done in several shades of red.

"We need to find out how to change like that." Sophie brushed the fabric with the palm of her hand.

"No shit." Norah laughed. "Why aren't we bursting into flame? Did those French freaks lie about that, too?"

She looked up into the sky that was an impossible blue of all the most perfect memories of childhood mixed together and straight enough into the sun to burn double images of it onto her corneas.

"Magic. Haven't you figured that out, yet?" Sophie intended sarcastic, but the tone was rather strained as she ran her fingers through her hair and glanced around like the White Rabbit was about to burst out of his hole with an Uzi. "We're here for a reason . . ." Sophie continued. "Here to find Suki." She was lost, and scared. Mainly really scared.

"You're here already." The two women spun around at the sound of the voice

Where the path through the trees abruptly ended and the fluttering grass began, an odd sort of man stood regarding them with an inscrutable expression. His hair fell in thick, straight locks past his shoulders—lilac and gold, violet and white—all of the hundreds of shimmering colors flowing together in what could only be the exact *right* way. The bones of his face stood out sharply in the bright sunlight, his large eyes slanting slightly at the corners. His skin was pale and slightly iridescent in the bright sunlight. He was breathtaking in a surreal way.

"That's a damned *elf*!" Norah said in the tone she normally reserved for cockroaches and telemarketers.

The man made a face, exactly what sort of face, and what it meant, Sophie could not begin to say. "You are expected to be ignorant, coming from a time and people who have lost the capacity to comprehend anything but the most mundane of topics, but as my guest I would ask that you not insult me with such a name."

At first, Sophie had no idea what the hell he was talking about, but she went through his sentence word by word and realized: he didn't like being called an elf.

Norah had beat her to the realization, as per usual. "What should we call you, then? Fairies?" Norah hated fantasy novels and sci-fi of any kind, but she'd always been swift, clever, and Sophie was glad for that.

The touchstones for reading human expression didn't flutter under the iridescent skin, didn't trigger any recognition in Sophie's mind. He gave her nothing to hang her expectations, hope, fear, loathing, on. "Modern humans are so ignorant even as they think they are advancing so rapidly. When you see a fairy, I shall point one out to you, impudent vampire. I am of the Fair Folk."

Norah turned to Sophie with a thankfully easily readable expression: annoyance. "Isn't that what an elf *is?*"

"Who knows?" Sophie was as confused as her friend. Nothing seemed real anymore. All the insubstantial, internal bricks she'd constructed her life from had been obliterated one by one. The construct of who, of what, she was lay demolished somewhere on the streets of Chicago. And she wasn't even sure the city was real anymore. Legolas, therefore, was out of her depth. How was she supposed to hold forth on the species difference between creatures she'd never cared about, much less believed in?

Creatures spilled out of the woods and across the turquoise veldt laden with every sort of something a large, ravished horde would need for an al fresco supper—daintily stitched sheets of iridescent silk in the colors of exotic butterfly wings, trays stacked in intricate patterns with bizarre fruits and improbable cheeses, pitchers and ewers and goblets. All of the picnic accoutrements were totted to and fro by regular, human-looking people, some were even dressed in jeans and T-shirts, others in garb closely resembling the not-Elf guy—all flowing, medieval tunic type get-ups with bare legs and slippers on their feet. As the last tray was set just so on a piece of silk, others like the haughty, unreadable personage began to stalk and glide out of the woods. ·

Sophie had a hard time differentiating whether they were male and female or hermaphrodites since they all stood of a height, had varying degrees of flowing hair, and seemed to all favor dresses with hemlines ending haphazardly at different lengths. Their eyes flashed and glittered in the magical sunlight in improbably colors; their faces angled in painful, sharp beauty, opalescent skin stretched over sixty degree obtuse cheekbones. Her fear bent back in on itself, feeding like an ouroborus of regret for not listening to Olivier, of her own self-loathing that Suki had tried to warn her, of the great yawning void of fear of what the outcome of this would be.

"Sit; you were invited as true guests. You are most welcome amongst us." The multi-colored hair of their host curled around itself, strands twining together into straining, slithering locks. His long, thin fingers extended towards a rectangle of silk Sophie had no name for, a combination of dark orange and bluish-green, and indicated that they should settle in. He alighted in the middle of the sheet and sat cross-legged, his feet bare, with toes as long as his fingers promised.

Sophie glanced at Norah for some guidance—as misplaced as it surely would be.

"Why the hell not?" said Norah. She plopped down next to where a servant with long, black hair that obscured her face piled something similar to watermelon with no seeds onto a plate that looked suspiciously like something from Ikea. Sophie hoped this situation wasn't about to go bad. Norah's obvious comfort made Sophie want to run home. These people—elves, Fair Folk, whatever—were just too strange. Stranger than magic-wielding Cathar vampires, anyway.

Sophie wondered if maybe, once she was exposed to magical creatures, the instances of magical creatures in her life was *supposed* to grow exponentially.

She decided to go home, just like she'd decided to arrive—but when she focused and then blinked, she opened her eyes to the sparkle of the fair folk instead of the sparkle of Paul's white tile kitchen.

"We're blocked from leaving," Sophie hissed at Norah.

"Whatever," Norah replied in a normal tone of voice. "If we get into really big trouble, your boyfriend will come save us."

"He is *not* my boyfriend," said Sophie. "I hate you."

"You love me," said Norah, and she reached out a hand to pluck a piece of the pale, pink fruit off the dish to sniff it.

Sophie shot out her own hand and grabbed Norah's wrist. "Don't eat anything."

"Yeah, I've heard that one before, too." Norah looked thoughtful.

"Oh my God!" A servant girl sat her tray on the silk ground sheet with a plunk. Sophie got a good look at her face.

"Suki?" She raised up to her knees, intending to scoot over to her friend. How was she here? What the hell was going on?

"Didn't I warn you?" Suki was furious, her face like an apple and her hands on her hips. "Do you know what I went through to warn you and then you didn't pay any attention to it at all? What the hell is wrong with you two? How stupid can two people be? Didn't your vampire parents tell you not to trust every non-human creature that came along?" She let out a frustrated screech the brought further unreadable expressions from the assembled fey folk.

Suki dropped to her knees next to Norah and Sophie. "You are so stupid!" She threw her strong arms around them, pulling them toward her. They both returned the hug.

Their host laughed to himself, and Sophie glared at him, then turned her attention back to Suki. "I was trying to find you!" she said. Sophie didn't understand

Suki's anger—but then she did. She pushed back so she could look directly into Suki's tanned, freckled face. "You didn't send the message through Paul."

"No, that was me, vampire," said the elf-guy. "I thank you for binding him to you—a soul I marked so long ago, casting a binding spell on a human, hollowing him out, making him easy to reach from this plain. Ah, with my witches there was no effort at all." His voice was smoke creeping into a pattern, circles and cones, reaching for an equation that would explain the universe.

Her thoughts refused to shape into patterns she recognized. In the corner of her mind, she knew there was something important that needed to be considered, a thought that she wanted to have, but instead she focused on the pink-haired man and his stained-glass eyes. "What're you talking about, marked soul?" It was like a script, she opened her mouth and the words dropped out.

"Can we live off elf-blood?" Norah asked menacingly.

Norah didn't seem to be affected by the strange vortex that was pulling at Sophie. She felt some sort of familiarity that resonated in a way she didn't understand.

"Because I'm willing to try," continued Norah. Sophie shivered.

This was wrong; wrong and really horrible. Was this something that happened to every new vampire?

Then Suki wedged herself between the vampires and the fairies, and pushed at Sophie until they broke eye contact.

"Don't you know *anything*?" said Suki. She sounded annoyed.

"I wish Luc had given us that handbook," Norah quipped. "We could definitely use it right now. First up: what's the difference between elves and fairies and the Fair Folk? Next: can we eat Fairyland food?"

"I bet you could find some willing donors among the people I live with," said Suki. "But not from me. Forget it. It's your own fault you're here. Because you're idiots. It took me ten years to find the spell to warn you, and that was completely pointless. I could've been playing Ultimate. I suppose you're both too stupid to fight the geas."

"Ten years? You've been gone for two days," said Sophie.

"You think time here works the same way? You really *are* an idiot." Suki put her hands on her hips and looked down at Sophie. "Every dimension works differently. You're in the realm of the Fair Folk, and time works here the way they say it does."

"Thanks," said Sophie sarcastically. "That's way helpful."

"*Witch*." A voice like chimes in an a scale unheard by human ears rang out. "You begin to tire me. Your betrayal will be remembered." Their host's hair curled and uncurled like a ribbon as he stared at Suki.

Her reaction wasn't exactly what Sophie expected. Suki turned from Sophie and glared at him. "Yawn. When you escape and rule the world, yeah, I've heard it all before. You will rule with the vampires and the demons at your side, world without end, blah blah, antichrist antics." Suki sat down next to Sophie with a look of complete boredom on her face.

Sophie knew that look was cultivated, though. She didn't buy it. She'd also missed her friend, and her little speech grounded her, reminded her that even here, even with everything else in her life wrong and going wronger, Suki was Suki: a total bitch.

Sophie wondered for a moment what it said about

her that one of her closest friends was almost a sociopath, and the other was a stone cold bitch.

"I'm hungry." Norah made that into a threat intended for their host. It wasn't lost on him.

"Why would you want our thin, weak blood when you can have this?" Extending his long, pale hand, their host offered a golden bloom, shaped vaguely like a Chinese lantern with papery skin and heart-shaped petals that formed a pod.

"What is it?" Sophie accepted the bulb dubiously. There were many stories of people trapped by fairy lures, and she was sure this was just one she had never heard before. Besides, she'd already been tricked once. Her pulse picked up, and she looked to her friends. Their gazes were trained elsewhere, at each other trying to communicate silently. So what, was she supposed to distract the fairy?

"Bloodbloom." His face rearranged. On the edges of his expression she almost recognized something, and she knew he was trying to be reassuring, trying to push his Otherness away and appear safe, known. Sophie wondered how she knew for a fact that this androgynous individual was, in fact, male. His attempts to soothe her made her more frightened.

Norah and Suki had finished their silent communications.

"What's your name?" Norah's tone was bleak, condescending and violent all at once, a tone that had made more than one man vomit in the past.

Opening her mouth to second that question, Sophie locked eyes with the fairy, and felt laughter tumble out of her mouth one tinkling, shocked bubble at a time. His name! That would explain everything; she knew that was true on some level that was like breathing, like sex, like the blood in her veins. Her stomach felt light, her blood beat through her veins with exultation. She could hear Suki and Norah also laughing; the humor must flow from him.

His expression was mostly unfathomable, but amusement was as plain on him as on any mundane human being. Bits of ivory and lavender hair caught the light as he regarded her.

"Since you ask, I must tell, but can I ask a boon before I do?" A whisper threaded through her mind that this was part of a plan, but as soon as she tried to chase that back to some source, some knowledge she knew was there, it faded like an old memory.

"Don't grant a boon!" Suki clutched at Sophie's hand, but Sophie didn't look over at her. How could she look away from his beautiful eyes? They were almost—almost faceted, like diamonds.

She knew Suki was right, that anything the fairy could ask of her would screw her up, make everything difficult, but she didn't *care*. She also knew the desire to agree stemmed from *him*, the fairy. He had to be controlling her thoughts somehow, but she didn't care, wasn't interested in finding out how, in making him stop.

"What the hell is a boon?" Norah choked on the laughter still constricting her words. Sophie could feel the pulse of the unnamed fairy, the humor he felt. Even as she struggled to revert to neutral, she knew he was imparting some deep amusement into her blood and into the minds of her friends.

"If I can," she said to the fairy, ignoring Norah.

Altruism and humor suffused her, and even as she couldn't explain why she felt that she had to offer something in return for the Fair One's name, she *knew* she did. Magic on top of magic, one fey creature to another.

"Extend the same hospitality to me that I did to you." The sound of chattering voices broke off, and the flat plane of grass stretching around them was eerily silent.

"Naturally, you're more than welcome to come to by our place. Anytime." The thick hum of friendship, of blood, of kinship overwhelmed her and she couldn't imagine telling him no. The conversation picked back up, louder than before with a more manic edge to it.

The bloodbloom felt heavier in her palm. She had forgotten about the flower.

"My name is Ankou, and you have my undying friendship. Which is nothing new, as you have had it for five hundred mortal years." His smile obliterated the question his strange words brought to her lips.

"I suppose there's blood inside." Norah's words caused Sophie to assume she now also had one of the pods.

"Why would it be called a 'bloodbloom' if not?" The voice that answered her friend's was so melodic the spoken words were close to a song.

"You people are very literal. You have poets and songwriters in to do up your music, right?" Norah continued the conversation. Sophie ignored her until Ankou broke their eye contact with a trilling laugh, and a little leap, like a dance.

"We have beauty and immortality while human folk have creativity and hip-hop," a Fair One replied.

Sophie shook her head, felt a headache begin behind her ears, felt her eyes ache. She leaned over and whispered in Norah's ear. "I'm wondering how much of what he says is true."

"Probably none. And he probably has superhearing," Norah replied in her normal voice. Sophie cut her eyes back to Ankou. He was watching her steadily. Suki was sitting white-lipped next to her, her hands twisted in her lap.

"Trust me," he whispered to her seductively—which really was the statement most likely to cause Sophie to be absolutely distrustful, not to mention his lame attempt to be sexy.

Reaching out his pale, rosy-tipped fingers, Ankou waved another of the gold blossoms before Sophie's face. The unmistakable scent of blood wafted up her nose setting her teeth to sliding around in her mouth.

She popped the bud into her mouth. The universe disintegrated into copper and fire and pure bliss beyond anything she had ever conceived. Lights burst behind her closed eyelids, a kaleidoscope of red and hungry golden sparks. Her inner ear could faintly hear a tuneless melody pricking at her to follow, follow. She felt the weight of sable and feathers on her skin; the scent of narcissus and cinnamon filled her nose.

Her eyelids were almost too heavy to open as her Self, the Sophieness, began to coalesce. Norah's jubilant face was the first picture she could piece together through her slitted eyelids.

"Down the rabbit hole." Norah laughed, full of genuine humor instead of her usual sardonic chortle.

When she twisted her limbs into a sitting position, Ankou was gone. Vampire soma.

He had tricked them, then drugged them, and then fled. Sophie felt like a total idiot, but the lingering effects of the blood drug—deep well-being, contentment, aftershocks in her nerves like orgasm wavelets—made her almost too mentally lethargic to care.

"So you—do this all the time?" Sophie said to Suki, slurring her words a little.

"What, drink blood? No, remember, I'm the witch. *You* are the vampire." Suki rolled her eyes.

"No, I mean, hang out with guys like Ankou?"

"Yeah. I'm not really a servant or anything," said Suki. "Mostly I just hang around. And, I mean, I would have never *said* to anyone that my life's ambition was to be a slave to the Fair Ones, but it's better than nine-to-fiving it." Suki flipped her hair over her shoulder.

She wore a sheath dress with tiny pink and yellow flowers embroidered all over it. Not anything like her normal attire.

Sophie tried to comprehend what she was saying. She liked it here?

Norah turned her attention to the Fair One to Suki's left. Her expression was softer than normal, but she was hardly friendly. "Who do you lure here?" Sophie could see that Norah was disturbed by the reality of fairy kidnapping. Her moral compass had definitely been demagnetized.

The Fair One appeared unperturbed at Norah's insolent tone. "Mainly folk who can build."

"We're unable to build or make non-organic products," a Fair One with silver and white hair chimed in.

The first speaker continued. "We can't sit stone atop stone and make castles nor can we weave clothes to cover our nakedness nor forge gold and silver and gems into jewelry."

"So, engineers, smiths, weavers and seamstresses, anyone who can do anything?" Norah asked.

Sophie was truly interested now and tried to force herself to string words together. She sat up a little straighter and breathed through her nose.

The woman turned her gaze and smile onto Sophie. "Yes."

"What did you do before you could kidnap people and get them to make you things?" With a meaningful look at several of the serving humans, Norah tried again to start an argument.

"There was never such a time," a third Fair One responded.

"But what about caveman days?" Sophie knew there was something wrong with what these fairies were saying, but she couldn't get to what in her hazy state. She couldn't believe how well Norah functioned while drugged.

"Human folk were smelly and sewed us pelts to wear," the fey woman said. All of the Fair Folk in earshot of that remark burst into laughing.

Chapter Fourteen

THE DAY AFTER Sophie moved her most valuable possessions from the place where she had lived as a human, Olivier spent drinking in the false safety of his loft. The light streamed in the windows, weak, desultory city winter light, and he sat in the grey light drinking vodka. Drink after drink until his eyes shut themselves, and he collapsed where he sat in sleep closer to stupor than rest.

Dusk had marched into night by the time he finally convinced his dreams he should leave, the last one tugging at him even as he pulled a hand through he hair and levered himself off the floor: the horrid smell of crackling flesh mingled with green wood smoking, bridle bells tinkling over harp strings plucking out a cradle song, the sky too low to the ground threatening to drop the rest of the way, the overwhelming feeling of futility. His mind presented the images as a dream, but he recognized it as memory. Wished he didn't.

He considered giving Sophie up as he made coffee

and showered. She belonged to herself, had her own intentions and choices to make that had nothing to do with him and his desires.

Life was what it was, and he had lived his extremely extended one as well as he could, without forcing others to obey his whims.

Pulling on his shoes, he listened as a car alarm went off below his windows starting a chain reaction of every car on that side of the block. One of the collages he'd begun since meeting Sophie lay on the floor between the bed and the door, and he had to step over it to leave. The canvass brought to mind the child's earnest attempt to render a pear tree hanging on the wall of the Great Gallery. He knew as soon as he woke up that he was going to try one more time with Sophie—to tell her that what he was after was so much more than yet another doomed relationship in the grand parade of the same—but the thought of the painting, of what it could represent, allowed him to rationalize it all the more.

Through the lobby, down the sidewalk, on the train and off again, he tried to remember Phillipa. Not just the echo of the color of her hair or eyes, but her voice, the feel of her in the room. Luc had forced him to name the truth to his greatest fear—that his memories were truly fading. All of the people they had sacrificed everything for were not only beyond this world but also beyond even recollection in it.

He was in a fine mood by the time he arrived at Paul's. Twisting open the doorknob, he shoved the door inwards. Standing on the other side was Paul himself. But something was extremely wrong with him. His hair moved, curling and looping around itself like a male Gorgon, but there was no wind. His face, so expressive and open normally, was rearranged into an unfathomable stare, something other than blankness, something less than emotion.

He smelled of mercury and sage.

"Oh, excellent. I was having trouble with that." Paul's face ripped, pulled into something approaching a smile. He was wearing purple corduroy pants and a red shirt, no hat or coat or shoes.

"Trouble with what?" Olivier had the sliding feeling of recognition. This was something he had seen before, long, long ago. Mercury summoned fairies; the scent of sage was the sign of witchcraft. Olivier wondered what fairy trick was afoot here.

"The complex human mechanism that allows one to exit the dwelling." He attempted to brush by Olivier.

Yes, naturally he couldn't open the door, since the knob was made of steel, and fairies were allergic to iron. "You will find that most doors here have similar mechanisms. Where are the females who stole this home from the rightful owner?"

A person had to be very careful with the phrasing of questions to fairies, and if asking a question one should offer some information in return.

"They are in the Blessed Realm."

Olivier was surprised and pleased that he hadn't had to resort to physical violence to illicit a response to his question. His unease grew as the scent of Otherness plucked at him, the greenness of fairy blood tasting tart on the back of his tongue.

"Have you trapped them there?" There must be something else that fairies did, but he surely didn't know of anything besides kidnap and murder and mayhem of a pattern only they comprehended.

Paul cocked his head, his hair standing further from his head, waving in what could have been agitation. "I

offered them an invitation. They have trapped themselves." He peered around Olivier into the street.

"How can I get them back?" He stepped to the side
to allow the fairy access to the outside, not ready to attack him, not sure how to trap him. Every encounter
with one of their kind had a different set of rules. But
this was just too much of a coincidence with what he
suspected of Sophie.

Phillipa had been lured by the fairies, lured by one of
the oldest, most powerful. She fell to their tricks, despite
her age and wisdom; the fairies were older, wiser.

Could this really be the King of Death? After all of
this time? Was he not bound?

"You must fetch them, of course!" Sparkling laughter sprang from his throat. "You know this story, as old
as you are!" He looked Olivier up and down. "You are
stronger than when last we met. I will find excellent
uses for you in my Court."

With that, Paul—or Ankou in Paul's body—jauntily
hopped out the door, down the steps, and onto the sidewalk. Olivier watched as the snow melted and evaporated where he stepped, greenery poking through the
snow. Humans walking close enough to feel his breath
continued on their oblivious ways without any notion
of the trouble they were in. Olivier knew how great a
risk it was to let a fully grown fairy out amongst a
modern, disbelieving population, especially this particular fairy, but he simply couldn't leave Sophie in the
Fairylands while he dealt with that situation.

He had done this, taken so long to tell Sophie what
he suspected of her soul, that she was his old companion, his greatest love reborn. The search had been so
futile for so long, he had lost hope himself, had
thought his suspicions were created by his need to be-

lieve in something. His self-doubt had crept in and allowed this to be set in motion.

To be *reset* in motion.

IN A VERY luckless week, Olivier finally had a stroke of it—or perhaps fate, feeling sympathetic, intervened on his behalf. When he returned home, it was to find Luc cooking in his kitchen.

"Do you like curry? I don't really care, but if you do, this will be much more pleasant for you." Deftly maneuvering, Luc chopped a chili into shreds.

"I need your help." Olivier knew that even attempting to trick Luc into this would be an abysmal failure, Luc being the tricky one between the two.

Bending over to light the stove, Luc hummed to himself. "This sounds suspiciously like work."

"I need to rescue Sophie and her friends from the Fairylands."

Luc's sharp laughter indicated to Olivier that perhaps he could have finessed that slightly, or constructed a speech about how many favors Luc owed him before launching into the meat of the issue.

Luc was even less thrilled than Olivier by the prospect of rescuing two—possibly unwilling—women.

"A quest to the Fairylands? I would rather be burnt alive."

Olivier really hated it when Luc said that, but he didn't comment. He had planned to spend the next few days working on some poems and inviting Sophie out to dinner, maybe tapas or one of the small, quiet Italian places—not prying arcane knowledge out of reluctant underworld dwellers.

Sure, he had, in recent centuries, warmed back up to

fey creatures, but that didn't mean he wanted to spend any time with fairies of any variety.

"I'm considering using guilt or invoking the concept of honor here, but first I have to figure out which part of the Fairylands the girls have fallen into and how we can gain entry into it. And—"

"If you plan to call them girls to their faces, you might want to simply leave them where they are and spare your eyeballs from being ripped from your face." Luc smiled. Olivier read truth behind his words and decided to be more careful in how he formed his thoughts about women in the future.

"Will you please help me find the women?" The *please* came out fairly sarcastic, but Luc saluted him with his fingers to his temple, mouth, and heart all the same.

"I pledge to help you in any way I am able in your quest against these devious Fairy Folk, up to, but *not* including, venturing into any other worlds. Mainly because I hate all fairies, but also for the fun of it." With that solemn pledge, Luc got up and began rattling through Olivier's wine. "So, did you see what sort of fairy it was that tricked them?"

He watched as Luc poured the wine, considered lying or ignoring the question, but what would be the point? It would only obscure the issues, make everything more difficult, and make it take longer to get the women out of the Fairyland—possibly long enough that they would be dead. "Ankou."

In less time than it took Olivier to blink, Luc had vaulted over the kitchen island, teeth extended, body poised with feet set at exactly shoulder width apart. "You lie."

Normally, Olivier would be angry at the accusation,

but shock did horrible things to vampires, causing great massacres, rape, horrors beyond human reckoning.

"Do you believe Sophie may be someone we knew, now?" said Olivier.

Olivier had been sure the second he saw Ankou, certain in a way that only something as unexpected as the fairy's appearance could invoke.

"Rosamund," Luc snarled. "It is her revenge as much as ours."

"There's no time to send for her." He'd already considered that—the honorable way was to send for her, to give her an opportunity to revenge Phillipa upon her tormentor. The friendship between Phillipa and Rosamund extended back as far as Olivier's fading memory could delve—they had been inseparable, in life and in the night-life they had shared for hundreds of years. They had shared everything, until Rosamund had caused Phillipa's death by tinkering with fairies and magic and Ankou. "Rosamund forced his binding the first time. It's enough."

"There is no enough." Luc was gone like a creature from a child's nightmare, full of murderous intention and righteous fury. Olivier didn't bother to follow him and remind him that was exactly what Ankou lived to incite—or to tell him what body Ankou was in. If Luc killed Paul in a fury, who knew what that could do to Norah and Sophie? The only instances of thralled and bound humans being killed happened right before their vampire owners were killed as well—Olivier didn't know what could happen to the vampires if one of their thralled was murdered.

Not to mention what could happen to Luc, since Luc was bonded to Paul through Norah and Sophie and his stupid alchemy ceremonies.

Olivier sighed; perhaps he was just getting older, but people seemed to get more and more annoying.

THE BLOODBLOOM HAD a lasting effect similar to vampire pot. As the human servants of the Fair Ones packed up their picnic, Sophie and Norah almost frolicked in the citrus-scented grass of the prairie. Suki cut their romping short, demanding they accompany her on her walk back to where she lived. The stroll through the woods was less real than a dream, like stepping into a movie set while breathing Jell-O.

"How did you get here?" Sophie touched Suki's shoulder, just to make sure she was real. This was all so wrong. So very wrong, and the echo of familiarity was trying to induce panic, shoving out the drugged haze.

Suki turned her brown eyes to Sophie's face. "I was lured here with music, like in a fairytale, with music like you've never heard." Her voice was distant, not like Suki at all, serious and drained of sarcasm. Sophie wanted to say something comforting, meaningful, but the lingering effect of the bloodbloom made her giggle slightly.

Suki glared at her and Norah giggled in response to that. The two of them began a loop of glaring and laughing that continued as they followed the path through the woods.

But there was more Sophie wanted to talk about, and even the lures of Fairyland weren't going to stop her from asking her questions. "You haven't said anything about us being vampires. Don't you care?" Sophie was slightly affronted by that.

Suki swept her eyes over Sophie. "What can I say? You're a total moron, and Norah was bound to end up as some sort of murderer sooner or later. Besides, I knew."

Norah cracked up at that, laughed hard and genuinely.

"Plus," said Suki, "I've seen weirder since I've been here. And I was trying to prevent all this all along." The tone left Sophie with no doubt it was frighteningly so.

"What in the hell is that?" Norah pointed, as though a visual aid was needed. Sophie's mind stuttered, like film with every fifth frame removed, but she could definitely see the scary wall thing Norah meant. They emerged from the wood in a clearing before the wall. Sophie gazed at it with confusion.

"The wall around Provisional City." Suki stepped onto a pathway made of thousands of metal bottle caps. The soles of her shoes made tinny clicks as she beckoned the vampires to follow.

As she began to wander off, Sophie followed, mouth agape at the wall. The section nearest where they emerged from the woods stood more than two Sophies high, consisting of badly laid concrete with every sort of broken pottery and bits of colored glass imaginable jammed in it for decoration. Next to the spout from a Delft teapot, tiny imprinted hands touched little finger to thumb circling a decayed flower. The top of the concrete rippled in uneven waves.

What made this truly strange wasn't so much the concrete and crockery but how they abruptly merged into blonde brick mortared with a bright teal. Sophie turned to observe Norah watching the wall with a raised eyebrow as though she was just on the edge of figuring out the entire point. The wall didn't seem to interest Suki.

Sophie hustled to catch up with her, snatching Norah by the arm near where the brick gave over to rough-hewn logs held together with what appeared to be gallons of tree sap. "Come on," Sophie said, yanking Norah up to the other woman.

"Hey," said Sophie. Suki's head swiveled, but she

kept on walking. "This place is sort of freaking me out." Suki laughed at Sophie's anxiety, and Sophie felt a little better—that was familiar, that was known, Suki was here. At least Sophie was with her friends, right? Not like that would keep her from getting murdered at the hands of crazy fairies. She also seemed to be way more in the know than either Norah or Sophie. How had she known what was going to happen to them?

The wood logs of the wall ended at a blue ceramic archway embossed with catawampus birds and quadruped creatures painted in bright, primary colors. Sophie found the effect disturbing in a way she couldn't explain.

"Is that some kind of hieroglyphic language?" Sophie asked Suki. She peered closer at that figures.

"Uh, I think they're just decoration?" Suki spoke with the sort of up-inflection at the end of statements that Sophie usually mocked. "Do you know what a geas is?"

Sophie turned to look at her as Suki walked under the arch. Norah answered, "A male skeaze?" without a trace of humor in her voice.

"You get on my nerves." Suki glared at her.

The bottle cap path continued into the town, threading between buildings just as quirky and strange as the wall. There was series of wicker bushes whose branches had been molded into onion-shaped structures with elliptical gaps for windows. Like giant, living baskets.

"It's a kind of curse, right?" Sophie asked in response to Suki's query. And considering the other things that Suki had said, Sophie didn't like the direction the conversation was going at all.

"Yes, a curse that has several components, that's bound to specific actions. The Fair Folk love them, because they're so complex and can go wrong in so many ways. They have a wagering system based on geas-related fiascos." She looked Sophie in the eye. "I think you're under one. The vampire thing, that I tried to save you from, may I add, is one part of it."

Sophie gaped. Norah grabbed Suki by the arm hard enough to leave a bruise in the shape of her hand. "And?" she demanded.

Suki sighed and tugged her arm away. "I can't tell you anymore. If I do, you'll be trapped here forever." When both of the other women made scoffing noises her expression turned dark. "I did everything I could do to save you from like even getting this far into this mess. You need to take some responsibility for your own lives." The last bit was punctuated with a hair toss and her hands affixing to her hips. In a softer voice she added. "Make normal conversation, okay? I'm going to try to help you two morons, but if anyone catches on, we're sunk."

Sophie fumbled for chit-chat, her mind whirling in chaos with Suki's speech. This was weirder than she thought. And that was a feat.

"Do you live here?" Norah voiced Sophie's question.

Suki shook her head and looked over her shoulder. "Hell no! But we have to pass through it to get to where I do. It's cool here, just looks weird." Sophie's unease at the extreme oddity wasn't assuaged.

"How long you been here?" Norah didn't look at Suki but at the scenery they were strolling by.

Suki stared at the side of Norah's face. "We don't have clocks here. A long time. A really long time." She paused. "Time passes in loops and jags here; we tried to keep a calendar, but I lost track at fifteen years."

Sophie almost gasped. "You don't look any different."

"People here never do." Suki looked her in the eye, and Sophie shivered.

"How long do you think it's been since we were in Chicago?" she finally asked, and Norah sighed impatiently.

"Sophie, what do you *care*?" she demanded. "It's not like it even matters!"

Suki nodded. "The world is different when you're not human," she told Sophie.

"Yeah, thanks, like I hadn't noticed? Maybe you guys don't care about your parents or anything, but I do—what about my mom? My sisters? What about Sathan?" She looked from Norah to Suki and back again; they both shrugged at her.

"Sophie, you chose this," said Suki coldly. "Now you have to deal with—"

Suki was interrupted by a yell from across the street. "Hey!" shouted a voice, and Sophie turned to look.

On the other side of the "street" stood an open-air pavilion consisting of a canopy of what could have been woven leaves interspersed with shiny objects held up by four glass poles. Sitting around on bean bag chairs in the tent were several tweens.

"Hey!" shouted one of the tweens. Her ash-blond hair was braided in two Heidi-esque plaits on the side of her head. They reached all the way to her waist to be tied off with leather strings bedecked with tiny bells. She wore a flared a-line skirt that ended well above her knees and a cropped pull-over shirt—both in bright pink.

"Hey back." Sophie thought the girl was cute—and would make a good dinner. She pushed that thought to the back of her mind; *inappropriate!* she snapped at her vampire innards. She noticed a set of what looked like wire clippers in one hand and a riot of metal wire in the other.

"Are you on a quest?" The girl smiled brightly, and Sophie would have guessed her to be about thirteen.

Hm, a quest? This could be where the real danger started. Sophie gazed around for Monty-Pythonesque shrubs or Knights that said Ni.

"Uh . . ." She met Norah's eyes, but Norah was too annoyed at her to help.

"Oh my God! You totally are!" The girl shrieked a little, bouncing up and down, and turning around to run back to the clutch of other girls sitting around the tent. Two more shot up and the scampered back over to Sophie and the others.

One of the new girls had chestnut curls cut into a bob, dark olive skin that looked vaguely middle-Eastern to Sophie, and appeared maybe a year older than the first girl. The other had afropuffs pulled back with satin ribbons, dark chocolate skin, and seemed of an age with the other two.

The blond girl exclaimed, "I'm Amy," she pointed to the brunette "this is Huda," then at the black girl "and Jackie." She directed her introductions to Norah.

"We want to give you something!" Jackie jumped in place then hightailed it around the strangers and towards a clutch of teepee-like structures. Each teepee twinkled with semi-precious stones and bits of mirror set on brightly colored cloth. Sophie could tell these three were just the advance party of the Teepeeites since there seemed to be at least fifteen of the structures.

"Are these beads all over here?" Norah reached out a hand as they passed the first one and poked at one shining object. The bead shone amber in the hearty sunlight, flashing a brighter yellow at its heart. A citrine, Sophie thought.

"Yup," replied Huda. "We, like, make jewelry and stuff. There's always left over stuff."

"These are so cute." Sophie couldn't believe how each teepee seemed to be an expression of some personality—

one burnt orange with yellow spangles and bumblebees painted from top to bottom, one black with silver bugle beads and what had to be a poem painted on close the ground, another baby blue with white and clear beads in complex designs that looked like Arabic.

"Okay, this is so cool!" Amy pulled back the front of a hot pink teepee and beckoned everyone to follow. Cool would not have been the word Sophie chose, but it was better than fucked-up, which might have been.

They all slid into the opening flap, ducking under and stooping over. Inside, the teepee was quite spacious. Sophie crawled in and shuffled over to the far side, plopping down on an embroidered pillow adorned with five pointed stars in pink and white. She looked up and was amazed to notice that at the exact right height to get a clear view of the sky, apertures had been cut in the fabric allowing airflow.

Everyone took seats on pillows sort of like what Sophie remembered seeing in *National Geographic* about Native Americans as a kid. Except in the middle there was no fire, but instead a pallet that looked way more comfortable than her bed at home. It was like a kid's fort with more stability, a permanent sheet tent.

"What sort of quest are you on?" Huda asked. Sophie gazed at her exotic, animated face. Her lashes were so long she'd never be able to wear mascara and glasses. An odd thought, but Sophie decided she was welcome to those in the Land of Nod.

"You can't ask that!" Amy threw a pillow at the general direction of the offending head.

"Oh my God, seriously, Huda, what's your problem?" Jackie sounded highly annoyed.

"We're not on a quest." Suki sounded bored.

"See! Totally secret!" Amy rooted around under one of the hundreds of pillows strewn across the floor, then jumped back clutching a box in her had. She turned around and offered it to Sophie. Oh, Sophie wasn't loving this development. Was this when things went really badly? Was her soul in the box? Why couldn't she be a dramatic, violent vampire who just killed everyone here and ran away like a bad-ass?

"What's that?" Norah scooted nearer. Suki leaned over Sophie to see what Amy had. So, she might not be a bad-ass, but they definitely were.

"This is my gift." Amy smiled. Sophie thought she looked like the original model for cute, blond, American girls. The worst sort of danger generally came in the most appealing packages.

For about a minute, everyone sat breathing hard as Sophie considered what to say. This situation was perhaps the strangest in her life aside from waking up a vampire. Something very weird was up. She really wished she had listened to Olivier and learned what she could about the supernatural. In fairy tales, specific details were always really important. Like how they got tricked into being here. "What sort of gift is it?" She planned to ask all of the specific questions she could.

Amy's smile dimmed a tad. "I was told to give this to someone, and I would know that someone when she came along." A red light went off in Sophie's head.

"Okay, I would die from curiosity if I didn't take it." She nodded at Amy, who smiled a smile far older than her years. A stray breeze blew into the teepee through the windowlets, ruffling everyone's air and flapping their clothes about them. Very ominous. Sophie immediately regretted the choice before she even saw what was inside.

Amy opened the box. Inside was ring of gold, ruby, and pearls. Picking it up, Sophie lifted it into a shaft of light to get a better look. The goldwork was ancient;

the stone wasn't set on teeth, but welded directly into the metal with the pearls likewise set around the ruby in the gold.

"How do I use it?" She looked Amy in the eye. This girl was more than she seemed, she was sure.

"Uh, you wear it?" The crease above Amy's nose was cute, but Sophie felt her vague fear increase.

Sophie grabbed Suki's hand. "Grab Norah." Suki complied. Awkwardly with her hand holding Norah's, Sophie put the gift on the ring finger of her right hand. Closing her eyes, she expected to open them again in Chicago. That was too logical, though. No, she closed her eyes and the world dropped away. Spiraled away into a lifetime of memories, into two lifetimes, ten, a hundred.

Years and years marching on and on and on back to a mountain, her home, the land of her blood, of her people, so long ago even the stones have been lost, the names of the land, the history of her life, had changed. She saw herself, not herself, her other self as she was—*Phillipa d'Alairac*—falling into the Otherlands before, this time alone. Rosamund's magic gone awry again, as always. Phillipa had told her that magic couldn't bring their people back to life—that sorcery always rebounded on the practitioner. Ankou pulled her into the Fairylands with him when Phillipa conjured him and he mocked her attempts to bind him.

She saw herself running from Ankou, running from his mad dreams of ruling the human world, using vampires to control the human world, unleashing pain and death and terror. And her own terror so utter, her belief in his powers so complete she wanted to die.

The Fairylands had been appealing in a strange way, though. She had wanted for years to go beyond the endless questing of Rosamund and Olivier and Luc, into a life that was lived just to live. She had been so young when she chose to live forever. Young enough to have no idea what she was choosing.

She could see herself giving the ring to a girl—*not this girl*—fleeing from Ankou back into the human world, his spirit following, but not his body, just his spirit, but enough to start the riots—*Witch! Witch! Burn her!*—to churn up the chaos, to end her endless marching years, to let her go—*start over*.

But there was no starting over, only going forward, never understanding completely that all our actions lead to the next action and the one after that. Only for people, for those ruled by human rules who lived in the human world. Fairies lived by another rule in another world.

His spirit form called to her:

"You came to me, chose me. Even as I chose you, before you were born into this body, before thirsty iron drank the blood of your family, my thoughts found you and knew you for my own. You were chosen for death, to bring death and suffer death and witness death, and I knew, ah." His voice like starving children, poison on the tongue, looming disaster, chased her as she ran, tried to hide from the approaching villagers. If she could find Rosamund or Luc they could fix this, save her somehow . . . not Olivier, she couldn't bring this abomination to him. He hated magic, knew it for a guise of the Evil One.

"I will find you, as you quicken in your new mother's womb, as you love and waste your few years in your new life. I will be in every heartbreak, in every nameless fear in the dark, and I will be part of you, always part of you. Because once you taste darkness you belong to me forever." His words poured over her, rattling her bones and shaking her nails in their beds. His words bled into every hair on her body, crept into her

skin as though they had some power in their own right. The villagers no longer scared her, the inevitability of lifetime after lifetime of being the puppet of something worse than herself, something that with no logic or foreseeable ends who could possess what was left of her soul was beyond comprehensible fear.

She stopped running from the villagers and their bobbing torches. The scent of lavender and wet earth filled her mouth and nose. Her death paraded through the low-crouching lavender bushes in lines through the furrows between cultivated rows. She walked calmly, sure now that death was coming, toward the pear orchard on the far side of the break in the lavender.

His voice followed her. "Your kind are unruly. We like that. Keep trying to make your own choices."

She opened her eyes to Suki coughing meaningfully. Everyone was staring at her with odd expressions, even her traitor friends. She definitely should have listened to Olivier. Oh, this was a deeper game than she could have ever, in five hundred years of Sophieness, guessed. She looked at Norah and felt a ping, a weird ping, and she knew that was something. She would never deny that again, those feelings, her dreams, that she had ignored her entire life. This life.

"Those ain't the ruby slippers." Norah laughed. "And you ain't even in Oz, bitch!" Sophie laughed along with her, at her own stupidity, a stupidity none of them could guess at. She turned her eyes on Suki. Who stared right back. Maybe one person could guess at.

"You shouldn't speak like that, it reinforces stereotypes," Jackie informed Norah haughtily, her best "adult" face twisting her features into a parody of grown-up.

"Wait, what? And who are *you*?" Norah snatched her hand away from Sophie and was clearly about to start a whole episode. Which was tedious to Sophie. Especially now. They had to get out of here, stop Ankou. Stop the cycle she had started—had started twice now. Would she never learn? Was she going to continually be reborn to set Ankou free amongst the humans, for all their silliness—and her own, very much human stupidity—didn't really deserve the God of Death cavorting around in their cities.

Sophie reached out and patted the girl's leg. "Relax, she just likes to annoy people. So how did you all get here?"

"Oh, this is good!" Suki burst out, chuckling softly. Both vampires cut their eyes to her, suspicious. They had always had that personality trait in common.

"That's easy. I asked to come," Amy flipped a braid over her shoulder, looking bored.

"Me too," Jackie said.

"Totally," Huda chimed in.

"What?" Norah looked at Suki then at the girls.

"Okay," Amy began. "I wanted to get this piercing . . ." She pointed at where her adorned belly-button peeked out from beneath her top. "And my dad was all, *What would my boss say if he saw you at Family Day parading around like that?* And my mom was all, *Where do you get these slutty ideas?* and she smacked me. So I went to my room crying and I wrote in my diary how much I hated them and I fell asleep. When I woke up I was here. But not here here, I mean, the Builders made the teepee."

"What?" Norah voiced Sophie's confusion.

"Why are we looking for logic in Fairyland anyway?" Sophie muttered to Norah. She knew better, but she had expected that this girl might have some secret she needed to escape, that her arrival story might help Sophie figure out how to escape.

"No way. Just like that?" Norah asked. "You were mad at your parents and you wished really hard, and then you woke up here?"

"Totally, that's how it works," Huda informed them, one eyebrow raised, as though they were really stupid for not seeing the inherent logic in this method.

"Is that what happened to you?" Sophie turned to Jackie.

"It's magic," Huda explained. Almost laughing, Sophie nodded. Oh, *magic,* of course! What the hell else would it be? But who was she to throw the first bag of plasma at that explanation?

Jackie spread her skirt over her lap. "It didn't happen exactly like that for me. Not *exactly,* I mean, I wanted to go out of town with these friends of mine that my parents never liked. Mama called them trashy, and I always thought that you can't help your family, right? Whatever. So, they wouldn't let me go on the trip and told me if I tried to sneak out I'd have to go stay with my granny, which would be all bible reading and QVC, so I was not about to do it. I wrote it all down in my journal. I went to sleep and then I was here." Sophie saw Suki looking at her fingernails, obviously uninterested.

"We need to head." Suki scooted towards the flap. She looked back at the women. "You need to come with me, you don't belong here. And we have things to do."

And that didn't sound scary, right? Everything was scarier to Sophie now. She knew that was far more horror, evil in the world than them. They were tiny players in a panoply of terror.

"They can stay." All three girls yelled at once. Sophie decided they wanted them to stay way too badly.

Not a good sign. Maybe their main dietary intake was fricasseed vampress?

Sophie headed for the flap, giving her excuses as she did. "The quest and all, gotta keep all that moving along." Which sounded pretty lame even in her head.

"Lame," Norah whispered, laughing slightly. *And thank you for getting my back,* Sophie thought.

Right behind them, the three tweens emerged from the teepee. They hugged the vampires tightly, crying pretty tears in the sunlight as the women took their leave. Sophie was overcome with a floaty vertigo, a sense of wrongness tinged with horrible loss. Suddenly, she recognized Amy.

"Thank you for my gift." Sophie kissed Amy's cheek. "We've met before, haven't we?"

Amy nodded and turned around. Sophie watched her thin back as she re-entered the teepee, Sophie's existence probably already forgotten, and felt Norah's hand on her arm.

Sophie had met Amy, but then she'd had a different name, a different set of abusive parents, and she'd been a meal, long, long ago, when her braids had been longer, her smile shallower. She wondered if this life was some sort of reward for being born a victim more than once. Looking up, she expected her friend to press her about what she'd just said. Instead, she saw that Norah was also discombobulated, but about something else in her own head.

"Thank the gods I never kept a diary as a kid." Suki sighed as they worked their way down the bottle cap path.

"Why? You're here *now,*" Norah said as Sophie goggled at a house constructed of old toilet paper rolls and gumballs set next to one that looked like a replica of a flying saucer. That tableau was doing nothing for her sense of weirdness, but it certainly helped her focus on concrete strangeness and not on her double set of memories . . . Olivier. Her heart thudded and she wanted to run, but that would do no good.

They had to find a way *out*. And Suki clearly had one, so it would be nice if she'd share the information.

Suki snorted. "Yeah, but I'm fully grown, too."

"Oh," Norah said. *Sarcasm*, thought Sophie, *is a fine art, like painting a person's name on a single grain of rice.*

"This is a city of lost children?"

"More like a City of Stolen Slave Children. But they seem happy enough." Suki sounded sort of repulsed.

"They all make bead jewelry? What, for an army of middle-aged white women?" Norah plucked a candy cane off a bush that exuded them. She gave it a lick. "Marshmallow flavor."

"They make everything. The road we walk on." Suki tapped her foot. "Those insane houses." She pointed to a giant papier mache fish. "They weave and forge and build."

"Holy." Norah exhaled a long breath. She dropped her candy cane on the ground, and Sophie fought her reflex to pick up the litter. Vampires did not care about litter. Olivier had always—*always*, Sophie knew now—been sort of interested in garbage, but that was just one of his many oddities. When he was still a fighter, a knight, he used refuse to track, to keep them out of the path of those they wished to avoid.

"How do they know who can make stuff?" Sophie tried to keep herself focused on the here and now. They entered a town center where several boys sat on white and blue ticked mattresses, sewing clothes. Papers fluttered out of the clear blue sky to be engulfed by a blue and white flame sprouting from what would normally be expected to be a fountain.

The boys waved. Sophie waved back. "How do they know who to kidnap? I mean, how do they know who can make things?"

Suki lead them through the boys, then past an exquisite statue of a hummingbird perched on an alabaster peony that marked one of the many paths out of the square.

"Everyone can do something." Three, black, fat, sassy puppies capered by, their tails wagging, their tongues happily lolling out of their mouths. Sophie fought the urge to snuggle them. That would not be badass in the least, but they were very cute. Was she thinking as herself or as who she used to be? She looked behind her and saw Norah was similarly affected by the puppies and smiled.

"Puh-leez. There are lots of losers in the world who can do nothing." Norah messed with her hair in an ineffectual way. "However, I can do origami." She laughed, obviously being stupid.

"There are a group of Fair Ones who only wear dresses made from origami flowers. The kids who make them live on the other side of town." Suki looked over at her with a twinkle in her eye, and Sophie couldn't tell if she was for real or not.

She knew she had at least one talent, though. "I knit."

They passed a row of houses whose doors were painted into the likenesses of different gaping mouths—a monkey, a snake, a pig.

Suki marched on, the line of her back a silent indictment of some sort. Finally she blurted out, "You shouldn't have taken that ring. Didn't you think that was fucked up?"

Sophie's stomach dropped to the bottoms of her feet. Yeah. She did.

"So, weird on what scale? This whole thing is beyond fucked up." As she often managed, Norah's bored tone was at odds with her pointed words.

"That ring is obviously part of the geas. Those children are part of the series of events that have to happen for some plan of Ankou's. I know it." Suki sighed.

Sophie didn't like the sounds of that.

The houses ended at another rectangular arch set in a weird part of the wall constructed of old shoes and straw. Beyond the arch, the bottle cap path ended and an expanse of beautiful, bluish grass began. Sophie wasn't exactly sure she wanted to leave the confines of the city. Who knew what was out there? Paper tigers? Pencils with legs? Voldemort? She—*the ring*— remembered monstrous beasts with multiple heads and sharp teeth, of women who lived in water and ate souls, of fish with legs and lungs.

Suki waved them on, and they followed, Sophie linking an arm into Norah's for support. "Do you think those kids are happy?" She really wondered if anyone could be happy here. But she also knew what it was like to want to escape her life.

"They looked like it. Did you see those freaking teepees from hell?" Norah looked down at Sophie, grinning. "They'll be the cheerleading squad for life. It's better than disappointment that life isn't really all pink sparkles and calling dibs on boys."

Sophie considered that. "But they live in a sweatshop Never Never Land. It sounds great, except the work part, but should we try to save them or something?" This was where she truly knew she was failing as a decent vampire. She was supposed to want to *eat* babies, not save them, she reminded herself. But something about that didn't ring true anymore. She knew that life, especially as a nonhuman, was far more complex than that, that there were many paths, not just one fork.

Suki stopped. "They're happy. Don't worry about that. There're real things to worry about here, those kids aren't one." Uh-oh. Confirmation on something Sophie didn't want to think about.

"I hate kids, let them live in sparkle-covered misery." Norah tried to growl, but it sounded more like indigestion.

"How do you know they're happy?" Sophie didn't like the idea of child labor at the best of times, but child slavery was quite a bit worse.

Suki sighed impatiently, and when Sophie looked over at her, she said, "Because the ones who are unhappy can leave any time they want." Suki started walking again through the hip-high grass parallel to the horizon.

"Is this one of those 'because I say so' things?" Sophie hadn't ever been able to let something go. The savannah rustled around her, long blades of grass rubbing against themselves and sighing with something close to a voice.

"No, they just wish on a shooting star to be home, and they are." That sounded exactly right, so Sophie let it drop even though Norah burst out laughing.

Norah and Suki began a chat about a better surfacing agent for streets than slick, metal bottle caps—the soles of old shoes, credit cards, broken remote controls from televisions—and Sophie examined her feelings as they walked. She realized she was still herself, just herself with some added features, knowledge she couldn't have acquired with five Ph.D.s.

Luc's face suddenly popped into her mind, and she wanted to laugh at her previous reaction to him. She knew him almost as well as herself, or had for many

many years. He was dangerous only to himself, and she knew that the threat she'd seen in him was all in her own mind. The weight of her ring dragged at her hand, familiar and not at the same time. Olivier's face flashed into her mind, the serious, dangerous expression he wore as he told her of his convictions in the Great Gallery, the soft, beautiful elation over her simple conversation with him, the quizzically amused face he wore the first night they met. Not the first night now.

The grass at her side waved of frantically, arresting her steps. She looked down to spy a set of tiny wings bearing an even more miniscule figure. About the size of a chickadee, the body was chubby, naked, and quite blue. It shot out of the grass and buzzed around Sophie's head.

"Hey!" she shouted, and the other women turned to observe Sophie and the source of her distress.

Suki let out a peeved huff. "Just wave it off. Like this." She marched over and swatted the blue cherub with an open hand. It stuck out its tongue and flew off wagging its bottom in the air.

"What the hell was that?" Sophie followed Suki up a slight slope, the ground had turned hilly all of a sudden.

"We think they're some offspring of Krishna's and either a pixie or an insect." The delivery was deadpan, and Sophie accepted it as an honest statement and not a practical joke.

"Krishna?" Then they crested the biggest hill yet, and Sophie's interest in Hindu gods sort of evaporated at the sight that greeted her.

"Hobbitses!" Norah wailed.

The hill on which they stood was just one of many stretching beyond their sight. Each was covered in a waving rainbow of exotic flowers, separated by wide lawns of flat grass crisscrossed with meandering pathways. In the side of most of the hillocks was a recessed door in various shapes from octagons to ellipses.

"This is so cute I might be ill." Sophie caught site of several figures below skipping about, hugging each other, and just basically cavorting.

Suki turned to them and smiled. "Most of my crew lives around here. We play Ultimate, bet on pixie races, have parties, hang with the Fair Ones, you know, just chill." She started down a set of steps worn into the hillside. The others followed, agog. She glanced over her shoulder "And I spent so much time trying to warn you about Ankou's plot. Waste of fucking time."

At the bottom of the steps a path wandered away in several different directions. Suki pointed at each. "Down there are bards and minstrels. That way are poets. There most of the beautiful damsels have a gang, don't go that way; they pull hair." She chose a path she hadn't explained.

"What part of the dell do you live in?" Sophie was kind of surprised that Suki wasn't a beautiful damsel, but then again she didn't seem completely helpless and stupid, but who knows?

Suki laughed and kept walking. She threw over her shoulder "Oh, I live with the rest of the witches."

Chapter Fifteen

THE SIGN READING *Evil, Soul-sucking Magic-Doers Cartel Stay OUT!!!!* over the entrance to the magic ghetto was a little misleading. Sophie thought all the witches were pretty friendly, and the roast unicorn was tasty. They even tended several bloodbloom bushes for magical purposes, which Sophie and Norah were more than pleased to discover.

A huge lawn spread between several of the barrows, for playing Ultimate Frisbee, a game of which always seemed to be on. All of the doors faced in weird directions according to some magical feng shui that one of the male witches had tried to explain in excruciatingly boring detail.

"I missed you." Suki said it like it was the most natural thing in the world. "Now you're different, and so am I." She paused and licked a finger, leaning forward to wipe dirt off Sophie's face. "I knew trying to prevent this from happening wouldn't really work, but I had to try."

"What is actually happening?" said Sophie.

"It doesn't matter now. Ankou is free and you're here," replied Suki. Sophie scowled at her.

"You said that all we had to do to get back is wish on a falling star. How hard can that be?"

"What, are you stupid? Did you wish to be here in the first place? There are different rules for everyone." Suki rolled her eyes, and Sophie felt her teeth start to shift, felt violence well up inside her, and she clenched her fists.

"Listen," she said to Suki, "I need to get back to planet Earth—to my mother and *your* freaking cat, and the fucking zombies that Norah conjured up, and—"

"Chill *out*," said Suki, and she didn't look at all perturbed at Sophie's vampire visage, which just pissed Sophie off even more. "There's a whole *thing*," she added. "You'll see. I think because of the geas I can send you home. There's no way your part in that is done. So we'll try this whole system I know. I think it will work, since the most unlikely things are the most reasonable when someone is set upon by a geas."

That didn't do much to calm Sophie down. She studied Suki more closely. She was attractive with a heart shaped face and full lips, freckles sprinkled under her almond-shaped eyes along her cheekbones and wavy hair cut chin-length.

This was her friend—her real friend—but there was far more at play now than their shared history, which for both of them was now just a small part of their lives.

Sophie was way creeped out. "How did you get here?"

Suki tilted her head. "A spell gone very wrong, but I don't think it was an accident. I've spent a lot of time thinking about that. When I found out about Ankou and his crazed plot to escape . . ."

"How did you find out about that?"

"Seriously, the Fair Ones have no shame and they're totally sure of themselves. Ankou tells everyone about it all the time. It's not like it's a secret. I heard him talking about you."

Sophie boggled at this. Everything here was counter-intuitive. Maybe fairies were the inspiration for stupid movie plotlines where the villains confess their entire, complex plot to the hero when they capture him.

"But how did you find out the rest?"

Suki screwed up her face. "Well, duh, I asked him."

"Um, okay." Sophie was still overwhelmed by the hundreds of years of new memories, and she was starting to feel like her brain was going to explode. "Won't you get in trouble trying to thwart Ankou's whole big plan thing?"

Suki shook her head and sighed. "Don't you get it yet? This is all part of his plan. I mean, why else would I end up here? Why right at the time you were going to be vamped? Jimbo, this guy I know, he's sort of an expert on curses, hexes, jinxes and geas, he told me not to bother trying to help you, that I'd just end up pushing the geas forward. Blah. I think he was right. Besides they aren't our bosses, I mean they don't think like us. We do what we want here."

Finally Sophie decided to drop it, and said, "What can you tell me about the Fair Ones?"

An excited smile lit Suki's face. "Well, the Fair Ones live for eternity, so it gets boring. Like they're always coming up with ways to wreak havoc amongst humans and other fey creatures. Starting wars, inventing cults, encouraging interbreeding between humans and nonhumans, leading people into untimely deaths. I mean, why do you think you're here?"

That all sounded very bad for anyone that wasn't a fairy. "To get my memory back. So that Ankou can win

because of me. So that I know he won." It came out almost as a whisper as Sophie became afraid again.

Her smile faded, and Suki bit her bottom lip.
"Pretty much. He's evil. More evil than the rest of
them. Which is why your old companion bound him,
long ago, after you died before. You weren't there
then, you were long dead, but your companion bound
Ankou so that he couldn't escape into the human
world." Suki tilted her head to the side. "But when she
died, when the body that cast the binding on him died,
he knew it. He knew he could try to escape again,
even though her spirit would be reborn. He hates her,
for binding him, but he wants to destroy you. Why?
Who knows."

Infinity yawned at her feet again. Sophie looked at
Norah who was dancing with a warlock, her hair bobbing around her elated face. *Rosamund*. And *Phillippa*.
Two souls together again—with Olivier and Luc, they
were back to being a foursome.

She should have seen it, should have known it right
from the beginning. She felt stupid—and then reminded herself that it was easy to understand when
everything was explained by a magic ring. There
wasn't a reason why she should have put the pieces together before. Who woke up in the morning and
thought, *I am the reborn soul of a crazy vampire's life-
mate*? No one, that was who. Except for maybe some
people on thorazine in the psych ward.

"When did she die?" whispered Sophie.

"I'm not sure. I just know that it had to be both of
you." Suki stood up.

"He will make it worse for her. Because she pro-
tected me, bound him." Sophie wanted to cry. Why did
everything have to be so horrible? A part of her oldest
self whispered that Olivier should have been able to

save them, that was his job. How much horror had Ankou done in the human world already?

Her face softening again, Suki reached out a hand and patted Sophie, wrapped her hand around Sophie's. "It's too late to worry about how many people Ankou has tricked into suicide or falling in front of a truck. Obviously, you're on a quest now to bring him back here and win something for yourself in the process."

"Win what for myself?" Her voice was soft, whispered.

"A chance to be happy again? To live your life for yourself, not for a dead religion or to further the plots of the King of Death?" She smiled, tried to be comforting, then turned and tugged Sophie with her.

A barrow with a leaf-shaped door nearby was filled to overflowing with witches merrily getting their mead and dance on. Norah was dancing with a witch who was taller than she was, and had blond hair down to her ankles. They waved at the two women as Suki led Sophie around the party and towards a narrow valley between two other mounds. Fiddle and fife and drum flowed over her and Sophie couldn't help but dance a few of her steps, laughing with a strange euphoria. Several of the partyers pointed at her and beckoned her over, but Suki grabbed her arm.

"Hey! Back up off my vampire! Do you have the other one in there?" Suki arrested her forward motion, and Sophie did a long-forgotten tap-ball-chain in the grass, laughter tumbling from her mouth that seemed to motivate the handsome band all the more. "Hey! I'm frickin' serious here!" Suki punctuated that pointing her finger around at anyone who moved.

One of the pipers broke off a long trill and waded back into the burrow with a frown. Sophie happily danced on, tap dancing away, thinking of Christmas with her family, Olivier inexplicably present, of home-made pecan pie and seven-layer cookies and fresh nutmeg in homemade eggnog. Of her father, not dead, not in the ground—with her, dancing with her.

She gazed up at the turquoise and fuchsia sky, watching as a heron-shaped cloud floated over-head, her feet keeping time with the music, and she day-dreamed on, imagining everyone she loved deeply and genuinely happy, and the lights on the Christmas tree glimmering in all their wonky glory. She remembered carols in the snow, the moon shattered on the snow in endless white light, Olivier singing in her ear, his breath puffing into crystal clouds.

A hand grabbed one of hers, and her eyes floated from the sky to the burrow to Suki's reddened, angry face, to Norah tugging her into another dance, an impromptu waltz.

"They have Turkish Delight in there, and fairy cakes and ambrosia, and impossibly beautiful people." Norah smiled, full and red and white and lurid in the bright daylight. Sophie let her lead the dance, with Suki prodding them through the valley between the hillock homes.

"You can buy Turkish Delight anywhere." Sophie had tried it several times, just to make sure she hated it. "It's icky licorice."

"No, not that shit! The real thing! It tasted like dreams and hope." Excitement and pleasure fluttered around Norah's words, and Sophie believed her about the candy.

Oddly, she began to feel less like dancing at exactly the same instant that Norah halted in mid-turn, dropping her arms from the rigid form of the dance. "This is eff-ed up." Her face scrunched up in an attempt at a frown, but her ebullient mood somehow prevented a peeved expression.

"What the crap just happened?" Norah bitched. Sophie disengaged completely from her. "What is this crap? Okay, why can't I say curse words, drat this hoopla!" Her voice remained cheerful through her negative comments, a smile firmly on her face.

"See what crap?" Sophie experimented with the cursing.

"Oh, heck no!" Norah pointed at Suki who strode away from them into an open area between several burrows.

They followed her. "She was doing the cabbage patch inside," Suki shot over her shoulder as she walked. Sophie elbowed Norah in the side laughing hysterically.

"I will love you and hug you." Norah snickered. "What? That's not what I meant!"

"It's the spell they cast on you freaks," Suki didn't even bother to look over her shoulder at them. "You're happy and can't curse, can't do harm to others, there are several riders. The guys are still experimenting with it."

They emerged completely from the valley, and Sophie felt her jubilant mood evaporate immediately. Fear and anxiety and an underlying hostility reasserted themselves.

Norah let out a long sigh as though all the forced cheer had been almost too much to bear. Scoping out the hollow where they stood, the vampires really couldn't miss the honkingly huge copper cauldron situated in the exact center. The cauldron that Suki made a direct line for and stood next to with her hands on her hips.

"That stuff is better than smack. You could sell it and clear up inner-city problems." Norah's face was serious and considering as she spoke.

"Yeah, heard all that hippie stuff before." Suki patted the rim of the cauldron. "Okay, hop on in and get out of here. You wanted to leave; here's your thing to go."

"Isn't that kind of . . . easy?" said Sophie dubiously.

"Easy? I'm not even sure this will work. I mean, it might. You also might end up in Nepal, or worse France. Maybe even another dimension. I'm just hoping that Ankou has rigged everything up so that whatever I do will send you home. I figure that's how things are working now." Suki frowned at Sophie. "Don't put your vamp face on. You know it's true. Put your teeth back where they belong and get your ass to earth. Didn't I tell you you're on a quest now? You have to live through the geas, figure it out. That's the only reason you can leave here. If you weren't cursed, you'd be stuck."

"I don't want to be on a quest," said Sophie, and she knew she sounded petulant, but she didn't care.

"You have to be on a quest because you are the idiot who didn't listen to my warnings. Although I guess you were never going to listen to my warnings because that's both of our fates." Suki shook her head. "Go find a magician or a wizard and bind him up again. Go on. Hop in."

Pointing as she spoke, Norah scoffed. "Hop in?"

Stepping forward, Sophie examined the etchings around the side of the huge pot. Apples, grapes, pears, bananas, every kind of fruit imagined or real rioted around the rim. The next band of images depicted capering men and women next to vivisected corpses, one after another in an unbroken chain, one body touching the next. She touched one of the dismembered etchings.

"This is Cauldron of Plenty." She looked hard at Suki who didn't blink, then leveled herself up with her barely utilized vampiric strength and hopped into the bowl. Norah's shouts and screams chased her down, down as she tumbling into blackness, echoing off the dented metal of the conduit between worlds as she fell forever, fell and kept falling.

Chapter Sixteen

FALLING OUT OF thin air onto a maple floor can take a lot out of anyone, even a rapid-healing, generally physically impervious vampress. Writhing into an almost sitting position, Sophie rubbed the back of her head gently, feeling out the lump that, if she were human, probably could have killed her. The bone was slightly cracked, a fact she noted as her skull began to knit itself back together. Both of her elbows and her tailbone had absorbed the remaining momentum that her head had barely arrested.

She groaned in the sort of self-pitying fashion that she generally reserved for high drama or moments of pathetic self-indulgence. Squeezing her eyes shut, she gasped as the blood vessels in her tailbone began a very painful healing process.

"Here, let me help."

Her eyes snapped open at Olivier's voice. His face was its normal mix of elusive and genuine, a small smile lifting one corner of his mouth. Sophie was beyond dissembling and hauling her own, sad carcass off the glassy wooden plank floor. Her pulse fluttered irregularly in her throat as she looked at him, so very glad he was there. Would he know that she remembered him, see it in her eyes? She flipped through her memories for incidents of mind-reading and only came up with superstition and sorcery.

She began to offer her hand, but as she did, Olivier snatched at her wrist and lifted her fingers to his face; all traces of his smile fled, the alienating coldness from the Great Gallery returned. Her smile died stillborn.

"Where did you come by this?" His voice rumbled low, the cracked whisper making the hair on the back of her neck raise and her nipples to harden but at the same time raising an answering anger in her chest. It was hers!

And he had done next to nothing to prevent her trip to the Fairylands, to protect her and Norah, to teach them what they needed to know. She could have easily died ten times over from lack of the knowledge that he had, that she had now, and the hundreds' of years worth of more that he had she didn't.

"A child gave it to me." Her voice matched his, the whisper seemingly yanked from her throat by his unblinking stare, the tremor in it not nervousness but anger. He didn't know her that well, didn't know Sophie, and that's who she still was. Sophie with memories of another life, another life that was hers and not at the same time.

"A changeling child who was one of three?" The tips of his fingers dug into her wrist, and she tugged her arm back towards her body. His grip only tightened, making her madder.

This was hardly the strangest situation she'd been in recently—Olivier's intent gaze, his tight mouth, the unspoken threat in the tension in his muscles all tilted Sophie into rage.

"There was a prophecy? There was a *prophecy*! And you told me nothing!" she yelled. Olivier blushed a little, looked uncomfortable, and that just made Sophie angrier, because he *knew* that he hadn't handled this shit right and he wasn't going to apologize. "You said nothing while you waited and kept silent and let everything play out? You could have prevented this—"

She was just getting her flow going as a *whoosh* sounded from the ceiling and distracted her.

Norah drifted like a feather from the ceiling, hair trailing lower than her body, back in the clothes she'd worn when they had crossed over, instead of fairy saris. Sophie looked down at her own clothes to see they were jeans and a pink sweater, as Norah swung herself forward when she neared the ground, and landed lightly on her feet.

Gaping at her, Sophie let Norah help her off the floor. "How did you *do* that?"

"Unlike you, I asked Suki for directions and a small tutorial on the whole cauldron thingy." Norah fluffed her hair, and then roughly dusted off Sophie's clothes with the flat of her palm.

"Lay off! I'm the walking wounded here." Scrabbling away, Sophie bumped into Olivier who steadied her without remark. She was glad of that, because she'd hate to have to open a can of whoopass on him in front of her friend who would mock her for it . . . forever.

Suddenly, Sophie's new lifespan—deathspan?—didn't seem like a cool thing at all.

"I can't believe you just landed on your feet and I broke my tailbone." She spoke to Norah, but her eyes never left Olivier's face. His eyes narrowed slightly and the corners of his mouth hardened.

"You deserve what you get for being stupid. Who wants a drink?" Norah sauntered out of the parlor, obviously not impressed with the trip to Fairyland and the subsequent exit. "Screw all this quest shit."

Sophie's anger hadn't really dissipated. She was good at masking her emotions from Norah, for a short time anyway, to save herself from long conversations about things Sophie would rather bury. Like her father's death, like her lack of a love life. The second part had been rectified anyway.

"And what're you doing here anyway?" she tossed at him as she shuffled out of the room, intending the salvo as a blistering commentary on both his continued existence and invasion of her ersatz home.

She, unfortunately for everyone's safety, heard him following her. Not with the click of a step or creak of a floorboard but the soft shh-shh of his clothes rubbing against themselves and the steady burr of his breathing. The pattern of his breathing was rapid and through his mouth, and she knew without thought that he was confused and worried. He *should* be worried, with Ankou loose and the way he'd screwed this up.

Sophie felt slightly guilty about being so mad at him, but not enough to apologize or try to make up in any way. Why couldn't he be more consistently proactive? Probably because he'd been conditioned to let the women in his life lead from the cradle. She had faint memories of his mother's towering personality, of her own easy manipulation of him in another life.

Olivier followed them into the kitchen, where Norah was mixing up a batch of *mojitos* with extra lime. Olivier grabbed her arm, turned her around physically, and when she stared at him—glared at him, really—she realized that he looked worried, that he looked angry, that he looked annoyed, that there were all kinds of emotions flying across his face . . . emotions he was allowing her to be privy to.

"I am glad for your safety," he said to her in a low tone.

"Puke," said Norah. Sophie shushed her, didn't break eye contact with Olivier.

"Suki is there," she told him, feeling all of her anger draining away. "She wants to stay."

"That is how it often is with those who are marginalized and pushed aside in this life." Olivier nodded, and his firm grip on her arm turned into a caress. Sophie felt her nipples harden as his thumb swept over the vein located right below the skin on the inside of her wrist. Her heartbeat slowed, matched with his; his pupils dilated and his mouth parted and suddenly she was aware of his every breath, movement, every moment of his existence.

"I'll miss her," said Sophie.

"There are ways," replied Olivier.

"You two are seriously making me sick," said Norah from behind Sophie. "I hate you," Sophie said to him, ignoring Norah. "I hate this."

"I have felt it for a thousand years, two hundred lifetimes, and will feel it for a thousand, five thousand, ten thousand more," said Olivier. He pulled his hand away from hers, turned sharply and left the kitchen. As his hand slipped from hers, he left slip of paper. A poem was scribbled in smudged pencil.

Words drop and dip like freeze frame
meaning evaporating as breath meets the air.
You speak and I think of Toulouse.
I speak and you think of dying.
We construct each other in the dead spaces,
*   the silence between the words.*

Sophie closed her eyes and breathed through her nose, and *felt* Olivier leave Paul's house. She stuck the paper in her pocket, not wanting to deal with who she knew he really was.

"You two are nauseating. *Los Vampiros* ain't got no plotlines like this," said Norah, and pushed a glass into Sophie's hand. Sophie drained it without pausing for breath.

"He loves me," she said to Norah.

"Duh, idiot," replied Norah. "Even the zombies knew that."

"But . . ." Sophie stared into her glass. Norah slid an arm around her neck and an arm around her waist and pulled until they were flush against each other. Sophie breathed in the scent of Norah, underlaid with blood and magic, and let her head fall back to Norah's shoulder.

"But nothing," said Norah into Sophie's ear. Love and friendship coursed around them like a protective blanket—okay, maybe Norah was kind of a sociopath, but at least Sophie could trust her to be there when Sophie needed her. "But this is the kind of thing you dreamed about as a kid, don't shit us both by denying it. I know you, Soph, and—"

"We've known each other for a thousand years."

"I ain't getting you killed in this lifetime, bitch," said Norah, and there was none of Rosamund in her voice.

"How did you know?" asked Sophie, twisting to look at her. She was stunned, for a moment, by Norah's beauty, the smooth skin stretched over perfectly symmetrical bones.

"Luc told me, of course. You mean Olivier didn't tell you?" Norah snorted, stepped back, and poured herself another drink.

"What?" Sophie blinked, tried to reconcile the information.

"Yeah," said Norah. "First he made a tree dance, then he taught me some magic, then we conjured up my soul and examined all my past lives. It was a fucking hoot."

Sophie looked at the empty glass in her hand, then pointedly at Norah's pitcher. Norah took the hint and poured her another drink, and Sophie took a sip before she said, "Okay, first of all, I won't rip your throat out for not telling me all this."

"Whatever, like I knew about the fairies and shit? I just knew that we were crazy religious cult freaks, with Kool-Aid and everything."

"There was no Kool-Aid in the Middle Ages," said Sophie dryly, and took another sip of her drink. "What about the geas, does Luc know that we're somehow cursed and bound to Ankou?"

"Yeah, whatever," said Norah, and waved a perfectly manicured hand. "I don't even know what "geas" means. Cursed does not sound good, though."

"Yeah, whatever," mimicked Sophie. Internally she agreed wholeheartedly that cursed did not sound good. Cursed sounded very bad, and a curse that was tied to their souls, that followed them from life to life sounded particularly bad. "So tell me, what else do you know about this that I don't? And since you know everything—does Olivier love *me*, or does he love Phillippa?"

"Can't the man love you both? Dumb-ass," said Norah, and turned away to cut another lime.

Sophie's gaze followed her, dropped to the counter to watch her deftly wield the knife and slice a lime in half, and then her gaze traveled to a desiccated pod resting on the countertop.

"Tell me that isn't what I think it is," she said, and finished her drink again, needing the layer of disconnection the alcohol would give her.

Norah looked up and held Sophie in place with her eyes, concerned friend left behind. Her eyes were total vamp sociopath, uncaring of the human elements.

"So we can sell this to all the other vamps," she said as she stirred the huge pitcher of rum mixed with mint and limes. The spatula clinked against the sides of the crystal pitcher; with every clink, Sophie winced, expecting the delicate crystal to break. "Don't worry," Norah continued, "we'll hook ourselves up first."

She winked at Sophie, who was mystified, and poured another round of the drinks up, adding more lime into the one for herself.

"What are you talking about? Is that a bloodbloom pod?" She pointed. This had the makings of a scheme. Sophie wasn't in the mood for a scheme; her life was screwed up enough. So, Norah's new plan was to become vampire hustlers slinging vamp-crack to the masses? That could only go wrong about ten million ways. Even if it did have potentiality for limitless amounts of cash or services that didn't involve violence or bloodshed.

Plus, they kind of had a pressing mission on their hands here, what with their curse and the evil fairy king and all.

"Yup." Norah handed Sophie her drink and watched as she drank it all in two gulps and handed her glass back for more.

"Where did you get it?" Swigging down her second drink, Sophie looked behind her for Olivier, but he didn't appear.

"Suki gave it to me." The world's allotment of smug was being sucked up by Norah at that moment.

"She did? How come?" Norah was entirely too good at getting people to do what she wanted. Sophie stared at her wondering if she had extra vampish powers that Sophie didn't. Then she decided that it had nothing to do with being a vampire in the least—with the exception of the Paul situation, Norah had always been able to get people to do what she wanted.

Norah shrugged. "I asked."

That was nowhere near the whole story, but whatever. "Uh, yeah I heard somewhere that could work." Sophie held out her glass for another drink. Sophie turned and looked at the empty doorway. "So she's staying."

"*Yeah.*" There was a tone there. A tone that told Sophie that Norah had tried to reason with her, to bring her back, to cajole, but that Suki was Suki. Or maybe not so much anymore, Sophie thought. How long had she been in the fairylands? More than thirty years, she had said—was that long enough to become a different person? Long enough to have better friends, more important things to do than hang out and shop and have cocktail hour or play in a band? Sophie felt a sharp thorn of regret in her chest. They should have tried harder to find her. Sophie should have tried harder to find her; she'd known it was something supernatural and she hadn't tried hard enough.

But Suki hadn't wanted to be found. Sophie considered that too. It was so easy for Sophie and Norah to leave Fairyland—how come Suki couldn't have just jumped into the cauldron herself, found them, warned them, and then gone back to be a servant to the Fair Ones, or whatever she'd been doing? It was all just as much Suki's fault as it was Olivier's; Sophie decided that she didn't actually need to take any of the blame at all.

Norah pulled a rock, a tiny cauldron the color of

dried mud, and a lock of black hair tied with a sad piece of blue string from her pocket. "We mix all of this whacked-out shit together and stick the pod in it, and tomorrow we'll have magic blood."

Sophie kept silent. Sathan padded in to twist around her feet as Norah assembled the ingredients for her grow operation. When Sophie looked down at him, he made his disdain for Norah and Sophie quite clear with a snotty "Meow."

"Shut up, you," said Sophie. Sathan turned and lifted his tail into the air, and licked the side of the mojito pitcher, where a thin trickle of the alcohol was dripping.

Her eyes swept over the counter, watching Norah's strong, brown fingers manipulate her accoutrements, and she noticed there was something out of place. An ancient book, mottled with mold spots. It smelled like cat butt when Sophie picked it up and started flipping through it. A scrawling, heavy script bled over yellowed, vellum pages in untidy lines of undecipherable text.

"Read it." Clink, click, Norah planted her bloom, demanding Sophie perform like an academic trained pony.

She tried but rapidly assessed that she didn't recognize the words. "Uh, do you think I read every single language you can't?" That was a rhetorical question.

"Yeah." Norah maintained the straight face of the truly flummoxed—or consummate joker.

"Okay, just so we're clear: Latin, Greek, some Romance languages, Finnish, Russian, no gibberish." Sophie wanted to mock more, but she was distracted thinking about Olivier and his consistently bizarre behavior. Because he had obviously left this book. He had probably been trying to find a way to rescue them. Rescue was definitely in his repertoire. The literal knight savior.

A knight in dented and scuffed armor with a serious

addiction to blood, and that was perfect for Sophie's dented life.

Where was he anyway? She figured he'd have followed them into the kitchen to lecture them on their stupidity. Maybe it was time to demand that guidebook from him.

"I always wondered what gibberish looked like written." Acting like she was truly interested, Norah leaned in closer, and suddenly flipped the page. "Hold up, look at this shit! It's Crazy Elf Guy!"

And, indeed, in pen and ink, it was. High cheekbones, wild hair flying in a textual mariah, long fingers pointing, it was definitely Ankou.

"Where did that book come from? Is Paul secretly a wizard? Why was he reading about Ankou?" Norah scanned her eyes around the kitchen looking for more evidence of the arcane arts, and accidentally summoned Paul himself.

"How can I serve?" His flushed cheeks and tousled hair made his sea-green eyes appear all the more gorgeous, causing Sophie to grow really uncomfortable. She was a complete slut now. Every hot guy that crossed her path was within her grasp; she could have anyone she wanted, and her body knew it. Her treacherous body.

Sophie wondered how vampires worked relationships. Were they monogamous? Did they have big, epic, vampire love? She kind of wanted big, epic, vampire love with Olivier—or, at least, she got really annoyed when she thought that maybe he'd have sex with someone else. Was that love? It was better than anything else she could think of to feel about him. Sophie tried to remember how they were in the past, call something up on marriage or monogamy—and got nothing. She had been on a mission in her other life, trying to protect and then resurrect the religion she and all her people had died for. There hadn't been much time for casual sex after she'd been turned.

Sophie was disappointed.

Paul made a small sound, almost a chuckle, and Sophie narrowed her eyes at him. His lips were set in an unusual twist, maybe a smile, maybe an approbation towards them for something. Something was wrong here. Maybe the thralling was wearing off and his natural haughtiness was returning?

To further unsettle her, he reached out and flicked Norah's hair out of her face for her, pushing a corkscrew curl behind her ear, smiling slightly.

Sophie watched that with a weird flutter in her stomach, fear. "Seriously, you haven't, you know, *used* him in any way?" She probably should have asked Norah that before, but she hadn't been able to do it.

"Don't make me puke up my drinks." Norah turned to Paul. "Speaking of which, make us more drinks, bitch!"

Paul burst into life—no, Paul lost all semblance of life. It creeped Sophie out. His huge hands deftly squeezed two limes at once, but his expression was flat, hard, no hint of smile anymore.

"So, your boyfriend was here while we were gone, researching ways to save you," said Norah, watching Paul.

Sophie blushed at the comment and averted her face to watch Paul to disguise it. Sudden exhaustion tugged her towards an immobile state. Her body wilted into submission toward sleep, with lazy eyelids, chin tucked to chest, and fingers relaxed into a curl. The one-sided conversation from her friend plucked at her hair, teased her with single words like "import", "magic beans", and "empire". The calming, familiar voice broke off, and Norah barked "Go to bed, idiot."

Sophie complied, but not without serious effort. Every step of the staircase applied to be her last, offering to let her sleep there for the day. She lumbered on, clutching at the banister. Her bedroom was the closest to the stairs or else she might have slept on the landing. The duvet caved in the middle and plumped around her body as she landed. Dreams met her as her hair settled around her face.

Chapter Seventeen

SOPHIE DREAMED.

Green, living notes from a harp's strings darted into the room. Somewhere outside, a child called to another, their voices unknown and neither male nor female, just young. Hands holding several scraps of parchment rested in a linen-covered lap. The fingers move on command, her lap. The fingers raise the scraps of paper to present writing:

I've made this rhyme completely free
of sense—it's not of you and me,
or youth, or doings he-and-she,
or springtime thoughts.
It came to me while I was sleeping
on my horse.
What planet ruled when I was born?
I'm native here and still feel foreign.
Can't be contented, or forlorn,
or change myself:

*I was the midnight work of freaking
magic elves.*

The script bled on the edges with a familiar, heavy hand pushing a dull quill. Bits of paper slid and skittered to the stone floor unexpectedly as the body pushed forward and stood. *Did I want to stand?* The thought formed and fled. Feet carried the body to the window, and the hands rested on a dark, scarred, wooden sill and pulled shutters inward to let the eyes peer outside. Fruit trees and moonlight and the scent of dirt and sap and roses. Light fired the dark heart of the ruby on one finger, broke the white light into bloody prisms. An edge of a white veil fluttered out of the window, riding the summer scents and false brightness of the moon.

"You were in my papers again," said the voice, the voice that matched the scrawling letters.

The body turned, and the eyes saw a well-loved face, a warrior with more love than hatred in his broken breast and poems choking his throat.

Her mouth moved. "I won't evade my path. We invoked the fairy. We must abide what our actions bring."

The face fell from pleasure to rigid blankness. "Your life is your own to escape or live as you choose, but I would live out a full one with you and die not because of the vengeance brought by a creature we could kill."

Anger pressed against the interior of the body, thrum, thrum, breaking through the strange fog. "Fate has played with us since before our births. I will not leave Rosamund alone to deal with what we have done in concert."

Hate and anger and love erupted from some hard, secret place inside the body and smoke clogged the throat, burnt the eyes, and caused the nose to run. Smoke so thick it wouldn't allow enough breath for a scream.

* * *

ROLLING OFF THE mattress and hitting the scratchy Berber carpet, Sophie sucked lungful after lungful of air into her chest fast enough to spur hyperventilation. Tiny, short bursts of air flooded her mouth but barely made it to her lungs. To calm herself she imagined the smell of sugar cookies, the shimmer of fresh snow in the full moon, her mother singing the wrong lyrics to songs on the radio. Her breathing settled into an almost normal rhythm. Hair clung to her face and she reached her hand up to brush it away and caught the heavy ring in it. She didn't have to look down at it to know it was the exact ring from the dream.

Because the dream wasn't a dream at all.

It was a memory of the aftermath of what had set everything, *everything*, that she was living now into motion. She and Rosamund—Norah—scouring the countryside for alchemists and sorcerers, conjurors and true villains, anyone who claimed to control souls. They wanted a spell, any spell, that could cast across the world and seek the souls they could not find. Couldn't find after five hundred years! They had struggled for so long, so very long, seeking as far as the icy wastelands of the far north, for nothing.

Rosamund had said "They think us witches, then let us be witches." The alchemist told them only fairies could do the magic they needed. Only a Lord of the Fey could search all the souls of the living in a blink of an eye and tell them what they wanted to know.

How ignorant they were. The fear was right there again, Sophie tasted it in the back of her throat. They summoned Ankou, and instead of giving them anything, he set his sights on them, wanted to mark them, own them, set to work as puppets, slaves. He offered them nothing but slavery or death. Her own anger had been the match of Rosamund's, the fact that their tampering with evil had led to nothing, to worse than nothing, to unleashing something horrible into the world.

His banishing had unleashed the chaos that caused her—*Phillippa's*—burning, Ankou's curse on her—*on Phillippa*—for defying him, for not loving him at first sight and bowing to his will.

She pulled herself into a semblance of calm and took herself into the bathroom for a shower. She always thought best when she was doing something else, something that would allow her mind to enter into the repetition of a task. Sophie turned on the hot water, lathered her body with her favorite frou-frou soap from Lush, and let her mind examine the situations.

Who had left the ring in the Fairyland? Rosamund, surely, but how had she known? As Sophie washed her hair, all that long blond and red hair, heavy with water, pulling her head back, straining her neck, she wondered if there was another piece of the puzzle to unlock Norah's memories, surely Rosamund learned how to bind Ankou for good if she planted the ring.

The ring tangled in her hair and the pain distracted her for a moment, but she didn't want to take it off. She wanted to keep it with her, because what if once she took it off, she lost all the memories it had allowed her to regain? Were they even her memories, by rights belonging to her?

The ring had been from Ankou himself, so that when he set his long-planned revenge into motion she would know why, remember everything, and he could relish it more. That seemed like a very human motivation, though. Human, vampire, same thing in those thought patterns.

But fairies didn't think like people in any way, as

different in intelligence as those who believed in angels thought them.

Sophie turned off the water and stepped out of the shower, wrapping a huge, soft bath sheet around her body. Another plus to Paul's house: no old, frayed, rough towels. She wrapped another sheet around her hair, turban-style, and began rubbing lotion into her skin.

Revenge plots usually backfired. Sophie could hear Olivier in her head, saying it calmly, as though he didn't know she'd done all this before. If only Olivier had explained things! Norah would not have listened, but Sophie would have. Maybe enough to stop Norah from enthralling Paul—maybe not, but Sophie would have been *prepared*, could have confronted Luc and Olivier with her knowledge, made them put in safeguards—would have insisted that she not be bound to Paul as Norah was.

That thought stopped Sophie's thoughts cold, and she stared at herself in the mirror, wondered who she had become with this vampire blood, this—this *midnight work*, like in her dreams, changing her into a being who—*that*, a being *that* would kill *its* best friend to stop this death fairy.

Because Sophie *knew* that was important. It was important that she was no longer human, because a human binding another human would never have drawn the interest of Ankou. No, Ankou must have realized it only when the mystical forces—Sophie snickered at herself, but allowed her mind to continue—showed him another mystical being creating a vacuum. So he could control Paul enough to send the invitation, could control Paul from Fairyland, and that could be bad. It would be bad, Sophie knew it, knew it like she knew she'd lived before, lived several times, knew it like she knew, now, that the devotion she'd had to her belief system when she lived as Phillippa did no one any good.

Paul was the conduit. Sophie thought of the night before, of Paul's odd expressions when he was first summoned, before he had been instructed to do anything more than appear . . .

Sophie suddenly pieced it together. Ankou was inside Paul. Normally her insightful intellectual leaps were only employed to academia, but she had been in school her entire life, she wasn't slow.

The very idea of it made her blood feel cold. She shivered, and returned to the bedroom.

The overhead light came on with the flick of the wall switch, illuminating all the details of the room she had yet to notice in her exhaustion of the morning. The duvet cover on the expensive, down comforter was her own—a pink and black kimono pattern her sister had sent her from Tokyo the year before. The hula boy lamp from the flea market sat on the table by the bed. The walls rioted in zombie-inspired juxtaposition with all the artwork that had lain on the floor of her bedroom unhung.

With a flash of odd inspiration, Sophie remembered the Angel-Tree cards in the pocket of her coat at the exact same instant she realized she needed some comfort. She wanted to get a Christmas tree. A white, flocked, tacky-as-hell, just like her grandma always had, Christmas tree. Good excuse to see Olivier and lay her theories on him about Paul. She felt like she needed an excuse. Not that she didn't have a good *reason*.

As she dressed, she considered her options. She didn't fool herself into believing she could rip Norah away from her pet planet/new criminal enterprise to research exiling Paul into the Fairyland. Would Norah even let her? Would she laugh that Sophie was completely insane? What if Ankou was running around the city somewhere masquerading as Paul? He could use Paul to kill them at any time. When they slept, or through poison, the possibilities were endless. Unless what Ankou wanted was more complex, slavery, mind-control, yeah, that sounded more logical. He wanted to use them in some plot to take over the world.

Sophie was glad that Norah was just Norah and not Rosamund when that thought struck. Norah could be a bitch, but she didn't have any hardcore magical abilities . . . but Luc did. Okay, there was far too much co-incidence converging for her to cope. The only real option was to call Olivier and pretend like it was natural to ask him for cash and company and lay the reality of the situation out on him. Besides, she had taken those Angel-Tree cards, and she might be a murderer, but she wouldn't disappoint children at Christmas no matter what sort of creeping crisis they were about to be confronted with.

She felt a serious pang of regret that she had been so nervous that day and had taken those cards. There were real issues to deal with here; her life was bigger now somehow than random acts of charity. When she thought that, she checked herself. Was that some sort of evil creeping up on her? First she was considering killing her best friend by killing her best friend's thralled zombie-guy, and now she was considering cheating some poor ghetto children out of their Christmas gifts.

When she shelved the self-exploration over her po-tentially evil self, she realized she was singularly lack-ing in a phone number for Olivier. Did he even have a phone? He was really weird, so maybe not. She would have to show up at his door and hope that he didn't have anything better to do than hit the toy store. Were vampires morally opposed to charity?

She thought hard, focused on the ring, and she could remember Olivier giving alms, bread, possessions to the indigent. Charity was definitely fine by him. She was a little more concerned that he might not want to fork over any cash without a whole conversation as to why she expected him to do so. Would he accept "Well, you're old, feel the gender stereotypes"?

For a second, she thought about waking Norah and asking her to jack money from Paul's bank account for her, but then recognized that as the red-herring for avoiding Olivier that it was. Maybe Sophie wasn't the most courageous woman alive, but she wasn't going to avoid a guy just because she remembered loving him like no other, just because she remembered another life when he and the Good God were her whole existence, just because she could remember *this* life, his bed, the calluses on his fingertips, the spiciness of his mouth, his tongue rough on her body, *in* her body—

Sophie took a long, shaking breath, and decided to avoid the zombies milling around in the kitchen. It meant forgoing coffee, but she could get some on the way.

Dressed in comfortable yet chic boots and jeans and an old, pink sweater with a black poodle design on the bottom left corner that her aunt had knit her, Sophie was ready to do good for the better of the humanity from which she now sucked the life-blood. She also had plans for side orders of tree-getting and fairy-thwarting.

By thinking hard about them, she instinctively knew that Norah was still asleep and that Paul wasn't in the house. She focused even harder, but couldn't locate Luc—and she didn't really care. That stupid alchemist should have known better, should have warned her, even if Olivier hadn't. He'd always been the practical joker, had always lured she and Rosamund—*Norah*—and Olivier into his bizarre plans.

Sathan sat next to the front door when she walked up to grab her coat, hat, and scarf from the one of the pegs on the wall of the foyer. His green eyes flashed reflective silver, making him look like a demon. He meowed loudly, protesting being left alone, and she had to shove him back with her foot, gently.

She didn't bother to lock the door behind her.

FRESH SNOW PRESSED against the side of buildings and kept jaywalkers at bay on the sidewalks as Sophie scampered along the last block from the train to Olivier's building. The whole car issue was going to have to be addressed soon. How could they be proper villains if they were forced to wait on taxis or the El? Not the Sophie would herself ever be much of a villain, but she could watch and root on the evil. In theory.

The frigid air smelled of pretzels and nuts roasting at a street kiosk, car exhaust, and animal—so many people swarming the sidewalks and bustling along in Decemberitis—or genuine holiday spirit. It made Sophie think of her mother, who, despite the death of her husband, had never flagged in her devotion to the holidays. She would have to use Olivier's money to buy her mother something beautiful, something nice, something Christmasy. Maybe she would even buy her mother's new husband something. After all, he'd never said, "You should feel free to call me Dad," and that gave him points in Sophie's book.

A gaggle of teenaged girls cut through the crowd, tittering and screaming into brightly-colored cell phones, and Sophie knew her limits, remembered her new predilection that she wasn't sure bloodblooms could staunch. Just as the hundreds of heartbeats around her started to press with urgent immediacy, she ducked into the coffee shop in the first floor of Olivier's apartment building.

A puff of warmed air huffed out of the door as she swung it open, flooding her nose and mouth with the homey, comforting smells of fresh ground coffee and the holiday smells of nutmeg and cinnamon. A patron knocked her across the threshold as he badly maneuvered his three paper cups and small bag of treats. He apologized, but as she looked up and met his eyes, they glazed over in a sudden panic, the pupils narrowing to almost nothing, his nostrils flaring in his average, middle aged face. She raised an eyebrow, curious about how she was sure, bone-deep positive, that he was a philanderer, a sexist, and that he started a pyramid scheme that bilked countless seniors out of their life savings. He dropped one of his cups as she turned away. Had some memory unlocked the ability to read humans in some way? Was this a talent that Phillipa had had? Her memories remained mute on the topic.

"You're not my type, but I wish," she mumbled as she shoved the man slightly and made her way through the line at the coffee bar towards the door leading into the lobby. Coffee wasn't going to do it—she wanted blood—but maybe it would staunch the craving until she and Olivier could find some willing victim in a back alley somewhere.

"I thought he was a dead man." The gravely tone sent claws scuttling up the back of her neck. "But I like this place and am glad you didn't make me kill everyone here to clean up after you."

Turning, she saw Olivier sitting in a retro vinyl

booth, sparkly red in the fluorescent lights, against the front window. He was far too distant to have whispered in her ear, or for her to have heard his soft comment at all. A trick she would have to learn, definitely. Or remember? She met his eye and slid around a loud young man on a cell phone who was "very pissed over this whole white poinsettia thing, all right?" and slithered into the seat opposite the biggest enigma of her life.

Far bigger than fairy justice or reincarnation or vampirism.

"I was coming to see you." She smiled despite herself. Strewn across the Formica tabletop were pieces of wire, a couple feathers, several charms—a horse shoe, a four leaf clover, a replica coin—and a whole slew of photos that had been cut up and reconstructed in bizarre ways.

"And here I thought this was a total coincidence." The sarcasm was tempered by his dimpled half-smile. He picked up some of the wire, bending it into an ellipse with a loop at the apex, then took up another piece and bent it similarly so the wires began to form a cage-like structure.

She watched him for several seconds. He seemed comfortable with her silence, twisting the wire into what had to be a Christmas tree ornament, two of the strange, photo collages pasted back to back and trapped in the oval frame. At this juncture, she felt really stupid asking him for anything, let alone money and accompaniment when she knew they had so much more to discuss. But she just didn't feel ready, and he hadn't been forthcoming himself when he'd had every opportunity to explain himself, his—*their*—history, and why he had turned her into a vampire. He had to suspect something about her, had to have suspected from the beginning, with the emails, and he had told her nothing.

That fit a pattern in the back of her mind, and she knew his art was how he tried to say what he couldn't directly, poems and paintings in the place of conversations he couldn't bring himself to have.

"Were you doing something tonight?" His words drifted into her ear, and her eyes jumped up from where they had been observing his stringing the horseshoe charm onto the top of the ornament. His hair obscured half his face, his left cheek was dotted with a spray of blue paint flecks, and he exposed his dangerous, dangerous teeth as he smiled.

"Somehow wheedling you into shopping with me for a Christmas tree and Angel-Tree kids." Usually he responded to genuine remarks even if he had trouble with them himself, maybe because, not even if.

His smile broke into a bright laugh that turned several heads. "Off the tree here?" he gestured over his shoulder towards the lobby. She knew he meant had she taken the cards off the tree in his lobby.

A shrug was the only response.

From the seat neat to him, Olivier produced a box that he flung all of the bric-a-brac on the table into. "Hm, you're always interesting." His eyes flitted over her face, then dropped to the ring on her hand. "You 'accidentally' kill yourself, seem to hate me, have a friend sure to cause mayhem for generations, unleash the King of Death into this world, and somehow acquired an object I thought obliterated long ago."

That was all he offered—no theories or elaborations on any of the observations—before standing and striding out of the coffee shop and into the lobby. He left all his arts and crafts on the table, as though he was sure they would all still be there when he decided to come back.

Sophie wasn't sure if that was a blow-off or not, so

she got up, and instead of following him, got in a line and ordered a pumpkin latte with soy milk. Could she do this? Could she play his game, the back and forth of half answers and enigmatic questions? Could she play him that way now that she had the very information he had to have been seeking from her from the first instant message exchange they'd had?

An arm slid around her waist, and the smell of linseed oil and bay rum soap momentarily obscured that of coffee as Sophie produced her wallet to pay.

"Oh, no charge." The boy behind the counter waved her off, and directed his next statement to the right of her. "Hey," he said, and when she turned, there was Olivier, smiling at the boy and steering her away from the counter, bending over to sniff her drink, and wincing at the smell.

"You get free coffee here?" She found that really amusing for some reason. "Like a cop?"

He shoved the door to the street open and pushed her through with a gentle nudge at the small of her back. "No, like someone who gives old art supplies to the kid who works here."

Sipping her coffee, Sophie considered that, along with everything else she'd seen in and about him. "You aren't even slightly evil."

He cupped a hand around her ear and whispered, "I don't recycle," triumph and humor in his tone.

"Well, I guess it doesn't matter, since I don't *feel* evil, or anything but confused." After another sip of her coffee, she decided it sucked and tossed it into the garbage as they passed. The caffeine from the espresso was already coursing through her veins anyway, warring with the hunger for blood, drowning it out.

"You weren't confused before?" His tone was light, but she felt the accusation underneath the surface. He had known her, in a way that many people who saw her every day and loved her—her family—never could, because the anonymity of the Internet had allowed her to open her mind and pour forth every minor and major thought that even hovered at her awareness.

Maybe she felt so confused because she hadn't written an entry in her online journal for a while, for days, since before meeting Olivier at the bar, since before her life changed.

But what could she write?

Dear Diary, she composed mentally. *I'm a vampire now. It's pretty cool, except I'm also the reincarnation of someone who's got a beef with some kind of fairy of death, and since I accidentally set him free, due to my own ignorance and also due to the fumblings of my soul mate from a thousand years ago, now I have to figure out a way to get him back into his little genie bottle before he destroys the world. Also, I've discovered that I really don't like pumpkin spice lattes.*

She looked over at Olivier; he was watching her, waiting for her answer. She finally said, "Confused in a different way."

"And that is?"

"Now I don't have to be scared of dying for a while. Since I did that and I got a free trip to Fairyland and some kind of deranged relationship out of it."

"You and Ankou are dating? Tall men that look like models and have seven digit bank accounts get all the girls. Even the vampire girls." As much as she liked him like this, amused and easy, Sophie felt her stomach clench. He didn't have any answers, yet he was sitting in a coffee shop making Christmas tree ornaments?

"Wait." She grabbed his sleeve, and they stood facing each other on the sidewalk. His mind had been honed for longer than she could still really comprehend. He caught up with her immediately.

"You know," he said reprovingly.

"Ankou is in Paul somehow?" She framed it as a question, because she hadn't *known*, she'd suspected. They weren't the same thing at all. She had always believed in the law of the worst case scenario, and this Paul situation was definitely ruled by it. "He was at the house last night. He didn't do anything to us." And here she was trying to work through her own thought process through Olivier's inscrutable responses to her observations.

"His plan is probably deeper than that, or he can't harm you for some reason. Fairies do not follow patterns we would recognize—you should have realized that by now. Perhaps his plans are nothing we could ever figure, like eating eight avocados while being dressed like a chicken." His delivery was deadpan. Looking up at his aquamarine eyes, she saw mischief. He'd known about this and done nothing so far. Fairies weren't the only ones with deep plans.

"Why didn't you capture him or something if you knew? What were you waiting for? This is your dumbest mistake yet!" said Sophie. She had only *thought* it might be the case; if she'd been *sure*, she'd have even braved the gauntlet of waking Norah—horror of horrors!—and gone after him with whatever half-baked plot they could cook up.

He sighed and started walking again. She followed behind slightly, grabbing his arm to keep him from getting away. He didn't turn when he spoke. "You and Norah—and, peripherally, Luc—are bound to Paul's body. I don't know what effect casting Ankou out would have on you." He didn't say "all of you," and she liked pretending to herself he meant only her, even with his long-standing relationship with Luc.

Also, he had a point. What would it do?

They stopped on a corner for the crosswalk signal. Watching the side of his face closely in the cluttered city light, she saw the muscle in his jaw throb. "Revenge schemes always go wrong," she repeated to him. "Why didn't you—"

He turned to her, angry. "You know me," he said to her, and she *did,* but that didn't mean she couldn't be annoyed.

"I didn't know you until yesterday," she replied. He'd always been that way with women, couldn't bring himself to contradict a strong-willed woman. A product of his upbringing a thousand years later.

Around them, a throng of people crossed the street, leaving them standing on the corner.

"I'm sorry," he said, and she lifted her face up as he bent his down, and he kissed her, brushed his lips over hers.

"Okay, so we've both made mistakes," she said, slightly breathless, but refusing to give him the satisfaction.

"Have you ever heard that song?" he asked against her lips. His tongue licked over her mouth. She pulled away.

"We really need to figure out what to do," she said to him.

"WE NEED TO get you a Christmas tree," he said, and smiled. He pointed to a Christmas tree lot looming on the corner.

"No, toys first." Sophie shook her head, and pulled him into the street without looking at the light. It was green for the cars. He tugged her back onto the curb, and when the car that almost hit her zoomed off, he didn't pull away and she didn't resist his second kiss. She tasted like coffee and nutmeg, of something long desired and distant. Cold shocks exploded on his neck as her hard fingers bit into the flesh, pressing her fingerprints deeper than his skin, into the muscle beneath, where she already lived.

Cinnamon and cocoa butter and fabric softener, the scent of her pulled him away from himself, into the world of her tongue on his lip, against his teeth, skimming his tongue and rolling in a way that promised screams and moans and exhaustion. His world was her mouth and the potential in it. Dancing her away from the corner, he withdrew from their embrace enough to tug her down the street slightly, into the relative privacy of an empty bus shelter. A constitution with biological imperatives vastly different from humans allowed Olivier to will his fingers warm, grabbing Sophie's hand to pass the warmth to her.

Without further encouragement, her fragile hand scrabbled into his coat, beneath his shirt, and popped the button on his pants. The pins in her hair pinged off the glass of the bus shelter as he pulled the heavy weight free, pressing his face in and breathing deep everything waiting here. Allspice and blood and thin, strong fingers wrapping around him, pulling with just the right twist, her voice strangling him, calling his name in a chant that wanted to yank his soul from its moorings, wanted to own him. Her hand stroked harder; his mouth attached to her neck, sucking and licking and the taste was too much, everything he had every wanted beneath his teeth and claiming him with the second hand pressing that secret spot behind his balls, his knees gave out as he came.

He blinked up at her, her hair falling around her face

and body like a veil, her head backlit by a flickering streetlight. Our Lady of Sex and Death. Her smile was the lie in the night that was impossible to ignore, impossible to not trust.

He loved her.

SHOPPING WASN'T REALLY at the top of her agenda anymore, her lust pricking her skin and making her hyperaware of Olivier's scent so close to her, all over her—but they were out, and it was her stated purpose, plus Christmas was a time for charity and children. The odd feelings he engendered in her—longing, familiarity, a lingering anxiety—mixed into something like a splinter in her veins that prodded her when she shifted the wrong way.

Preoccupied, she let him lead her down the sidewalk, sidestepping when he did, stopping when he did, until the tug at her hand was more insistent. "Does this look all right?" he asked.

Her eyes focused on the life-sized, soaring, fiberglass pig flapping on the sign of *The Flying Piggy Children's Emporium*. A pair of harried parents jostled them at they exited the store, and Sophie wondered why they had waited so late if they found crowds so tiresome. They frowned at her and Olivier, and she found that if she concentrated hard enough, she could prevent her teeth from shifting as she bared them.

"Yeah, this is great," she said, reversing the pressure of the pulling, and yanking him into the brightly painted store. "Okay, we need stuff for kids from two to six, boy and girl, let's get cracking!" Dropping his hand, she foraged in her pockets for the cards that gave the names of the children, their ages, and descriptions of what they needed and wanted for Christmas.

She wanted this over. They had other matters to handle, ones that were more important to more people. She wasn't a deity, though, and she couldn't choose one person's happiness over another's. The cards were her responsibility. Once discharged, she could confess to Olivier about her memories, maybe get some sex in for good measure, and go questing for Ankou.

"I thought you weren't into shopping?" Olivier trailed behind her at a leisurely pace as she made a beeline for the clothing section of the multi-purpose boutique. That's right: she complained about Norah's shopping addiction all the time in her blog, plus she hadn't been too thrilled when she'd made him buy her clothing.

Socks in various sizes and thickness, tights in four colors and a pair of tiny running shoes in hand, Sophie glared at him. "What? This is totally different." *Totally different,* she thought; shopping for herself was a tedious parade of clothes-on, clothes-off, but kid's stuff was all so wee and adorable. Besides, these children might have nothing if not for what she—well, Olivier—bought them.

He stared at her for a moment, and she felt uncomfortably like he was taking her measure, filing away information about her. "I'll be in the toys." He didn't stay to pick a fight or make fun of her, just faded into the crowd to let her spend his money—an unspoken fact he didn't seem to care about anyway. She watched him saunter around in the preschool area, picking up blocks and toys of unimaginable utility, mothers openly staring at him with flushed cheeks and saucy mouths. She watched him as they did, his large paint-stained hand threading through his hair, the sauntering shimmy of his hips that promised talent in bed, the casual grace that was the gift of his death. The fact that she knew he wasn't just a collection of frightening beauty, but so much more, was a private thrill.

Turning back to the cutest lion-suit thing, like, ever, she realized that what those women imagined—a man who loved kids and possibly was the best dad in the world—was about as far from the truth as anyone could get. Their jealousy towards her felt like a knife at the small of her back. All the same, she decided to let them have their fantasies about him. She had a few of her own, after all.

Skirts and tops and snowsuits and pants of every variety loaded Sophie's arms by the time she was ready to check out. She tried to think of everything, even underwear, that a kid could need and a harassed parent might not have the cash to provide. Silently, Olivier slid into line beside her, a full smile on his face.

"This mom, over in the Lego area, pinched me on the ass," he staged-whispered, tapping his credit card on his chin.

Sophie laughed with him, covering a jealous annoyance she wasn't ready to acknowledge.

"Did you find everything?" The sales girl looked about twenty, probably a college student, with drooping brown eyes and hair that refused to stay in the ponytail holder at the back of her head. She was clearly exhausted.

"Yup," Sophie stacked her purchases into individual piles. "Each of these needs to be in a separate bag with . . ." She looked over at Olivier to see about the toys—which he was not holding at all.

"Oh, those over there." He pointed to a massive pile of games, stuffed animals, books, and primary-colored, shiny toys.

The girl looked behind her. "Big family?" She giggled to herself, raking her eyes over Sophie and Olivier.

The damned blush crept over Sophie's entire face. Olivier's arm came around her shoulders, pulling her flush with his side. "Actually, these are Angel-Tree children. My wife and I are, sadly, childless." He turned to Sophie with a mock concerned look. "It's all right, baby." The backs of his fingers smoothed the burning flesh of her cheek, making them flame even brighter. Okay, she could admit he might be worth keeping even if he was an unforthcoming moron who let his offspring run amok. Which made her smile—they had one child after all.

Stuttering, the sales girl replied "Oh, ah, I'm really sorry, crap, do you want to arrange things how they're supposed to go?"

Sophie nodded, biting back a guffaw.

Olivier paid as Sophie sorted all of the gifts, arranging with the manager to have the gifts delivered the next day to the charity headquarters.

FEELING REALLY GOOD about herself, what with Olivier in fine spirits and hanging off her arm, and having just created the best Christmases ever for several kids and their families, Sophie figured it was now or never to broach a thorny subject.

"So, why is Ankou called the King of Death?" She made her tone as light as possible to mask how much she pretty much knew everything, with strange gaps in her memory that she couldn't exactly explain.

Rolling her ring around her finger with one of his, Olivier waited a few beats. "We both know you're smart enough to figure that out on your own."

Yeah, okay, that *was* pretty damned obvious. He killed people. A lot. "Okay, fine, how do you think Ankou will end up killing people?"

"You shouldn't say his name a third time." His eyes darted a sideways glance at her that was half warning, half joke.

The three-time invocation? Suki's various rants filled that in. He was superstitious. It came from his lack of knowledge of magic. She smiled to herself. "Isn't that superstition?"

Ahead of them, the same Christmas tree lot they had passed earlier, sprawled in a lot, and it didn't appear that a single tree had sold. Two men in parkas and huge boots patrolled as close to the tent with the generator and coffee pot as they could, nodding to Sophie and Olivier as the stepped between two poles and into the constructed wood. Spruce and pine mingled with no apparent order, unlike in many Christmas tree lots where species ghettoization dominated.

An irrational annoyance at the lack of planning irked Sophie, brought her hunger to the forefront of her consciousness. She dug her nails into Olivier's hand.

Olivier shook out the limbs of a long-needled pine. "About two hundred years ago, when Luc went into hiding, I decided to live fully among humans, because I knew that no one would ever guess what I was." She was interested, and followed his movements closely. He looked over his shoulder and shook his head at the tree, or at his remarks, she wasn't sure which. Stepping away from that tree, he continued, "Ever. Science filled in blanks that myths used to. People could see the benefits of science, feel the weight of centuries of labor fall off their shoulders because of it." He paused, shaking out a tree. "After that, the psychiatric industry did humanity a great disservice in mocking them for fearing the oldest stories."

She wondered how he didn't understand that modernity had made their prey more readily accessible. Humans didn't even believe in them anymore. They were unsuspecting, easy.

Trying to decide what exactly to say, and where this odd conversation was heading, she stepped up to a tree that looked almost too perfect to be real. Every branch stood out in symmetry; shooting from the trunk was a straight, proud finial, and she couldn't see a single brown needle. When she pushed aside a couple branches to get a look at the trunk, a tiny figure scuttled along the end of one the branches she held. Sophie leaned closer to get a better look. Hovering in the juncture of two limbs of the scotch pine was a blue, winged creature chomping on a tiny pine cone.

"Oh my God!" Sophie gasped.

"Don't let it bite you," Olivier swatted at the pixie.

"I saw one of those in . . ." she looked behind her as the owner of the lot came jogging over with a hacksaw in his hand. "Whoa, running with that is a bad idea."

"These things are vermin from the Fairylands. You'll notice them everywhere now, like a vocabulary word you never knew the meaning of that you look up the definition to and suddenly see everywhere." Olivier glared at the pixie, which turned to show him his butt.

Nodding, Sophie replied. "Ubiquitous."

"Yes, everywhere." She laughed at his annoyance that she just repeated what he had said.

"No, I did that vocabulary thing with ubiquitous last year." The bleed-over of fey creatures really bothered her. That was a sign of something, something doubtless very horrible.

The pixie did a little dance punctuated with thrusts of its exposed rear in Olivier's direction to Sophie's amusement. The imp was cute, but it shouldn't be here.

"So, you guys like this one?" The hacksaw-running guy held out the saw with a frown.

"Can you flock it?" Olivier asked. Annoyed, Sophie wondered if it was because of the pixie, that he decided that they had to remove the tree from the lot for other people's protection. Maybe she wanted an old, bent, wonky tree. He was annoying.

"You really want to do that to a tree this nice?" The beefy, red-faced man reached his free hand out and pulled the tree out of the hole it rested in, knocking it against the ground a couple of times to let the limbs fall better.

"Did we ask your opinion?" The words shot out of her mouth before Sophie really considered speaking at all, but who was this dude to make fun of what she wanted? Who was he besides food, period?

Shooting her an eat-shit-and-die expression, the employee shrugged. "We don't do that here," he ground out, tight-lipped. The remark was an obvious lie which spiked Sophie's blood-pressure into stroke range. The man smelled like pork rinds and beer, and even though Sophie thought pork rinds were kind of gross, she wanted to eat him for her own snack.

Olivier wrapped an arm around her shoulders and his hand against the side of her neck. "We can do it ourselves, no problem." He reached into his pocket and pulled out several bills. "Do you deliver?"

Cutting his eyes over at Sophie, the guy was obviously about to say no.

"My love." Olivier ran his thumb over the bump behind her ear. "Take this." He shoved a couple hundred dollars into her fist. Her eyes flayed him; she saw his recognition that he was the new target of her anger. He was willing to make that exchange and was remaining dead calm himself.

"Why should I?" Words fought to escape past her clenched teeth. Rage surged from the bottoms of her feet. Churning through her body to set her fingers tingling and hair shocking with static.

"You seem a little hungry?" His smile seemed pleasant enough, but she saw how forced it was, recently lived memories augmented in her shattering state. He didn't want her to eat the tree lot employee, but she didn't understand why he cared.

What was one useless human to another? They were all walking death anyway.

She hated Olivier.

"Whatever." She stomped off in the direction of the diner on the corner, trying to nurse her anger, and Olivier turned back to the placated Christmas treemonger to give him the address of the condo.

Chapter Eighteen

TINY, FERN-LIKE tendrils bounced and bobbed in the air given off Norah's passing body as she thumped around the bloodbloom bush. Sticking her face right up to the foot-high shrub, she inspected the delicate, gold-toned stems. Normally she didn't think solariums were good for much aside from cat habitats, but in this case having one had proved fortuitous. Or not so much fortuitous as expected since they had picked one of the nicest homes of anyone they knew; it was bound to have a sunroom.

Instinctively she knew that Sophie had flown the coop, but she decided all worrying should be saved for post-coffee consumption.

Norah glared at the zombies as she flounced into the kitchen. There were four of them, all clustered around the small television on the counter near the sink. She shoved one aside to fill the kettle, and as the water boiled, she ground coffee and put it into the bottom of her French press.

The zombies were dead silent, but the television was

loud, and tuned to PBS, a station Norah never watched. The program was some sort of mockumentary about Santa being a sweatshop owner. Children were dressed in thread-bare, patched jerkins and hose and chained to benches. Santa loomed over the "elves" with a whip in his hand. The elves worked furiously building the latest in trademarked toys that Sophie didn't recognize.

"The quota is fifteen Big Birds an hour, Bippy, get cracking!" Santa barked.

Norah rolled her eyes. A buzz hummed in the back of her mind, and she knew there was someone in the room below her. After she finished making coffee, she decided to investigate. The door in the kitchen that Norah had assumed to be some sort of broom closet stood wide open, exposing carpeted stairs. The basement—she was quick like that. Plus, she could hear the television murmuring, contrasting with the noise of PBS.

Negotiating the stairs with the coffee pot and her cup in her hands was no fun. The scene in the basement was pretty much what she expected from a bachelor love pad. Every square inch of the basement of Casa De Paul the Thrall crawled with conspicuous consumption of a magnitude only achievable by a single, ambitious, insecure man. Decadently soft carpet in a neutral color that had to have been chosen by a professional decorator cushioned feet and dampened sound from wall to wall. On it rested Italian, leather furniture in a bright red in counter-point to the carpet. Even the most prosaic of toothpaste commercials on the plasma screen television blared out from speakers set invisibly in the walls at perfectly engineered intervals to give a theater quality experience. Recessed lighting burned natural enough to cause Norah to shade her eyes at first as she surveyed the scene.

She set down her mug and the French press—why oh why couldn't magic make coffee take less time to brew?—and then settled herself on the chaise. She flicked her eyes towards the television. "This place makes me puke," she said.

Even though she'd smoked a pack of cigarettes after Sophie had gone to bed, her voice trilled melodious and not a bit scratchy.

Luc looked up from the couch, his hair falling into his face, an ashtray balanced on one knee, a long French cigarillo in his mouth. He was watching the news, but not the PBS news. "Did you know that Olivier has no television?"

Norah stared at the coffee, willing it to get thicker and darker faster, then decided to give up. She pressed on the top, and poured herself a cup of coffee, blew on it to cool a sip.

If Luc was here, there was a reason, so she'd play along with his inane conversation for now.

When he'd first taken her off with him the other day, she'd assumed it was for sex. On one hand, that was awfully presumptuous. On the other hand, he was gorgeous. She decided to wait and see how he played it before she decided how to react—but instead of taking her to a sumptuous hotel room or a gorgeous house somewhere on the Gold Coast, he'd dragged her to a bunch of magic stores in the slums. Everyone knew him—old, gnarled men, black women wearing white turbans, Wiccans with long hair and too much silver jewelry . . . Everyone knew him. And he never touched her, not even to show her how to do something. She still wasn't sure she trusted him, physically, but she figured that if worse came to worse, she could stab him with a pencil or a chopstick or something, right through the heart, just like in the fourth season finale of *Los Vampiros*.

"What did you need to see on television?" She assumed he was already playing games, ready to give her enough information so that she could figure out his plans herself. From the first time she saw him, she'd assessed him, labeled him, found his power alluring and his French accent annoying.

He surfed through several stations.

We interrupt our scheduled programming to bring you this breaking news story. Good afternoon, this is Juan Carlos Fanjul in the WGN newsroom. We have just gotten word of a bizarre incident in downtown Chicago that has resulted in at least three deaths. A donkey that was being transported to a living crèche escaped from a trailer on the Michigan Avenue Bridge during the evening rush hour. In the chaos, it appears that two people flung themselves off the bridge into the Chicago River. One motorist who abandoned her car insisted she saw "elves." A bike messenger who claims witnessing the theft insists that "a male model in the weirdest clothes ever totally broke the donkey out of the trailer." A third reported death remains unexplained. The exact series of events has yet to be determined. Tune in to WGN News at Nine for more developments.

What Norah found remarkable wasn't the story about donkeys or people leaping off bridges.

"Why isn't Paul reading the news? I gave him a direct order to go to work." She took a mouthful of coffee, then played over what little coherent information had been in that report and paired it with Paul's absenteeism. "No way."

"What do you know, if anything, about fairy possession?" Luc lit a cigarette from the butt of his finished one. A cloud of blue smoke surrounded his head.

"You're kidding. You have got to be kidding." Even as she said it, she knew there wasn't enough coffee in the world to get her ready for the night ahead. She reached over to snatch the remote out of Luc's hand and changed the station to an old Jay-Z video.

"Wait—what does *another* bizarre death mean?" She flipped the station again and landed on a how-to show on redecorating a living room.

"Usually *another* means there has been something that came before of similar nature." His amused tone did nothing for Norah's mood. Although if she were in better spirits, his sarcasm might be attractive.

"Okay, please feel free to die." Norah watched a home decorator apply packing paper to a wall. "Is it our job to stop the evil elf guy? That's the only reason you'd show up like this, right? Unless you're really unbearably attracted to me and couldn't admit to your feelings the other day."

Mr. Artfully-Disheveled definitely did raise an eyebrow and curled his lip at her. She smirked back at him.

"I'm sure that's a problem you have often," he said, and recrossed his legs.

She rolled her eyes and took another long sip of coffee, then said, "Have you ever heard of vampires that help people and shit? This ain't a television show, bro." She really, really did not want to go out and catch some supernatural creature—especially one that was apparently possessing Paul the Thrall. So, that whole thrall thing might have been a bad idea. Everyone made mistakes, but that didn't mean she had to be the one to fix it. "I don't do useless charity," she continued. "That's Sophie's domain."

Luc continued staring at her. Norah stared back, refusing to let him discomfit her. Finally he said, "Paul belongs to you. If—" He cleared his throat meaningfully—"the evil elf guy destroys Paul's body, it will affect you *and* Sophie. That *is* the point of the Thrall; he's yours forever, until *you* decide to destroy him."

"So all I have to do is kill him, right?" Norah lifted one shoulder and let it drop, half in mockery of the movement Luc used on her all the time, and half in genuine spirit of shrugging. "No problem."

"Ah, it's lovely to see the young embrace their true natures like this," said Luc.

"Shut up," said Norah. "Didn't you used to do everything Rosamund said? I do recall you telling me a story or two about—"

"*Norah*," said Luc sharply. "If you kill Paul, Ankou will only jump into another empty body—a zombie, someone else's golem, someone else's Thrall. You have made this mistake and now you must rectify it."

Norah stared at him suspiciously. He looked way more intense about this than normal—although normal for Luc, at least in Norah's experience, was shallow like a mud puddle. And that was kind of what she liked about him. Now he was solemn. That scared her some. People who were as vested in their façades as Luc didn't drop them unless there was no other option.

He was letting her peek inside, and she didn't think she really wanted to.

"Don't get all serious on me now, Sire," said Norah, and poured herself more coffee. She changed the channel again, this time flicking through a hockey game, three different cooking shows, and a rerun of *CSI*. Luc groaned in what was probably annoyance as Norah alighted on an old *Space Ghost Coast to Coast* rerun.

"If you ever call me Sire again, I will be forced to address all of our correspondence to Norah, Child-with-an-E, of the N-Y-G-H-T."

The intense look was gone from Luc's face, replaced with his usual sardonic expression, and Norah felt much more comfortable.

"I don't write letters, baby, that's why I have a thrall," she scoffed. "Is this the episode with Bjork?" She looked up from her coffee cup to see Luc staring at her. "Okay, okay, okay. What do we have to do? What do *I* have to do? We'll get rid of the elf, bring Suki back from Fairyland, and take over the world with the bloodblooms, right?"

"One out of three, anyway," replied Luc. He exhaled a thin stream of smoke from between his lips. It stung Norah's nostrils and made her long for her first cigarette of the day. But she'd smoked the rest of her pack the night before. She looked longingly at his cigarette. He passed it to her.

"How do we do it?" she asked, then put his cigarette to her lips. The tip was slightly wet, slightly salty, slightly sweet. Mmm, sexy vampire spit. If this was how it was, it was. Norah didn't believe in fighting too hard against the current when the ride could just be a float down the river instead. "I can get behind some mayhem," she added as she exhaled, and handed the cigarette back.

"We should find Olivier and Sophie; we'll need them for the ritual. Of course they are involved . . ." He sighed and stubbed out his smoke in the ashtray.

"I'm sure they're screwing in a doorway somewhere," muttered Norah. "Do you have more cigarettes?"

Luc's smile was unexpected, luminous, his mouth redder than sin. "First you get dressed, no?"

SOPHIE'S HUNGER SEETHED into something more than need when she left Olivier at the tree-stand. Why did he choose to relate to the prey on its own terms rather than take what he wanted? A tree belongs to no one.

From every direction on the sidewalk blood pounded in over-taxed, narrowed arteries, the blood of athletes, of addicts, or diabetics, and she was offered ashes and sorrow to drink instead.

Olivier brought her nothing but pain and torment. He was the source of all troubles, all horrors. Her body burned, her mind twisted—

Ankou appeared in her mind's eye. His iridescent pink skin stretched over his bowed neck, her teeth sinking into the taut barrier with an audible pop.

"This world consumes you in this life as you rejected it in the last, my Lady, the eternal law, and I knew, yes, I knew you would *crave* and *strive* and *need* enough for this . . ." His voice whispered in her swiftly-fragmenting mind as hunger-madness began to take over.

His words sounded like wind through dead leaves.

Need decimated her, tore her from herself inch-sized bit of awareness at a time. Her feet carried her at a clip barely maintained by world-class sprinters, clack-clack-clack, away from anything, everything, life and meaning and thinking. The night, the arid chill in the frozen air, the ghostly heartbeats somewhere in the distance—that was eternity.

"I mean, like, he was totally checking you out." A stray voice floated into her ear.

Half a block, that was all.

The crackle and hum of the cell phone made Sophie's elongated teeth itch.

"Well, duh. He is totally hot."

Angel perfume by Thierry Mugler, raisins and pop-corn and butterscotch and licorice and innocence parading as cynicism . . .

Sophie knocked the phone so far with a backhanded

swat that when the police found it, their search radius was off by three blocks. The girl was probably twelve, thin, too thin, and as Sophie tore into her throat, she knew it was from an eating disorder. Anger, longing, confusion, hope in something unknown, pink sparkles and clarinet lessons and self-hate so bright—

Sophie drowned in the girl and only came up for air when her consciousness struggled up from where it had fled. With it came the sound of other heartbeats close by, coming in her direction. She dragged the body into the closest crevice between buildings, and searched around for something to obscure the wound. Her eyes lit on a Snapple bottle. She wrapped the girl's scarf around her hand and used it to hold the bottle—as far as she knew, her prints weren't on file, but no sense in borrowing trouble. She broke the bottle against the brick of the building's façade. Tears smeared the clotting blood on her face as she set to work.

Wind froze the blood and tears on Sophie's face. Wiping at it with the sleeve of her sweater, she wept silently at the images in her head. The girl hadn't even had time to scream as Sophie descended on her, fangs bared, hands outstretched as claws, bodyweight sending the tween sprawling on her back with a loud crack of her spine. At this juncture, with hindsight, Sophie knew that even if she hadn't fed from her, the girl would have been paralyzed for life from a broken spine. Still, having to slash her throat with a broken bottle after the fact, to cover the bite marks, had turned her stomach and almost cost her the meal.

She considered her options: pretending nothing happened seemed pointless since she, her hair, eyebrows, and eyelashes were spiked with frozen blood; going crying to Olivier seemed even worse since he had tried time and again to keep her from doing exactly what she just did, and shame wouldn't let her attempt to find him anyway; going back to Paul's and getting really drunk did appear to be the most expedient option, even if she didn't know how the hell she would get there looking like an escapee from an horror film.

A part of her thrilled at the kill, a winding memory like the wire Christmas lights are connected to. Of course. She had always been this way. From the very start. Phillipa had fed from blossoming girls as well, and that was one more reason to curse Olivier for never saying anything. Yes, he'd tried to stop her, tried to keep her from living with the guilt, but he didn't tell her why. Never why. He had to know who she had been—had to have suspected.

There was nothing she could do that moment, not until she'd bathed and talked to Norah about catching Ankou, Paul, whatever, so she turned to the street and tried to hail a cab. It wasn't all that late, probably around 11, not that Sophie was wearing a watch. She could *feel* it—not the time itself, but the sun, how far away it was, how long she had until it rose above the tops of buildings.

She wondered if it was true that vampires burned up in the sun. In *Los Vampiros*, the vampires could survive in direct sunlight if they'd fed until they were almost overfull. They could also survive in the sunlight if they were from a particular tribe.

Sophie wondered if real vampires had tribes, and added it to the list of really specific questions she wanted to ask Olivier and/or look up in the mystical vampire guidebook—the existence of which Sophie was beginning to doubt.

In under five minutes, a checkered cab pulled up to the curb, and Sophie flung open the door and stepped into the backseat.

"Where to?" The cabbie turned over the meter and looked at her in the rearview.

"Sheffield Avenue, just south of Irving Park," said Sophie shortly. She met the cabbie's eyes in the rearview.

"Lost your coat? Midnight's cold with no coat," was all he said as he kicked the car into motion.

People were definitely becoming far too jaded.

ARRIVING AT THE condo, Sophie realized she had no cash. Should she kill the cabbie? She explored her feelings. Nope, that still sounded bad and wrong.

"Wait here, I'll be right back." She didn't give the guy an opportunity to lock the doors and trap her inside, leaping out of the car with her preternatural swiftness.

The cabbie turned off the car as she sprinted up the stoop, calling the cops she was sure. That would be a very very bad thing.

The front door was unlocked, as per usual, and Sophie bounded into the condo calling Norah's name. Sophie hoped she was home and that she had cash, neither of which was a sure thing. Although maybe Olivier had beaten her back.

Norah almost ran around the corner of the kitchen with her hair flapping behind her, panic straining her face, all very un-Norah. "What? What happened? Oh shit!"

"What?" For a second Sophie had no idea what the problem was, and when she remembered the blood all over her, she felt even worse for forgetting.

"I just need some money for a c—" Her explanation was cut short by an underwear-clad Paul jogging down the stairs. The boxers left absolutely nothing to the imagination. "Um . . ." Sophie blushed and turned to Norah. "Uh . . ."

"Get your wallet, moron!" Norah barked at Paul, who obediently headed back up the stairs just as the cabbie flung open the cracked front door. "You have to tell him specifically what to do all the time."

"What?" There had obviously been some development on the capturing Paul angle since she'd gone out earlier. Norah knew Paul wasn't Paul for one thing, which was weird. Sophie squinted her eyes at her friend.

"Yo, only reason I ain't called the cops yet is you look like you got beat the fuck up, and I ain't go out like that with the ladies, so you better get your white ass in there and find that money tree I know you white folks got in yo' house!" The cabbie appeared on the stoop behind Sophie. His dreadlocks shook with the vehemence of his anger.

Sophie was about to cough up an excuse when Paul bounded back down the stairs, dressed the same as before, but this time with his wallet in his hand. His normally dim expression was enigmatic and distant.

"Day-um, some kinky shit up in here," the cab whistled.

"Pay this guy," Norah commanded Paul. "Then shut the door."

Direct commands, huh? What did that do? Keep Ankou at bay? How?

"What happened?" Norah steered Sophie into the kitchen, sat her in one of the armchairs, and went to the sink to wet a tea towel.

"You're kidding, right?" Her head fell back onto the chair. The sound of the girl's cracking spine echoed in her ears, and she ground her teeth to drown it out.

Paul shuffled into the kitchen—she could smell him. Burnt sugar and recycled air and deodorant. And something else, something, complex, textured.

"Paul, why are you in your panties?" Sophie asked around Norah's wash cloth.

"My master thinks that unclothed I won't leave the house unattended." The voice had Paul's timbre, but nothing of his personality. There was something strained about his vowels, something sparking in the way he bit his words off. Normally Paul was languorous and unhurried in his diction, someone who didn't give two shakes what anyone else thought about him. Sophie grabbed the wash cloth out of Norah's hand.

"Why isn't he tied up?" Paul turned his eyes on her, the blue-green had become a lavender blue. "Why isn't he bound? Tie him up!" Sophie ran from the room, overcome by Paul's regard, Ankou's eyes staring out of Paul's face.

She heard Norah laughing behind her, always laughing when she shouldn't. Sophie was terrified as she ran up the stairs and into the bathroom to shower and change. They needed to find out what Ankou's exact plan was, discover why he had chosen now as the time to emerge into the world. That must be related to some arcane series of events that they had accidentally set into motion by first thralling Paul and then inviting him back to their place.

And by "they," Sophie meant herself and Norah—and Olivier, because Olivier was *so* not getting out of the blame for this shit. He should have just let her die when she broke her neck.

On the other hand, Sophie really wasn't all that excited about death. Being a vampire didn't suck—being an vampire ignorant of what her actions could spur *totally* sucked.

At least focusing on the suck took Sophie's mind off the guilt she felt over the girl's death.

Stripping out of her bloody clothes in the bathroom, she felt totally lost. The water burned her skin as she stepped under the flow. She rubbed her fingers over the ring, leaned against the cold tile, and closed her eyes.

Images rushed through her mind: Ankou bound in the alchemist's circle laughing, the sound like shallow stab wounds all over her body, his voice in her mind telling her she'd never be free, Olivier's face as she left to go with Rosamund, his voice reading poems on a night far colder than the one she now lived through.

> Time was the invention of men who would confine the
>   ocean and bottle the wind.
> Eternity is too short to fulfill the promise of love my
>   soul holds for you.

When she got out of the shower, she was calmer. They would live through this, or they wouldn't.

How many times had she died?

A whisper in her mind told her infinite times only to live infinitely more lives. There were circles within circles that dictated her life—*lives*—that she would never even begin to realize.

She wandered downstairs to find Norah again. She passed through the kitchen into the solarium. Planted in a suspiciously authentic yellow cloisonné urn, the magical bloodbloom shrub was more of a collection of vines than a proper bush. Willowy, pinky-thick vines twisted together for about a foot forming a stalk before separating to form a canopy of arced branches. Each branch supported a riot of chartreuse leaves and a couple of scarlet blooms hanging underneath the branches by a single tendrily stem.

"Paul, your stupid ass better not have knocked the bush over again, or I swear you're wearing a thong!"

Norah's voice, as usual, preceded her entrance into the room.

"Didn't you tie him up?" Sophie's stomach sank into her feet.

Norah slithered into the kitchen in a white silk kimono painted with a pond full of multicolored koi, a cigarette in her hand. "Oh, hey!"

Her scowl brightened into a nuclear smile, wide enough to make Sophie smile back, even if she was even more curious about the Paul situation now. Who made someone run around in their underwear as a form of restraint rather than just tying them up with duct tape and sticking them in a closet? Someone with a freaky agenda, like Norah's sick ass.

"Whatever." Norah flipped Sophie off. Which meant she hadn't tied him up. At all. Oh fantastic. "What happened?" She gestured with her cigarette to indicate she meant Sophie's ruined clothes and nasty hair from before.

Sophie was going to kick her ass. Right after they got the homicidal fairy under control.

"*Paul!*" Sophie screamed. There was no answering thumping from upstairs or rustling from near by. Without bothering to call again, she concentrated, searching for him in the house. Nothing.

Lifting an eyebrow, Norah flicked her cigarette into the sink. "Everyone has their bad days." What? That was her apology/explanation?

"You're so stupid! God, I hate you! I bet you didn't even capture him before, right? He just came home on his own?" Sophie shot out at Norah's back. The lack of any response indicated Sophie had made a direct hit.

She hated everyone and everything, and she planned to get a totally new set of minions tomorrow. Or at least get some minions.

Chapter Nineteen

LUC AND NORAH had arranged to meet later that night. Sophie didn't want to think about that on about fifty levels. What everyone on earth needed right now was for those two to hook up—*again*—and bring about Armageddon.

"What did Luc tell you to do if Paul came home?" Sophie stomped along the sidewalk glaring at Norah. She didn't answer.

"Tie him up, right? He told you to tie him up and wait for him to come back so he do some magic crap and send him back?"

"That was hypothetical and therefore not binding." Norah tossed her cigarette in a wide arc into the street.

"You were more worried about your damned blood-crack empire, right? I mean, did Luc mention the King of Death part? Did he tell you the guy can cause riots and jihads and might have incited the Crusades? Have you even though about what this guy could do if he hit

Iraq? Afghanistan? *Israel*!" Sophie was just working up into a real rage when Norah started to laugh.

"Um, you know none of that sounds all that bad to me—"

"If the world ends in a nuclear holocaust," said Sophie snidely, "you won't get to cause any more mayhem."

"But if you're upset about it," continued Norah, ignoring Sophie as usual, "I won't let him escape again." Her smile was pure, just happiness, no sarcasm. The idea of real violence and chaos appealed to her. It had always appealed to her on some level, which, now looking back on it, should have registered with Sophie's human self as odd.

The only thing that saved Norah from a real talking to was their arrival at the Orchid.

Ray Ray didn't bother to brandish his club at them. Norah gave him a wink.

"What's cookin,' good lookin'?" His smile bared perfectly white pointed teeth, like a child drawing a series of Vs for grass.

"Looking for Luc . . ." Norah glanced back at Sophie who seethed in her general direction but knew automatically that Norah was asking her to fill in the surname.

"I don't know his last name." Sophie wondered if vampires had last names. She thought about it, and still had no answer. Her memory wasn't going to be as useful as she'd hoped. "Do vampires have surnames?" she asked Ray Ray—if anyone knew, he would.

"Some do, some don't, depends on how ancient the vampire." He withdrew his Palm from under one of the jewel-toned pillows resting on his stool. "If he comes from before surnames were in wide usage, probably not."

"Huh," Norah replied wittily. One didn't need witty repartee when one could chew out someone's throat;

Sophie could see that thought-process as though it were written out on a chalkboard. "Do you know a vampire named Luc? Black hair, stubble, Pepe Le Peu accent."

"I knew who you meant. Warlock, big ol' ho, who don't know the vamp? He was here earlier, maybe still is. Waitin' on you baby vamps, I bet." Apparently Ray Ray considered their discussion complete, because the duo fell through the portal into the bar without warning, landing on their feet clutching at one another to maintain balance.

"I guess we're on the VIP list now," said Sophie as she straightened her clothes. She smiled to herself as she watched Norah futz with her hair from the corner of her eye. Her anger evaporated. It wasn't going to do her any good to focus her energy on blaming Norah when all Norah was doing was being herself.

Plus, if Sophie didn't focus her energy on blaming Norah, she could focus her energy on blaming herself for turning Norah into a vampire before she'd really thought through the repercussions.

Of course, if Sophie had to do it all over again, she'd probably do it exactly the same. Maybe not. Maybe instead of ripping out Olivier's throat, she'd have stolen his vampire guidebook instead.

She sighed impatiently at herself.

"I think we should name the house," she told Norah as they made a wide loop around the tree in the middle of the bar, skirting the walls and coming close to some dodgy looking booths set in the deep shadows.

"You do, huh?" She sounded amused. Sophie became preoccupied with the darting lights set in the higher branches of the oak. White, blue, yellow, they flitted with no apparent pattern. They hadn't been there the last time they visited the bar.

"Check out the lights in the tree." Pointing for emphasis, Sophie tripped over a chair leg, almost fell in a comic routine reminiscent of a bad Jerry Lewis film, with arms pin-wheeling and feet scrabbling to catch on the worn wood of that portion of the bar floor.

"I read somewhere that vampires have the natural grace of the predator," a lazy, male voice intoned from one of the booths near the two women. "This, I think, is not true." He used the trick to sound like he was whispering in her ear when she knew there was no one but Norah close by. Concentrating on his face, his smell like wine and cigarettes and sage, she threw her voice into his ear back.

"It's easy to be cool when you sit in the dark, you could be wearing a lime green polyester track suit and no one would know." Sophie's ambivalence towards Luc teetered into severe dislike at that moment. He laughed with real delight that she had turned his own trick back on him. Her natural distrust of him was offset of memories she tried to ignore. He was flip and shallow to cover his emotional turmoil. She knew that but it didn't make him any less annoying. "You always manage to show up right when you're needed."

"And not when I'm not, but this doesn't *always* work, as you say, as some people are *always* in need of me." The laughter fluttering around his words might have been sexy to someone else—was probably sexy to *Norah*, ew—but Sophie just wanted to smack the hell out of him.

"Why didn't you wait with Norah to make sure she didn't fuck this up?" demanded Sophie. "You know better than to let Norah be the person responsible for capturing Ankou." Maybe he had a weakness for her that Sophie didn't understand. Maybe he just had an inexplicable agenda that Ankou didn't really fit into.

Luc laughed. Sophie scowled. Norah pinched her arm.

"Bitch," said Norah, "shut up."

"You shut up," said Sophie. "Deny it. I dare you." Focusing, she narrowed her eyes and the darkness clinging to the walls dissipated. The shapes of old fashioned, European booths with doors to shut out prying eyes popped well-distinguished from the gloom. Luc waved to her from one of the booths slightly down from where they stood.

"You're a moron," she said to Luc.

"What, can you see him or something?" Norah turned her head from side to side in a futile search. Sophie wished Olivier was there. Why wasn't he there? Why did she have to deal with Luc and his sliding scale of bad and worse than bad, and Norah who didn't even know better than to tie up a captive?

She didn't think she'd get over that soon.

"Norah, vampires see in the dark and shit, just think about it really hard, like keeping Tinker Bell alive, wish with all your heart to see Luc so I can kill him, and you will." Turning from her tutorial on the finer arts of vampirehood, Sophie scanned the rest of the bar for Olivier, but already knew he wasn't there; she couldn't smell him, couldn't feel his blood in the back of her throat.

"Oh damn. This is like one of those 3-D puzzles from way back." She started towards Luc's table, tugging on Sophie's sleeve to follow. Sophie allowed herself to be dragged along. "He just popped right out, like the picture of the ship."

Luc tilted his head and propped it on his arm resting on the marred wood of the table. "Ah, my beautiful damsels." His smile hinted at things best left in the dark. "What can I do to smooth your path through life? Capture a wicked elf perhaps?" He made a mocking sad face. "One that someone should have tied up, perhaps?" Good. They were on the same page about something.

"Why didn't you tie him up yourself?" Norah snapped. "I'm pretty sick of you and Sophie being on my ass about this crap. Whose fault is it that we don't know what to do?"

"I told you what to do," said Luc coldly.

"*Yeah*," said Sophie. She didn't want to agree with Luc, and it felt both bad and wrong, but Luc was *right*. Of course, Luc had trusted Norah to do what he told her. "*Wait*," she said to Luc. "You trusted Norah to do what you told her."

"I follow no one's orders," said Norah blithely. She reached into the inside pocket of Luc's leather jacket and pulled out a slim pack of cigarettes. Luc held out his finger and a flame danced upon it; Norah lit her cigarette and sat back in the booth, looking very satisfied with herself.

Sophie fought the urge to just ditch these two and find Olivier now. But she knew if she did they were most likely to do something even stupider, like maybe open a portal into an alternate reality called Upside Down World where people only ate shrimp and the sky was orange.

"Seriously now," she began. Luc winked. If she had to watch them flirt, Sophie was going to have to haul her butt up and hang out with whatever slug-creature she could find lurking in the shadows. "What are those lights in the tree?"

Which really wasn't what she needed to ask, but Sophie was groping for a distraction.

Tilting his head back, Luc examined the canopy. "Solstice sprites that linger?" He shrugged. "They are pretty from here, but don't climb the tree for a better look. Ginger candy?" He offered Sophie a piece of candy wrapped in wax paper, when she didn't take it, he laughed and offered one to Norah, who did.

"I don't like candy." She didn't, but she said it like it was a euphemism for 'fuck you'—and it was.

"Or me." Laughing again, Luc lit a cigarette off his finger and watched Norah unwrap her treat. "That's nothing new." The way he said the second part froze her.

"How well did we know each other?" she asked him in a voice that was closer to a whisper than a snarl.

"Do you really want to know?" asked Luc, and he leered at her, and Sophie's stomach dropped.

Either he was being a jerk for fun, or they really had—

Oh, ew.

Sophie twisted the ring on her finger and focused on breathing.

"Will you help us capture the fairy?" She felt like she might as well ask him, even though she knew he'd do it to get into Norah's pants. Not that Norah wore a chastity belt, so the effort was absolutely wasted. Sophie wouldn't mention that.

He took a long draw off his cigarette and blew the smoke straight up. Gesturing at her with his free hand, he leaned back in the booth bonelessly. "First you will tell me some things."

Norah stifled a sigh next to her. Oh, please! He was French, that wasn't even Norah's type. Gah. This sucked. "What sort of things?"

"What do you dream about?" She thought there would be at least a few more passes before he started the inquisition, and was knocked off kilter by the swiftness of the question. Which was exactly his intention, no doubt.

She glanced at Norah who didn't seemed to see any threat yet, and was calmly awaiting the reply. Way to get my back, bitch, Sophie thought.

"If I said I dreamed my father was dead, what would you say?" She stalled with reference to one of Freud's famous patients, causing Norah to smile. They had both hated psych at school.

"That Freud was boring even when he was new and supposedly enthralling." Luc blew smoke out of the side of his mouth with a frown, using a loaded word and pretending like he wasn't.

Sighing, Sophie relented, wishing she was clever enough to construct a decent, believable lie. Part of her wanted to taunt him for suspecting the truth and being subtle and vague about it. Wasn't it her *right* to know these things he suspected about her? Who were Luc and Olivier to choose for her what she would know, and what she wouldn't? "Sometimes, I dream I'm in a castle, and it's springtime. Sometimes I dream about fires."

Luc leaned on elbows, his hair swinging on the sides of his face. "What happens?"

She hesitated again, wondering how much she'd have to say, feeling that something very personal was being exposed. These were her memories, some shared with him, but she didn't pry into how he configured his internal world. Worst of all, the vague feeling of lingering shame constricted her throat, reminding her of her mistakes, how all of what was happening now was her fault.

"Different things. Sometimes I hear music. Sometimes I'm really scared. Sometimes I argue with someone."

Without warning, Luc sat back and rapped the table with his knuckle. "*Who* do you argue with?" His anger twisted the words into a completely French cadence, making the question almost unintelligible.

"Olivier! God, chill out." Her body tensed for a fight. Norah laid a hand on her arm and glared at Luc, showing where her loyalty truly fell, in case he was in doubt. "Olivier is in the dreams. But he looks different, his hair and how he's dressed."

"Dressed different how?" With another swift personality shift, Luc raised an eyebrow and affected aloofness. His bottom lip twitching slightly and the pattern of his breathing gave him away.

"In mail and a tunic." She thought she might as well tell him the truth, but it seemed wrong to tell Luc before Olivier, and she hadn't gotten her chance to tell him. He knew, knew instinctively, but she wanted to *tell* him, to talk to him—the human side of her wanted to *communicate*. The vampire side of her just wanted to eat, and didn't care that she hadn't gotten her chance to talk to him, what with her blood lust overwhelming her. And the handjob in the bus shelter.

Sophie blushed. Luc raised an eyebrow.

"I won't ask the . . . theme of these dreams." His smirk made her teeth itch. "What device does he wear on his surcoat?" She almost smiled. What device, indeed.

"Sanguine pomegranate on per bend of white and green." In her mind, Sophie could the standard, sharp and crisp like a digital image.

"Excuse me, per what? Huh?" Norah snatched Luc's cigarette from between his fingers and pulled a long draw from it. Sophie saw her from the corner of her eye looking back and forth between her and Luc.

He remained frozen in mid-motion, his head cocked slightly to the side, an enigmatic expression on his face. What had he expected? Did he really not believe it until he heard that? With the suddenness he was inclined to, he smiled, swung his head around to Norah, and plucked his cigarette back from her mouth.

"This insignia was mine as well, but in my upper sinister corner rested a crescent moon . . ."

"You were a second son." Sophie watched him closely. "Was Olivier your brother?" That was a hole in what she knew, her memories not connecting everything for her, leaving huge patches of nothingness and void.

His eyes flashed back to her. "Alas, no, just my cousin, but his father was also a first son, so the honor of the standard, this was his."

"Hold up! Pomegranate? What the hell?" Not one to be left out of any conversation, Norah was annoyed.

"The pomegranate stands for the Tree of Knowledge, that whole apple thing is from the Renaissance." Sophie looked at her, and they understood each other. For the first time, Sophie thought, Norah began to realize how old the new men in their lives were. She shook her head slightly to negate it. When Norah said that Luc had told her everything, obviously she meant that Luc had told her that she and Sophie were the reincarnations of two chicks who used to hang out with Luc and Olivier.

Way to go with the sharing information, Luc.

Sophie opened her mouth to chastise him when a figure slithered out of the shadows surrounding the booth. She was tall, dressed in skin-tight red leather making a half-hearted go at being a dress. The material shone with oil or wax or some substance Sophie didn't want to explore too far.

"Is the darkness in here somehow manufactured?" Sophie squinted into the absence of light encircling them, but no matter how she tried, she couldn't make out the giant tree growing in the center of the bar nor the lights she knew flickered amongst its branches.

"The green on the standard is for evil, the white for good." The woman in the dress flipped her waist-length black hair over her shoulder and looked haughtily down her nose at Norah. Luc patted the bench next to him with a flourish, scooting over for the woman. If Norah could have snarled, Sophie was sure she would have.

"This is ridiculous," snapped Norah, and stubbed out her cigarette viciously. "Am I the only person here who doesn't have a Ph.D. in medieval symbolism?" Norah looked from face to face, sneering at the interloper. She turned her lack of knowledge into other people's mental deficiency with a tone.

Sophie admired that about her, definitely.

"I picked it up playing EverQuest," Sophie said patting Norah's arm. What that meant was, "I got your back, friend."

Laughter met Norah's snort and the look of disdain on the new woman's face. Everyone had to decompress somehow. Can't play Ultimate Frisbee in the winter in Chicago, so Suki had played EverQuest. Sophie didn't have to share that it wasn't *her* hobby.

Sophie knew the pale sneering chick was there for a reason and wouldn't give Luc the satisfaction of asking what. She watched as Luc ran the back of his fingers over the girl's arm. She seemed entranced. Sophie blinked. No, she *was* entranced. And human. That meant she was a witch of some sort or soon to be an ex-human. Either a tool or food. Luc was capricious, but not fond of humans, not ever.

"Are you playing EQ2? I was thinking of switching over," Luc stubbed out his cigarette and grinned at Sophie through the fall of hair in his face. He was flirting with her now, trying to unsettle her, tipping his cards so she'd look there and ignore the knife in his other hand.

He never gave up, which earned him points for nerve; he refused to be anyone but himself, which earned him more.

"You can*not* be serious," the human lady intoned with great loathing. "Video games? I thought you were serious night stalkers on an important quest. You are nothing but posers." Snatching her arm out of Luc's grasp, she slithered away the best she could in her constrictive garb.

"Luc? You get one chance to explain that." Using the tone that Sophie avoided at all costs, Norah pulled a huge grin from him. Not all of his strings were tuned if he thought Norah wasn't a threat. Violence had been almost casual with her before her change, and Sophie knew she felt no remorse for the people she was killing nightly, nor would she feel remorse for him if he had to lose his throat or heart.

Maybe a twinge if she didn't get to sleep with him first, but that was about it.

Sophie felt guilty that she was sometimes glad to have a friend like that—who she knew would do the things Sophie knew she never could herself. This was getting boring, though. Luc was in, she knew it, so now she needed to find Olivier and talk to him, fix things between them as best they could before finding Ankou. And also . . .

"Can we figure out how to get Suki out of Fairyland? asked Sophie.

Norah turned an ice glare onto her. "Sophie, get real, okay? Suki ain't coming back, Suki don't want to come back, Suki ain't interested in us no more. And who would be? Come *on*."

Sophie looked from Norah to Luc. Luc lifted his shoulder and let it fall, in a movement he'd done hundreds of thousands of times before.

"We can't just leave her there," Sophie insisted around the lump in her throat. Maybe she and Suki weren't always on the best of terms but—

"Suki wants to be there, sweetheart," said Norah. "Suki *wants to be there*. What part of that did you not get when we jumped home through the cauldron and she didn't come?"

"I don't want to leave her there," said Sophie, wanting to cry and also feeling grumpy. "Where's the waitress, I need some blood before I rip your throat out."

"You can *try*," sneered Norah. Then she turned her sneer to Luc: "Answer my question. Who was that bitch all up in your shit?"

Sophie blinked back tears. She didn't want to leave Suki in the Fairyland. She wanted her friend back. Plus she didn't want to have to be responsible for Sathan for all eternity.

Oh. Could she turn Sathan into a vampire? The sadness she felt at the thought of never seeing Suki again transmuted very suddenly into curiosity, and she tuned back into what Luc was saying.

"—so Scarlet has sworn to help us find La Roi." Scarlet? Lamey McLame!

At Sophie and Norah's frowns he shrugged and kept grinning. Right. Something screwed up was definitely happening.

"Why?" Norah hit Sophie's main question in one. "Why would she agree to help you and what help can she give us?" She was a reporter, after all. Maybe Luc didn't know that? Sophie wondered what Luc *did* know about either of them, about Sophie and Norah, not about who they had been once.

Luc threw his head back and laughed. "I have my charms. *They* have their weakness." The second part was delivered with a tone that could cause a human heart failure, cold, like the abyss staring back.

Definitely a meal. Miss Scarlet, in the bar, with the haughty voice would be a meal.

She wasn't going to let him play her with his vampire tricks. "And they're just stupid?" Sophie had serious doubts about that. He had offered them something. She could guess it was the obvious something—eternal life. She wondered how often people fell for that trick.

"Is it stupid to want what we offer?" Luc knocked a knuckle against the table softly. His tongue flicked over an exposed canine for comic emphasis. He had also evaded her question, her real, unspoken question which was how this fit into some plan for sending Ankou back where he belonged. She knew she would never get anything out of him he didn't want to give; a thousand years is a long time to learn how to manipulate.

"Death?" said Norah.

"So suddenly you're all 'oh, *we* blah blah blah'?" Sophie wondered if there would ever be a time when she didn't find Luc insufferable. There was no way they'd ever slept together. None.

They understood each other on a certain level, despite so much unsaid between them. He had asked her who she was, using an old tool that they had all employed to find their lost ones, something Olivier had been unwilling to do—although she was willing to bet that Luc already *knew*. He didn't offer her anything in return, though, didn't give her any information, but he was willing to help on a quest that he found useless and boring. Luc was shameless, but he got what he wanted more times than not.

The question, as always, was what did he want? Maybe revenge. She held his amber eyes.

"Ah, *oui*, don't be so angry with me." His face pulled into a pathetic paroxysm of sadness, eyes dropping from hers. "It was a favor for my cousin who was never going to ask." Olivier had spoken to him about it. Luc offered her some measure of honesty, because he thought she was ignorant, but honesty all the same. The sentimentality underneath seeping out. Reaching out two fingers, he wound them briefly in the curl resting against Sophie's cheek. Just as she was about to push him away or swing her head out of his reach, he withdrew his hand and slapped both of his palms against the table. "We need a steel cage, a ferret, and three wooden dolls."

"A friend of mine has a cage in her basement." Norah sounded bored, like always. She was not bored. More than likely she was pissed off at Luc's antics with the leather chick and getting into Sophie's personal space. He would pay.

Luc, however, was extremely interested in Norah's friend's cage, and oblivious to her real mood. "Yes? Is there a story or two to be found there?" He raised an eyebrow and winked.

"You're an idiot." Norah rolled her eyes. The flirting was back on.

"Please shut up." Sophie had had enough.

"Will you spank me if I'm very bad?" How he managed to deliver that line with a straight face, Sophie had no idea.

"Okay, ick, please shut it. Where do we get a ferret?" Sophie looked at Norah, who generally knew where to get anything.

"You're joking, right?" Her tone was more a straight forward, *How could you be so dumb?*, rather than *This is so not for real.*

When Sophie didn't get the connection, Norah sighed and made a long-suffering look towards Luc. They had *looks* already? This shit was wrong. "The wereferret." Norah filled in the gap.

"Oh great, breaking and entering, my favorite." Sophie sighed and rubbed her temples.

"Wereferret? I've seen a wererabbit, but never a ferret," Luc lit another smoke. "For this, a wereferret is okay."

Sophie ran a hand through her hair, frustrated, wanting to laugh at Luc's comments but not willing to give him that advantage. "It's not really a wereferret, Luc! God, it's just an evil, bastard ferret that Norah hates, and I think we should find a different one—like *any* other ferret in the *world.*"

How many ways could this ferretnapping go wrong? She summoned her most serious, business face and turned it upon Norah. "Seriously, no."

"Okay, so how do we get the ferret? Lure it out with a snake?" Norah completely ignored Sophie's serious face and her refusal to participate.

"That's a mongoose who hunts snakes." Luc imparted this wisdom with undue gravitas.

"How is a mongoose different from a ferret?" Norah asked him. They jumped right in on the game of pretending Sophie wasn't sitting right there dissenting from the Very Bad Plan. She hated them both, and the world in general. There was a serious existentialist crisis looming in the near future for her; granted they were both mainly unaware of that—Luc less so—but that didn't alter the fact that their flirting was getting in the way of her ditching them and finding Olivier.

"How are you going to get the beast?" The whole ignoring game meant that Sophie had to be proactive in her attempt to steer the activity.

With her eyebrows lowered and chin raised Norah waved a couple times to indicate her boredom with this tact. "Murder."

Pretty much what Sophie had anticipated, and Luc didn't possess Olivier's scruples about killing for fun. She examined his leering face for any hint of a misgiving. Nope, absolutely none.

"The wooden dolls I have covered." Norah sat back in the booth and knocked her leg against Sophie's as she stretched out. Playing footsie? Bah.

Luc clapped his hands together twice and smiled with his too-red mouth framing his too-white teeth. "It's done! Now we drink and I seduce you!" Sophie was not at all sure who the "you" in that sentence was. Which was his intention, she was certain.

"Why don't you tell us the details of the plan instead?" Norah lifted an eyebrow and linked her fingers together across her midriff. Sophie sat back and silently thanked her friend for being the one to ask that. Not that she believed there really was a plan. Okay, no.

"Look, why don't you two masterminds cook up the 'plan,' and the sarcasm you hear in my voice is intentional. I have things to do." She shoved Norah over so that she could get out of the booth.

"Like my cousin, my lady?" Smarmy got him no concessions, just a blush, which was probably enough for him.

"Wait, you're ditching me for a guy?" Wounded was not what Sophie expected from Norah. Not when she was on the make. Definitely an act.

Shrugging into her coat, Sophie negotiated the pins in her hair and winked at her friend. "I'm sure Luc can keep you busy. Be careful. Don't go looking for La Roi." She shot a hard look at Luc. "Or kill too many people."

Luc straightened slightly. "This banishing? It has to be done at exactly midnight. The parting of the veil." She lifted an eyebrow as he slouched back against the booth. "Important information for someone who will maybe spend the day in someone else's bed."

For the love of . . .

Sophie stomped off. She had wasted enough time

with those two idiots. She needed more blood and she needed Olivier—in that order.

THERE WAS ABSOLUTELY no way, whatever else she felt, that Sophie was going to face down any kind of monster without Olivier there to make sure Luc didn't get them all killed. Sure, she knew Luc didn't have anything actively against her, especially considering their history, but he seemed far too addicted to mayhem and chaos to be trusted.

Riding in the elevator to Olivier's floor, Sophie alternated between two thoughts: *I hope he takes this well* and *How does one use a ferret in a banishment spell?* She highly suspected that Luc was making shit up to cover up ulta-violence and virgin sacrifice.

Plus she was nervous about seeing Olivier. Confession might be good for the soul, but she wasn't even sure she had one anymore. She felt the weight of the girl's death earlier weighing on her along with the knowledge that her behavior since returning from the Fairylands had been ridiculous at the least and manslaughter-level stupid at the worst. Her most prudent order of conduct should have been to confess to Olivier as soon as she fell out of the ceiling and demand he tell her every single thing he knew or remembered about their past and Ankou and then forced him to force Luc into helping them figure out what to do.

Hindsight and all that crap.

How old would she have to get before she started thinking fifteen moves ahead like vampires in television shows and movies? Obviously a thousand wasn't old enough if her two role models were anything to work from.

The light in the short hallway from the elevator to

Olivier's door flickered. She wrapped her hand around the doorknob and twisted. It wasn't locked and turned easily. The week before she would have never simply opened some man's door and strode in as though she had the right to. However, he wasn't just some man, and on several levels she did have the right—she knew it was unlocked specifically for her.

His back was to her, and he didn't react at all as she stepped into the apartment and shut the door behind her. The click of the mechanism was loud in the stillness of the room. Across the open loft, Olivier knelt over a large canvas, at least five foot by five foot square, almost the same height as her. He was dressed in old, ratty shorts that might have once been light blue but were mainly holes and paint and a white t-shirt just as splattered as the shorts. Red and aqua paint melted into each other in the upper left corner of the canvas, the texture built up into a mound that dropped off towards the middle of the work into a flat, reflective, silver metallic surface. The silvery paint bled into an area of ink sketches overlaid with words she was too far away to read.

Most of the recessed lighting in the ceiling was still off, and illumination came mainly from the glaring, fluorescent kitchen lights. His hair hung past his shoulders, caught in a ponytail holder at the nape of his neck, the rest swinging around his face, hiding it from her view.

"I killed a girl tonight. After you sent me away from the trees." The words leaped out of her mouth. She wanted to say so many other things, too, too many to count, but the confession was the first to get to her tongue. She had two confessions to make, and that was the easier of them. Which scared her.

He didn't react, his right hand pressed palm down on the surface of his painting, red and yellow paint almost obscuring his skin completely. "That is who you are, the sooner you embrace that fact, the easier it will become to control your impulses."

His voice was a soft burr that tripped into her ear sounding damaged, abraded. Even so, even though he was attempting to hide his face and emotions from her, she could tell there was something very wrong.

"Are you mad at me for leaving you at the Christmas tree lot?" That was something she hadn't expected or even thought of. He was so mercurial himself; she thought running off to feed would be normal to him, something he understood. Her victim, maybe *that* was an issue, but the urge to run, not so much. She stepped away from the door and towards him. Dropping to her knees next to the painting, keeping a little distance from him, Sophie ducked her head to look up at his down-turned face. His eyes flicked up to hers, and she felt the immediate jab low in her belly that he could invoke just by breathing near her, by existing at all.

His pupils dilated until only a thin rim of turquoise remained captured between the white and the black. He trailed two fingers down the side of her face, leaving cool paint behind. "I loved a woman once, so long ago that I can't remember the sound of her voice or scent of her skin." He drew a silent breath, long and through his mouth. "I lived in the syllables of my name from her lips, in the roll of her walking hips, in the fury of her righteousness."

Her world collapsed in on itself. He still loved Phillipa. He didn't want Sophie for herself, he just wanted to recapture something from his past. Memories are only facets of a person, and Sophie *wasn't* Phillipa, she couldn't be. Could never be. Her heart broke for both of them. Him for his loss, her for the love she could already taste in the back of her mouth, like the memory of something that never happened.

Yes, she remembered some of what Phillipa did, what she saw, but she had no access to *who* she was, what made her *her*. Knowing a person's favorite color or flower or that they preferred white wine to red didn't mean they were truly known, definitely not enough to play-act and stand in for them. Even that wasn't complete, because Sophie had huge gaps in what she could remember, like she'd been hit in the head a few two many times and lost big hunks of time.

All the same unlike him she could remember the exact sound of Phillipa's voice, but only how it sounded in her own ear, that internal voice everyone has but no one else can ever hear. She could hear the strange—but not strange—tumble of Olivier's name from her throat. She could remember the scent of him and match it to the scent she smelled even then under the acrylic paint. The memories were there, with her all the time, along with the dreams that were memories of a life that was hers and not hers, like looking at a well-known face portrayed in a blurry photograph— the shape was right, but the details were obscured.

"You want me because of who you think I might once have been—I want. I want." Sophie swallowed hard, choked as she tried to breathe. "I want to be loved for myself, not—not for some creative fiction, not for someone—not for. Pretend." She drew in a quavery breath. Yes, once she had looked through different eyes, felt the world on different skin, heard Olivier's voice with ears attuned to ancient cadences. That was simpler to accept than she would have ever imagined before it was just true, just her life. Like being a vampire, Sophie took what she was given. She found it easier to accept transmigration of the soul than allowing herself to get involved with someone who wanted who she was in another life. Someone who wanted her to replace something he could barely remember having.

Olivier slid on his knees until he brushed against her. She didn't protest as he unfolded her from the Indian-style position she sat in, placing her legs over the top of his thighs and pulling her into his lap. With every touch, he smeared more paint onto her. He slid his hand into her hair, and she felt the sticky wetness swirling from her throat up the side of her neck.

"Love is unique, like the taste of each person's blood. I remember that I loved her, but you tear at my insides and try to be borne in my understanding." Words vibrating against the space between the back of her ear and her hairline, sending gooseflesh popping out from her scalp to the soles of her feet. His lips followed his breath, moving back and forth in a pattern on the sensitive patch of skin.

"I'm not really sure what to say to that." She was also having trouble thinking at all, forming words. Levering her up by her thighs, he pulled her more securely into his lap, and she knew that she had to get away soon. Immediately, or she would give in to this and hurt more for it later.

"I'm used to that response from people." Lips skimming up from behind her ear to the side of her face, smearing paint as he went. "I love you. Sophie."

"*I am Phillipa.*" Whispered admission into his hair, a rush of words tangling together and becoming one long word.

"Of course." The tip of his tongue, flexed and pointed, outlining her lips punctuated with the shove of his hips against her, the hard thickness of him wedging along right where they both want him to fit. "I loved her, too. But you are you, and I love you."

And this was impossible. She could barely breathe, couldn't explain herself, and the imperative was there. His hips starting working in a pattern, and she knew he was on the verge of flipping them over. Threading her hand in his hair, she yanked hard enough to pull his head away from hers and take some of his thick, coppery hair with her.

He smiled. His laugh broke free from his mouth and jumped down her throat into her belly, and down, down, down to where his cock jumped against her— hard enough to feel through her pants and his thin shorts. Undone and glad to be, she tried to remember why him loving the wrong part of her was a problem.

"Harder." He tugged his head away from her hand as she groaned. Fire shot along the nerves of her clutching fingers. He ripped her pants open at the same second she snapped his head back with the force of her fist in his hair.

"Olivier—"

She had to tell him, really, because the guilt would overwhelm her later if she let it go. If she felt like she was using him for this, for the dilated pupils and strong fingers with nails that broke the skin on her inner thighs and the rattle of his breath as she tossed her shirt directly onto his painting and his broken voice begging her to hurt him. "I remember. All of it, everything—I remember—not everything—but—"

"I *know*!" His roar shocked her into stillness. How he managed to stand with her attached to him she had no clue. Carrying her to the bed he bit her neck, over and over, just hard enough to bruise but not break the skin, and she convulsed against him. Pain was very good; she agreed with him.

He knew.

He threw her on the bed with enough force to break

one of the slats under the box springs. He knew and he didn't care that she knew. When he sat back on his knees to peel his shirt off and fling it away, she used it as an opportunity to pay him back, just a little, for stringing her along, not giving her what she needed when she needed it and letting her run around half-cocked like an idiot.

His shorts rode up high enough that all she had to do was lean up and pitch him back and her teeth found his femoral artery. His thigh flexed under her lips and restraining hands, shaking, and the combination of his moan and the taste of his blood made her wet almost to her knees. His hand pressed against the back of her head when she withdrew her teeth and dug the tip of her tongue into each tooth mark, one by one, pressing her hand against the straining material of his shorts. Rolling her cheek along the seeping wound, smearing the blood along the whorls of yellow and aqua paint she met his eyes. He rested on one elbow, tendons in his neck straining to keep his skull from lolling back.

"I could bite you there. I know it's what you want." She squeezed him, and his head hit the bed as he came in his shorts so hard even her bite mark bled in a rush, his muscles constricting and forcing the blood from his leg.

Using the time he needed to recover, she stripped her clothes off, shirt and bra, ruined pants and underwear, aware that he was languid, but watchful. She unbound her hair completely, tossing the pins and ponytail holder onto the floor by the bed, and crawled up his body, stopping to raise his hips and yank his shorts off. Straddling him, her knees against his ribs, she sank both hands into his hair. His long lashes brushed his face as he blinked slowly, full lips parting, expecting a kiss.

Leaning close enough to lick a line from his top lip to the indentation below his nose, she stopped and whispered against his mouth. "Do you want to hurt me back?"

Her hands were restrained above her head in one of his hands, and his teeth were breaking the skin of her chest, severing the large artery running right by the crease of her armpit before she had time to draw another teasing breathe. The biting didn't hurt, no, that felt right, natural, like fire on a cold night, his fingers on the inside of her thigh hurt.

He yanked her to him, the bones in his fingers pressing so hard she was sure it would break the skin, that they were breaking something, ripping muscle and popping the cartilage of her hip, and when the bruises were turning to something more and the hurt was too distracting to enjoy the pleasure of the bite, he shoved inside of her, and that was everything right about life.

"Olivier," she moaned. He couldn't bite her and fuck her at the same time because of the height difference, not where he had chosen to bite, and she knew that was his place. She pulled his head up by his hair and offered him the inside of her elbow instead. His eyes met hers, and she saw he wanted something else.

His mouth against hers was worth two more deaths at least, the sticky brush of his ribbed bottom lip against her slick one, the sly flick of the tip of his tongue against the middle of her top lip, then the drop into oblivion when her blood on his tongue met his blood in her mouth. She bit him as her teeth tried to snap together as she came, his mouth catching his own name. The words to an old song floated through her mind . . . *I love you, but I don't want to love you.*

"I love you," she whispered against his mouth.

Chapter Twenty

SOPHIE WOKE LESS sore than she felt she deserved to be, totally naked, on her back with the lights from the kitchen glaring on her uncovered form. She had a Midwestern mentality after all—you should pay as you go—and she thought as much pleasure as she just experienced should be bought with a little suffering. Not the sort of suffering she would enjoy.

Paint and dried blood cracked on her skin when she shifted. Maybe she would settle for the mental anguish of having a couple new fetishes. She wasn't a fetish kinda girl. Or she hadn't been last week.

"Who gave you the ring?" His always bruised voice sounded tortured. She resisted the urge to reach over the edge of the bed for a sheet or blanket now that she knew he was awake. What they had done negated a need for embarrassment between them—for good. His worldview was elastic, and he never judged where people found their pleasure. Her memory filled in that crack in her self-image. When she apparently took too long to answer, his hand lifted from the mattress, and he splayed his hand over her stomach like a starfish around her bellybutton.

She glanced at him. He lay sprawled on his stomach, head turned away from her, knee cocked up and to the side, other arm hanging over the side of the bed. When she brushed her thumb over the dimples above the swell of his perfectly rounded ass, he clenched his fingers on her belly, but didn't turn his head. This was his way of giving her space while still trying to reassure.

"A girl. A girl I know that I knew, once, but I'm not sure how. In the Fairylands. When I put it on, I remembered. Not everything ever, but enough." She skimmed her hand up his arm, brushing the golden hair in the wrong direction, the thick muscle clenching slightly.

"Rosamund." It wasn't a question, but she treated it like one.

"Yes, I think; Norah wouldn't remember. I don't know how she did it, but I gave her my ring . . . before the end." That—that was something she didn't want to talk about. She remembered the frenzy leading to the bonfire only too well, remembered sending Rosamund off with her ring before the mob closed in, remembered telling her that one of them should survive, at least one of them.

But she hadn't survived, because Norah was alive. Uh, well, Norah was undead, anyway.

And Ankou had, somehow, ended up with her ring, given it to the child, and . . .

Olivier's face was hovering over hers, his hair brushing her face, blocking out the light, before she could taste the smoke in the back of her mouth. "I tried to kill her. I tried, but she was too powerful." He pressed his cheek to hers moving it around in a broken circle.

"It was my own fault. I'm glad it wasn't you who killed her, because she'd be really pissed off now." Whoosh, flash, and he sat up with his arm across her back, tilting her head towards the light.

"What does that mean?" Oh, he didn't know. Should she tell him? She tried to move her head, to look him in his eyes, but he wouldn't let her. His hand was as big as the back of her skull, and the curve of it fit in his palm in a way that wouldn't let her budge.

"Rosamund had to die for Ankou to escape," Sophie told him gently. "She bound him and when she died, her magic died. But he needed a conduit. When we bound Paul, he had a connection to her and to me, a body to inhabit, a way to break free. I mean, I guess. It's not like Luc has been too forthcoming with the information about all this mystical crap." The fingers squeezed a little harder; not hard enough to make the hurt count, enough to make her shift to straddle his thigh.

"Norah? I figured." He was amused.

"You knew Rosamund was dead?" She wedged her hand into the hollow between her breasts and dug her nails into his chest in answer to his behavior. He let her go.

"Yes, Luc and I felt it, like a void creeping on the edges of consciousness."

She settled back on the bed, looking up at him as he moved out from under her completely, back enough to be in range but not touching. "I think Norah is almost exactly like her."

"That's amusing. In a way you're not like you." Leaning down, he pushed her hair away from her face.

"I think it's because I was dead for so long, that's all I can figure." Leaning down, he licked a patch of dried blood on her neck, dissolving it and sucking it away.

"Maybe we should not worry about that until you're comfortable with it." Yes, that sounded good to her. Not worrying about anything but his tongue sounded good to her. His breath chuffed, chuffed against her wet skin, curling her toes, the sound drifted to her ears—laughter.

"I'm worried about leaving her alone with Luc. He knows—"

"He knows?" Olivier sounded surprised. Of course he would be—Luc knew and didn't tell him.

"Yes, he knows . . ." Sophie's voice trailed off into a sigh as Olivier's tongue moved lower, to her breasts. "Mischief paired with ambition in heels. Not good for anyone who isn't them."

"Luc is invested in sending Ankou back to the Fairylands. Rosamund will die again and again in payment for her crimes."

"I don't like the way that sounds," said Sophie.

"Neither does Luc." Olivier sucked on one of her nipples, his tongue rough against her skin. She writhed against him.

Even fluorescent light couldn't rob the sharp planes of his cheeks or the dramatic sweep of his eyebrows of their intrinsic beauty, his smile of its deep dimples, and Sophie fell a little bit harder as Olivier's face loomed closer to sink in her hair just as his hand sank between her spread legs.

THEY DIDN'T LEAVE the apartment for the rest of the night nor the whole of the next day, not until well into the following night. Olivier assured her that Luc would contact them when he was ready, and sure enough, the phone rang and it was Norah.

"Game on," she said, and she either sounded tired or

drunk or really turned on, or all three. Sophie couldn't tell, and didn't think she wanted to know.

She and Olivier had slept and made love and slept and made love and slept and talked. Olivier read her poetry and painted her body with his acrylics. He washed her hair and brushed it dry, photographed her spread out on his bed. He talked to her about their life, what he could remember, stories of taking her virginity, of her belief in the Good God. He fed her blood that tasted musky, not human, but no animal she could identify.

And when he fell asleep in the watery light of dusk that eve, she whispered into his hair, "I love you," and he turned and his eyes blinked heavily and he said, "I love you," and she felt that he was saying those words to her, not to Phillipa, not to the ghost of a past neither of them truly remembered or wanted to repeat. She slept on his chest and awoke to an empty bed, with him watching her from a corner, his fingers black with charcoal, a sketchpad propped on his knee, an American Spirit cigarette dangling from the corner of his mouth.

The Christmas tree he'd purchased flashed behind him. Somehow, Sophie wasn't surprised that Olivier was partial to the colored running lights that would cause anyone epileptic fits.

Chapter Twenty-one

CRISP, SEPIA-COLORED snow drifted to the ground back-lit by streetlights. Olivier followed flake after flake float by markers that meant nothing to anyone else: China Station Restaurant, Sophie's left cheek, a *Chicago Tribune* box, the tip of Sophie's scuffed boot. One finger-wide hank of hair had escaped the complex system of hair restraint on the crown of Sophie's head, and the snow collected in the curve of the curling ends. He didn't want to be there at all. But his addiction to her had to be tempered for the sake of the world—that's all that drew him from his apartment.

When Luc informed him there was a serious time constraint on capturing Ankou, Olivier believed him without question, therefore he and Sophie had come to meet Luc and Norah to assist with the capture and banishment. Luc's idea of a reasonable plan, and Olivier's idea of a reasonable plan hadn't met very frequently in their history together, and tonight didn't look like it would break that mold.

The plan hadn't been explained to him, nor to Sophie, when Norah had called the telephone Sophie was shocked he owned. He used the internet; he had no idea why she had expected him to not own a telephone.

Norah and Luc said come, and they came. Now he realized that with Luc it was always better to get the facts up front. Norah, dressed all in black leather from her zip up shirt and pants to her boots, had no sympathy in her tone, when Olivier tuned his ear to her. She stood about thirty feet from him, negotiating turning a clutch of young people into vampires in exchange for their "help."

She wasn't elucidating what that word might involve. That was a bad sign for the wishful fledges.

Olivier foresaw their horrible deaths in the very near future. He turned his eyes to Sophie, her hair curling along her face and the top of the turtleneck he'd lent her. Even his protestations that Luc and Norah were both also vampires and unlikely to do more than mock would dissuade her from covering as much as possible.

The familiar weight of Luc's hand descended onto his shoulder. "The sand shifts, but it's still the beach."

"Zen koan?" Olivier had never considered Luc much of a philosopher, but he knew he could never really know anyone as much as he assumed he did; no matter how long nor how well he knew a person, he also knew they would always shift to the right when you expected them to shift to the left, and that flux of personality was endlessly fascinating to him.

Luc laughed softly. Olivier kept his eye fixed on the blush of Sophie's cheek, snow slowly melting on the collar of her pink coat, the minute alterations in her tight mouth. She was anxious about what Luc and Norah planned. He couldn't help but see the echo of long dormant memories in that.

Luc was still Luc, and Rosamund had been too old, too strong, not to bleed through into Norah. Sophie was right to worry.

"*You* told that to me once, when I despaired over the swiftness of time." The pressure on his shoulder increased, and Olivier tried to remember ever saying that, or Luc ever worrying over too little time.

"When did I tell you that?" Turning his eyes from the curve of Sophie's jaw, Olivier watched Luc's eyelashes brush his cheek, his own gaze resting in the shadows where the children stood being instructed by Norah.

"In the first trembling of the spring, when I was too young to understand how old I would become," said Luc. He stepped away, towards the fluttering shadows arcing inside the alley. Tall buildings hulked on all three sides of the narrow space and a solid brick wall stood at the far end where one would expect a fence or a thin driveway for emergency vehicles. Olivier followed his progression until Luc stood one step behind Norah, hands in his pockets, one foot out in front of him, one shoulder dipping. Fear fell on him with the increasing snow. They would kill all those people. Kill them with a finality that did not allow for them returning to life as one of them.

Olivier had realized this when he and Sophie had arrived to find the eleven humans huddled together in a quivering clutch. He'd encountered people like this often enough, but only when companioned by Luc. His cousin had an odd fondness for thwarting the hopes of those who sought purposefully to become what they became out of conviction, out of a loyalty to their fallen comrades and co-religionists. Luc believed people who sought endless life in order to gain revenge upon their childhood enemies or become rich and lead a soft life of being served did not deserve eternal life.

Eternal life grew tedious, Olivier knew, without the fire of conviction, without a true purpose. He wondered what his purpose would be, now that he had Sophie beside him—perhaps Sophie would be his purpose.

Olivier didn't think he would mind that. He could happily watch Sophie for hundreds of years without losing his focus on living to breathe the same air she did.

His hand tightened around hers; she stepped closer to him, pressed her body against his, dug her nails into his hand.

Norah pointed to a girl in a white dress and barked out an order for her to perform an odd series of movements, hand to belly, hand to space between her breasts, hand over her eyes. Olivier recognized the beginning of a ritual, even if he wasn't an adept himself. Luc looked up at him, tossing his head back in the casual sexuality he owned like his name. They were all definitely going to die.

"Sophie." Her head swiveled with the sibilant hiss of the first letter of her name.

"What's wrong?" If the situation wasn't so urgent, he would have asked her how she could tell something was.

"Luc is going to do something horrible."

"I don't see how they can do anything without Paul being here," said Sophie. She licked her lips.

He leaned down and licked her lips for her, kissed her, sucked her tongue into his mouth. "He'll come," he said, and gave her his air when she gasped.

Flicking his eyes from her back to Luc and Norah, he saw that Luc had begun instructing another of the humans to blink his eyes exactly eleven times and pull out a lock of his hair. Pointing to specific spots, Norah indicated that the humans who had already performed their movements should line up according to chalk marks on the ground. They swayed towards Norah, flesh and bone and hair like stalks and petals and sap swaying towards the distant sun. Olivier could imagine her as a major player in the underworld, a dangerous leader.

She smiled at them, reassuring, moved her hips, sex like they had never known, and snapped her fingers, commanding with a threat more deadly than anything they had ever experienced.

"If you don't want to see, you don't have to watch. But you have to be here. Your blood is needed." Olivier grabbed Sophie by the arm and swung her into his chest, but held one of her arms out toward Luc, who was striding toward them.

"I know what they're doing," snapped Sophie. "I'm not an idiot. I just—" She gasped. Olivier looked over. Luc had sunk his teeth into her wrist. Sophie moaned and her hips canted into Olivier's. He wondered if she knew Luc was her brother, decided not to tell her. After all, he wasn't her brother any longer; they were connected by blood, but not the sort that would matter in Sophie's modern human world.

Luc's mouth was full of Sophie's blood and Sophie was falling backward over Olivier's arms. Olivier could feel Ankou coming toward them.

"They're calling Ankou to this spot," said Sophie, and Olivier realized that he'd lifted his mouth from hers. "They're calling him with death. It's the only way. I know that, and so do you. These lives for all the others he would take."

He stared into her face, its natural flush stolen by the

moon and sodium lights overhead and Luc's stealing of her blood.

Stepping back slightly so her neck wouldn't have to bend as sharply, she met his eye, the hazel he expected to see washed to grey.

"Olivier . . ." she began, but a single scream followed by several others joined in a horrifying chorus, pulsed from the blackness of the alley. The scent of blood poured out of the stillness that followed the first rush of sound. Sophie looked up at him with eyes that hungered, half-feral.

He pulled her wrist up to his mouth, sank his teeth into the same spot Luc had, finding the teeth marks that were already not puncture wounds but minor divots in the skin. His tongue laved her skin, tasted himself and Luc and salt and metal and—

Olivier hadn't spent much time with fledges, never longer than it took to read their souls, and he suddenly wondered how long it would be before she settled down. Before she could smell blood and not lose her mind to it.

The scent of blood washed over them. Sophie moaned and writhed in his arms and her blood flowed into his throat.

SOPHIE ENTERED THE alley blinking snow off her eyelashes and fighting the blood lust. It was hard, harder than not eating chocolate on a diet, harder than not confessing an unrequited love when the object sits so close you can smell them. She didn't run. She did rub her wrist a little—Olivier's teeth had chipped a bone, she could feel it regrowing under skin that had already grown back.

If Ankou appeared, she wasn't going to fly heedlessly into death . . . or anything else. She'd known what Luc and Norah were doing when she counted the number of humans wandering around in the alley like cows in a pen. The number was symbolic, odd numbers important for some ritual something, but her knowledge—Phillipa's knowledge—was still limited. She'd known it was a summoning ritual, but not exactly how it worked.

The whole charades aspect had been surprising and amusing.

She was still wondering about the cage and the ferret and the dolls.

She watched as Norah fed from a boy in a see-through shirt and vinyl trousers. Somehow the victims were all anchored to their ritual locations. Luc was good. The screams had become begging, a complex sound of several voices twisting together in terror. Not everyone had been bled yet. Illumination from the streetlights faded to almost total blackness about six feet into the alley. She could only see what was happening due to her heightened night vision. The screams were loud, very loud, pathetic, and her blood lust shut out her ability to feel pity for the struggling, writhing prey.

The question of why no one had come running to rubber-neck or help did strike her. Had to be another spell. Was it limited to shielding the alley, or could no one but those Luc wanted to hear the ruckus? Sophie decided magic was fascinating, worth studying for sure.

She started toward the prey, but found she couldn't move. Olivier had her around the waist.

"This is my battle more than yours . . . and I'm enjoying this. Which is weird," she said thoughtfully. Because she knew she shouldn't want to see this at all, that some part of her later would hate herself for not trying to stop it, like how she knew killing the cabbie had been wrong, killing the girl, killing anyone—but right now, with the magical stink of ozone and sulfur in the air, the taste of blood so thick in her throat it was like she was drinking herself . . . and then she knew she was, that she felt the languor, the almost feeding haze because she was, that Luc and Norah could never have drained eleven people between them, that they were somehow receiving part of the feeding.

"Do you . . ." She looked up at Olivier's face, at his averted eyes and knew he felt it. And that he was angry. This was probably some sort of violation, but Sophie didn't care. One of those kids had been a virgin; her knees began to buckle, and she leaned into Olivier.

He smelled like safety, and not at all like magic. He smelled like art and—and *life,* not the end of the world.

She felt it when his anger softened, the tense muscles in his chest and arms relaxing. Her mind drifted, sated, Olivier's scent everything that wasn't the scent of blood. Why did she want revenge against Ankou? The idea of it felt right, dripping through her like blood from the back of her throat, but somehow she suddenly thought it was ridiculous. Revenge was one of their weaknesses. She understood that then. The reason that even Luc—*Luc!*—warned her and Norah against thralling Paul was that revenge wasn't just an act of retribution for vampires, like it was for humans.

Revenge was a craving, something that burrowed inside and could come to own a vampire, obsess a vampire, take over the afterlife, take over the existence of any undead. And Rosamund's revenge plot against the Catholic church, which had decimated her people, had led to Ankou's unleashing and Phillipa's death. Even knowing that, Sophie still felt the human impulse that revenge was an end in itself, something pure and right.

Pulling back from Olivier, she stepped towards the buffer of Norah and Luc. Norah knelt on the ground by her last victim, Luc stood behind her, almost touching.

The smell of power rode the air, salt and copper and recent death and lingering agony. Not all of the victims were dead yet. Paul's voice crackled from the middle of the arranged bodies of the sacrifices. He wore pants of indeterminate color and a girl's half-ripped orange tank top.

"These pathetic creatures die so easily, children. But you, you are something different." His voice was torment and suffering, endless terror and the certainty of worse to come. He paused. A wet popping noise issued from the ground. One of the begging voices fell silent. "You will be the terror in the night, the voice in the dark, the fear under the bed that will bring the humans crawling on their bellies to me. To worship me. This sacrifice is flattering."

Sophie wanted to sigh. He thought they were enough to bring the entire human population of the earth to their knees? Maybe Luc and Norah and a thousand more just like them, but Sophie wasn't really up for hiding in the closet to scare children. Ruling the world sounded great on paper, but the constant need to punish and dominate would be too much.

Allowing Ankou to get even a toehold in this world was beyond imagining. Sophie had made some bad mistakes in her life, but none before this that lead to mass murder. She wouldn't let that continue. Feeding to survive was one thing; bringing about the complete subjugation of the human race was on another scale.

Plus, humans really had their own agendas, and should be left to them.

A sharp scream broke her musing. The scream took shape becoming a reverberation:

"NOOOOOOOOOOOOOOOOOOOOOOO!"

A scuffle began, and Sophie wanted to yell to the humans not to struggle to get away from their marks or draw attention to themselves.

Olivier brushed her back in what Sophie assumed was supposed to be a soothing gesture, but it only reminded her that he'd screwed up not telling her to look out for fairies. Luc touched Norah's shoulder, and she stood. When she did, Sophie realized Norah'd been shielding the lower half of Luc's body from Ankou, blocking his line of sight. She felt like a coward then because she knew she was the only one not watching the people die. She was purposefully not looking at the ground. She was ashamed.

Ankou inside Paul was luminous, radiant. She hadn't needed to use her vampiric sight to watch him watch her.

Concentrating, she blinked once, and when she opened her eyes back up, she saw it all. All eleven bodies, sprawling in a pattern, interlocking around Ankou who knelt in center of the figure. One body with no head, another with a cracked sternum and no heart, another had her entrails hanging out of her belly. The woman who had sat with them at the Orchid the night before—Scarlet—lay in front of Ankou with blood covering her, clots splattering the side of her face, deep scratches running up her gore covered arms.

Ankou was pristine except for two splatters on his cheek. The scene made no sense. How could he be so clean?

The woman raised her hand to her throat, fingers pulled into a claw. Sophie watched in horror as she ripped out her own throat with one swift motion. Ankou's face was blank as he watched, neither excited nor disturbed by the show. Sophie hated him, truly hated him. Paul also didn't deserve this. Was he inside there with the fairy, aware enough to see the show? Could he hear Ankou's thoughts spiraling through his own mind? Did he think it was his own will to do these things?

Sophie had done this. She had allowed Norah to enslave Paul, and that had killed these people, made Paul a victim twice. Would she outlive the guilt?

Light spread from near Luc towards Ankou, purple neon light crept along the ground inch by inch, drawing his attention. "Do you think this will hold me?" demanded Ankou.

Sophie guessed he couldn't get out of the—she didn't know what an eleven-sided figure was called.

"Long enough." Luc made a sweeping motion with his hand and the light whipped out lightning fast, capturing Ankou in a halo of gently glowing lavender. Royal purple for the king.

He was caught tight, not even able to struggle, the haughty disdain for their actions caught on Paul's face.

THE SIGHT OF blood didn't bother Norah, unless it was hers or someone's she cared about, but there were limits. Such as trying to converse with someone covered head to toe with gore and bits of stuff while he arranged vampire carcasses into some arcane symbol.

"So, evisceration, who knew?" She gave Luc a look to indicate that she knew *he* had known.

"Summoning the power to capture Ankou takes an offering," Luc grinned, his face streaked with blood that began at the corner of his eye, like tears. She grinned back. He was too hot for her own good. Even covered in bits and pieces of ick.

"I'm always down for some ultraviolence." She squatted down next to Luc and wiped a wad of something unidentifiable off of his cheek. In response he smeared blood on the side of her face.

"I like that in a woman."

A cough behind her drew her attention. Olivier stood looking up at Ankou, as inscrutable as ever. He didn't seem too upset to her. Sophie, on the other hand, didn't look too thrilled, maybe preparing to puke, actually.

"Soph, you okay?"

"Luc is kneeling on an entrail." Sophie unnecessarily pointed to the evidence of that.

Olivier brought Sophie's hand to his face, brushing her knuckles against his cheek, then kissing the tip of a finger, before releasing his grip and stepping around her. "Luc," he said in a low voice that brought Luc's head up in a snap.

"You should have told me." Olivier grabbed a body and hauled it into another position.

Luc laughed, his cheery face lurid in the unnatural light surrounding Ankou. Luc responded in some foreign language Norah couldn't understand.

"She can't understand you, you know." Olivier turned another body so that its head rested in the lap of one of the others. Norah liked Olivier. Luc looked up and met her eye.

"I said that I didn't want him to know I still kill to impress women." Her stomach flipped over when he licked a bit of blood from the corner of his mouth.

"Norah?" Sophie touched her arm, and she turned. Baby girl did not look good. Norah wiped a piece of something off Sophie's cheek with the edge of her sleeve.

"You'll be buying me a new shirt." She smiled and pushed Sophie's hair over her shoulder thinking about how much blood she'd gotten in her own from the splatter.

"Do you believe in reincarnation?"

Norah sighed. *Here we go,* she thought. She loved her girl, she really did, but she thought too much, even when she was drunk.

"No." She didn't. Maybe Luc and Olivier were right, maybe she and Sophie were totally their reincarnated bitches from a million years ago, but she didn't *care*. She didn't really like to think about religion at all, boring—and now she didn't have to, not ever, or, at least, not for a long, long time.

You don't know someone for fifteen years without getting to know them well, even if it's someone you don't like. Sophie Norah liked. So, when she threw her head back and laughed, choking out "Oh my God, this is good!" she knew the joke was probably at her expense.

Behind Sophie, she saw that Luc and Olivier were done with the bodies and were standing casually touching from shoulder to hip, watching them. She had a heavy wave of déjà vu, but that happened constantly when Sophie was around anyway.

"Yes, would you like to share with the class?" Norah put a hand on her hip and cocked it out.

Tears ran down Sophie's face, and her hand came up to clutch Norah's shoulder. She couldn't help it, Norah started to giggle in reply to Sophie's cackling, the joke not even mattering.

"You know—" Choke, laugh. "—how boring you think all the religion stuff is? Irony!"

Over Sophie's shoulder she saw Olivier lay his hand on Luc's elbow. He whispered, "Rosamund *is* dead." Several expressions chased each other over Luc's face.

"Non," he said with an incredulous look and a gasp. His eyes met hers over Sophie's shoulder. The eye contact zinged in a way that it shouldn't have. Something was happening, something important. Her eyes were drawn up to Ankou's suspended body over Olivier and Luc's heads.

"They're talking about you." Sophie had stopped laughing, but Norah hadn't even noticed.

"What?" Her eyes swept down to her friend's softening face.

"Okay, so one time, we were best friends, a long time ago. You were very bad and I was less bad, and Luc was in love with you." She paused. "Let me know if anything seems familiar."

"Tell me we weren't in their stupid cult." Norah believed her. She always believed her. About being a vampire, about moving to Chicago, now about being reincarnated. Why not? Friendship was about trust.

Luc barked out a short laugh and said something in his secret language with Olivier. Sophie turned and looked at them, too. "We'll find a way to get your memories back."

Ah. "You understand them?"

"Yeah, Luc's glad you're hot." Sophie futzed with her hair. "Don't think I'm not pissed about the fucking mass murder thing here, okay? I just had to tell you, because it's a little much. Olivier's great in bed, but a little weird."

"Yeah, yeah." Norah didn't really care about their other lives, whatever, she had this one, and she didn't care if Luc had been pining after her for a thousand years, if he got on her nerves, she would bounce his ass.

Ankou seemed to be following them with his eyes, which unnerved her even further.

Without warning, there was a flash of golden light bright enough to blind her and a cascade of glitter fluttering from the sky. The purple light was gone, instead Ankou stood in the middle of the weird design created by the vampire corpses, blinking and twisting his head around like a confused bird. The golden light was more purple than the purple, and it gave off enough light to expose the disgusting gore covering Luc, Olivier, and Norah.

"I beg your pardon, but I demand an explanation for all of this." Paul was becoming more and more Ankou. His face was starting to be oddly angled. He glared from face to face. The voice was purely Ankou, like an echo in the dark creeping up Norah's spine.

Luc turned to Norah. "Go over there by Sophie." He pointed to where Sophie had stepped close to Olivier. Was he telling her what to do? Oh, hell no.

"Feel free to fuck yourself." She glared at him, intending to huff away. No one told her what to do. Even if she would have just walked over to stand next to Sophie naturally. But there were ways of doing things, and points to be made. She did not let men tell her what to do.

"*No!*" Luc screamed at her back. Whatever. Like she cared what he thought. She was going to get a cab, go home, and wash the blood out of her hair. Heading for the end of the alley and the street, she wondered what all the business with the damned fairy had been about anyway. Who was he and what was his deal? He seemed sort of familiar. The ground gave way, and she pitched onto her face. Right onto a huge flower.

*   *   *

"WHERE DID SHE go?" Sophie screamed, running for the mouth of the alley, as Norah blipped out of existence. *"Norah!"*

Olivier caught her by her hair, and she wheeled on him, baring her teeth, terrified. "Where is she? What happened?" She wanted to scream, cry, pull out her hair from fright. Olivier released her hair and wrapped his hand around her forearm, tugging her back to where Luc stood. Luc just looked puzzled and shrugged.

"How do I know? Fairyland." He turned to Ankou with a frown. "You're my thrall, no?"

Ankou lifted his chin and blinked twice slowly, keeping his eyes narrowed. "I could say no . . ." Ankou began.

"Tell me only the truth," Luc cut in.

"I am your thrall, you vile creature." He sniffed and looked away, directly at Sophie. Paul was one of the hottest men she'd ever met—that, combined with Ankou's essence, made him formidable. He wanted her, she could feel it, taste it. She wished she was gay. Would she obey him if he asked her to? He waved just the tips of his fingers at her with a small smile. That was enough for her. She was scared.

"We have to get rid of Ankou and help Norah." Sophie grabbed Olivier's arm. "Hurry, she's in some hell place where Ankou comes from, what if she's hurt or . . ."

"It doesn't work like that," Olivier rested a hand on her shoulder. "There's no way to pick where your opening will lead you. There are no rules and laws of physics there."

"He did." She pointed at Ankou, thinking about the tea party.

"He can't do anything but maim and kill. Someone

else from the inside must have done that, a witch—
they have powers alchemists don't, and that's why
fairies take them so often." Luc grabbed Ankou by the
hair and yanked him towards the invisible door into
Fairyland.

Sophie knew he was wrong that Ankou couldn't do
anything but maim and kill, intrinsically she knew that
was wrong. He had other abilities, but she had no access to what those were. They weren't a sweet singing
voice and ability to drive a standard transmission, that
was for sure.

"We have to do something!" Sophie began to cry,
and felt embarrassed for herself.

Luc smiled at her, his blood-streaked face terrify-
ing. "I haven't rescued a beautiful woman in at least
five hundred years," he said. "I'll get to it in a minute."
He twisted his fist in Ankou's hair.

"I am greatly affronted by this treatment. This
woman is mine. I shan't have her taken from me again!
This a great indignity." He sniffed again skewering Sophie with a hateful glare that promise torments beyond
her comprehension.

Luc blew a kiss, and stepped in none of the gore as
he hauled the struggling fairy along with him.

Sophie turned to Olivier. "How do we save them?"
She thought about it for a couple seconds while she
waited for him to form a plan. The fact that Ankou
needed someone to open a portal into Paul's body
struck her. "Suki! Suki is back there. She can help
them!" What would happen to Paul? Would Ankou be
automatically cast out, or would he live in Paul's body
forever? Would Paul still be their thrall? Where had
Norah landed? How far would Luc be from Norah?
Would that put Ankou near Norah, put her in danger?

Olivier's face broke into a smile, "I was thinking

that we could leave them there for a while anyway." He stepped into her, the sweet tang of blood strong on him. "Luc is powerful, and Norah is clever, they should be fine." His lips trailed over hers, just a brush. "Maybe I can teach you what I know of being a vampire."

She didn't want to leave Norah to fate, but Olivier's tongue touched the corner of her mouth. It moved along the line of her lips until she parted her mouth to him moving to suck his bottom lip inside when she tasted blood there. His hand slid down her back and into his borrowed jeans, right over the swell of her ass, and she gave in, just a little, just enough for him to be complacent. Wedging her hands between their bodies she shoved him back. He stumbled slightly.

"I'm not making out here where the cops will find us, and I'm sure as hell not leaving Norah to Luc's so-called rescue. I lost Suki—I won't lose Norah, too." Sophie pushed her hair away from her face and walked towards the street.

The only thing that kept her from falling through alone was that Olivier had reached out to grab her right as she stepped into the closing portal and back into the Fairylands, and when they landed on a giant mushroom, they landed together, entwined, kissing.

Epilogue

"YOU ARE, PERHAPS, lost?" A voice like every dream she'd ever had twisted together wrapped around her, eliciting a childish giggle. She sat up.

The most beautiful man in the universe sat opposite her. His face was perfectly symmetrical, arched eyebrows and the largest eyes she'd ever seen with an upwards tilt at their outer edges. His nose was strong and straight. His cheeks were both rounded, plump in the middle and sharply angled at the high bones. His mouth was a red with no name, but the Mouth of God. His lustrous, thick black hair was tied in a knot on top of his head, his arms and neck wrapped by gold bands, his blue skin painted with black symbols. He opened his palm and a flower sprung from nothing. Extending his arm, he offered her the sweetly scented bloom.

Love exploded inside Norah's body, blocking out all fear, hate, insecurity, negativity she had ever experienced.

"Krishna?" she said, and laughed when he winked at her.

Author's Note

Throughout human history, religions have cropped up that explain the universe as a system of one thing in constant conflict with an opposite thing. Orthodox Christianity is a system like this—God as a force for absolute goodness and the Devil as a force for absolute evil working in the world to influence humans. This sort of explanation for the cosmos is called dualism— dual, from *duo*—two.

Catharism (or the Albigensian heresy, named for the village of Albi in France) was a dualist belief system. Sometimes called a Christian heresy—that is a deviation from accepted, Papal-approved Catholic theology—Catharism was, in truth, not even Christianity at all. Adherents believed that the human world was made by the Devil—the Evil One, or the Dark One— to both tempt and torment human beings. The goal of the Cathar faithful was to escape the world of the flesh into the pure world of the spirit—a construct similar to Christian heaven.

While their wacky theological hijinx angered the Catholic church, what really got them into hot water was preaching a sort of early hippie-ism. Men and women were equal—a concept that is still not accepted worldwide to this day, but in the 1200s was revolutionary. Women often functioned as clergy, called Parfaits, or Perfects. These Perfects denounced the world as corrupt, abstaining from meat, dairy, and sex (i.e., vegan monks and nuns who stayed in the community rather than withdrawing to abbeys). Your average Cathars further subverted the status quo by having few sexual scruples and no prohibitions against drink and debauchery of any sort—since human bodies were made by the Devil, why deny them any of the Devil's evil fun?

Unfortunately for the fun-loving (or hating, in the case of the Perfects) Cathars, they had one more belief that really peeved the Pope—they refused to take oaths. Back in the Middle Ages, oath-taking was the system that held society together. A man's word was his bond, and anyone refusing to swear an oath, who also preached that the common person was equal to a king, was a serious troublemaker. What would happen if no one obeyed commands and began demanding equal treatment? Many nobles were either suspected or confirmed Cathars, and the concentration of power in the hands of those sybaritic wackos was just not going to do.

A crusade was dispatched, and the Cathars were wiped out. For the most part.

Rumors of their survival persisted for centuries. The best known myth of their survival pertained to four Cathars escaping from the mountain fortress of Mont Segur on the eve of their final destruction. These survivors supposedly carried the Cathar Treasure to safety. What that treasure was has been speculated upon ever since. Some say it was the Holy Grail, others vast wealth. Since I can't imagine anyone scaling a cliff face laden down with gold after being starved for months on end, I speculate that these survivors carried their only real treasure—their faith, which they believed had been passed from believer to believer since the dawn of time.

Here's a sneak peak of

THE
ULTIMATUM

BY SUSAN KEARNEY

coming in February 2006 from Tor Romance

SOME SPECIES LIVED to make love. Why did hers require mandatory sexual encounters—not just to procreate— but to survive?

Once again Dr. Alara Bazelle Calladar's goal of creating the DNA she required eluded her, and she rubbed the bridge of her nose in disappointment. Her search to free Endekian women from the curse of their genetics was turning out to be extraordinarily complex and laborious. But all her effort would be worthwhile if she ever succeeded in putting women's hearts and minds, instead of their biology, in charge of when they had sex.

Under normal circumstances, finding a solution to achieve her goal was difficult, but during the beginnings of *Boktai*, Alara's female hormone levels made unclouded reasoning as elusive as a Denvovian sandworm who'd grown wings. As if in anticipation of a kiss, her lips already tingled and the increased blood flow from arousal had caused her breasts to become tender.

"Alara," her assistant and good friend, Maki, interrupted, her words echoing through the com system and over the lab's DNA maturation receptacles that housed Alara's hopes for the future of every Endekian woman. "You have a visitor."

"I'm busy." *Busy* was their private code word for put whoever was interrupting her work off until another day, a day when she wasn't so frazzled.

"He's . . . insistent."

"He?" Alara snapped her head up from the array of test samples, every one of them a failure. Science required patience and normally she had plenty. But with her blood simmering from the onset of *Boktai*, just the mention of a man caused her heart beat to escalate, her patience to dwindle.

"Oh, he's one hundred and ten percent male," Maki practically purred, and Alara imagined how the Endekian male would preen at Maki's compliment. He'd no doubt entered the reception area, puffed up with confidence that he was wanted and that he was worthy of female attention. Very likely, he wasn't. Endekian men didn't need to treat their women well, not when women had to offer up their bodies to them on a regular basis to stay alive. While it took a lot to impress Maki, she still wouldn't have interrupted unless she believed the man important.

"*Krek*," Alara swore under her breath, annoyed that in her current biological state she would react to a male just like every other Endekian woman with her hormones demanding sex. After inhaling male scent and male pheromones, she'd find him irresistible—even if he turned out to be an absolute idiot, or an uncivilized brute, or simply an unskilled derelict. In the early phase of *Boktai*, her enhanced senses would enflame her, deepening her desires, quickening her yearning until she transformed into a female she loathed—an undiscriminating female who required sex with every needy cell in her body.

Alara didn't want the temptation of a male in her lab, or in her life. Not unless she chose to invite him, but that wasn't damn likely. She had no use for men— not until she was caught deep in the clutches of *Boktai*. In fact, the few rare males who deigned to enter her laboratory were often those who sought to discourage her from continuing her work. Oh, yes. Endekian men were quite content with the status quo, and if Alara hadn't been a war heroine, the male-run government might have shut down her facility from the start.

Some heroine she was. While everyone else had died during the Terran terrorist's bombing of her city, her presence within an underground laboratory had saved her life along with her mother's. But due to an preposterous calamity of nature, Endekian biology tied a wife's death to her husband's. After the Terran bomb had killed father, her mother had suffered a slow, painful death.

Alara had gone on . . . alone.

She had raged, mourned and buried both mother and father. And then she'd repressed her grief in work. As the sole survivor of the vicious attack that had killed her parents, she'd studied harder and become more determined than ever to unravel the secrets of Endekian biology. She wanted women to be free of the curse of *Boktai* and an odd fame had given her the means to follow her dream.

She could never have foreseen the results of her survival, that the government would chose her as the symbol to rally the masses to their cause against the Terrans. Alara had used her new-found celebrity and government connections to help fund her research.

However, as the anger against the Terran attack abated, she'd become less useful to the government and had fallen out of favor. With the current unpopularity of her work, she wouldn't be surprised if her visitor was here to close her lab.

"Alara." Maki's voice dropped to a whisper. "He's bristling with attitude."

"Tell him I'm *busy*."

"I already tried." Maki's tone conveyed vexation. "He refuses to make an appointment."

"Well, use your imagination. Get rid of him for me."

"I'd be perfectly willing to take him home for the night." Maki breathed out a delicate sigh. "I tried. But he wants you. He said he's willing to wait as long as it takes."

"Oh, for the holy structure of atoms," Alara cursed and shoved back from the table. "He can wait all through the dark hours if he wants. I'm leaving through my personal entrance."

Alara picked up the disk to start her flitter and headed out the back of the building. She intended to go home, soak in a hot bath and take care of her growing arousal. Using self gratification to ease her cravings was only a temporary solution, one that would work for a short time and only if no males were present. Out of distaste, she would delay approaching a man for as long as possible to ease her need. Alara's personal physician had warned her that repetitive delays were detrimental to her wellbeing, that her cells required regular sexual activity with a male for healthy regeneration, and Alara fully understood that relief from her inborn biological drive to mate would be fleeting. Experience told her she couldn't hold out much longer and that within a day, two at most, she would lose control of her psi and herself and be forced to seek out a male partner.

With a quick retina scan, Alara unlocked her back door and stepped outside into the balmy dusk. Automatically she used her psi on her suit, the type worn by every Federation citizen, to shield her from the cloying humidity. Anxious to be on her way, she didn't pause to take in the city lights beyond her building and headed straight for her flitter, climbed in, inserted the disk and revved the engine.

"You were leaving without speaking to me." A deep male voice that was filled with vitality arrowed from the back seat and struck her full blown, causing her to jerk in surprise.

She held her breath, refusing to allow his scent into her lungs, but just the sound of his husky male tone kindled inevitable biological reactions. Her nostrils flared, automatically seeking his provocative scent. Blood rushed to her sensitive breasts and her suit cupping her skin seemed inadequate. Her pulse between her thighs quickened. Her flesh yearned for male hands to caress her, seduce her, satisfy her.

However, she was not yet so far into *Boktai* that her brain had abdicated completely to the demands of her body. She still maintained enough control to keep herself clothed, but thinking was becoming more difficult. The man had asked anticipated her escape. He had some nerve following her. Even if he recognized her needy condition, custom dictated that the female choose her mating partner, not the other way around, so she answered without bothering to conceal her annoyance. "This is *my* flitter. Get out."

"Not until we have a conversation," he countered.

Conversation? Ah, the combination of her needy

cells plus the rumble of his voice must be clouding her thoughts. He was not here to mate. He was probably here to speak to her about the laboratory and her work. She refused to turn around. She knew the moment the receptors in her eyes detected his male shape, her hormones would elevate to the next level. In her worsening condition, he could be the ugliest male on the planet and if she stayed in his presence long enough, her will to resist wouldn't matter—she'd still find him handsome and her interest would flare into a kaleidoscope of basic need.

She spoke through gritted teeth. "Make an appointment with my secretary."

"I don't have time to delay. Neither do you."

"Exactly. We agree. I don't have time." Totally irritated by her reaction to him and how badly she wanted to climb into the flitter's cozy back seat and rip off his clothes, she practically growled, "Go away."

"Are you always so friendly?"

"Are you always so annoying?" she countered and took in a breath. Clean, musky male scent wafted to her nostrils, down-shifted into her lungs and revved her olfactory nerves into third gear. *By the mother lode*. Why did his aroma have to remind her of sweet grasses and summer rain? Surely no other Endekian male had ever smelled so incredibly delicious.

She tried not to savor his wondrous scent and to distract herself with analysis. There was something odd about him. Something strange. Her mind tumbled and then settled. He didn't smell like an Endekian because . . . he *wasn't* an Endekian.

"Who are you?" Forgetting caution, she turned around. He was one giant of a man, one fantastic male specimen.

At the sight of bronze *male* skin molded over a powerful physique, her mouth watered. With his black hair clipped short to reveal a very *male* neck that was supported by cords of muscle, her gaze skimmed from his bold nose to his lush mouth to his dazzling cheekbones. But it was his compelling violet eyes, the color of precious nebula flame gemstones, that sought her out with male curiosity and which almost did in her rioting nerves.

Except his harsh expression stopped any inclination to move closer. He wasn't gloating with the usual I-know-you-can't-resist-me arrogance that she hated from the men of her world. Actually as he returned her stare, he appeared to be attempting to conceal distaste, but he couldn't hide his reaction in those grim eyes.

He held still, not crowding her. "Let me introduce myself. I am Xander from Mystique."

"You're a Rystani warrior," she accused him, still managing to keep her tone antagonistic, but barely.

Oh-*Krek*. He was one gorgeous hunk of a man. Even if she hadn't been entering the early stage of *Boktai*, he would still have been dazzling. Dealing with him now when she was in such a vulnerable condition was frustrating.

He spoke as if he had no inkling of what his presence was doing to her. "After Endekians invaded our homeworld, those of us who survived emigrated to Mystique." His tone was cold, his eyes direct. Despite the clamoring-for-attention need that she couldn't subdue, she shivered under his austere expression. But perhaps she was reading more into his demeanor than was there, coloring it with her own past.

She couldn't imagine any Rystani warrior had any love for Endekians. Her people had invaded his world fourteen Federation years ago and the rightness of their actions, the political reasons for war, had no bear-

ing on the suffering they'd caused. Many Rystani had
died in the invasion as had countless Endekian males.
Her own brother had not come back from the war.
When one lost loved ones—no reason was good
enough to fill the emptiness, stop the pain, ease the
sleepless nights. She ignored the sympathy and compassion that urged her to touch him and give comfort.
Doing so would set her on an irrevocable path. It was
bad enough to mate with an Endekian when neither
participant had feelings for one another, but to mate
with a man who had every reason to hate her people
would be abhorrent.

She turned off the flitter, opened the door and exited
her vehicle, hoping the fresh air would blow his scent
away. But of course the weather didn't cooperate.
When Xander unfolded his big frame from the vehicle,
he revealed he was larger than she'd realized. Inside
the flitter, she'd only viewed his upper half, but his flat
stomach, narrow hips and long legs with muscular
thighs made him seem more intimidating, more domi-
neering, more male. If the battle for his world had
come down to hand-to-hand fighting, if all the Rystani
men were this large, his people would never have lost.
Luckily for Endeki, they'd had superior technology
and fire power.

Too bad there was nothing superior about her situation right now. As his scent swirled and eddied around
her, her irritation with his determination to force her
into a conversation warred with bubbling desire.

Even through her growing need she understood that
he wouldn't leave until he'd said what he'd come to
say. Rystani warriors had a fierce reputation. Known
for their stubborn traits, she should have felt fear. She
didn't. She should have felt relief that he wasn't here
to shut down her facility. She didn't. She couldn't relax

the tension that gathered inside her like thunderclouds before a storm, especially as she realized that the sooner they had their conversation, the sooner she could depart. He wouldn't allow anything less.

"So why are you here?" she asked, deepening her voice to compensate for the breathy teasing tone that her biology so urged her to emit instead.

"I need your help."

The only way she wanted to help was to find a private place. She imagined shadowy lighting, mellow music, hot sex and his mouth and hands roaming over her flesh. With determination she shut down the fantasy thoughts. "What kind of help?"

"Could we go somewhere more—"

"I'm not going anywhere with you." No matter how strong her hormones, no matter how badly her cells wept for satiation, she could not have sex with an off-worlder. She was already at odds with her government. Taking a Rystani into her bed would be seen as a betrayal by her people.

He chuckled, his tone so warm and inviting that she barely restrained a gasp of delight. At the change in his demeanor, she forced herself to listen while she tried not to stare at his full mouth, tried not to wonder what it would feel like to have his lips skim past her ear, down her neck.

As if he could read her thoughts, he frowned. "Is it true that you need merely look at a person to read his DNA?"

She shrugged and folded her arms beneath her aching breasts, hoping the light was too dim for him to see her hardening nipples. Why was he interested in her peculiar ability, albeit one she found useful, though her skill mattered little to the non-scientific community? "So what if I don't need a microscope to read DNA?"

He ignored her sarcasm. "It is said you can spot a flaw in the double helix chain at thirty paces."

She'd be willing to bet her last batch of test samples that Xander had never seen the inside of a lab, never mind looked through a microscope. He appeared to have spent his entire life outdoors, exercising and eating and growing muscles over his well-shaped bones. Ah, what she wouldn't give to spend more time with him. His intensity intrigued her and although she put her impression down to *Boktai*, she suspected under other circumstances he might still fascinate her. She'd noted a keen intelligence in his eyes, a glimmer of humor in their depths even as his voice carried overtones of compassion. Yet despite the intensity of her attraction to him, the offworlder's interest in her skill made her wary.

The war between his Rystani people and hers hadn't been over for very long. Although the Rystani had left their homeworld and emigrated to Mystique, Endeki still ruled Rystan. The peace between their people remained uneasy, and she suspected only the most dire of circumstances could have caused him to come here.

She eyed him, wishing the light was better so she could read his DNA. While chromosome combinations wouldn't reveal his motivation or his purpose for seeking her out, she had never before had the opportunity to examine Rystani DNA in a living male. Science would do her no good. She'd have to rely on her instincts and her chaotic senses.

"Why are you curious about my work?"

"I have no interest in your work. My interest is . . . in you."

Bloody Stars. Endekian men didn't speak with such directness. Then again, they didn't have to. They simply waited for a woman to choose and took their pleasure. Conversation was rarely part of the arrangement, so Alara found his bold declaration of interest in her odd, yet exciting.

Reminding herself that her brain couldn't possibly be functioning on all neurons, she eyed the big warrior with renewed caution. "What do you want?"

"I'd like for you to join me on a mission."

Before she told him that she was not about to give up her work to join him, or leave her friends and her home, she freed her curiosity and asked, "What mission?"

He shot her a charming, come-to-me smile that almost stole her breath. "I'm seeking the Perceptive Ones."

Despite his charisma, she snorted. "The Perceptive Ones haven't inhabited this galaxy in eons. They are legends. We aren't certain they ever existed, never mind that they still live."

"Have you no faith, Doctor? You wear a suit that was manufactured by machines the Perceptive Ones left behind." His voice turned earnest, youthful, and she suspected he was younger than she'd first thought. "They existed, all right. And according to ancient records, out near the rim is a system named Lapau, colonized by a humanoid race called the Lapautee. Not much is known about them. However, legend suggests their planet may be an outpost for a protector, a Perceptive One. I'm hoping that since their machines lasted through the millennia, perhaps they did as well."

She didn't know if he was insane or on a grand quest. Either way, she couldn't help him. "I'm sorry. I must decline. I have my own work."

"This is important."

"And my work is not?" She arched a brow, daring him to put her down because she was female and her purpose inconsequential.

But he didn't. Instead he tried another tactic. "My

mission to find the Perceptive Ones is necessary to saving the lives of billions."

She narrowed her brows, unswayed by his earnestness. "Then I wish good fortune to be on your side." She turned away to dismiss him.

He clamped a hand on her shoulder and electricity shot straight to her core. She barely restrained a gasp. The Rystani warrior's hand was gentle, strong and warm—warm enough to fire her flesh. Ruthlessly, she clenched her jaw and tamped down on her need.

His voice hardened in demand. "You will at least do me the courtesy of hearing me out."

Like she had a choice with his big hand on her? She forced herself to shrug it off, and no doubt sensing she would listen, he allowed her to free herself. He couldn't know that his touch had set off a storm of need so great that her ears roared. He was speaking, but at first she couldn't think beyond the rushing sensation that threatened her composure. But finally she regrouped.

"The Perceptive Ones are believed to have been responsible for seeding life in our galaxy with DNA."

"That's legend. It may not be true." She took deep breaths and as her chest raised and fell, she gave him credit, his gaze didn't once drop below her neck.

"My goal is go to Lapau in search of the Perceptive Ones and a pure strain of DNA."

"A pure strain?"

"For Terrans. They—"

"Terrans?" She felt the blood leave her face. She'd thought he was trying to help his *own* people, not the despicable race that had killed everyone she held close to her heart.

He continued as if he did not know of her hatred. "Terrans have polluted their planet and their DNA is damaged. Soon they will be dying by the millions. To save them, I'm looking for a pure strain of Terran DNA, without it . . . they will all die."

Groaning, she leaned against the flitter, raised her hands to her pounding temples. She had to think past the river of passion bubbling through her veins. Just mentioning Terrans to her had likely set off her fervor. Anger could trigger lust, the strong emotion set off signals, one emotion feeding the other.

She'd had no intention of helping this Rystani before. She certainly wasn't going to help him save cursed Terrans. She hoped they all died, and she would dance a celebration to the Goddess if she could rid the Universe of every last one of them.

Terrans had launched the bomb that killed her family, several friends and a coworker. Terrans had destroyed her life. She wouldn't lift one finger to save such a savage race. But she kept her reasons locked down tight.

"You don't need me," she argued. "Any scientist with a microscope can do what I do."

He shook his head. "We may not have the opportunity to examine each species in a laboratory. You can walk on their worlds and merely look—"

"That is where you are wrong. Even if I wanted to help, and I don't, Endekian females are not permitted to leave our homeworld."

Clearly stunned, he dropped his lower jaw and a muscle tightened in his neck. "Why not?"

She would not reveal her shame. She refused to tell him that their men didn't want their women to approach offworlders for life-giving sex. Selfish to the core, their men kept that pleasure for themselves. Still, she didn't lie, either. "It's the law."

Anger flickered in his eyes, whether it was for her inability to leave her homeworld or frustration that she couldn't accompany him, she couldn't discern. But all that male heat spiked her hormones another notch, flaying her with endorphins. *Krek*. Forget the scientific explanations. She was ready to pounce. On him.

She had to get away before she did something really stupid, like leaning into his chest, wrapping her hands around his neck and pulling his lips down to meet hers in a kiss. Like rubbing her skin against his. Like grinding her pelvis against his sexy hips.

Reminding herself he was a stranger, a Rystani warrior and forbidden to her, reminding herself that contact with him would ruin everything she'd dedicated her life to, would only keep her at bay for so long. Her starving cells demanded regeneration. She needed sex so badly she shook.

And damn him, she needed him to be out of sight so her gaze couldn't dwell on what he concealed beneath his plain black suit that molded to his frame with a precision that seared the image into her brain, branding her with a flaming heat. Moisture beaded on her upper lip and seeped between her thighs.

But she would not yield to her need.

She could not have an offworlder—especially one who was a friend to her worst enemy.

She would not succumb.

She'd remain strong.

Opening the flitter door, she eased inside, sensing he would not pursue her. Even as she escaped his presence, his words rang in her ears like a whispered promise. "Laws can be changed. We are not done, you and I."

The
Dark Horse

Patricia Simpson

"Claire?" he asked, tilting his head for a better view. "You okay?"

"You—" She broke off, too stunned for words. Her mouth was full of cotton. Her legs were shaking. A chill of fear and awe coursed through her, setting her teeth chattering. She glanced at Jack's face to find him staring at her, his gaze boring into her as if seeking the image she still held in her head. He grabbed both her arms, intent on keeping her on her feet, even though her body hovered precariously out of her control, as limp as a rag doll.

"Claire?" he whispered, his voice cracking.

"I saw a—" she gasped, and Jack bent down to her. She couldn't believe he was going to kiss her, not after all the angry words they'd flung at each other. And yet, she didn't want to pull away.

He spoke her name again as he drew her against his tall frame, and then his wide mouth sank upon hers, claiming her, demanding that she come into the searing reality of his embrace.

Again Claire saw the horse, heard each heaving breath as horse and man merged into one—hot gasps and silken hair on her neck, hard muscles rippling beneath her palms heat and power crushing her breasts as she was gathered against what she could only define as a pillar of strength.

The kiss shocked her into the here and now, tearing through her body with the force of a wildfire.

. . . Now Available from Tor Romance
ISBN 0-765-35324-5, $6.99 ($9.99 CAN)

Colliding Forces

Constance O'Day-Flannery

D. shrugged. "I don't know the future—but reality has shown me that marriage isn't an easy institution."

"You have been married?"

Throwing her head back with laughter, she said, "Absolutely not! The only institution I've been in is one of learning. And college wasn't that easy."

"I see," Marcus murmured, smiling gently into her eyes.

All right. This was progressing well. Time to wrench it up a notch. "What do you see, Marcus?" She hoped her voice was as sexy as she felt now that her body temperature had regulated back to almost normal.

His smile remained gentle. "I see a lovely woman who has turned her back on fairy tales and romance. Such a shame."

"Hold on. I didn't say I didn't believe in romance. I'm all for it. Just that it doesn't last." She paused, letting out her breath. "But I'm all grown up now and know how the game is played." She paused again for effect. "Any time you want to play, Marcus, just call." There. That was more like it. She was back, no simpering little female at the feet of a Roman god.

Smiling as her gaze slowly left his chest and trav-

eled up to his eyes, she added, "I'm easy to reach."
And with that parting shot, she started to walk back to
the party. That was better. Let him do the chasing.

"Deborah . . ."

She stopped and turned around. Against her will,
her breath caught in her throat as she took in the sight
of his tall frame against the sunset, the breeze playing
with his dark curls. Curls her fingers were itching to
touch.

Swallowing, she asked, "Yes?"

"I just called."

. . . Now Available from Tor Romance
ISBN 0-765-35102-1, $6.99 ($9.99 CAN)